5⁰⁰

2008

Lisa Manuel

Fortune's Kiss

Medallion Press, Inc.
Printed in the USA

DEDICATION:

*For Benay Unger and her mother, Pauline Unger,
whose encouragement and enthusiasm for the romance
genre are reason enough to keep a writer writing.*

Published 2008 by Medallion Press, Inc.

The MEDALLION PRESS LOGO
is a registered tradmark of Medallion Press, Inc.

If you purchased this book without a cover, you should be aware
that this book is stolen property. It was reported as "unsold
and destroyed" to the publisher, and neither the author nor the
publisher has received any payment from this "stripped book."

Copyright © 2008 by Lisa Manuel
Cover Illustration by Adam Mock

All rights reserved. No part of this book may be reproduced
or transmitted in any form or by any electronic or mechanical
means, including photocopying, recording, or by any information
storage and retrieval system, without written permission of the
publisher, except where permitted by law.

Names, characters, places, and incidents are the products of the
author's imagination or are used fictionally. Any resemblance
to actual events, locales, or persons, living or dead, is entirely
coincidental.

Printed in the United States of America
Typeset in Adobe Garamond Pro

ISBN# 1933836350
ISBN# 9781933836355

ACKNOWLEDGEMENTS:

With heartfelt appreciation for:

The untiring efforts of The Florida Romance Writers to advance the careers of its members, and for always having chocolate on hand during good times and bad.

Special thanks to my agent, Evan Marshall, and to Helen Rosburg and the professionals of Medallion Press, whose collective vision and hard work help keep this industry exciting and innovative.

CHAPTER

Sir Graham Foster sucked blistering air into his lungs, gave his Arabian gelding a firm pat on the neck, adjusted his feet in the stirrups, and raised his saber high above his head. Glaring sunlight arced along the steel, sending a shimmering signal to the men assembled before him.

Boot heels dug into drought-scorched earth. A plaintive creaking arose as hemp ropes tightened and clenched. Some two dozen workers strained forward beside ten of the best camels British pounds could buy. Slowly, painstakingly, and with a screech that set Graham's teeth on edge, the barrier to the tomb inched open.

He prayed the ropes would hold. And that the laborers handpicked from a local tribe of nomads wouldn't choose that moment to start an uprising or observe one of hundreds of incomprehensible religious rituals. Or simply decide it was time to return to their colorful tents on the desert.

He gripped a handful of damp shirtfront and unstuck it from his chest. It had taken three months to find this tomb, a modest vault of stone and mud brick laid out on a rectangular slab about twenty feet below ground. It hadn't always been subterranean, but part of the once-prosperous village of Deir el-Medina, now buried beneath centuries of blowing sand. It wasn't a place one would expect to find the remains of a pharaoh, but rather a pharaoh's master craftsman.

Which suited Graham Foster fine. He wasn't searching for a king's treasure or anything of great historical value. Not this time. A text in the Alexandria archives had indicated this to be the burial site of a wealthy goldsmith from the second millennia BC, and Graham expected a handsome return for his pains. He only hoped the poor dead chap wouldn't mind extending him a bit of a loan for a good cause.

It had taken another two months to raise the money and manpower needed to excavate. An additional four weeks to successfully bribe Pasha Mohammed Ali, Egypt's temperamental Turkish ruler, into allowing the "pesky British swine" access to the area. Of course, this excavation was merely a means to a more important end. If it proved fruitless, there would be more searching, more money to raise, more bribes to offer, and more nomads to deal with.

"My lord! My lord!"

Shaun Paddington, his friend, assistant, and, when necessity dictated, imposter British consul, hailed from the top of a rise some thirty yards away. Graham swore under his breath. What could be so important that Shaun would interrupt him at such a crucial moment?

A high-pitched groan snared his attention. The workers were moving too fast, putting undue strain on both the ropes and the entrance slab. Too much tension on the stone could literally rend it to pieces and cause a cave-in.

Graham cupped his hands around his mouth. "Slow down before it shatters!"

The perspiration rolling down his sides had little to do with the hundred-degree heat pounding down from an unimpeded sun. He sucked another breath in preparation of a second warning when he saw the lead camel drivers signal to their snorting, spitting charges.

Graham held the searing oxygen in his lungs. Done without the proper skill, the drivers could stop the progress altogether instead of simply slowing it. The momentum would be lost. That meant starting over.

"My lord!" Shaun shouted again.

Damn. From the corner of his eye, Graham saw his friend descend a sand dune at top speed. As his image undulated in the heat waves, Graham noticed something white flapping in Shaun's outstretched hand.

"Blazing hell, Shaun, not now."

But within seconds, the overseers had brought the

pace under control. The whining complaint of the ropes and the slab ceased. With a whoop of mixed relief and triumph, Graham swung from the saddle.

"Did you see that, Shaun?" he called to the panting man, whose running steps kicked up whorls of sand around his legs. "Can I pick them or what? Are these fellows not princes of their trade?"

They weren't completely out of danger yet, wouldn't be until the slab cleared the tomb and was secured with more ropes and scaffolding. But already Graham felt the charge of adventure, the anticipation of entering the three-thousand-year-old grave site.

Shaun loped to a halt a few feet away, waving what Graham now identified as a sheet of paper practically under his nose.

"What have you got there?" Graham asked. "A grant from the same university that sent me packing ten years ago? Tell them I don't need it."

"No, it's. . .a letter. . .from your. . .solicitor." Puffing, Shaun bent full over, resting a hand on his knee in an effort to recapture his breath.

"I don't have a solicitor."

His friend maintained his bent posture and continued gasping. Finally, hand pressed to his chest in a manner that would have worried Graham if he wasn't familiar with the man's dramatics, he straightened. "You do now. And it seems you're needed at home."

"The devil I am. Bad joke, old man." An oddity

struck him. How had Shaun hailed him? With cries of *my lord*?

He'd been Sir Graham Foster since his twenty-fourth birthday, after presenting His Majesty, King George, with assorted artifacts from various digs. Tanis had yielded a gilded ebony statue of the god Osiris; from Karnak came a bejeweled pectoral pendant featuring the eye of Horus; and from Akhenaten, an elaborate burial mask. Baubles that had granted him a solid footing on England's social ladder.

But a lordship?

"Shaun, my friend," he said with a laugh and a swat to the other man's broad shoulder, "you've been baking in this sun too long. Go back to your tent. Have a little nip. It'll restore perspective to that addled mind of yours."

Shaun shook his head and the paper at the same time. "There's nothing wrong with me, my lord. Your cousin twice removed and then some," he jabbed at the information with his forefinger, "Everett Foster, has died and—"

"Who?"

"Your second cousin twice removed. Or is it thrice? Here, it lists the lineage tracing you to him."

Scowling, Graham peered at the page. "Oh. Old Man Monteith. Only met him a couple of times, and that was years ago. But this is absurd. He has a nephew."

"Dead, as well, within weeks of his uncle." Shaun squinted down at the page. "Says here you're the great-

great-grandson of the first Baron Monteith's younger brother." He dropped the paper to his side and met Graham's gaze with a mixture of disbelief and amazement. "It would appear you've been the new Baron Monteith for quite some time now, my lord."

"Call me that again, and I'll knock you a facer. Now tell me how I can avoid this calamity."

Shaun stared back, lips compressed. A hot gust nearly ripped the letter from his hand, but he whisked it tight against his chest. Then he said, "There's more."

"Out with it."

"Your solicitor sends his apologies for having allowed your family access to your new London town house. He didn't think it would be a problem. They are your family, after all." Shaun paused to swallow. "But it seems they've amassed some debts."

Gritty sweat trickled into the corner of Graham's eye. He swiped at it with his sleeve. "Blazing hell."

Moira Hughes threw her weight against the cottage door and shoved. It stuck for an instant, then gave with an abruptness that nearly sent her headlong across the foyer floor. She clutched the doorknob and anchored her feet, managing not to fall but only just. Then she took her first glimpse of her new home. It was. . . Awful.

Dim. Shabby. An enormous disappointment. She

stepped across the threshold.

To her left, an archway opened upon a cramped parlor. She spied, between two dust-laden windows, a diminutive fireplace that promised to smoke the very instant anyone dared ignite a blaze. To her right, a decidedly rickety staircase ambled its way to the second floor. Ahead, the foyer narrowed to a tight corridor that must surely lead to an equally oppressive kitchen. Moira could only imagine the amenities to be found there.

She sighed. Until this morning, Monteith Hall had been her home. Sprawling, elegant, *large* Monteith Hall, a mere two miles and a world away. There had been servants, gardens, fine carriages. Not that Moira and her parents had used the latter for much besides excursions to church on Sundays. They had settled, these past several years, into the uneventful routine of country life. But there had been security and a sense of peace, a dependable contentment.

That had ceased to be true some four months ago. Until then, she had been the beloved stepdaughter of Everett Foster, Baron Monteith. Then one frigid November morning, she had watched his coffin lowered into a fresh grave in the family cemetery. Influenza turned into pneumonia, the physician had informed her and her mother. Through their grief, there had at least been a sense of reassurance, of continuity, for Moira had for some months been engaged to Nigel Foster, her stepfather's nephew and heir.

But there would be no marriage now, nor had Nigel enjoyed his inheritance for long. Poor Nigel. Dearest Nigel had been thrown by his horse and laid in his grave not two months after Papa, leaving Moira and her mother alone. Quite alone. And what a great irony, for Nigel had been the most proficient of riders. Something, a rabbit perhaps, must have spooked his horse and, in a freak occurrence, Nigel had fallen and broken his neck.

At the moment of his death, Moira and her mother had lost all claim to Monteith Hall and become merely the distant stepcousins of the new baron. A baron who very much wanted—needed, his letter said—to take up immediate residence in his country estate, and would Moira and her mother please make the necessary arrangements as soon as possible.

Those arrangements had thankfully materialized in the form of this cottage, offered to them by St. Bartholomew's Parish. St. Bartholomew's had once been presided over by Moira's natural father, the Reverend Mr. John Hughes, and she found the congregation's gesture touching, indeed. Not to mention a tremendous relief. If the accommodations were somewhat inadequate, the rent at least was cheap. Needless to say, she and her mother hadn't rushed to pack their things, but this day had arrived in a dizzying blur all the same.

Uncertain footsteps picked along the path behind her. Moira backed out of the cottage, pasted on her most cheerful smile, and turned. "Oh, Mother, isn't it wonderful? Just like in a fairy tale." Seeing her mother's brow pucker with doubt, she added, "Think how cozy we'll be here in winter. And once the furniture arrives, you'll feel right at home."

Putting a spring in her step, she went to her mother's side and linked arms with her. "Come, let's explore."

"Do you think your father will like it, dear?" Estella Foster raised a skeptical glance to the stone and timber facade. "It seems rather limited. You know how Papa likes to roam the house at night when he cannot sleep."

Moira regarded the hazy confusion in her mother's eyes. A weight that had become a familiar burden these past months pressed her heart. She patted a wrinkled hand, kissed a careworn cheek.

"You know Papa is in heaven, Mother," she said quietly, and paused to let it sink in. Again. "And yes, I do believe he would be quite pleased with our snug new home. Come, let us have a look about. We must decide where to place your settee and armoire. And the petit-point chair and footstool."

Yes, those items had been part of Estella Foster's dowry, and so they were allowed to take them from Monteith Hall. Most of the other furnishings must stay, of course, part and parcel of the new baron's inheritance.

"And don't forget your father's chair, dear." Estella's grip tightened on Moira's arm as they entered the cottage together. "He'll want it just so beside the hearth. Is there a window nearby? Your father is most particular about having natural light to read by during the day. You know how he disdains lighting the lamps before tea."

Moira sighed and nodded.

Hours later, when the scant furnishings had been placed to their best advantage and Moira had tucked her bewildered mother into bed, she stole outside. Mrs. Stanhope, still at work organizing the kitchen, promised to check on Estella often.

Thank heaven for Mrs. Stanhope, something of a saint in Moira's estimation. She'd been housekeeper at Monteith since before Moira and her mother's arrival when Moira was only three years old. Favoring loyalty over her enviable position in the manor, Mrs. Stanhope had chosen to accompany them to their new home, such as it was.

Exhaustion clawed at Moira's limbs, but she trod a resolute path to the remnants of what had once been a kitchen garden. No one had lived here for years, and the cultivated rows had long gone to weeds. She would have to hoe and rake quickly in order to plant in time for the growing season. Even then the first yield would be negligible at best. There would be little money besides. The vast bulk of the fortune was entailed to the estate and belonged now to the new Lord Monteith.

Moira curved her tongue around his name: Graham Foster. She wondered who he was, what he looked like. As to the sort of man he was, she wasted no time in pondering. His nature had been made plain by his curt request that they vacate the Hall.

Over the years she had heard rumors about him, mostly from Nigel. Tossed out of Oxford for cheating, Sir Graham Foster had become something of an adventurer, an explorer who dug up ancient treasures in Egypt and claimed them for England. He'd won the king's favor for his efforts. Now he was coming home to claim the only security Moira and her mother knew.

She bit her trembling lip and vowed not to shed a single tear. She'd shed plenty for dearest Nigel. Many more for Papa.

Of her natural father she retained no memories, for John Hughes had died before her second birthday. She had always thought of Everett Foster as her father with no other word attached, just as he used to sit her on his knee and declare her his bonnie little daughter. He'd called her *his* child for the last time as he lay dying, and whispered of a recent change in his will that would ensure his family's welfare.

Where had that money gone? Mr. Smythe, their solicitor in London, had written to say he knew of no funds other than those entailed to the estate, except for the small sum her mother had brought to the marriage. Hardly enough to see them through the coming months. Although the rent was paid for a full year, they'd need food, fuel, and clothing, and Moira couldn't expect Mrs. Stanhope to stay on for free.

Something was very wrong, and it now fell upon

her shoulders to discover what that something was. The thought of leaving her mother, even temporarily, brought on waves of numbing doubt, but she knew Mrs. Stanhope would die before she allowed any harm to touch her mistress.

She and her mother would never again have a home such as the one they'd left. They would never again enjoy the privileges so recently stripped from them. But the other things—security, contentment, a feeling of home—those Moira believed—hoped—she could provide. She must first go to London and press for their rights. She must summon every ounce of her courage, barge into Mr. Smythe's office, and demand to see her stepfather's financial records. Somewhere a codicil to his will existed, and she intended to find it.

In the fading twilight, she scanned the surrounding countryside, the gentle hills and meadows of Shelbourne. Deeply she inhaled the piney-sharp scent of the village's evening fires. From a quarter mile away, the church bell struck a single peal, ringing in the half hour.

The very thought of leaving produced an ache so sharp it nearly cut off her breath. Although the family had many acquaintances in London, in truth she could count none as close friends. Certainly no one in whom she felt an inclination to confide. She could not have borne the pitying looks, nor the whispered gossip about how low poor Estella Foster and her daughter had sunk.

So then, where would she stay? Not in the family's

Mayfair town house. That belonged to Graham Foster now. There was Uncle Benedict, but the letter she had sent him nearly a month ago had brought no reply; he must be traveling at present. No, she would be on her own, and on such limited funds she despaired of eating more than one meal a day. But what other choice?

With no man to champion her cause, she must act as head of the family, no matter how inappropriate, how frowned upon. For there was nothing genteel about poverty. Nothing to be gained from an empty stomach. No, indeed. She must plant the garden and see her mother settled into a pleasant routine with Mrs. Stanhope. Then she would pack her bags and set out for London.

CHAPTER 2

I'm afraid you can't go in there, Miss. . .ah. . ."

"It's Miss Hughes, and well you know it by now, sir." Moira made it as far as the inner door that led into the private offices of *Smythe and Davis, Legal Consultants* before the secretary barred her way. He was a new employee, someone Moira had never met before this week. Wedging himself between her outstretched hand and the doorknob, he regarded her defiantly.

"Mr. Smythe is presently engaged with a client and must not be disturbed."

"Mr. Pierson, I've called three times this week, and each time I've been turned away with promises that Mr. Smythe would schedule an appointment at his next possible convenience. He has failed to do so, and my patience has quite run out."

She drew a breath she hoped showed no trace of the turmoil pitching inside her. She loathed forcing her way into a man's world and issuing demands with feigned bravado. If only Nigel were here. Ah, but if Nigel were here, she wouldn't be in this predicament.

She became uncomfortably aware of the person sitting in the waiting area, a well-dressed man with a thatch of black hair whose face must no doubt be turned in her direction.

The secretary sniffed. "Mr. Smythe's appointment calendar is quite full, Miss Hughes. He has had urgent business—"

"No more urgent than mine, I assure you, Mr. Pierson." She stopped a tad short of becoming shrill. Both the secretary and the blasted door stood like stone walls between her and the sole reason she'd traveled to London. Her stomach clenched around a clawing sensation that never left her, a hollow ache only partly due to hunger, more to sinking desperation. She couldn't give up now, simply wouldn't turn away in defeat—

The door abruptly opened.

"Is there a problem out here, Pierson?"

Moira surged forward, nearly knocking the secretary out of her way. "Mr. Smythe, *finally*."

The solicitor stared at her a long moment, his obvious irritation tinged with an impatient curiosity. "Miss Hughes?"

He said it as though he hadn't spared her a thought in months; as if he hadn't received multiple messages from her these past several days.

"Yes, Mr. Smythe, and if you have but a few moments—"

"I'm afraid I haven't, not at present. I've a very important client in my office." He began retreating through the door.

A surge of panic sent Moira's hand clutching at his coat sleeve. He regarded her with no small amount of consternation, but didn't pull away.

"Mr. Smythe, my stepfather was a very important client of this firm for many years. Please speak with me." She held her breath.

He gave a nod and reclaimed his arm. "Very well. Perhaps I can spare you a moment. Step this way."

He led her past the first office and into another that lay empty. Mr. Smythe walked several paces into the spacious, well-appointed room but didn't sit, nor did he invite Moira to make herself comfortable in one of the armchairs set before the desk. Just as well. She presented a much more formidable impression, she thought, standing rather than sitting.

"What may I do for you, Miss Hughes?"

"It's about my stepfather's will."

A decidedly uncomfortable cast settled over the man's aging features. "The will has been read and executed accordingly, Miss Hughes. And I must point out you were not directly mentioned in it."

"May I see a copy?"

"That would be most irregular."

By the depth of his frown, she knew he meant impossible.

"Then can you tell me please, sir, did my stepfather make any recent changes to the will, perhaps a few weeks or months prior to his passing?"

"Again, Miss Hughes, your inquiry is most irregular. You were not, after all, Everett Foster's natural daughter."

A near sob of frustration escaped her.

His expression softened. "In answer, no. Lord Monteith made no changes to his will. You must realize the document was merely a formality. The original patent quite clearly established the line of inheritance."

"Are you entirely certain?" She wanted to grasp his lapels and shake him, make him remember what must— simply *must*—be so. "Could there be a codicil? You see, Mr. Smythe, as Papa lay ill, he told me he'd made a change, one that would. . ."

She trailed off, unwilling to disclose to this apparently indifferent man how very badly she and her mother needed whatever provisions Everett Foster had made for them.

"If there is a codicil," Mr. Smythe said at length, "I'm afraid I am not aware of it, which prompts me to state with certainty that none exists. Lord Monteith always discussed his legal affairs with me. He wouldn't likely have taken such action without consulting me." He smiled gently, his first real show of sympathy thus far. "I know he was very ill in the end, my dear. Could he perhaps have been delirious when he made this declaration to you?"

Moira sank into the nearest chair. "Perhaps. I don't know." She cradled her forehead in her gloved hand. "Couldn't you please make an exception and allow me to view the will?"

"If it were up to me, I would. But you see, since the will has been executed, the document has been registered and filed with the Prerogative Court of Canterbury."

"Very well, then, I'll go there."

"Miss Hughes, one can't simply *go there*. One must first file a request to view the documents in question and wait for the next available appointment. This being London's busiest season, it could take weeks or even months."

"Months?" Her throat closed around a lump of despondency.

"I'm sorry, Miss Hughes, but I must be getting back. . ."

"Yes, to your important client." She placed her hand in his offered one and rose to her feet, feeling the slightest of thrusts as he turned her toward the door. So much for sympathy.

He escorted her into the corridor. "How is your mother?"

"Quite well, thank you. Enjoying our new home."

"Give her my regards."

"I will. Good day."

"Good day, Miss Hughes."

She barely had time to turn away before the tears began stinging her eyes. Clenching her teeth and wanting only to be gone, she quickened her steps.

The door to the first office lay partially open. At her approach, a man sitting inside turned his head toward her, revealing a strong chin; a fine straight nose; a brow hidden beneath a careless shank of tawny brown hair. He saw her, stood partway up, and made a little bow, his head cocked in polite acknowledgment. His eyes— cool, clear, starkly blue against an unusually tanned complexion—met hers, and he flashed a grin that took her aback with its impertinence, its brazen assessment.

To Moira's complete chagrin, his disarming smile brought her to a dead halt. Like a simpleton, she stared at the teasing curve of those lush lips, the whiteness of his even teeth, and the deepest, most captivating set of dimples she had ever seen.

And then, dear God, a tear spilled over, trickling hot moisture down her cheek. At the same time—oh, the shame of it—she emitted a small but undeniable sniffle.

Mortified, she hurried to the door of the outer office, praying the man hadn't noticed her sorry state or, if he had, that she'd never cross paths with him again.

♥ ♥ ♥

"Mr. Smythe, who was that lovely but woefully tragic young lady walking by just now?"

The solicitor rounded his desk, adjusted his trouser

legs, and settled into his creaking leather chair. "Yes, that was Miss Moira Hughes, the late Lord Monteith's stepdaughter."

"Really? Then why the blazes didn't you introduce us? She and I *are* practically related." He bit back a grin. This might prove one instance when a family connection came in handy. "She seemed rather upset. Is there a problem I should know about? As head of the family, I mean."

"No, my lord, not at all." At Graham's skeptical look, Smythe released a lengthy sigh. "I'm afraid her stepfather's death has left the lady most distraught."

"Have she and the widow been provided for? Is there anything I might do for them?" Yes, he'd be more than gratified to offer his services to the darkly stunning Moira Hughes; would graciously lend a sympathetic ear to her sorrows and extend a benevolent hand to wipe away her tears, albeit they magnified those midnight eyes until they gleamed like newly cooled obsidian.

"You needn't concern yourself." The solicitor held up the flats of his hands in a gesture of reassurance. "They've a house in Shelbourne and an annuity. I assure you they are quite well taken care of."

"Do you know where she's residing in London?"

Smythe glanced at him from over a sheaf of papers. "She used to reside where you're presently residing, my lord. Beyond that I couldn't say. She didn't leave her card."

"A pity. I shall have to make inquiries." He grinned

at the other man. "Tell me again, Smythe. Exactly how much money have I inherited?"

♥ ♥ ♥

"What do you mean, they've vacated?" Graham ran a hand through his hair, then remembered the pomade his new valet had saturated his head with earlier. He resisted the urge to wipe his fingers on the front of his formal tailcoat and vowed to duck the next time Baxter came at him with a comb and an open jar.

Then again, Baxter's fashion sense appeared to be dead-on, judging by the number of heads glistening beneath the lanterns strung throughout Mr. and Mrs. Ralph Jarvis's formal gardens. That is, where heads were visible. The affair was a masquerade ball with an Italian Renaissance theme, and a good number of the crush sported wigs and masks.

Graham had flat out refused to attend in costume. Despite his mother's and sister Letty's protestations, he'd worn black evening attire whose sole concession to history was a cravat pin of lapis lazuli carved in the shape of a scarab. It was Egyptian in origin, but who here would know the difference? He'd threatened to come in a fig leaf and nothing more, effectively silencing Mother's and Letty's nagging.

Beside him, his mother tsked at his question. "Perhaps *vacated* is the wrong word, dear. Lady Monteith and her daughter have simply moved into a home that is more suitable to their needs."

"At whose insistence?"

"Their *own*, to be sure," his sister said. "They *certainly* must understand that you, as the new baron, have need of the house or will shortly, once you've married and set about producing an heir."

The beginnings of a headache grazed his temple. "I see you two have my future well planned."

"Yes, and after all," his mother went on, shaking her head and setting the peacock feathers on her mask fluttering, "what need would a widow and her spinster daughter have of such a vast estate?"

Spinster? Hardly the word Graham would use to describe the dazzling beauty he had glimpsed in Smythe's office yesterday. Somewhat flippantly he had termed her *tragic*, but the notion kept returning to haunt him. He couldn't erase from his memory the single tear that had traced a glistening course down her lovely cheek.

The woman had lost her stepfather and her fiancé all in the same year. She'd left her home of many years, as well. Everyone jumped to reassure him of her well-being, but he wondered. Had the move been a voluntary escape from too many rooms and too many memories, or impelled by far less sentimental forces, such as the two ladies currently affecting innocent expressions, or trying to.

"*Really*, Monteith, you needn't sound as if we tossed them out into the *rain*. We hear the parish has offered them a perfectly *charming* cottage." Letty waved a beaded fan before her face while peering over its rim to see who might be watching her. In her jeweled headdress and draping, shoulder-baring gown of red and gold, his sister appeared an odd mixture of Roman goddess and Italian courtesan.

Graham suppressed the urge to point this out to her and said, "For the umpteenth time, Letty, it's Graham. Not Monteith."

No, his title sat heavy with him, more a burden than a boon after so many years in the desert. There, such respect was typically reserved for men who'd truly earned it, rather than those who claimed it on the successes of their forebears.

"How *provincial*." Letty tossed her golden brown curls. "Monteith *is* your name now, like it or no. Furthermore, while you were away digging for skeletons, I grew up. I prefer Letitia. I *despise* Letty."

Yes, so did their mother. Graham still remembered the exact moment Augusta Foster had realized her colossal error in naming her infant twins Frederick, for their paternal grandfather, and Letitia, for a great-aunt. She'd entered the nursery one sunny morning to hear their nurse cooing ever so gaily above them, "Good morning, Freddy; good morning, Letty. Time to get Freddy and Letty all ready."

Their mother had gone utterly still, open mouthed and aghast, only to burst into a tirade an instant later.

She'd berated the nurse never to use those pet names again if she valued her position. Too late. Nine-year-old Graham, perched on the window seat, had taken an immediate fancy to the rhyme. He'd devised dozens more over the years.

"I'll certainly try to remember that, Letty," he said now with a wink that made his sister's eyes narrow and her lower lip droop.

A crescendo from the orchestra drowned out her huff. Graham's gaze drifted to the couples waltzing on the terrace. This gathering was about as exciting as life in London ever became, and he feared he'd drown in the boredom of it.

Like Letty, the city had grown up while he was away, burgeoning with new streets and squares, becoming ever more intricate, sophisticated, fussy. And as with Letty, he rather disapproved of the changes that made London a stranger to him.

An increasingly familiar yearning took hold, an acute craving for baked desert winds, the piercing brightness of sun and sky, the unpredictable adventures of hidden temples, cursed tombs, and Bedouin-guarded treasure.

How long before he settled his inheritance and returned to Egypt?

"Where has your brother run off to?" His mother's question broke his reverie. She craned her neck to scan the gardens. "I do hope he hasn't. . ." She trailed off as frown lines arced above her feathered mask.

She needn't finish the thought, for Graham to understand her apprehensions concerning her younger son. Freddy, too, had undergone changes since Graham had seen him last, not the least of which was a troubling fondness for brandy. "Would you like me to find him, Mother?"

"Would you, Monteith? Yes, do be a dear."

A dear? Not exactly how he felt, especially when he would mostly likely want to box Freddy's ears when he found him. As he started away, his mother's eager voice carried above the surrounding din. "See there, Letitia. I do believe that young man is a viscount. Come, let's wangle an introduction."

"Yes, but is he a *rich* viscount, Mama?"

Ah, Letty. When Graham left England ten years ago, his little sister had been scrambling to follow her twin brother up into trees and anywhere else their tutors' lessons might be avoided. She'd thumbed her nose at party dresses and any pastime considered conventionally feminine, much preferring to ride, swim, or shoot a bow and arrow. And her hair had been pleasantly wavy, not this ridiculous mass of corkscrews that jiggled whenever she moved. What in blazing hell had happened?

His reunion with both siblings had been strained at best. He'd been away so many years. . .and there had been that letter they sent him not long after his departure from England.

How could you disgrace us? We're so terribly ashamed. Don't ever return. . .

He shook the memory away, blinked. . .and saw her. He had no idea who she was, but he couldn't take his eyes off her. Downright stared as she proceeded in his direction. There were at least two-score ladies strolling the gardens tonight, but this one stood out, seized his notice, spiked his curiosity. It was, perhaps, in the way she moved effortlessly through the crush, as if she had nowhere in particular to be—unhurried, serene, her hips swaying with the languid grace of a temple cat.

Like him, this woman wore simple evening attire: a sleek gown of midnight blue, a velvet mask trimmed to match. A gossamer veil of the same hue draped from a coil of ebony hair at the crown of her head. Unadorned, unaffected. . .and entirely intriguing.

Their gazes met, hers a dark mystery behind the mask that covered half her face. A smile eased across her lips. Then, quite abruptly, she changed direction, but with a parting glance that set his feet in motion.

Suddenly London seemed a good deal less boring.

CHAPTER
3

Moira pivoted and set off at a brisk pace, away from Graham Foster. She had been watching him for the better part of a half hour, after learning his identity from an acquaintance. She had known the Fosters were attending tonight, and so she had managed an invitation through the wife of an old friend of her stepfather's. But until some thirty minutes ago, she'd had no idea this man was the very same who had witnessed her utter humiliation at Mr. Smythe's office yesterday.

Good grief.

Tonight, as yesterday, he was affecting her in the most alarming manner. As she strode off, her hand flew instinctively to her mask to ensure it was still in place. She resisted a peek over her shoulder. Was he following, as she had intended? She listened for the clip of pursuant footsteps, but heard only the dull roar of voices and the musicians on the terrace.

Then there he was, not behind, but right in front of her, stepping out from behind a topiary elephant. Flashing that disturbing set of dimples, he pinned her with a stare as piercing as cut crystal. "Good evening."

His voice was deep, as fiery and rich as brandy and altogether too intimate. The sort that made pulses race, cheeks flame.

She pulled back, and the wineglass she'd been holding slipped from her fingers. It shattered against the paving stones, sending up a shower of white wine.

"Good heavens," she mumbled, instantly forgetting all the carefully rehearsed witticisms with which she had planned to seduce information from this man. "How horribly clumsy of me."

When he didn't immediately respond, she wanted to dissolve into the footpath. Oh, whatever had made her—inexperienced, country-bred Moira Hughes—think she could charm a confession out of a scoundrel the likes of Graham Foster?

She braved an upward glance, straight into those clear blue eyes, which on second thought possessed an intriguing hint of green. Not to mention laughter. Yes, Graham Foster's eyes smiled down at her even before his lips parted and curled.

Something bracing and sharp tripped her heartbeat. She whisked her gaze away. Would he recognize her eyes within the mask's slits?

"The fault was entirely mine, I assure you," he finally said in that too smooth, far too sensual voice. On either side of a broad grin, the dimples that had flashed in her dreams last night cut even deeper crevasses into his cheeks. "The shattering glass didn't catch you, did it?"

"The glass?" She gazed at the ground, at bits of crystal sparkling in the lamplight, then at her wine-soaked hems. "Oh, dear. I'm quite all right, but my dress is ruined. Your trousers, too, I'm afraid. Oh, what a mess."

"At least we can be thankful it wasn't port."

"Ladies don't generally drink port, sir."

"Don't they? A pity." He leaned in closer, and she caught the scent of his shaving soap, crisp and invigorating, like clean canvas sails stretched in a high-seas wind. "I believe ladies should grasp at life, and convention be damned." The last word plummeted to a growl that raised a shiver down her spine.

She stepped back. "I should call someone to clean these fragments away."

"No need. Here comes a footman now."

Indeed, a man in livery trotted down the terrace steps, broom and dustpan in hand.

"I'm so sorry," Moira said to the servant.

"It's what the good man's paid to do." Graham Foster took possession of her elbow in his broad palm. "Come, we'll find you another glass, shall we?"

"Oh, but. . ." She trailed off. Hadn't she come here

for this specific purpose? To strike up an acquaintance with the new Baron Monteith, beguile him, and steal inside his conscience. An unshakable suspicion convinced her that Mr. Smythe had been withholding vital information yesterday. Could he have been acting upon his new employer's orders?

Goodness, Moira Hughes, you're in it up to your ears now, aren't you?

As he guided her along the garden path, a sense of laughter hovered about him—in his eyes, in his voice, even in the way he claimed her arm with a breezy familiarity that set her on her guard.

They passed one of a half dozen refreshment tables ranged through the gardens. Upon arriving earlier, she had set about quieting her growling stomach by discreetly consuming an entire Cornish hen, a healthy slice of roast venison, asparagus in cream sauce, potato pudding, and several ratafia biscuits so luscious she'd nearly sighed her pleasure aloud. This—and only this—allowed her to pass the refreshments now with the air of disinterest expected in a wellborn lady.

With a fluid sweep and without the slightest break in his stride, he lifted a glass from the linen tabletop. An equally smooth flourish transferred the glass to her hand.

"Champagne, madam."

"Why, thank you."

As they walked on, her free hand somehow traveled to the snug, warm, quite solid crook of his arm. His considerably larger hand descended to hold hers firmly in place. She became exceedingly aware of the masculine weave of his coat sleeve beneath her fingers, the rougher contour of his palm against the back of her hand. A tremulous sensation traveled through her.

"As long as we've baptized one another in your wine, madam, perhaps you'll tell me your name."

He guided her past the central fountain and down a tree-lined path that disappeared beneath an arbor. Covered in climbing honeysuckle, the latticework formed a sweet, dusky tunnel. A little warning trilled inside her, along with a tremor of expectation she liked not at all.

She knew she should divert him in another direction, but trees and tall hedges barred that option. He ushered her steadily forward into the fragrant twilight of the arbor. She drew a breath that quivered and slowly released it. "You've yet to introduce yourself, sir."

"Indeed, madam." He chuckled as he brought her to a halt, then twirled her as if leading her in a dance. "Graham Foster, at your service."

"Sir Graham Foster," she said with feigned surprise. To have *not* done so would have seemed odd, indeed, for these days nearly everyone had heard of the exploits of the daring Egyptologist Graham Foster.

"Not *Sir* Graham any longer, I'm afraid." His grin turned wry. "Seems I inherited a bit of a barony while I was away. Now I'm saddled with a title, property, and the lot. Keep hoping to wake up and discover it's all just a perplexing rumor."

Moira stiffened. A rumor? Had rumor dislodged her ailing mother from the home she loved, from all that was familiar and comfortable? Indeed, not. The new Lord Monteith had done that, though it seemed little more than a joke to him.

"Why don't you give it back?" she murmured through lips gone stiff with fury.

"Can't. It's all entailed, and I have the dubious honor of being the last available heir. Besides, I believe I can find good use for my inheritance. But we digress. You still haven't told me your name."

She concealed her outrage behind her champagne glass, letting far too much of the sparkling liquid pass her lips before remembering how quickly the bubbles tended to affect her judgment. She slipped her hand from his arm. "I am Miss Houser. Miss Mary Houser."

She'd hesitated the smallest fraction of an instant in speaking the name, and—confound the man—his eyes narrowed in acknowledgment. But speculation quickly vanished within the laugh lines fanning from the corners of his eyes.

"Very pleased to make your acquaintance, Miss Mary Houser." His tone mocked ever so subtly. He reclaimed her hand and shook it, then continued to hold it, confine it really, within the confident sprawl of his long fingers. "Especially as you took such great pains to make *my* acquaintance."

Her chin snapped up. "I beg your pardon."

"Don't deny it." Even as his voice dipped to a sinister baritone, his grin widened. "If that smile of yours earlier didn't say 'follow me,' I've lost all power of perception."

"You assume too much, sir."

"Now, now, Miss Houser, let us be frank. You wished to meet me, and I am equally delighted to meet you."

Oh, such an insufferable flirt. Such a coxcomb. Her hackles rose. She tried to tug her hand free, but like a clever snare, his grip tightened and trapped her fast.

"You know, Miss Houser, you still have me at a distinct disadvantage." His fingertip stroked her knuckles beneath her lace glove, sending her pulse for a gallop. "You have full view of my features while yours remain hidden beneath that mysterious mask of yours. Won't you remove it so we might become properly acquainted?"

With a jolt of alarm, she pulled free. "I think not, my lord, for were I to remove my mask, my coif would fall to shambles." Turning to prove her point, she allowed him to see where the silken ribbons twined into her coiled hair and helped hold her veil in place.

A colossal mistake on her part. He eased closer, his solid chest radiating heat against the thin silk covering her back. His hand slipped beneath her veil and descended on her nape with a whisper's touch that made her skin sizzle. "You are correct, Miss Houser, this is quite an entanglement. You may never free yourself of it."

At the sound of his throaty chuckle, she whirled, only to find her back tucked against the trellis. Delicate tendrils of honeysuckle curled about her shoulders while its heavy perfume blanketed her senses.

"Here, my lord." She thrust her glass at him. "I've discovered I have no taste for champagne after all. I must go."

A nimble side step blocked her escape. "Have I offended you, Miss Houser? Please forgive me. I've been away many years, so long I am now a foreigner in my own country. It would seem I've become woefully ignorant of English manners and customs. To be frank, I feel out of place at affairs such as these, and when I saw you walking alone. . .well, I thought perhaps I'd encountered a kindred spirit."

He raised her glass and drank from it, from the place that still held the moisture of her lips. As his gaze held her, the air around her thickened and warmed. Her mouth tingled as if his lips had touched her and not the glass; an achy sensation gathered deep inside.

"Th-there is nothing to forgive, my lord," she assured him, and shook her head to clear it. The past moments had quite convinced her she would never glean a bit of useful information from him, not here beneath the dark and fragrant arbor; not with those laughing blue eyes making her forget everything she'd planned to say to coax the truth from him.

"If you'll excuse me, my lord, I—"

"Won't you call me Graham? I cringe at the sound of 'my lord.'"

"Certainly not."

"No?" He touched a fingertip to the underside of her chin, sending a mortifying blaze of heat to her cheeks. "I suppose it will have to be Foster then, won't it? For I simply will not abide 'my lord.'"

How dare he belittle the title borne with such dignity by both her stepfather and Nigel? She clenched her fists in the folds of her gown. "Mr. Foster, I must bid you good evening. I did not attend alone, you see. I was escorted by. . .my brother, and I'm afraid he'll be searching for me."

"Brother. Blazing hell." His groan dissipated into the honeysuckle. "I'd forgotten. I'm supposed to be searching for a brother myself. We'll have to excuse each other then, Miss Houser."

He lifted her hand to his lips. When she thought he would release her, he didn't, but contemplated her glove with a vague frown. She had sold all her full-length evening gloves and had to make due with these lace mitts. Now her wrist felt naked and vulnerable beneath his scrutiny.

Gently he turned her palm upward. Bending his head, he pressed his open lips to her pulse, just beyond the edge of her glove. And then. . .great good heavens. . .she felt the moist graze of his tongue against her flesh, leaving a trail of fire that burned all through her, straight down to the tips of her toes. Her knees wobbled, threatened to give way. A gasp broke from her lips.

Graham Foster straightened, smiled into her eyes, turned, and strode away. Her heart pounding against her corset stays, Moira stared after him and shivered.

♥ ♥ ♥

"Shaun, my friend, I think I'm in love."

"You don't say." Shaun turned from whatever he'd been contemplating outside Graham's sitting-room window. Eyebrows as black as coal arced in genuine interest. "With whom?"

Graham stretched out his legs on the chaise, tipped his head back, and slipped another orange slice into his mouth. He'd purchased two crates in Spain on the trip back from Africa. Now he wished he'd brought three, as Letty threatened to exhaust the supply within days. "I wish I knew," he replied.

"A little early to be drinking, isn't it?"

"I haven't been. Did you see me walking with a woman at the ball last night?"

"I saw you walking with a number of women." Shaun moved away from the window and threw himself into a nearby armchair. "To which are you referring?"

"You saw me *escaping* the advances of a number of women. Only one caught my interest. The one in dark blue with the matching mask."

"Ahhhh. Intriguing, that one. You ever discover what lay behind that mask?" Shaun leaned to pluck an orange from the bowl at Graham's elbow.

"No, damn it."

"More intriguing still. And since you no doubt tried, I'm quite certain your failure to do so has you stewing."

"I want you to make inquiries."

"Will do." Shaun pierced the orange rind with his thumbnail, sending out a tangy spray of juice. He licked the tip of his thumb and made a face. "Too tart. I did manage to find out where that Miss Hughes is staying while she's in London. Got Smythe's secretary to spill his guts."

"So Smythe lied."

"Like a Gypsy horse trader."

"I wonder why. How thickly did you have to line the secretary's pocket?"

"Not too much. Just sat there cleaning my fingernails with that serpent's-head dagger I found in Dendera." Shaun shrugged. "It seems the lady has rooms at a boardinghouse on the Surrey side of the river."

Graham jerked his chin toward his friend. "The Surrey side?"

"Southwark."

"Why the devil would she take rooms there? She might have stayed here if she'd only asked. It was her home, after all, before it became mine."

"You know how ladies are. Probably didn't want to share the place with a new mistress."

"New mistress, indeed." Graham scowled and rolled his partially eaten orange onto the table beside him. "I wasn't at all pleased to arrive in England to find my family already installed in my new home and amassing debts I'm now expected to pay. Talk about taking without asking."

"Have they spent all that much? Relatively speaking, that is."

"That's not the point. They had no right."

"They *are* your family."

"Are they? They disowned me quick enough ten years ago over that cheating incident." Graham suppressed a shudder at the memory of the injustice. He'd never felt more betrayed before or since.

Shaun furrowed his brow in sympathy. "Didn't help matters that your own uncle took sides against you."

"The old cobra isn't my uncle. Just another of my numerous distant cousins. We're a far-flung family, one whose reach far exceeds its regard."

"Still, your immediate family has tried to make amends over the years," Shaun reminded him, not for the first time.

"Ah, yes, *after* they heard I'd discovered treasure in Egypt. But I haven't tossed them out on their ears yet, have I?" Shaun said nothing as Graham ruminated for several moments. Then a thought occurred to him. He swung his feet to the floor and sat up. "I have a sneaking suspicion they might be the same person."

His friend nodded, unperturbed as usual by Graham's abrupt leap in conversation. "Miss Hughes and the mysterious woman in blue, eh?"

"She called herself Mary Houser."

"Moira Hughes, Mary Houser." Shaun shook his head. "Quite the amateur, isn't she?"

Moira. Like Maura, but not quite. No, one must achieve a quick realignment of the mouth to make it come out right. A pursing of the lips and a slight flick of the tongue, clever little motions that pleased him. Rather like a kiss. Moira, Moira. "What do you suppose she might be hiding?"

A knock at the door prevented Shaun from answering.

"Come."

Baxter bowed his way into the room. A dismal expression dragged at his otherwise stoic features. "I've brought the requested items, sir."

"Good. Bring them here."

The valet stepped gingerly across the carpet as if afraid of disturbing someone, then reached into his coat pocket to extract a cloth bag cinched tight with a drawstring. Graham reached for the sack and held it to his ear.

"Are they alive? I don't hear them buzzing."

"Quite alive, my lord." Baxter's lip curled. "Sleeping, perhaps."

Graham nodded. "Thank you, Baxter. That will be all." But just before the servant closed the door behind him, Graham called, "Oh, Baxter, have you seen my brother yet this morning?"

"No, sir. I don't believe Mr. Frederick returned home last evening."

"Let me know the moment he does."

"Very good, sir."

"Brothers, sisters, cousins. . .ah, Shaun, life was so much simpler in Egypt," Graham grumbled as the door closed behind his valet.

"You didn't think so when Hakim al Faruq threatened to slit your throat."

"The man was making a point."

"Yes, against your jugular."

"It turned out well, didn't it? I miss the old boy. By God, I miss that life."

"We'll return soon enough, and when we do, we'll have virtually unlimited funds." The armchair creaked as Shaun leaned forward. "We won't have to search out the graves of goldsmiths and minor nobles any longer. We can head right for the important sites and get on with the work we set out to do."

"How right you are." Graham glanced down at the sack cupped in his palm. His mood brightened considerably. "Isis is sure to be hungry by now, but perhaps I should wait and allow Freddy the honor when he arrives home. Or perhaps you'd prefer to do it."

Shaun flicked the fingers of both hands as if to dislodge something sticky and unpleasant. "Unless you wish to create a panic, you'd best do it. I'll lock the door, just in case."

♥ ♥ ♥

"Why, Miss Moira, what a surprise. A *wonderful* surprise, my dear. But why are you sneaking in through the garden?"

Stout hands encased Moira's shoulders as Mrs. Higgensworth drew her into the kitchen.

Moira indeed felt like a sneak. Having concealed herself in the laundry yard until dusk, she'd approached the house and peeked in through the kitchen windows, ducking whenever one of the servants passed by. It had taken a colossal effort of patience to wait until she finally glimpsed the housekeeper alone before tapping on the garden door. She drew a breath now to begin her explanation but Mrs. Higgensworth spoke first.

"You poor lamb, abroad this time of evening and all alone. Why I've never heard of the like. . ." Cradling Moira's hand in both her warm, ample ones, the older woman brought her into the servants' dining hall. "Have you had your tea? You sit yourself down while I ring for Susan to bring some."

Emitting little puffs of breath, the housekeeper waddled to the bell pull. "You're such a dear to visit me like this. We've missed you and your mother dreadfully these many months, and your stepfather, too, God rest his kindly soul. I daresay, things have not been the same

41

since he left us. Dear me, not at all the same. . ."

"Mrs. Higgensworth, I need to speak with you."

"Not until I've seen a hot meal go into you. You're as thin as a scarecrow, you poor little thing." She returned to the table and plunked down beside Moira. "I suppose I should bring you upstairs and announce you, though I confess I'd rather keep you to myself for a while, give us time to catch up and all. But, Mrs. Foster—oh, can you believe the woman ordered me to call her *my lady*, as if it were her birthright. No, it's her oldest son who's inherited the Monteith name, and all the rest of 'em are Missus, Miss, and Mister Foster as far as I'm concerned."

She went on, but Moira heard little after mention of the son who'd inherited Monteith. The very thought of him incited an infuriating flurry in her stomach. Her wrist still tingled, occasionally, where the rogue's lips— and tongue—touched it the night of the ball.

She suppressed a shiver.

"Please, Mrs. Higgensworth. I'm here because I need employment. As a maid."

Mrs. Higgensworth's mouth dropped open. Something between mild amusement and abject horror flickered across her face.

"Can you hire me, Mrs. Higgensworth?"

Moira's question roused the woman from her stunned silence. "Well, I. . .I don't know. . .I can't imagine. . .whatever do you mean, Miss Moira?"

"I wish to work here as a maid."

"But. . .you're a gentlewoman." Her voice plunged to an undertone. A wash of crimson stained her face. "You couldn't possibly. Oh, what on earth's happened, my dear, to drive you to such lengths?"

How Moira wished she could explain, yet to do so would only burden a kind soul who had no means of offering the financial assistance she and her mother so desperately needed. "I don't mean permanently. Just for a short time. You see, I believe my stepfather left something behind here, and I need to find it."

"Is that all?" The woman released the corner of apron she'd balled in her hands. "Why don't you just ask the new Lord Monteith for it, whatever it is?"

"Oh, no, I couldn't. You see, I don't believe he wishes me to have it, though it belongs to my mother by rights. Please, Mrs. Higgensworth, couldn't you fit me in as a parlor maid or the like? I need access to the library and study, and perhaps the master's private rooms, as well."

"Oh, now, Miss Moira, you're as sensible a girl as ever were born, but this plan of yours is foolhardy. What if the family should discover you?"

"The only one who might recognize my face is Lord Monteith. The rest of the family has never met me. And I understand most of Papa's staff has left. Is there anyone working above stairs who might recognize me?"

"Well. . ." Mrs. Higgensworth tapped her chin. "There's Stanley the groom, but you wouldn't cross paths much with him, I don't suppose. You're right, nearly all the old staff was either let go or left on their own as soon as new positions became available. As I told you, things haven't been the same around here, though better since the new Lord Monteith's arrival, I must admit."

"So, then." Moira held the other woman's gaze and her breath at the same time, and ignored her jolting pulse as she acknowledged how close she would be to Graham Foster during the next few days. "Will you help me?"

"Well. . .forgive me for having to ask, my dear, but. . ." Mrs. Higgensworth appraised her with a doubtful air. "Can you handle a mop and duster?"

"Of course."

"Carry large trays stacked with china and silver-ware?"

"Child's play."

"Be willing to treat this family with the utmost respect?"

The thought of Graham Foster's impertinence stiff-ened her spine. "Rather more vexing, but for a worthy cause, yes."

"Then you're hired, my dear. And may heaven preserve us both."

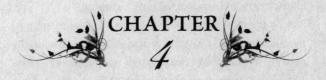

CHAPTER
4

She dreamed of Nigel. Nigel as she best remembered him—galloping his horse across the countryside, jumping hedgerows and streams, and sending her heart into her throat as she watched from her vantage point by the lake. Later she would scold him, tell him he'd break his neck one of these days. . .

Oh, Nigel.

A pounding at her bedchamber door scattered the memories. Beside her, Trina the scullery maid sat up, rubbed the sleep from her eyes, and delivered a hardy thwack to Moira's shoulder, still huddled tight beneath the blanket.

"Rise and shine, Your Highness. Sleepin' away half the morn won't wash round 'ere. You'll find your sorry arse in the street by luncheon."

Moira peered at the bedside clock. Four thirty in the morning—in the *morning!* Oh, what *had* she gotten herself into?

By day's end her aching back, sore muscles, and throbbing feet provided the answer, not to mention a new appreciation for the length and depth of the service staircase.

By the close of her second day in the Fosters' employ, she'd shaken out and rehung the velvet curtains in the drawing room, set and cleared stack upon stacks of dishes, and hauled linens from the laundry to the bedding closet and back. This morning she found herself on hands and knees scrubbing the hardwood floor in the morning room.

Mrs. Higgensworth hadn't intended for her to scrub floors. But minutes ago, after that dratted tray of porridge, scones, and clotted cream upended in her tired hands, the housekeeper reluctantly set her to work with scrub brush and bucket.

Miss Letitia Foster had insisted. Red-faced with fury, the sullen young woman had bewailed her ruined frock and threatened Moira with immediate dismissal if she didn't dispose of the mess instantly. Miss Foster had behaved like a spoiled child and really, only the smallest drops of porridge had spattered her pale muslin over-skirt. Nothing the laundress couldn't set to rights.

Moira certainly understood now why Mrs. Higgensworth had warned her to stay clear of Miss Letitia.

So far she had managed to avoid Graham Foster, for Mrs. Higgensworth carefully timed her duties before and after he occupied any particular room. Once, however, while traipsing from the kitchen to the conservatory with a brimming watering can in hand, she'd had to detour into the ladies' parlor as he strolled down the corridor. An ill-placed armchair—which would not have been set so close to the doorway in her mother's day for fear of a draft—had been the unhappy recipient of splashing water. The mishap resulted in a watermark on the fine moiré, which only a strategically placed pillow could conceal.

But not once in all this time—marked by arduous toil and near disaster—had she gained access to either the library or the master's study. The latter had been locked tight both times she had tried. The former presented a different sort of difficulty, one she hadn't counted on.

Upon tiptoeing into the library the first evening, she had been surprised to discover the same dark-haired man she'd seen in Mr. Smythe's waiting room—a man certain to recognize her should he get a close enough look at her. Graham Foster's friend and houseguest, as Mrs. Higgensworth identified him, seemed unfortunately fond of reading in the evenings.

The thought produced a pang. Everett Foster had enjoyed reading in the evenings, as well. Throughout Moira's childhood, they'd shared wonderful adventures, reading aloud from the novels and histories he loved. Moira had adored the stories, though sharing Papa's spacious wing chair and hearing his voice rumble against her ear had provided as much if not more delight.

"What on *earth* do you think you're *doing*?"

Oh, dear. The pointed toe of a delicate silk house

slipper rapped an angry tattoo practically beneath Moira's nose. Attached to it, the person of Miss Letitia Foster loomed above, her pale blue eyes positively glacial.

Moira hadn't seen the girl steal back into the room. Nor had she noticed the soapy rivulets coursing along the floorboards and soaking the rug beneath the breakfast table. Her heart sank. The crimson dye from the now-sodden needlework roses had stained the fringed tatting a bright pink.

"I'm so terribly sorry, miss. Perhaps I could. . ."

"Sorry? Yes, you'll *be* sorry when my brother hears about this." With a whirl that sent the hem of her gown flouncing into Moira's face, Miss Letitia stormed from the room.

Moira sat back on her haunches and, with another glance at the rug, admitted the girl could not be blamed entirely. She flung the scrub brush into the bucket, only to send another sudsy wave splashing onto the floor. She stared at this newest puddle and felt exhausted. Empty. Defeated. Then she gathered her weary legs beneath her and hefted the bucket. She supposed she might as well go pack her things.

"We must dismiss her at *once*, Monteith. Before she destroys something else."

Graham scowled at his sister but didn't bother correcting her on his name. She'd stormed into his study moments ago, figuratively but not literally dragging the housekeeper in behind her. Letty had delayed her tirade long enough to toss a pointed glance at Shaun, who took the hint and exited through the connecting door to the library.

"I fail to see why *we* need do anything," Graham replied. "The girl is Mrs. Higgensworth's charge."

The housekeeper folded her arms across her chest and gave a gratified nod. Graham responded with a little wink.

"But Mrs. Higgensworth *refuses* to sack her." Letty stood with hands on hips, chin in the air, feet anchored firmly to the floor. Her outrage had quickly consumed all her ladylike affectations; oddly, Graham rather preferred her this way.

"Perhaps she sees no reason to sack her," he said with feigned patience. "I respect Mrs. Higgensworth's judgment."

The housekeeper's self-satisfied grin faded when Letty narrowed her eyes in her direction.

"Pardon me, but in this instance Mrs. Higgensworth's judgment isn't worth a wooden *farthing*."

"Be nice, Letty."

"Have you *seen* what that chit of a maid has *done* these past few days? The drawing-room curtains are all awry—"

"So straighten them."

"The luncheon china is chipped—"

"Buy new."

"She just now threw the remains of breakfast all over the morning-room floor—"

"Were you planning to eat the leftovers?"

"And the lovely rug Mama purchased only two weeks ago is reduced to rubbish."

"Bother the rug."

"Monteith, how *can* you make light of this?"

"Because for one thing, it is no small matter to let go a servant. Even with a letter of recommendation, she could very well end up on the street. Secondly, I trust Mrs. Higgensworth. She has run this house for nearly two decades." He turned to the waiting housekeeper. "Mrs. Higgensworth, is the girl worth retaining? Is she salvageable?"

The woman stepped forward, her capable hands clasped at her waist. "I believe so, sir, for all she makes the occasional mistake. Ah, but she's a sweet lamb with an elderly mother to support. She means well and tries her best—"

Letty squeaked. Graham issued a warning glare and gestured for the housekeeper to continue.

"And I think in time she'll do quite nicely, my lord."

Graham nodded. "Good. Perhaps you might curtail her duties a bit, set her to some simpler tasks for the time being."

"Yes, sir. She could fluff pillows, dust—though not the fine porcelain—and I could send her to market each day."

"And trust her with *money*?" Letty gave a snort.

"We purchase on credit and pay the accounts

50

monthly, miss," the housekeeper calmly pointed out.

"There, then, it's settled." And none too soon, as far as he was concerned. Just prior to this interruption, Shaun had been about to confide some newly discovered detail about the mysterious Moira Hughes.

"Monteith, had you no servants at all in Egypt? Do you *not* know they're supposed to *earn* their keep?"

"Mrs. Higgensworth," he said quietly, "would you leave us, please?"

The woman curtsied and closed the door behind her. Graham allowed his gaze to bore into his sister until the self-righteous spark faded from her eyes and a mottled blush crept into her cheeks. Then he said evenly, "Tell me, what of family members who insinuate themselves upon one's generosity? Should they also be made to earn their keep?"

Her brow puckered, and her bottom lip slipped uncertainly between her teeth. She might have been nine again and caught stealing sweets from the kitchen. His question clearly perplexed her, so much so a watery sheen obscured her blue eyes just before she blinked and looked away.

"It was a rhetorical question, Letty, one you might wish to ponder. That will be all."

With something between a grimace and a nod, she swept to the door and was quickly gone. That door had no sooner closed behind her, when the one to the library opened. Shaun sauntered in, his features pinched with concern.

"I suppose you heard most of that," Graham said.

"Had my ear pressed to the door." Shaun settled into a wing chair. "Don't you think you were a bit hard on the girl?"

"After that sort of impudence?"

Shaun waved away the notion as he would a fly. "She's growing up, becoming a young lady, and experimenting with new ideas." He leaned forward, looking a good deal too animated for Graham's liking. "She needs some free rein, room to explore."

"And what would you know of my sister, Shaun?"

"Nothing." He sniffed, affecting a disinterested air.

"Then why don't you talk about Miss Hughes and leave Letty to me."

Shaun's mouth curved to a sly grin. "Did some snooping around that boardinghouse of hers. Miss Hughes hasn't been back to her rooms for the past couple of days at least."

"You don't say." Graham walked to the window. Above slate rooftops, London's constant haze presented a sickly contrast to the startling azure skies of Egypt. He stared past his own faint reflection to the carefully swept street below, again so unlike his adopted nation's sandy, ever-changing thoroughfares. A coach and four ambled by, rumbling along the cobbles. The gilt crest on its door caught the weak sun and tossed a glint in his eye. "Moira Hughes came to London for a reason, Shaun. An important one. I'm sure of it."

"Yes, but what? And why would Smythe lie about

not knowing where she was staying?"

"Good questions, both."

Down below, a woman walked past the house, her steps raising a crisp echo along the foot pavement. Graham watched her until she disappeared around the corner. Something about her graceful posture and imperious stride seemed familiar, and utterly contrary to the white linen cap, dark blue frock, and low-heeled boots that declared her a maid. With a shake of his head, he turned from the window. "And my brother? Have you discovered his whereabouts?"

"The Lazy Hound."

"God knows you're right, Shaun, but that is my brother you're talking about."

"No, the Lazy Hound Tavern. Over on Cheapside. That's where he is."

"Ah. Come along, then. Let's go and collect him."

♥ ♥ ♥

"Oh. . .roll your leg over, roll your leg over, roll your leg over. . .it's better that way! Oh, roll—"

"Stop it, Freddy. I'm warning you." Graham tugged his brother's arm for emphasis, producing the desired effect, but at the same time causing Freddy to stumble over his own feet. He'd have skidded face-first onto the graveled path if not for Graham and Shaun each having one of his arms slung across their shoulders.

"Pardon, your lordship. Don't like my singing, eh? Miss Ruby Rousseau liked it well enough. Want to know *how* she liked it, Graham, old boy?"

Graham turned his face to avoid a waft of secondhand whiskey fumes. Earlier, he and Shaun had discovered Freddy thoroughly cup-shot, lying facedown across a littered table in the Lazy Hound Tavern. Red satin dress hitched to her thighs, the famed Ruby Rousseau, in little better condition herself, had sat perched beside him, running her fingers through his tawny hair and humming the same sordid tune Freddy currently seemed so fond of.

After tossing down a shilling for Miss Ruby's pains, Graham and Shaun had hefted Freddy by shoulders and legs and carried him out of the dank, putrid-smelling establishment. He passed out during the ride home, regaining consciousness once and only briefly, to hang his head out the carriage door. The street sweeper would be far from pleased when he reached the corner of High Holborn and Oxford.

Upon arriving home, they bypassed the house and proceeded to the garden, where Graham and Shaun were presently walking Freddy back and forth in the hopes of establishing some measure of sobriety before their mother saw him.

"You're a disaster," Graham murmured as all three men struggled to remain upright where the path circled a birdbath. "Where's Baxter with that coffee?"

Shaun squinted over his shoulder. "Looks like refreshments are on the way."

Graham followed his friend's gaze. A small square table had been placed just beyond the terrace doors, and two footmen were now placing chairs around it. "About bloody time."

He began to steer his brother toward the house when a maid bearing table linens crossed the threshold from the Gold Saloon inside. With a brisk snap she opened a tablecloth and spread it across the polished wooden table, then began setting out napkins. Hunching over her task, she seemed in a bit of a hurry. A sudden breeze caught one linen square and whisked it from her hands, sending it floating over the flagstones. She scrambled after it.

Graham went still, arms falling to his sides. That dark coif, those delicate shoulders, the smart little flicking motion in her hips as she bustled after the errant serviette. . .

Thud.

"Ouch."

"I can't manage him all by myself, you know."

Turning, Graham witnessed a scowling Shaun struggling to lift a half-sprawled Freddy from the path. Freddy's legs, incapable of anchoring his weight, wobbled and gave way with each attempt.

"Sorry." Graham tugged his brother relatively up-right. By the time he looked up at the terrace again, the dark-haired maid had vanished, replaced by a redhead carrying cups and a coffeepot.

"Shaun," he mumbled as a nagging sensation took hold, "I must be in love."

"Why's that, m'lord?"

He ignored Shaun's flippant use of his title. "I'm beginning to see the lady everywhere."

"Big brother's in love, is he?" Freddy's knees buckled as giggles racked him. Graham and Shaun traded exasperated looks over his sagging head and hoisted him higher. "In that case, Graham, you lordly old boy, roll your leg over. . .roll your leg over. . .roll—"

Graham released his hold on Freddy's arm, and this time Shaun made no effort to catch the weight plunging to the ground. Another thud was followed by a groan.

"Coffee, Shaun?" Straightening his coat, Graham set off for the house without sparing a second glance at the heap his brother had become.

"Don't mind if I do, thank you."

"Do join us when you can, Freddy," Graham called over his shoulder. To his friend he murmured, "I'll send a footman out for him. Think I'll have Isis brought down, as well. She could use a bit of sunshine."

♥ ♥ ♥

Moira peeked carefully through the curtains of the Gold Saloon as Graham Foster and his guest took their seats on the terrace. There had been a third man with them, and she assumed by his striking resemblance to both Graham and Miss Letitia that he was the younger Foster brother. She no longer saw him and hoped he hadn't reentered the house. The fewer people about, the better.

Scanning the gardens, she spotted something long, dark, and sprawling on the path near the birdbath. It stirred and, raising up on elbows, revealed itself to be a man. A thatch of golden brown hair caught the sun for an instant before the figure flattened against the ground and went still.

The brother? Moira squinted, straining to see out the slightly wavy glass of the window. Why, Frederick Foster must be blind, stinking drunk. That would certainly explain the ribald crooning she'd heard a few minutes ago, lyrics that had made her blush.

Well and good. Mrs. Foster and her ill-mannered daughter had gone out for the day, so she needn't worry about them. Earlier, Mrs. Higgensworth had presented Moira with quite a boon. While rummaging through a cupboard below stairs, the housekeeper had quite unexpectedly discovered an extra key to the master's study. Now Moira slipped away from the window, tiptoed from the saloon, and stole across the house.

Minutes later, her throat closed as she stared into the velvet shadows of the room officially forbidden to her throughout her childhood, yet into which she'd been invited more often than not.

Moira, darling, come and help Papa decipher these figures. . . Moira, Papa's eyes are grown tired. . . Come read this passage for me, dear heart. . .

"Oh, Papa. How I miss you."

She blinked away a veil of tears. The room had changed little these past months. Though Papa's personal effects had been cleared away, the furnishings remained the same, placed where they had always been. Even his favorite chair, a leather wingback, sat beside the hearth at the precise angle Papa had always insisted upon. It wanted only for the master of the house to settle in, favorite book in hand.

A tremulous breath filled her lungs with Everett Foster's pipe tobacco, old and stale but lingering like a persistent ghost, a haunting reminder of the happy life they'd shared.

She hitched her maid's skirts in one hand and strode to the desk. This was no time for sentimental tears, but for decisive action. Who knew how much time she had?

Mrs. Higgensworth would steer the other staff clear of this room, and Mrs. and Miss Foster had mentioned a museum on their way out the door. They were going to view the artifacts brought home from Egypt by the new Lord Monteith.

Graham Foster, on the other hand, might decide to retire to his study at any time. Mrs. Higgensworth promised to keep watch and deter him if it proved the case, but even so, Moira must move quickly. Where would her stepfather have hidden something as vital as a codicil?

She opened the topmost desk drawer to discover a leather-bound notebook, a pot of sealing wax, a penknife, and, tossed in haphazardly, a pair of riding gloves. She leaned in closer, inspecting the buff leather. These were not Papa's gloves. They were far too large and too grayed at the fingertips, revealing signs of frequent use. Papa would have discarded them long ago in favor of a new pair.

With her forefinger she stroked the buttery kidskin. Then she lifted the pair, holding them in the light of the window behind her. She imagined them filled with the rugged contour of Graham Foster's hands.

Hands that had enfolded her own in confident strength, drawn her somewhere she hadn't wished to go, and held her there, nearly breathless. Remarkable, startling, disturbing hands. She raised his gloves to her cheek. . .

And remembered what he'd done next. Her wrist. . .his tongue. Oh, such insolence. Nigel had never. . .simply wouldn't have done. . . She tossed the pair into the drawer and snapped it shut.

The codicil was her only reason for snooping— yes, like a common thief—through the man's personal effects. To no other purpose would his private, intimate world ever intersect with hers. That she silently swore.

And yet. . .what else of his might she find?

The notion shocked her. Scandalized her. Why, to rummage through a stranger's possessions was bad enough. But to enjoy it, anticipate it, was wrong. Disgraceful. Beneath her.

As she opened another drawer, her fingertips quivered while her belly tightened around a curling sensation.

CHAPTER
5

"ongratulations, Freddy, on having made a first-rate ass of yourself."

As Graham spoke, the footman who had helped his brother to the terrace moments ago backed discreetly into the house. Graham lifted the silver coffeepot and filled Freddy's cup with the steaming brew made extra strong according to his orders.

Movement inside his coat pocket—fitted with a stiff, starched linen sleeve to prevent it collapsing—signaled Isis's awakening from her midday slumber. Graham set the pot down and carefully slipped his hand into his pocket. Once his Egyptian-born pet made her way onto his wrist, he extended his arm to the streaming sunshine. She rose up on eight bristling legs, basking in the heat.

"I dread to think what iniquities you might have committed last night, little brother," he said. "You didn't get married or anything to that effect, did you?"

Sitting opposite, Shaun snickered at the suggestion. Freddy slouched with elbows propped on the table, head anchored in splayed fingers. Suddenly, from that miserable huddle, a yelp emerged.

"Good God, Graham, don't move." Freddy's head swung upward, mouth agape. One hand inched toward his napkin. "Hold completely still, and I'll swat it away."

Graham's free hand shot up, creating a protective barrier between his pet and Freddy's improvised weapon. "Don't you dare harm a hair on Isis's, ah, legs."

Freddy's jaw dropped. "Isis?"

"Quite. She's an African sun spider." Graham brought the arachnid close to his face and stared into numerous bulging black eyes. "And what a lovely sun spider she is. Want to hold her?"

Freddy lurched away, nearly losing his balance and toppling his chair. He gripped the table's edge for purchase. "Keep that disgusting creature away from me."

"Disgusting? That's no way to talk about a lady."

With a sickened expression—though whether from drink or Isis's presence, Graham couldn't say—Freddy watched the spider's hairy-legged trek along Graham's coat sleeve. She stopped at his elbow and raised her burnished brown back to the sun, twitching her pedipalps to taste the air. Freddy grimaced, shut his bloodshot eyes, and cradled his forehead in his palm.

"She's really quite harmless." Graham leaned toward his brother, bringing Isis with him. Though in his younger days he'd consumed enough brandy to sympathize with Freddy's present condition, he couldn't resist teasing. "I think she likes you."

"Looks as though she wants a kiss," Shaun added with a wicked grin. Yet the direction in which he leaned and the wary narrowing of his eyes declared Shaun's relief that Isis's regard centered on Freddy and not himself.

Muttered oaths too garbled for comprehension streamed from his brother's lips, though Graham distinctly heard his name mentioned more than once.

"Would you mind leaving us?" he said to Shaun. "There's something I need to discuss with my brother."

"Right you are." Looking a bit disappointed, Shaun pushed to his feet.

Graham slipped Isis into his coat pocket; she scuttled into a corner and settled in. He didn't immediately speak, but stared out over the small but formal gardens he had the damnedest time thinking of as his. Fruit trees and box hedges bordered fastidious flower beds; marble benches, birdbaths, and statues graced several winding paths. Set near the rear wall, a miniature Grecian pavilion dominated the scene.

Such perfect, symmetrical artistry seemed to exemplify the well-ordered ideal of a gentleman's life—the elegance, the refinement, the ease. On the other hand, his brother, fast degenerating into hiccups, expressed the reality so often lurking beneath.

Hypocrisy. It was what had sent Graham seeking

adventures in far-off places years ago. It was what convinced him of the importance of self-reliance. It made him wonder now if he shouldn't simply get up from the table, set his feet in motion, and see how far he got by the end of the day. Hadn't he learned, in the harshest terms possible, that the concept of family—especially his family—constituted the greatest hypocrisy of all?

"Why are you doing this, Freddy?" he asked quietly, eyes fixed on the swaying tops of the pear trees flanking the pavilion.

"Doing—*hic*—what?" His brother eyed him up and down. "Where'd that thing go?"

"My pocket. You're safe for the moment, so do me the favor of satisfying my curiosity. Why do you seem hell-bent on destroying your life?"

"That's overstating it just a bit, wouldn't you say? And do you really—*hic*—think you're at all qualified to judge my actions?"

"No, not to judge. But I'm worried about you." The truth of that statement startled him, but there it was. For all his claims to the contrary, he cared. Very much.

"Ha." Another hiccup claimed Freddy's laugh, making it an ugly, clipped bark. "You're not permitted to worry about me. You relinquished that right years ago."

"I'm still your brother."

Freddy laughed again, a strident sound filled with scorn. "Who are you to point fingers? As I recall—*hic*—you didn't leave England in a burst of triumph. Or did you? Perhaps cheating at one of the most—*hic*—prestigious universities in Europe would be considered quite a coup in certain circles."

Graham lifted a weary gaze to his brother's face. "Do you believe that, Freddy?"

"Why shouldn't I?"

"Because it isn't true."

"Then why did you leave?"

"I seem to remember a certain letter signed by both you and Letty, informing me in no uncertain terms I'd done the right thing in leaving." The missive had caught up with him on the Iberian Peninsula, days before crossing the Strait of Gibraltar into Morocco. Until those bitter words had spread their poison through his veins, he had considered retracing his steps. . .

"We were children when we wrote that." Freddy's fist struck the table, sending his coffee cup toppling from its saucer. He seemed oblivious to the liquid soaking his sleeve as he gripped the edges of the table and hissed, "Why didn't you come back when Father died?"

Freddy's vehemence momentarily knocked Graham breathless. "I didn't return because I was angry. Damned angry. I'd been accused of an offense I didn't commit. My future, the future I'd been working so hard to achieve, crumbled before my eyes and no one—not Father, Mother, or anyone else—stood by me. So I left. I left England, with its sanctimonious rules and shallow standards, and washed my hands of the whole damned lot."

"And—*hic*—of me." The venom injected into those words stung no less for the hiccup.

A gulp of air lodged like a stone in Graham's lungs. "No, Freddy, not you. I believed you wanted me gone, yes, but that only garnered my regret, not my anger."

"No?" The younger Foster raised eyes burning from drink, and from a pain Graham realized he had put there. "I bore the brunt of it. Me and Letty both. While you were off hunting for trinkets, we lost our father. You're our elder brother. You should have become head of the household." His voice dropped to a caustic whisper. "You should have been here."

"Freddy, I'm sorry. I didn't realize. . ."

"Don't bother." His brother turned his face away and squinted into the gardens. "You think you can waltz back into our lives after a decade and express your disappointment in the way we turned out? The devil—*hic*—with you."

Freddy shoved backward and gained his feet, overturning his chair with a crash. A footman appeared in the doorway, but Graham gestured him away. A sound of disgust grated in Freddy's throat as he pivoted with a precarious stagger, caught his balance, and headed for the house.

"Where are you going?"

"To—*hic*—pack my things."

"You're in no condition to—"

From inside the house, a shriek blared—long, keening, outraged—taken up by frantic cries of *Help! Help!*

"What the blazes?" Graham jumped up from his seat.

"That's Letty." Freddy took off running. A clunk resounded when the toe of his shoe caught against the step-up into the Gold Saloon. He went down hard across the threshold, chin mercifully landing on the plush rug inside. He lay there stunned, blinking, then rose tentatively on his elbows and shook his head to clear it. Continued cries of "Help, thief!" roused him to his feet. Graham followed at a run.

♥ ♥ ♥

"Oh, do stop yelling. I can explain. Really. Please just shush!" Backed to the study's bay window, Moira wanted to clap her hand over Miss Foster's mouth to stop her from raising the alarm.

On second thought, that mouth was presently opened so wide she doubted one hand or even two could effectively seal it.

Poised at the center of the room, arms flapping and ringlets flailing like a raging Medusa, the girl shouted on and on until Moira's ears throbbed. She had been caught red-handed as they say, with desk drawers yawning, cabinets gaping, and a dozen or more books akimbo, pages fluttering in the breeze of the young woman's tirade.

"This isn't what you think," Moira tried again, raising her voice to be heard. Miss Foster's face, already an ominous scarlet, flamed hotter still, precipitating another hasty step backward on Moira's part. She found herself flush against the windowpanes and tangled in the curtain.

"I—I must have misunderstood Mrs. Higgensworth's instructions. . ." Even to her desperate ears, that explanation rang with idiocy. She might have done better had the clatter of approaching footsteps not sent the panic rising to her throat.

Several men burst in at once, a small but vigorous onslaught of trampling feet and booming voices. Their sheer ferociousness drove Moira tighter against the panes. Their entrance also silenced Miss Foster, thank heavens for that at least. An instant later Graham Foster, his brother, houseguest, and several footmen went silent, their fierceness fading to puzzlement as they took in the scene.

Frederick Foster was the first roused from bewilderment. "Letty, for pity's sake." His words were slurred and breathless. "Are you hurt?"

"I caught *her* ransacking the place." Miss Letitia jabbed a forefinger in Moira's direction. "She's a *thief*."

"Blazing hell." Graham Foster tugged his neck cloth and scowled. With a backward wave, he dismissed the footmen. "Letty, we thought someone had a knife to your throat."

"Look what she's *done*." Miss Foster swept her arm in an arc that encompassed the disheveled room. "We must have her arrested at *once*."

"For untidiness?"

"For thievery!"

"Good grief, there's nothing in this room to steal," Graham said. "I doubt she's loaded her apron with books and writing paper."

Letitia Foster hoisted her chin. "Then what on earth *is* she doing?"

Oh, dear. All gazes turned to Moira, huddled and shaking in the window recess. In that instant she understood the discomfiture of the fox held pinioned to a tree by barking, salivating hounds. She swore then and there she'd never join a hunt again, not even for the exercise.

Ah, but they were waiting for an answer.

"Yes, well, I. . .you see, I was in the process of. . ." She glanced at each expectant face in turn: Miss Letitia, Mr. Frederick, the houseguest, and, finally, Graham Foster. Her mouth ran dry. It was the way he peered back at her. Since entering the room he'd barely spared her a glance, focusing his annoyance on his sister. Now his scrutiny caressed her up and down and deepened with the inescapable dawning of recognition.

"Moira Hughes." His mouth curved with the familiar impudence, raising the hairs on her nape. "Moira, Moira. What a delightful surprise." He lengthened the syllables of her name, pronouncing each with evident pleasure as though savoring a spoonful of honey. "Or are you Mary Houser today?"

"The former, my lord," she returned as flames leapt

to the tips of her ears.

"You *know* this creature?" His sister flashed an incredulous look that turned speculative in the next instant. "Moira Hughes? Isn't that our. . ."

Miss Foster's question died on lips gone suddenly and alarmingly chalky. Her hand clawed at her throat as her mouth widened in terror.

Moira clapped her hands over her ears as Letitia Foster let loose a fresh round of screams that far outdid her earlier ones. The room once more dissolved into a confusion of voices and movement. The younger Mr. Foster scrambled away while their houseguest raised his voice in an explanation no one could hear.

To her own indescribable horror, Moira discovered the source of the uproar. It was. . .good heavens. . .the most hideous thing she'd ever seen in all her life. A spider, but bigger, thicker, uglier than any she'd ever imagined, a monstrosity from deepest, darkest nightmare, with fearsome clawlike pincers and furry brown legs that bent and stretched with a leisurely grace that made it all the more grotesque.

The leaded casements dug into her spine as she tried to shrink from that dreadful, hairy, revolting creature creeping along Graham Foster's coat sleeve.

And yet. . .*he* regarded it as calmly as you please. He even—ugh, Moira looked away, then couldn't help peeking—allowed the monster to crawl into his palm.

"Letty, do stop that infernal shrieking," he said with a weary roll of his eyes. "Isis is merely an African sun spider. She's quite harmless, completely tame, and certainly nothing to warrant permanently deafening the lot of us."

Letitia's mouth closed. She stared. Blinked. Swallowed with a gulp that echoed through the room. "Isis?" she whispered. "It has a *name*? It's a *pet*?"

"Of course, she's a pet." He smoothly deposited the creature into his coat pocket. "And I'd thank you not to terrify her in the future."

Letitia's head wobbled slightly as she nodded.

With an expression that made her spine tingle, Graham Foster's attention returned in full measure to Moira. "Now then, Miss Hughes, perhaps you'd care to explain why you've rearranged my study in this most charming manner? And why you're masquerading as a maid in my employ? Or have you, indeed, joined my staff?"

Before Moira could answer, Miss Foster pivoted to glare at her. "Better she saves her explanations for the magistrate. I'll have Mrs. Higgensworth send for one *immediately.*"

"If you'll allow me, Miss Foster." The houseguest pulled himself up with a flourish that might have made Moira laugh under different circumstances. "It would be my pleasure to be of service."

"Hm." Miss Foster regarded him down the length of her slender nose. "Yes, Mr. Paddington, thank you. Do hurry."

"There's no reason to summon anyone," Graham

Foster said, but too late. His friend had set off at an eager trot. He glowered at his sister, who produced a self-satisfied shrug.

"Leave us, Letty," her brother commanded. When she pouted and voiced a protest, he ignored her and turned to his brother, who had all but disappeared into the wallpaper at the far end of the room. "You, too, Freddy. Finish sobering up. Letty, did Mother accompany you home?"

"Mama's still at the museum, I suppose." The young woman tossed her curls. "I grew bored staring at all your relics, Monteith, so I begged a ride home with the Sanfords."

"Sorry to have disappointed you." His steely gaze traveled back and forth between his siblings. "Leave us, and don't either of you get into trouble."

Frederick Foster pushed away from the wall and sauntered into the corridor. His sister followed, after flinging one last derisive look at Moira.

The door closed behind the pair, leaving her quite alone with their perplexing older brother.

Yes, most perplexing, indeed. He stood staring at her, his arms folded across his chest. His dimples taunted while an infuriating half smile played about his lips. He strolled out of Moira's vision, and a moment later she heard the familiar creaking of the desk chair.

"Well, Moira Hughes, won't you come out from that recess?"

She much preferred not to. The very suggestion

emphasized the utter foolishness of her behavior. Her maid's uniform didn't help. The plain blue dress and starched apron smoothed away individuality and all the grace of femininity, leaving only the drudgery and burdens of being female. And in this instance, it lent Graham Foster one more seeming advantage over her, besides the obvious fact that she had trespassed in his home.

But with a deep breath she raised her chin and remembered who she was. Moira Hughes, stepdaughter—no, *daughter*—of the late Everett Foster, Lord Monteith, and every bit as good as the man confronting her. She walked out from the embrasure and stood tall before the desk.

It was a large block of carved mahogany, dark, imposing, impressive. Or so she'd always thought. Graham Foster almost dwarfed it. Even sitting, he met her eye levelly and made her feel small and defenseless and very much alone.

Through the window behind him, slanting sunshine burnished the top of his head. He was all golden light, deep shadow, and brilliant smile as he regarded her.

A devil in a halo. She must not forget what he'd done, how her mother had suffered loss upon loss because of this man. Estella Foster had been not only widowed—well, not his fault—but thrown out of her home—most assuredly his fault—within a few short months.

"Now then, Miss Hughes." He closed two of the books she'd left open on the desk, moved them aside, and leaned forward, his face expectant and still so damnably amused. "What have you to say for yourself?"

The scoundrel made her feel like a child. Saw her vulnerability and made full use of it. Holding her chin steady when it wanted to slink into her collar, she mustered the dignity of knowing she, in truth, was the injured party here. "What I have to say, my lord, you might not like to hear."

He held up the flat of his hand. "I'd much prefer you not call me *my lord.*"

"Very well, then, Mr. Foster—"

"Will you not call me Graham?"

"Most assuredly not."

"Because I'd like to call you Moira." Again that grin, those dimples. And that unsettling sensation that traveled through her and curled tight in her belly.

"You may not, sir." She squared her shoulders and glowered, then wished she hadn't displayed any emotion at all when his eyes flashed with mocking humor.

"A pity." He sighed, compressed his lips, and made a show of appearing uncertain. "Tell me, Miss Hughes, have I again departed the dictates of propriety?"

"You don't need me to tell you that, Mr. Foster."

"Perhaps not." He slid closed several gaping desk drawers. Before closing the topmost one, he reached into his coat pocket and dropped something—she could only assume that it was the repulsive spider—inside. After shutting the drawer gently, he flattened his palms to the desktop and pushed to his feet. His amusement melted away as he circled the desk, and with it went the boyish impertinence she'd come to associate with him. Suddenly he was every inch a lord, and very much in command.

She wanted to back away, thought with longing of the safety of her window recess. He came closer despite her willing him to stop a suitable distance away. He filled her vision. She had to look up and up to see the top of his sun-kissed head while the room disappeared behind the broad, hard curve of his shoulders. Waiting, she drew an unsteady breath that filled her with the taste of him, warm and exotic, a sun-drenched wilderness.

"What I need," he said when they stood nearly toe to toe, "is for you to tell me why you're here and what it is you want of me, Moira Hughes."

Goose bumps rose at the sound of her name, spoken in rumbling notes that grazed her lips and cheeks like a lover's gentle kiss. It left her trembling, confused. Frightened. How could the man make her feel seized and kissed without ever laying a hand upon her?

Abandoning subtlety and even pride, she backed a step away. So what if he deduced her need for safety? This man bewildered and alarmed her. His effect on her called for extreme measures.

She looked him directly in the eye. "I want what's mine and my mother's, Mr. Foster. Nothing less will suffice."

"You believe I have something of yours?"

"I do, Mr. Foster. And before I leave, I mean to have it."

He leaned closer still—much too close—and raised his hand to the sensitive skin beneath her chin. His fingertips barely skimmed her, yet commanded every nerve in her body to quiver at attention. "What makes you think, my dear cousin Moira, that I'll allow you to leave?"

Before she could form a reply, he tilted her chin and trapped her lips beneath his own.

CHAPTER 6

Shaun Paddington rushed along the foot pavement until a thought brought him to a dead halt. Where would he find a magistrate? Must he go all the way to Bow Street near Covent Garden? That would take considerable time. Or did every London neighborhood boast such an official, occupying convenient offices identified by bold lettering above the front door?

He glanced up and down the street, detecting nothing but the facades of Mayfair's lavish residences.

He had to admit he'd rushed off without giving the task proper consideration. Perhaps he should go back and seek assistance. But what would Miss Letitia think of him then?

Letitia Foster. Miss Letitia, of the golden brown hair and desert-sky eyes, sleek, willowy, a pharaoh's treasure. She was taller and a little more angular than most women, but he especially liked that about her. He adored the slender silhouette of her hips, the delicate lines of her collarbones, the grace of those long, lean arms. Ah, she fired his every instinct to protect, provide, good heavens, lay down his life.

She irritated Graham, but only because he didn't understand her spirit. He misinterpreted the spark and called it temper. But Shaun saw it—felt it—like the desert sun, bright and glorious and utterly without mercy.

Graham was right about one thing, though. Her name, Letitia, didn't suit her. Not at all. Too fussy and overdone, like hothouse flowers. But Letty—yes, that was pretty, vivacious, full of life. Just like her.

Letty. Let. He could just hear himself. *Morning, Let, shall we have a walk,* or, *Come give us a kiss, my Let.*

Or even, perhaps, *Marry me, Let.*

He groaned. Thus far the girl hadn't shown him the slightest regard. Better he returned to raiding tombs. That's where he was at his best, where he shined. He thoroughly enjoyed fooling sheiks into believing he was the king's ambassador. But with a woman like Letty. . .Shaun sighed. There could be no pretending.

Where the devil would he find a magistrate?

The king's ambassador. That gave him an idea.

♥ ♥ ♥

Moira Hughes's lips were all Graham had imagined. Soft, sweet, and as unpracticed as he had expected. And hoped. But certainly not without curiosity. Not without adventure.

He felt her astonishment in a gasp that filled the interior of his mouth. He breathed it in and pressed for more, refusing her time to think. She went as rigid as a startled rabbit, but lingered rather than pulled away. Then her lips moved against his with a shy taste, an exploring nip. No other part of their bodies touched, but even at that, or because of that, he experienced an immediate rise in his trousers.

Knowing she'd at any moment regain her ladylike sensibilities, Graham slipped his tongue into her mouth. He savored a moment of sheer bliss, fiery heaven, sweet sinner's paradise, before she broke away with a shove that resulted in a full stroke of his tongue against the entire length of hers. A lifetime's pleasure in one fell swoop.

Her hand shot up. It started for his face, but then, oddly, fell to her side.

It puzzled him, for he undoubtedly deserved the full force of her lovely hand.

Her eyes glittered volcanic fury. "How *dare* you?"

He wished he could say he was sorry. But blazing hell, he'd never been less sorry in his life. And for all the indignation flaming her cheeks, he'd wager that, for an instant at least, she hadn't been entirely regretful, either.

"You're a cur, a scoundrel, a—"

"You ransacked my study. I stole a kiss." He shrugged. "Shall we call it fair?"

"Fair?" Her black eyes snapped. "What can you possibly know of fairness, Mr. Foster? You, who has everything a person could ever want, who lives life with a devil-may-care impertinence. You should be ashamed of yourself." She swept an aggressive stride closer. "I'll have you know I'm quite aware of your past, Mr. Foster, and I. . ."

At those words, his enjoyment drained like blood from a wound, leaving a cold void inside him. It must have shown on his face. Her voice faded into uncertainty, and she stood balling the hem of her apron in her fists.

Would he never escape the unearned infamy of his past? Who was this woman to come into his home—albeit, it was once hers—rifle through his belongings, and hurl accusations at him? They shared no blood relation, yet here she was, denouncing his character as blithely as the rest of his faithless family.

"Miss Hughes, I still haven't an inkling why you're here or why you abhor me, other than the kiss, and in truth, I don't believe you found it all that loathsome." Her mouth opened on a retort that he spoke over. "Whatever you may have heard to the contrary, I am not without scruples and feel no need to apologize for how I've lived my life thus far. At least no more so than any other ordinary mortal."

She dropped the hem of her apron; no, she flung it from her hands. "No need to apologize?"

"None."

"Not even for dishonoring the memory of my affianced by making ill-mannered advances toward me?"

Her fiancé, Nigel Foster—how could he have forgotten? He supposed he wanted to forget, even now, especially now, with the sweet taste of her lips lingering on his. She was right. His lapse in memory showed a distinct want of respect. "Forgive me, Miss Hughes. I am indeed sorry for your loss. I didn't know Nigel well, but I certainly thought highly of him."

Not entirely true. On the few occasions they'd met, Nigel had treated Graham with outward friendliness. Yet he'd always detected an undercurrent of condescension, a haughty awareness on his cousin's part that while Nigel constituted the shining fruit of the family tree, Graham's hold was several branches lower.

Moira didn't look appeased. "What about forcing an elderly widow from her home of twenty years—" She stopped and gulped for breath. "Mere weeks after her beloved husband's death?"

"What?"

"You heard me. Why must my mother live in a ramshackle cottage when Monteith Hall stands empty?"

"Ramshackle? Forced out? Not by me, Miss Hughes."

"Most certainly by you, Mr. Foster. I've a certified letter to prove it."

Anger rose at a suspicion suddenly confirmed. Why, that family of his. . . He tamped the thought, for the time being. He'd deal with his mother and Letty later. "Miss Hughes, I think you had better slow down and tell me exactly what it is you were searching for."

"A codicil to my stepfather's will." Her nostrils flared. "Do you deny knowing of its existence?"

"A codicil declaring what? From what I understand, the inheritance was straightforward and unalterable."

She skewed up her lips on a rebuttal, which was interrupted by a knock at the door.

"Damn." Not now, not when he finally had Moira Hughes talking. He sighed. "Come in."

Flushed and out of breath, Shaun strode into the room, then held the door for an elderly gentleman who shuffled in as if each step caused him pain. He was stoop-shouldered, in need of a haircut, and his shabby frock coat was missing a button. Yet for all his physical shortcomings, the man met Graham's appraisal with an air of confidence, even authority.

"The Honorable Mr. Herbert Doone," Shaun announced.

Irritation prickled Graham's neck. "I told you a magistrate wasn't necessary."

Doone regarded Moira from beneath his tightly drawn eyebrows. "Is this the offender?"

"Indeed, Your Honor." Letty entered with an imperious rustle of petticoats, a bounce of curls. "Arrest her at once."

"That won't be necessary." Grasping Letty's hand,

Graham gently but resolutely drew her to stand beside the desk, out of the way. Moira's pretty chin swung from one person to the next while her dark eyes grew large with worry. He caught her gaze and tried to convey an assurance that she would not, in fact, be hauled away to prison. Not yet, at least.

"This woman is a relative," he explained to Mr. Doone. "Miss Hughes is my stepcousin and a guest in my home."

He heard Letty gather breath to speak and tossed her a don't-you-dare scowl.

The magistrate cleared his throat. "Cousin, you say. Then why, if I may be so bold as to ask, is she dressed as a maid?"

"Ah, yes. A practical joker, my cousin. Aren't you, Moira?"

She blinked. "I, ah. . .yes, I am. And I'm terribly sorry—"

"This is *absurd*." Letty pushed away from the desk and brushed past Graham's restraining arm. "Cousin or no, she's been prowling through the house without leave. Look at this room, Your Honor. I caught her rummaging through my brother's things. Red-*handed*, I tell you. And you should see all the chipped china and—oh!—the *rug*! You must see what she's done to the morning-room rug. She's a disaster, a menace, a—"

"Letitia." The first time Graham had ever addressed her by her full name, it rumbled like the dire warning he meant it to be. She flinched and went utterly still but for the quivering ends of her ringlets. "Another word, Letty, and I'll send *you* off with Mr. Doone."

She started to gasp, seemed to think better of it, and snapped her mouth shut.

"Now, see here, Graham." Shaun's attempted forcefulness failed to attain the necessary bluster. His expression urged Graham to be reasonable, to be nice.

But it was for Moira that he calmed. She looked genuinely shaken by Letty's charges, flushed and feverish, and while he wouldn't mind being the cause of that glow, frightening the poor woman was for deuced certain not the tactic he'd use. No, much more pleasurable diversions sprang to mind.

But first he needed to clear the room.

"Mr. Doone, please accept my apologies for this misunderstanding. Mr. Paddington will be most happy to compensate you for your inconvenience."

Shaun rolled his eyes.

"Well. . .if your lordship will vouch for the young lady, and if no crime has actually been committed. . ." The magistrate clasped his rheumatic hands and gave a satisfied nod.

"None has," Graham assured him. "And as head of the family, I assure you I take full responsibility for Miss Hughes. I'll see to it she behaves herself and comes to no more mischief. A good paddling, perhaps—"

"Oh!" With a delightful twitch of those shapely

hips, Moira pulled up straight. Had she possessed a bayonet, she'd have run him through on the spot, he felt quite certain.

"Shaun, please see our guest to the door and remember to thank him properly." His emphasis on the last word produced a grudging nod from Shaun. Graham turned to his sister. "I'd like a word with you later."

Without another peep, Letty darted past him and out the door. He followed her and closed it, leaving him once more alone with Moira.

She eyed him with no small amount of apprehension. "You stay away from me."

He couldn't help smiling. "Don't worry, my dear, your backside is safe with me." For the most part anyway, although what wouldn't he give to explore the luscious curves of that sweet little rump.

"I do, however, expect answers, Miss Hughes, and if you don't wish me to summon Mr. Doone back, you'd best be honest. Now then, explain to me about this codicil."

She hesitated, compressing her lips as she gathered her thoughts. A little frown creased her brow. "Another matter first, Mr. Foster. You mustn't think Mrs. Higgensworth had anything to do with this. I won't have you blaming her or—"

"I 'mustn't'? You 'won't have me'?" Her audacity raised a chuckle. "Bold talk for a maid who nearly found herself incarcerated for theft."

She paled, but held her ground. "I swear she had no idea—"

"That her former employer's stepdaughter had joined her staff? How much of a fool do you take me for?"

"Oh, but she didn't want to. I begged her to let me. I even threatened—"

Her sudden desperation produced a pang of guilt. Obviously her former housekeeper's future outweighed even her own concerns. However amusing he found the incident, this was no joke to Moira. "Mrs. Higgensworth's position is quite secure," he said. "Now, about this codicil business."

"Of course." She smoothed her palms across her apron. When her gaze met his again, she was all business, brisk with purpose. "Before my stepfather died, he confided to me that he'd secured my mother's and my future, that he'd made provisions for our well-being. He was most emphatic about it. Thus far these arrangements have failed to materialize, and even Mr. Smythe claims to know nothing about them."

"I know of no such provisions, either."

Her narrowed eyes proclaimed him a liar. "Do you swear?"

The question sparked a memory, a vile one. He'd sworn his innocence at Oxford, and no one had believed him. His pulse rapped at his temples. Good God, was her goading deliberate? Did she know how sharply her insinuations stung?

"No, I do not swear, Miss Hughes, for I've learned swearing does not a believer make. I tell you I do not have your codicil. Disbelieve me if you wish."

"But. . ." He'd called her bluff, and now her bravado faltered like Freddy on the foot pavement. Those exquisite obsidian eyes held him in a helpless, beseeching sort of gaze that made him regret his stern words.

Perhaps he'd overreacted. Yes, he probably had, letting past unpleasantness rule him in this instance, when Moira's foremost concern was for her and her mother's future.

He held up a hand and said more gently, "If it will make you feel better, I swear."

"Of course, if you did have the codicil," she tapped a finger to her chin as if figuring an arithmetic problem, "it would be in your best interest to deny it, wouldn't it, Mr. Foster?"

That went beyond the pale. The hair on his nape bristled. "Perhaps no codicil exists at all, Miss Hughes. Perhaps you resent my inheritance and have invented a ploy by which you hope to profit."

"How dare you?" Fury frothed in her eyes. The charges that followed, "cur," "villain," "blackguard'— he rather liked that last one—were fair enough, he supposed. Yet when she nipped her bottom lip to stop its quivering, he felt a scrap of remorse once again for not keeping tighter rein on his temper.

"You see, Miss Hughes," he said quietly, "accusations hurt, don't they?"

"Oh." Her expression relaxed as understanding dawned. "You were making a point. You didn't mean it, then?" She paused, searching for confirmation. He nodded, and the last of her frown smoothed away. "Because I would never stoop to anything so deceitful—"

She stopped again, glanced down at her clothing, and continued with a rueful grin that did much to lighten his own mood. "Well, perhaps a small deceit for a good cause. But I shouldn't have accused you as I did. I'm sorry."

"Apology accepted. And for what it's worth, I do believe that you believe a codicil exists. Perhaps together we might discover the truth of it."

"You're willing to help me?"

"I am."

"May I continue searching the house?" Her lips parted as if ready to smile, but not quite.

Ready for another kiss in his opinion, though that was best kept to himself. He smiled and gazed at the shambles she'd made of his study. "If you promise not to tear it apart bit by bit."

"I won't. I promise. Oh, thank you. . ." She swept forward, reaching out with both hands. Petite, delicate, they fit smoothly into his palms, her grasp almost childlike but with a warmth that proclaimed her very much a woman. Just as his body's response to her touch, to her nearness, was male in every way.

He wanted to pull her to him and savor another

sweet, virginal, yet ever-so-promising kiss while pressing her tight to his arousal. Yes, he could have spent the remaining afternoon hours doing just that.

Did his inclinations show on his face, or had she simply realized what she'd done, hurrying to him and grasping hold as she had? With a jolt, she reclaimed her hands and retreated, leaving him with the unsettling impression they were engaged in a bizarre kind of waltz, back and forth, side to side.

And perhaps they were. Despite his reassurances, he wasn't entirely convinced of her codicil story. If Everett Foster had made such provisions, why didn't anyone know of them? Why the devil would a man hide such an important change to his will?

Unless he hadn't hidden it, and someone else had already discovered it. His family had already taken up residence here before his arrival in England. . .

Would they stoop so low? They were a covetous bunch, to be sure. His father's legacy of debts had made them so, but Graham had alleviated that problem years ago with profits from his Egyptian finds.

Even so, they had claimed Monteith Hall without his authority, and without a thought for the women they displaced. And now, perhaps, a codicil went missing. . .his blood ran cold at the thought. He'd soon have a talk with his family.

"Tell me about this ramshackle cottage I've supposedly forced you and your mother into."

"Ah, yes, that." To his surprise, her cheeks burned bright. She drifted to the bookcase and became inordinately interested in straightening a row of volumes. "I exaggerated. The cottage is lovely, really, quite comfortable. It was a difficult move for my mother, I'll admit, but—"

"Are the two of you in financial straits?"

"Why, no, not at all." She seemed taken aback by the notion, a little insulted. She stopped fussing with the books. "Mother and I will do well enough, I dare-say, Mr. Foster."

"Graham."

She let out a sigh. "Mother and I deserve our fair share of my stepfather's legacy. I fully believe he set aside funds for us, a sum not entailed with the estate. This being the case, why shouldn't I see his intentions come to fruition?"

"Surely Mr. Smythe—"

She flicked her wrist. "Mr. Smythe was of no help when I visited him." Her lashes fell, shadowing another rise of color. Obviously she remembered, as he certainly did, their first encounter at Smythe's office. "He couldn't be rid of me soon enough. It was most suspicious. I'm convinced he knows more than he's willing to say."

"Perhaps you and I should visit him together. He's my solicitor now, and if he wishes to remain in my employ, he won't dare put me off."

Her lack of reaction surprised him. He had expected

some small show of gratitude. A sincere thank you, a warm handshake. A kiss would have been nice, but he knew better than to hope for that. Instead, those endless sable eyes narrowed once again, glittering inside lashes nearly as dark. "Why are you so willing to become involved?"

Graham circled the desk. Opening the top drawer, he offered his arm to Isis. Moira shuddered but craned her neck to watch the spider saunter to his shoulder.

"My dear, this is what I do," he said, enjoying the way she cringed when Isis burrowed against his neck. "I decipher clues and hunt treasure. In a city as boring as London, how can I possibly resist coming to your aid?"

That much was true. He needn't add that unlocking the mysteries of Moira Hughes presented an even greater challenge, one he couldn't ignore.

Her eyebrows shot up, though whether because his reply surprised her or because Isis had just scurried beneath his chin, he couldn't say.

"I don't like London, either," she said. "Much too dreary."

He grinned. "I've a hunch the city's about to take on a whole palette of new colors."

CHAPTER 7

Later that evening, Moira swept along the upper gallery of her former London home and wondered if perhaps she hadn't taken leave of her senses. She should have returned to her lodging house hours ago to plan her next strategy, but somehow Graham Foster had ceased being her enemy and become an essential element of that strategy.

Now she was his guest for the evening, and on her way to supper wearing a gown borrowed from his sister. The notion rather made her feet drag. She and Letitia had hardly started off on cordial terms. Would the young lady accuse Moira of plundering her wardrobe?

Halfway along the gallery, she came to a halt. Something felt not quite right, an odd sensation she'd experienced earlier but hadn't paused to consider. Now she examined her surroundings. The carpet, the wall sconces, and the three crystal chandeliers were as she remembered.

An irksome feeling of being spied upon made her skin prickle. She peered to her right, and understanding struck her in one indignant wave.

Good heavens. Great-step-grandfather Elijah Foster's portrait was no longer hanging in the space it had occupied for the past seventy years. In its place hovered the image of a man with sea-blue eyes and golden brown hair. A dimple in his right cheek lent a merry aspect to an otherwise serious expression, and as Moira stared up at him, she could have sworn he winked at her.

How very like Graham Foster. Yet not quite, for the artist's rendering placed the man securely within his fourth or fifth decade of life. Graham Foster's father, perhaps?

Undoubtedly.

She strode another several paces. Aunt Patricia and Great-uncle Darnsworth were missing, as well. From their erstwhile perches stared faces she had never seen before.

She continued to the staircase and turned to view the hall. Well, at least the portrait of her stepfather sitting beside his favorite hunting hound still occupied its usual spot, but who were those rather dour-faced ladies to the left of him?

Members of the new baron's lineage, to be sure.

With a harrumph, she pivoted to descend the stairs but pulled up short, her breath catching in a gasp she immediately regretted.

Graham Foster stood a few steps below her, leaning

against the banister with a careless slouch and a quizzical smile. Black evening attire, cut to display every broad, masculine line of him, lent an all-too-engaging contrast to his sun-warmed hair and skin, and to the brilliance of eyes that, like his father's, couldn't quite decide whether to be blue or green.

Oh, do stop staring, Moira. It'll swell his head.

"Good evening," she said, attempting to mix cordiality with a good dose of indifference. "You look rather nice tonight."

"Good evening. And may I return the compliment, but with a good deal more enthusiasm. You are a vision." He had the audacity to wink with the same impudence she had detected in his father's portrait. He climbed the remaining steps and stood beside her. "Ready for supper?"

She held out the rose silk skirts of her borrowed gown, hastily nipped here and let out there by a vastly relieved Mrs. Higgensworth, who was smiling again now that Moira's charade had reached its conclusion. "Do you think your sister will mind very much?"

"I fear Letty will burn with fury when she sees what that dress does on you." He tipped a bow and extended the crook of his elbow. "Shall we?"

She hesitated. "I'd like to set some things straight first, Mr. Foster."

"Graham." He lowered his arm to his side.

"Yes, in fact, that's the first matter—"

"It's Graham or nothing. I won't answer to anything else."

"We haven't known each other nearly long enough."

"Nonsense. We're cousins."

"Hardly. We are stepcousins several times removed."

"True, and I'm glad about it." He leaned closer, all but trapping her between his broad chest and the stair rail. "Glad we aren't too closely related, Moira."

A tingling sensation raised the hairs on her arms. "Do step away, Mr.—"

"Uh-uh. . ." He waggled a finger in front of her face.

"Oh, all *right*. Graham. There. Are you quite happy now?"

"Very happy, Moira. Did I mention how lovely you look?"

Oh, impossible rapscallion of a man.

He caught her hand and bowed over it, heating her skin with a touch of his lips. "At long last, I meet the true Moira Hughes. I must say, I approve of her wholeheartedly."

"You know nothing about me," she said, uncertain whether to laugh or scold at his impertinence.

A murmur of laughter rumbled in his chest. "Then learning you shall be all the more intriguing."

Her knees went a little watery. *Learn* her? As if he might hold all of her in his hand, turn her this way and that, explore all her parts, and. . .oh, dear. Her stomach dropped, contracted, then simply melted at the thought. Feeling rather dizzy, she let him tuck her hand into the bend of his elbow. They started down the stairs.

"So then. . ." His fingers caressed her knuckles. "What is it you wish to set straight?"

"Set straight? Ah. . .oh, yes." A cool drink was what she presently wished, to clear her head and moisten a mouth gone dry. "It's, em, about what you said to the magistrate earlier. I don't need looking after. I am quite capable of taking care of myself, thank you."

"Are you, indeed?"

"I most certainly am, Mr.—"

"Graham."

Oh, how did he manage to beguile and infuriate her all at the same time? "Graham. Yes. Your assistance is greatly appreciated, of course. But intrusion into my private affairs—"

"Won't be tolerated?" At the bottom of the stairs he stopped, turned her to face him, and gazed directly— brazenly—into her eyes. His own gleamed with challenge. "So, as I assist you, I am to keep my distance and mind my business, sweet cousin Moira?"

She didn't voice the retort that leapt to mind, didn't dare. No matter what she said, Graham Foster somehow twisted her words, giving them double meaning and using them to his own devious advantage.

His dimples flashed. "Shall we join the others?"

If the amber tones of the Gold Saloon were familiar

and reassuring, its occupants were not. These Fosters were practically strangers, mere acquaintances made under the worst of circumstances. Embarrassment over her earlier fiasco rose to sting her cheeks and scorch the tips of her ears. She found herself, much to her chagrin, clinging to the relative comfort of Graham's solid arm.

His brother, Frederick Foster, stood by a window overlooking the garden; he spared them nary a glance as they entered the room. Letitia Foster, her back also to them, hovered before the pianoforte, absently picking out odd notes with her forefinger. The Fosters' houseguest stood at her elbow, offering compliments on the lady's musical acumen. She acknowledged each with a shrug.

"Good evening, everyone," Graham said. "I trust you've all recovered from this afternoon's excitement."

Letitia turned at the sound of his voice, and as her gaze lighted on Moira, her face flushed several shades of crimson. "Why, that's *my* gown—"

Oddly, her complaint went unfinished. Or perhaps not so oddly. Glancing at Graham's profile, Moira saw the clear and quite stern warning he sent his sister.

"Is Miss Hughes borrowing a gown of yours, Miss Foster?" Mr. Paddington's voice rose in an obvious effort to diffuse the tension. "Allow me to compliment you on your excellent taste."

The young lady spared him a sidelong glance. "Kind of you to say, Mr. Paddington."

Her halfhearted acknowledgment raised a flush

to the man's face, cooled an instant later when Letitia swept from his side and plunked into an overstuffed chair. Chin propped in her hand, she continued eyeing Moira with a sullen expression until footsteps clattering down the corridor announced the arrival of the one family member Moira had yet to properly meet.

"Greetings, everyone, so sorry to be late. I do hope I haven't held up supper."

"No, Mama," Letitia murmured in a tone that suggested her mother often hurried in for supper at the last moment. "We've only just got here ourselves."

Like her daughter, Mrs. Foster was tall and fine-boned, her features delicate almost to sharpness. But where Letitia often spared little affability for anyone, Mrs. Foster was all smiles and eager, if slightly breathless, cordiality.

"My goodness, what an afternoon. I quite intended to be home ages ago," the woman rambled, "but the Mastersons insisted I join them for tea. Oh, Letitia, you really should have come along. Edmond Masterson came by unexpectedly. I'm told he has six thousand a year, and he's still highly eligible, you know." Her darting gaze lighted on Moira, and her eyebrows shot up. "Have we company tonight? How charming."

"Edmond Masterson's a toad," Letitia mumbled into her palm.

Her mother ignored the comment. "Do introduce our guest, Monteith."

"Mother, this is. . ." Graham began, but the appearance

of Mrs. Higgensworth in the doorway cut him short.

"Dinner is served."

"Ah, lovely." Mrs. Foster turned to lead the way into the adjoining dining room. "Oh, do forgive me, Monteith, you were introducing our guest." Mrs. Foster paused and held Moira in her gaze. "Dear me, but you seem so familiar. Have we met?"

Frederick Foster held her chair for her, and before Moira could answer, the woman sat and gazed up at her younger son. "Where on earth have you been since last night?"

"Here and there."

"Oh, such insolence." But with an indulgent smile, she watched Frederick shuffle to his seat. Obviously distracted from her initial question, the woman turned her attention on her elder son. "Monteith, you'll be pleased to know your artifacts have been displayed to their very best advantage. It made me so proud seeing your name on all those placards."

"Proud that I've taken treasures from one country and given them to another?" He winked at Moira as if she should understand the joke behind his words. As it was, she felt a sinking in her stomach. She hadn't thought of it quite that way before, but he did take valuables that rightfully belonged to one country and bestowed them on another. For profit.

As he held her chair for her, she thought of her codicil. But no, she had already laid those suspicions to rest. Graham Foster might be a rogue and a scamp, but a thief?

"You say such odd things, Monteith. Of course, I'm proud of your accomplishments. Oh, but our manners. . ." The woman's capricious attention finally wandered back to Moira. "I'm quite certain we've met somewhere. . ." Suddenly her smile waned. "Good grief. You're the new maid. By all that's decent, Monteith, how could you? You inherit a title and a fortune and all you can think to do is dally with the staff?"

Hunched in his chair, Frederick Foster giggled.

An insupportable weight of embarrassment crushed Moira's shoulders. Here she sat at her own mother's table—purchased on their honeymoon in Italy—while a usurper insulted her beyond endurance.

The back of her chair trembled slightly against her spine. She twisted round to discover Graham towering like a sentinel behind her, hands white-knuckled on the chair's shield back. No trace of amusement curled his sensual lips now; no mockery glinted from his eyes. Jaw locked, nose pinched, he was a narrowly contained explosion. He frightened her, just a little.

"Mother. That. . .is. . .enough." Little more than a murmur, but with an undercurrent that traveled under Moira's skin. Frederick closed his mouth on a chuckle. Letitia tensed, gaze darting from face to face. Seated beside her, Mr. Paddington pressed both hands to the table as if poised to push to his feet. "Miss Hughes is our guest, Mother, and we shall treat her accordingly."

"I don't understand."

"Then you should not jump to conclusions."

Flushed, Augusta Foster looked ready to burst into tears.

"This is our cousin, Moira Hughes," Graham said more calmly, yet not entirely without admonition.

"Everett Foster's stepdaughter," Letitia clarified with rather more emphasis on *step* than Moira would have preferred. As if to emphasize she wasn't truly their cousin.

"And she is here as my guest." Graham's tone clearly challenged anyone to refute the claim. No one did.

"Then, why. . ." His mother trailed off, her tongue flicking over her upper lip. With a breath she seemed to collect her composure. "If you'll pardon my asking, why did she disguise herself as a maid?"

The question had the peculiar effect of raising a sudden chuckle in Moira's throat—one she just as quickly swallowed. But she had to admit, Mrs. Foster could not be blamed entirely for her misconception, even if her outburst showed a want of decorum. Moira *had* deceived the family, and she couldn't help feeling Graham had responded rather too harshly over what was, truly, a rather comical misunderstanding.

He moved to his seat at the head of the table. "Miss Hughes has come to search for something her stepfather might have left here." One eyebrow rose to a bold slash above his eye. "For reasons you may be able to shed light upon, Mother, she doubted she would receive a warm welcome by our family."

Oh, why didn't he let it go? Why did he persist in making the poor woman squirm?

And squirm she did, while pressing a hand to her bosom. "Did you, indeed, my dear? I'm sure I don't know why you would think we'd receive you with anything less than open arms. Your dear mother, too. How is she faring?"

"Very well, thank you for asking." She answered this and a slew of other polite inquiries as the servants served the soup.

Thank goodness for Augusta Foster's endless questions about Monteith Hall and Mr. Paddington's eager observations about country homes in general, or the meal would have been as festive as a tomb. Frederick and Letitia spoke little, and Graham less, though Moira was keenly aware of his constant gaze upon her.

Was his scrutiny protective, or predatory? All she knew was because of it, the tension never lifted from the room; she was more than happy to make her escape as soon as the dessert course reached its conclusion.

Her exodus did not take her far. At Graham's insistence, she retired to a guest room rather than embark on a late-night journey across the river to her lodging house. She appreciated the gesture, but experienced a pang of regret when Miss Letitia breezed past her in the gallery, bid her an over-the-shoulder good night, and slipped into the bedroom that had once been Moira's own.

Alone in a guest room, she wrapped a robe around

her nightgown—the plain one she'd worn as a maid—and sat before the dressing-table mirror. These Fosters were a perplexing family, painfully ill at ease and on their guard. And resentful. Yes, resentment weighted this house like a pall.

As she ran a brush through her hair, she cringed to remember how Graham had taken Augusta to task for her mistake. What kind of son embarrassed his mother before guests?

What kind of man robbed a nation of its treasures?

What kind of rogue stole kisses from unsuspecting ladies?

A tap sounded at her door. Rising, she hoped it was merely the upstairs maid. She'd quite had her fill of Fosters for one day. "Who is it?"

"Graham. May I have a word?"

She might have guessed. Ever since he had discovered her identity, the man seemed intent on never letting her out of his sight. She opened the door an inch or two. "I'm very tired."

A candle in his right hand illuminated his crisp, white shirt, his bronzed cheekbones. A sense of impropriety rippled through her. She was, after all, clad only in a night shift and robe, her hair loose about her shoulders. She stepped behind the door, leaning to poke only her face into the opening. "Can't we speak in the morning?"

"It won't take but a moment."

She sighed and nodded.

"I wanted you to know that Mrs. Higgensworth spoke with the servants. They are now aware that you are a guest, not an employee. If there's anything you need, you have only to ask."

"I appreciate that." She grimaced. "I hate to think what they're all saying about their odd houseguest."

He flashed his devastating smile. "I suppose the tale will have spread through Mayfair by tomorrow at supper time."

"Undoubtedly." She waited, for he looked as though he had something more to say. He also looked far too casual for her liking, in shirtsleeves with cravat and collar gone. Didn't he know that was no way to appear before a lady?

Of course, the rascal knew, just as he undoubtedly understood the effect he was having on her at that precise moment. She pried her gaze away from the smooth column of his neck, from the sight of strong collarbones revealed by his partially unbuttoned shirt.

"Good night," she said, and tried unsuccessfully to close the door.

"May I come in for a moment?"

She frowned, considered delivering a blunt no, and hugged her robe tighter around her. "It's rather late."

His candle fluttered and sent a shimmer through the golden ends of his hair. "I wanted to apologize for this evening."

"Which part of it?"

He tilted his head and leaned into the gap between the door and lintel, bringing his face close to hers. "You know which part. My mother had no right—"

"She had every right." Knowing she should simply accept his apology and bid him a final good night, Moira ignored her better sense and opened the door wider. "It was you who behaved rather badly, if the truth were told."

"Me?"

"Yes. Under the circumstances, your mother's accusation was perfectly understandable. She thought I was a maid, and I'm to blame for that. When you think about it, the entire situation was funny. You might have laughed it off instead of embarrassing her as you did."

"I was defending you."

"Were you? Or was something more going on, something that had nothing whatsoever to do with me?"

His eyes smoldered with unspoken ruminations. "Since you won't accept my apology, perhaps you'll accept this. I'd like you and your mother to move back into Monteith Hall as soon as it's convenient."

Moira's heart made a little leap before plummeting with a thud against her ribs. Her throat stung with the desire to grasp this unexpected boon. She turned away from him and spoke to the shadowy bedchamber. "I do thank you, but that would be impossible, at least for the time being."

"What the devil do you mean?" He stepped over the

threshold and came up behind her, his breath warm on her neck. "Isn't this the very thing you wanted?"

"It was. But it's too late now." She turned to face him. "The first move. . .well. . .confused my mother. It affected her health. I fear another move, even back to the home she knew, would only upset her further."

"You keep insisting your mother is fine and that the two of you are amply taken care of. Is that a lie, Moira?" He took her chin, raised it, and lowered his own to meet her gaze. Their breath mingled, warm and sweet from the evening's wine.

Her thoughts thrashed, swam, foundered. What were they discussing? Her mother. Had she lied? Yes. And the truth. . .did she trust him enough? When he touched her, when his warm strength spread through her and her name became a rumbling murmur on his lips—yes, she wanted to trust.

Or did she? Why, for all she knew, he was here winning her sympathies simply to steal another kiss. That was a harsh assessment, she knew, but in her admittedly scant experience of him, that had been the one dependable occurrence.

Never before had she encountered a man like Graham Foster. When was he serious, joking, teasing, seducing? With this man she could never discern one from another.

Trust him?

She pivoted and made a tense circuit of the carpet

before halting a safe distance away on the far side of the woven medallion. "What I want, what I need, is quite simple. Self-sufficiency. Not charity, not the tolerance or indulgence of a distant relative, but the provisions my stepfather made for us before he died. Only upon that am I willing to depend."

"I see." His nostrils flared; his blue eyes frosted. "Then tomorrow we'll continue the search. Good night, Moira."

His shoulders squared like twin battlements as he strode from the room. Her words had hurt him, and that she regretted. But could she have framed her wishes differently and still made them clear? She wanted him to understand. Wanted him to stop confusing and provoking her. Needed him to stop making things like thinking and breathing so blasted difficult.

"Shaun, wake up."

Graham nudged his friend and ducked the resulting blow. Shaun's haphazard fist struck the bed table and upturned a glass of water, splashing the floor and Graham's foot. He caught the tumbler before it rolled to the floor and shattered.

Shaun flinched upright. "Who's there?" He squinted, sniffed, pushed higher, and blinked. "Good God, Graham. I was out like a baby. Take ten years off a man's life, waking him like that."

"I need to talk to you."

"Can't it wait till morning?"

"There's a matter that needs attending first thing tomorrow, and I'll be busy with Miss Hughes."

With a sigh that conveyed he'd much rather sleep than talk, Shaun nonetheless asked, "What's the problem?"

"Well, after supper I lined up that family of mine and asked them point blank if they'd come upon any documents left in the house by Moira's stepfather. Or if they simply felt the need to confess something."

"What sort of documents?"

"A codicil. One that would have left Moira and her mother far better off than they are now. But neither Mother nor the twins seemed to know a thing about it. After exchanging utterly baffled glances, they stared at me as if I'd gone daft. Couldn't help believing them, despite a lingering conviction that they *would* have interfered in Moira's finances if they'd known about the codicil."

"So where do I fit in?"

"I need your special area of expertise."

"Ah." The candlelight illuminated Shaun's burgeoning interest. "Another scheme, eh? What do you want me to sniff out now?"

"Moira's mother's finances. I want to know everything, including the condition of that cottage they've moved into."

Shaun scrubbed a hand across his face. "Why don't you simply ask Miss Hughes?"

"I have, and she's lying through her teeth. I'm sure of it. If my assumptions prove correct, I want to make arrangements, secret ones with Moira none the wiser. We'll get Smythe to manage it."

"You mean like an anonymous fund?" Shaun sat up, warming to this latest mission. His mouth skewed to a sly grin. "But why the secrecy? Seems like helping the mother would send the daughter straight into your lusting arms."

"Shaun, my friend, you don't know Moira Hughes. Whatever you would normally expect from a woman, she says and does the opposite."

"And that's precisely why you like her, isn't it?"

Graham lowered his candle and grinned in the darkness. "She's a challenge, by God."

"And you never could resist a challenge, especially one as fetching as Miss Hughes."

Graham nodded, and remembered another matter he'd pondered earlier. "That Mr. Doone. Not really a magistrate, is he?"

"Ah, you've caught me." Shaun shook his head and laughed. "I confess it. Hadn't the faintest inkling where to find a real one. Found Doone loitering near the park and did a quick once-over. Frayed trouser hems, missing button on his coat. . ."

"That's what tipped me off."

"Yes, a gentleman with too many gambling debts. Needed the money. By the way, you owe me four quid." Graham's mouth fell open, and Shaun shrugged. "He did a fair enough job, don't you think? Duped the ladies."

"Indeed. I'd say Letty was rather grateful for your intervention."

"You think so?" Before Graham could answer, Shaun's eager look vanished into a twist of his mouth. He flicked a hand against the bedclothes in a dismissive gesture. "If that's all, do you think a man might catch a few moments' sleep? Bloody middle of the night, for God's sake."

Graham lingered, regarding his friend. "You've gone and got all moon-eyed over her, haven't you?"

"Over whom?" Shaun stifled a yawn.

"Letty."

"Don't be bloody ridiculous."

"Ah, Shaun. . ." He drew a breath, let it out slowly, and shook his head. "She'll only bring you heartache."

"Haven't the foggiest notion what you're going on about."

"Just trying to save you a lot of grief, old man."

"Save someone else. Save Miss Hughes. Talk about moon-eyed." Hitching an eyebrow, Shaun crossed his arms behind his head. "Haven't seen you like this since that supposed sultan's daughter wandered into the Aswan camp."

"Now that's downright underhanded of you, Shaun. You promised never to bring it up again. Besides, this is different. Entirely."

"Mm." Shaun's eyes drifted shut, and Graham turned to go. It wasn't until he reached the door that Shaun's voice drifted across the room. "A supposed sultan's daughter is not what one would call marriage material. Miss Hughes, on the other hand. . ."

His hand on the knob, Graham turned back into the room. "Now who's being bloody ridiculous? Whether or not Moira Hughes is marriage material is a moot point. I'm returning to Egypt as soon as possible, and there's an end to the matter."

A resounding snore formed the whole of Shaun's reply, but Graham knew his friend wasn't sleeping.

CHAPTER
8

"Hold up there." Graham sprinted past the carriage house to the cobbled drive, where his coach and four stood ready. He signaled to the porter, just then opening the gates. "One moment, please."

The iron scrollwork barrier creaked to a stop, preventing the carriage from proceeding out to the lane that opened onto Brook Street. Graham came up beside the passenger window. Through reflections of the gatehouse's whitewashed brickwork, he spied Moira sitting stiffly against the squabs and looking none too pleased, at least not in profile.

The little sneak. Instead of ordering the carriage and waiting for it to come round to the front steps like someone with nothing to hide, she'd mumbled excuses after breakfast, slipped out through the terrace, and hurried off across the gardens like a wraith in the morning mist.

He swung the door wide and hoisted himself in. "So then, where are we going? Smythe's office?"

The corner of her mouth pinched inward. "*We* needn't go anywhere. I'm quite capable of—"

"Yes, Moira, I believe we established last night that you're a perfectly capable individual." He closed the door and slid closer to her. "We also agreed, however, that when you returned to Mr. Smythe's office, I would accompany you."

"I'm not going to Mr. Smythe's office. Not now, at any rate." Her tone implied an unwillingness to offer further explanation.

Ha. He rapped on the ceiling, and moments later the coach rolled through the open gates. Lounging beside her, he stretched out his legs, propping one across the other. Through half-closed lids he studied her. She was all rigid annoyance, simmering exasperation. Completely adorable.

"Trying to slink off without me, weren't you, Moira?"

"I was doing no such thing. I'm not on my way to Mr. Smythe's office. I've. . .other matters to attend to this morning, and there's simply no reason for you to tag along."

"Other matters? Such as?"

Her breath hissed. "I'm returning to my lodging house."

"Good. We'll gather your things and inform the

landlord you'll no longer need the place. You'll stay with us."

"Will I?" She bristled. "I don't remember being asked, or making such a decision."

"Then consider this a formal invitation."

Her gaze narrowed on him, then sharpened as she reached a decision with a shake of her head. "I think I'd prefer—"

"To what, Moira, pay for a place you don't need when there's a perfectly good room at your disposal on Brook Street? Or would you rather toss money away than accept my hospitality?" He leaned closer and spoke in a tone that always elicited a reaction that fascinated him—a shivering flutter she unsuccessfully tried to hide every time. "After all," he murmured, "it was your home long before it became mine. I couldn't sleep nights knowing we'd inconvenienced you."

Yes, there it was, that little shudder across her shoulders. "I. . .I suppose you're right." She compressed her lips as her stubborn resolve faltered. "Thank you, then."

"You needn't sound so irritated."

"I'm not. I appreciate your generosity." She shifted, broadening the space between them by an inch or two. "Still and all, there's no need for you to be here now. You needn't upset the routine of your morning."

"No bother at all."

The pull of her eyebrows declared she minded, very much. Was his presence so irksome, or was Moira Hughes once again concealing something? He knew better than to ask, but as the coach headed down New Bond Street and across Piccadilly, he wondered. Perhaps Moira didn't want him to see her lodging house. Could the place be as bad as all that?

He glanced out the window. They were skirting St. James Park and would soon come up on Whitehall and then the Westminster Bridge. Lambeth lay directly across the river.

Lambeth wasn't so bad. It even boasted a palace of the same name. When he left England years ago, plans were just beginning for the development of South London. If they headed west, they'd pass Vauxhall Gardens and the new residential neighborhoods of Church Street and Prospect Place. Not prosperous in the same sense as Mayfair, but certainly respectable.

When they reached the Surrey side of the river, however, the coach veered sharply east, away from Lambeth and toward Southwark. The sharp scent of fresh-cut lumber permeated the air, and within minutes a thin coat of sawdust clouded the windows. They passed one timber yard after another as they hugged the river. The street began to narrow.

The growing tension in Moira's bearing suggested he might as well expect the worst. The notion of her dwelling in some sagging old edifice framed in worm-eaten timber both twisted his gut and inflamed his temper. He stole a glance at her, thinking of how she had played maidservant to press her rights. So brave, and so damnably proud for not wanting him to know the truth.

Ah, she was something, this distant stepcousin twice or thrice removed.

Her left hand rested against the seat, fingers half-curled within one of Letty's kid gloves. Wrinkled and a little bunched between her thumb and forefinger, the glove made an ill fit, and Moira's hand seemed all the more delicate. Vulnerable. His own inched toward it, sliding cautiously like Isis approaching her prey, careful not to startle the coveted prize away.

She didn't notice, too entranced by the shops and buildings outside her window. His fingers made contact, just the tips to the side of her palm.

She started. "What are you doing?"

"What?" He looked down at their hands and pretended surprise. "Oh. Sorry. Close confines. Didn't realize."

"Stay on your side, please." She slid her hand into her lap. Her chin rose to a righteous angle.

"Didn't realize there was a boundary."

She slanted an eyebrow, pursed her mouth.

He slid closer to the door on his side.

But as the road became more rutted, he let the carriage jostle him back toward her bit by bit. The corners they turned worked to his advantage. Their elbows met. She shot him a look, and he moved his away, but before long his right knee swung to the side, bringing his thigh flush against hers.

"Will you stop that?" Her forefinger nudged his ribs. "This coach is plenty large for the two of us. Do keep your distance or sit there." She pointed to the seat opposite.

He hid a grin and shoved away, waiting for his next opportunity to steal closer. He simply enjoyed touching her—found it nearly impossible not to. Even in opposite corners, the dim confines of the coach created a closeness he couldn't ignore. Didn't wish to ignore. Everything about her sparked his awareness. The floral scent of her bath soap, the grace of her unconscious movements, the gentle rise and fall of her breathing.

She peered at him, her eyes flashing with alarm.

"Is something wrong?" he asked.

"You don't have that creature with you, do you?"

"Isis?"

Moira nodded and managed to squeeze a few more inches away.

"She's at home, safe in her crate."

"Thank heavens for that." She visibly relaxed.

"You needn't fear her. She's perfectly harmless. Besides Shaun, I consider Isis my best friend."

Her nose crinkled. "You have some rather interesting friends. Wherever did you find them?"

"Egypt, of course. Crawling round outside my tent, for one."

"And Mr. Paddington?"

"I was speaking of Shaun. Found him foxed, bruised,

and half-starved outside my tent one morning about four years ago. Been my best friend ever since. I discovered Isis sleeping inside one of my boots one evening nearly a year ago. Damned near jumped out of my skin. But then a local boy explained that she'd never hurt anything larger than a fly."

Moira made a sound between a chuckle and a snort. The coach gave a sudden pitch as it rounded a corner. She toppled sideways, her shoulder striking his. Another jolt landed her against his chest. Even as his arms closed around her, she shrank out of them, scooting into the far corner again.

"Sorry," she murmured and righted her hat.

He certainly wasn't sorry. He wished a rut would toss her right into his lap. What a flurry of skirts and indignation that would be.

Little chance of it now. The coach slowed along a street Graham ordinarily would have sped through. He looked out at a butcher shop that stank of last week's slaughter, a coaching inn that promised fleas, and, farther down, a stark, three-story abode with *Miss Ashworth's Foundling Hospital* styled in chipped green paint above the door. It was opposite this that the coach creaked to a stop.

Dear God, not here. Not Moira.

She wouldn't meet his gaze, but stared at her hands until the driver opened her door and let down the step. Without a word, she descended to the street and started toward the two-story dwelling that should have been torn down a century ago. When a round of obscenities drifted from the attached tavern, she made no sign that she'd heard.

Graham fell into step beside her. "So, this is it?"

She nodded, looking miserable.

It was worse than he had imagined, and worse still for the two of them now seeing it from each other's eyes. Had anyone else—even he—been forced to dwell in such a place, he might have found it, well, tolerable. But knowing lovely Moira had suffered this hellhole made it all the more deplorable. For her, he guessed, worse than living here was having him *know* she lived here.

If only he hadn't come along, he might have spared her this humiliation. He couldn't change that, but he could take pains not to increase her discomfiture.

"If you can manage packing on your own, Moira, there is a small matter I might attend to. Would you mind very much?"

She brightened a tiny bit. "Not at all. I don't wish to keep you from more pressing business."

"Would an hour be sufficient?"

"I believe that would do." Her look of genuine relief tugged at his heart and made him glad he'd posed the suggestion.

"Don't carry your bags down by yourself. I'll send my driver up when we return."

♥ ♥ ♥

A quarter hour later, Graham alighted from the coach, burning to smash something. Standing outside the offices of Smythe and Davis, Legal Consultants, he struggled to remain calm while at the same time attempting to estimate the force of a slam necessary to reduce the door's etched window to a glittering shower of glass. It wouldn't solve a single one of Moira's problems, but it would bring him a certain satisfaction.

Hands fisted, he drew breath in and out, steadying his nerves and reining in his anger. Shaun had discovered the whereabouts of Moira's lodging house from Mr. Pierson, Smythe's secretary. That meant Smythe also must have known. Devil take the solicitor for his incompetence. The man should have interceded, should have made arrangements more suitable for a lady.

Graham regarded the doorknob, a polished brass ball of reflected sunlight. One more deep breath enabled him to grasp and turn it, even if setting his shoulder to the door and ramming it down better suited his mood.

The jangle of a bell above his head nearly undid his tenuous composure. Seated at the paneled oak desk, Smythe's secretary squinted up at him from over a sheaf of papers.

"Your lordship." He lowered the documents and pushed his spectacles higher on his nose. "We weren't expecting you."

"No, you weren't." Graham forged a path to the door leading to the inner offices. "Is Smythe in?"

"Yes, sir." Pierson stood, gathering his coat closed with an air of impending urgency. "If you'll have a seat, I'll inform him your lordship is here."

"Don't bother. I know the way." Graham breezed past him.

"But, my lord. . ." Throwing down his pen with a thwack, Pierson tried to head him off. "If you'd be patient, sir—"

Graham moved faster, reaching the door first and capturing the knob in his fist. "I'll announce myself, thank you."

"This is highly irregular, my lord."

"Irregular?" He stooped and shoved his face close to the clerk's. "The matter I've come about is downright disgraceful, not to mention dishonorable. Believe me, Mr. Pierson, the responsible party shall rue the day I discover him."

He silenced any further protests with a look meant to intimidate the younger, shorter man. Pierson was only doing his job, he knew, but right now the secretary stood between Graham and his quest of attaining a measure of justice for Moira.

A muscle worked in Pierson's jaw, and a convulsive tightening of his throat pushed his Adam's apple against his collar. A shimmer of gold winked from inside the starched linen, catching Graham's attention for an instant before disappearing.

Smythe must pay his man exceedingly well, for him to be able to afford gold jewelry. So, why such paltry attention to Moira's welfare?

With a cough, Pierson retreated to his desk. Graham pushed through the door.

"Tell me why, Smythe." Inside the solicitor's private office, he all but charged the desk and hunched to grip its edge. "Why the devil is Moira Hughes living in a slum?"

"Lord Monteith." Smythe pushed back in his chair until it struck the wall behind him. "What can I do for—"

"You can answer my question, damn your eyes." At Smythe's hesitation, anger zinged through Graham like a buzzing wasp, furious and ready to sting. He canted farther across the desk, feeling no compunction about using his size to intimidate.

"A slum, you say?" The solicitor cowered in his chair, his knuckles white against the padded arms. "I had no idea."

"Don't act the idiot with me. What's happened to the funds her stepfather left for her and her mother?"

"But, my lord, surely you don't believe that story." Relaxing a degree, Smythe dismissed Moira's claim with a tsk that raised Graham's wrath another notch.

And yet the question struck home. *Did* he believe in this supposed codicil's existence? Was it merely wishful thinking on Moira's part, or perhaps the ravings of a dying man?

He straightened, tapping one fist against his thigh lest Smythe think his anger had abated. "I want to see everything—and I do mean everything—connected with Everett Foster's estate and will. I'll give you a day to prepare. When I return with Miss Hughes tomorrow afternoon, I'll expect every document ready to be examined with a fine-tooth comb."

"Tomorrow? I don't think—"

"Mr. Smythe, if you value my continued business with this firm, you will do as I say."

Smythe blinked up at him and swallowed. "Of course, my lord. It will be my pleasure."

Graham stalked out of the office, pushing past Smythe's startled-looking partner, Mr. Davis, who had been watching wide-eyed from the corridor.

CHAPTER
9

As the coach made its way out of Southwark, Moira didn't dare steal a glance at Graham. What must he be thinking of her former living quarters?

As long as she could remember, she had been a wealthy baron's daughter. Loved, cared for, indulged. Only now was she beginning to appreciate how much she had taken for granted, and with what unthinking ease she'd donned each new party frock and savored every lavish meal. Oh, the waste of it, especially when lost on the cheerful disregard of a child.

Really, she hadn't minded Southwark so very much. It had saved her a considerable amount in rent money, and she was perfectly willing to forego small comforts for the good cause of seeing her mother comfortably and securely settled. Yes, she might have continued enduring that lodging house, if only it had remained her little secret.

Well, never mind what Graham thought of the place. Necessity had brought her there. No use complaining, no sense regretting it. She was, of course, glad to be leaving. Except. . .

She caught her lip between her teeth as she remembered how Graham had admonished his mother at supper the previous evening.

Moira had been raised on certain principles. The head of a family should treat all those in his care with the utmost kindness and compassion. As Papa had done. Even at her naughtiest, she had never received anything more severe than a gentle reprimand. Firm, but never stern. Never angry. And neither had she ever heard Everett Foster speak an unkind word to her mother.

Graham Foster was a man who took liberties, who acted on instinct and made few apologies. A man who didn't stop to consider the right or wrong of his actions, or their effect on the people around him.

His effect on her. Far too often, he left her feeling breathless, turned about, a little out of control. She was not someone who enjoyed feeling out of control. Nor did she relish the idea of being dependent upon such a man.

The interior of the coach felt hot and airless. He insisted on sitting too close, on touching her and pretending he hadn't meant to. No matter her prods, exasperated sighs, or pointed glares. He returned each with a wide-eyed nonchalance that denied all knowledge of how unsettled he made her.

Then again, perhaps he didn't know. How could he? Only she could feel that odd twist in her stomach, the jump in her pulse, the nearly irresistible urge to press her face to his skin and breathe him in. And give in to his teasing.

No, surely he couldn't know any of that.

Their present direction restored a sense of, oh, safety, she supposed. A comfortable sensation spread through her as they turned onto Queen's Square in Westminster and a familiar brick mansion came into view. She knew this dwelling nearly as well as Monteith Hall and the Brook Street town house.

The carriage was admitted through the gate and traveled the short sweep of drive to the front steps. Graham peered out the window. "Where are we?"

"Trewsbury House. I'm hoping the bishop can shed light on Papa's last trip to London."

"The bishop?"

She nodded as she craned her neck to see around him. "I do hope he's returned. He's almost always in town during the Season, but last week when I stopped by, he was away on church business. Do you think he'll mind terribly that we've come unannounced?"

Graham shrugged. "Not knowing the man, I couldn't say."

She stared at him blankly. "Of course, you know him, silly. He's your cousin as much as he was Papa's."

"A cousin of mine?" He looked puzzled, then

wary. His voice dropped to a monotone that warned of impending anger. "What is his name, Moira?"

"Benedict Ramsey, the bishop of Trewsbury, of course," she replied, and watched his face transform in ways that made her breath catch.

Could a man be likened to an ocean storm? A black fury of cloud and wind and wave that takes sailors by surprise and only by the smallest margin leaves them with their lives? If so, that was Graham Foster for the briefest instant. Then he gave a visible shake that brought the tempest under control.

"Benedict Ramsey. . .a bishop? Blazing hell. I suppose I might have known he'd wangle his way to the top."

Taken aback, she frowned. "He's a respected clergyman."

Graham's simmering animosity could have burned a hole in the seat facing them. "I cannot accompany you inside, Moira."

"But. . .why ever not?"

"Because I would not be welcome, nor would I wish to be." He drew a sharp breath. "You would do well to beware of him."

"Nonsense. Besides being a relative, Benedict Ramsey was Papa's oldest and dearest friend."

"He's no friend of mine, I assure you."

"The bishop is an elderly man and half-blind. What could he have done to make you so bitter toward him?"

"He wasn't always so elderly, or so blind, Moira.

Once he was a deacon in his prime, wanting very much to rise in the ranks of the clergy. Ambition consumed him. So much so, he was willing to sacrifice a member of his own family."

Misgiving sank like sodden bread in her stomach. "You?"

He nodded, lips compressed. "Do you understand why I left England years ago?"

She hesitated. Beneath his exaggerated calm, rage pulsated, making her afraid to answer, afraid not to. "The. . .incident at Oxford?"

"Yes, my expulsion. My disgrace. Are you aware of how the bishop took sides against me in order to win the favor of a wealthy nobleman?"

Where were the dimples? The mockery? The flirtation? As much as she had wished them gone previously, she longed for them now. Preferred them to this sense of having committed some unpardonable sin beyond her comprehension.

"Graham, please—"

"Ah, you don't wish to speak of it, and I can't say I blame you. Unpleasant business, all of it." He turned away, knocked once on the ceiling, and waved his hand in a dismissive gesture. "Go, Moira. I'll wait for you here."

The coach listed as the driver descended from the box. A moment later, he opened the door and let down the step. Without a word and with an odd sense of loss dragging at her heart, Moira slid away from the almost-cousin twice removed who now seemed more a stranger than ever.

♥ ♥ ♥

Moira hadn't been gone five minutes when Graham booted open the coach door. Standing thankfully out of the way, his driver flinched but remained unharmed.

"Sorry," Graham mumbled and strode past.

At the base of the front steps, he stopped and considered the double front doors looming above. A portico supported by fluted white columns ran the length of the facade and wrapped around either side, allowing a view into the first-floor rooms. He loped up the stairs and, stepping to the right, gazed through the first set of tall windows. Behind sheer curtains he spied what appeared to be a waiting room furnished with uncomfortable-looking gilt chairs ranged along the walls. Detecting no movement and no fire in the hearth, he moved on.

It wasn't until he crossed to the left of the front entrance that he came upon Moira and the bishop. After nearly being spotted by two footmen rearranging furniture in the dining room, he darted around the corner and heard Moira's voice drifting on a billowing wisp of curtain from an open window.

He hugged the wall beside the wide window that

began at his shins and rose well above his head. The blowing curtain afforded him the advantage of peeking inside with little risk of detection.

Moira and Benedict Ramsey occupied armchairs several feet away. With a good view of his relative's face, Graham noted that the years had been less than kind. The once-energetic if parsimonious deacon had given way to a wizened, overweight bishop who squinted at Moira as though dazzled by the sun.

Yes, Graham found her dazzling, too.

"Thank you so much for seeing me," he heard her say. "I should have sent my card first. . ."

"Nonsense, child. I only wish I'd been at home when you called last week." Graham's temple throbbed at the sound of Benedict's voice. So cordial. So mild. Not at all as he remembered from years ago. "You must give me all the news of your dear mother."

"She's very well and sends her regards. She's enjoying our new home. . ."

And so the conversation went, with Moira doing her best to convince yet another individual how well she and her mother were doing. That made Graham angry all over again. Was there no one she felt she could turn to? If Benedict Ramsey had been Everett's closest friend, why couldn't she tell him the truth?

He heard tears in her voice. "We miss him terribly."

She was speaking of her stepfather.

"And now with Nigel gone, as well. . ."

The fiancé. Ah, Moira. She had endured so much. Graham experienced a stab of guilt. He tended to forget the tragedy in her life, tended to think of her simply as an enticing young woman he'd like to know better.

No wonder she held him at arm's distance.

"I know you saw Papa the last time he came down to London," he heard her say now. "Did he speak to you of matters concerning my mother's future?"

"Why, no, he didn't." The bishop's eyebrows rose, etching paternal furrows across his brow. "But at the time, there was no reason to believe Estella's future might be at risk. Everett seemed in the best of health, while you, my dear, were engaged to his heir, may he rest in peace."

She lowered her face, fingering a stray thread or piece of lint on her skirt. When she looked up, her features were taut. "And Papa never mentioned any changes to his will? He never discussed his intentions of doing so?"

Graham watched the bishop brush his hand back and forth across his flaccid chin. "Not that I recall."

"Are you quite certain?" A note of desperation clung to the words. Moira sat back—collapsed almost—in her chair. "I don't understand it. He was most particular on this point. Emphatic. He insisted he'd made changes to ensure the well-being of his family. Those were his words. He said we need never worry about anything."

"Are you, my dear? Worried, that is?"

"Oh, no, it isn't that." She straightened and pasted

on a smile that shouldn't have fooled anyone, unless that person wished to be fooled. "I only mean to see that Papa's wishes are executed accordingly."

The bishop patted her hand. "Have you asked Mr. Smythe?"

"He claimed ignorance of the entire matter. In fact, he hurried me out of his office as quickly as possible so he could return to a more important client." Bitterness edged her voice. "The new Baron Monteith."

The first time Graham saw Moira in Smythe's office, she had been crying, or nearly so. And he had made a devilish sorry joke of it. Damn his bones for that.

The old man settled back with a sympathetic shake of his head. "Have you had any contact with Graham Foster?"

Graham leaned closer to the window, ears pricked.

"As a matter of fact. . ." Moira sighed. "I've been invited to stay at Brook Street." After a pause, she said, "He's rather an enigma, isn't he? What do you know of Graham Foster?"

"An unpredictable sort, I'll say that much." Graham's blood simmered as Benedict hissed a breath through his teeth. "I saw potential in him once, but potential isn't always enough. Not nearly so. A man must have character, integrity. A sense of honor. I'm afraid events proved the young man lacking in all three. A pity. Perhaps it would be best, my dear, if you declined his invitation. You are always welcome here."

She didn't immediately answer. Was she considering the wisdom of Benedict's suggestion? She'd been hesitant in accepting Graham's hospitality, and it didn't take a fool to see that her trust in him was as tenuous as London sunshine.

Don't be fooled by the old snake, Moira. Don't look into those half-blind eyes and be blinded to the truth.

As he strained his ears to hear her reply, whistling echoed in the garden below. An instant later, a groundskeeper appeared from around a row of hedges, a rake propped on his shoulder. With nowhere to hide, Graham leaned his back to the wall and crossed one ankle over the other, trying to appear as though he belonged there. Just a guest of the bishop, out for a breath of air. He even rummaged through a coat pocket, pretending to search for a cheroot, which, of course, he didn't have.

The gardener glanced up, saw Graham, and touched a finger to his cap. Graham offered a nod and straightened his coat as if preparing to reenter the house. The gardener continued on his way, soon out of sight.

Upon turning back to the window, he received a shock that nearly sent him backward over the terrace rail. Moira stood just inside, one hand reaching to grasp the fluttering curtain. He considered slinking away along the wall, but her gaze lighted on him. Surprise elicited a gasp, which he diffused the quickest way he could think of—by flashing his most charming, disarming grin.

And there it was, the familiar, fluttering shiver across

her shoulders. She tried to hide it, tried to dismiss him with a quelling look and retreat from the window.

Ah, not so fast.

He caught her hand and tucked it inside his coat, pressing her palm flat against his chest above his heart. By heaven, it felt good there. Soft and slight, yet warm, steadying. Infinitely female, the sort of hand that held the power to change a man's life, turn a vagabond into a knight, a charlatan into a prince. God, the potential encompassed within that small hand. It made him want to promise her. . .ah, he didn't know. Things.

All that from a single touch. *Moira, Moira.* He breathed, and her fingertips moved, sampling the shape of him beneath his shirt. Her dark eyes glimmered.

Something inside him stirred. Something beyond simple attraction or seduction. Something far more dangerous.

He raised his other hand and pressed a finger to his lips, making a game of it. *Sh, Moira, don't give me away.* That broke the spell. He felt the pull in her arm as she tried to reclaim her hand. Her eyes narrowed with suspicion, censure. Her lips skewed with disapproval. He smiled and shrugged, playing the jester while an unexpected urgency knifed his insides.

Don't trust that old cobra over me, Moira. Don't make the same mistake I did. Don't believe his lies.

And, ah, Moira, please don't take your hand away.

Moira tried to tug her fingers free. Why on earth was Graham skulking like a burglar? And why did he squeeze her hand with such insistence while looking at her with that silly expression, as though this were nothing more than a schoolboy prank?

She had a good mind to yank him through the window right into the room, depositing him onto the floor at her feet. Oh, what she wouldn't give to hear his explanation to the bishop.

She knew she wouldn't. She'd keep his presence a secret in spite of, or perhaps because of, the way he was looking at her. And because of how his chest felt beneath her hand.

His heartbeat filled her palm and traveled through her, blending with the racing beat of her own heart until she couldn't tell which set the pace, his or hers. But wasn't that how Graham Foster always made her feel—overwhelmed and breathless and unsure of her own feelings?

He kept flashing those dimples just to confuse her, she was certain, and prevent her from knowing quite what to do. *Fiend*.

Behind her, Benedict Ramsey said, "The more I consider it, Moira, the more I believe it would be best if you stayed here while in London. I simply don't relish the idea of you being in that house alone with Graham Foster. It's no place for a young single lady."

She should have agreed with him; should have

jumped at his offer. After all, wasn't Graham at this moment proving those words true with his outlandish behavior? Yet she surprised herself by replying, "Oh, have no fears on that account. His mother and sister are present in the house. There's Mrs. Higgensworth, too. I'll be well chaperoned."

"Still, the man is a rake. Do you wish to be beholden to a—Moira, where are you going?"

Where, indeed? Graham was backing away from the window and towing her along with him. His grip allowed no choice but to either step over the sill, luckily no higher than her shin, or topple flat on her face onto the slate terrace floor.

"Stop it," she hissed. "What are you doing?"

Those brilliant dimples vanished within a scowl. "I've heard my character defamed quite enough for one day, thank you, and so have you. We're leaving."

"Moira?"

Uncle Benedict's puzzled face poked out the window just as Graham reached the corner of the house. With her hand firmly secured in his, he scooted out of sight. "Better come up with a plausible excuse fast," he whispered, "or we're done for. How the devil will you explain my spying at the window? He'll think you were in on it from the start."

"Cad."

"I prefer blackguard."

"You're absurd." Craning to peer over her shoulder,

she formed a smile while doing her best to conceal the evidence of her imminent abduction. Graham was right. By not immediately exposing him, she'd become his unwitting accomplice.

"I'm sorry, Uncle, I suddenly remembered a prior engagement."

"Good heavens, child. Do you always take your leave by jumping out windows?"

"It's the fastest route to my carriage. I really must be going or I'll be late. It's a very important appointment. I promise to call again soon." She smiled and waved, backing away until Graham gave a final tug that propelled her around the corner to the front of the house, and smack up against his chest. His arms went around her, holding her tight.

"Phew. That was close." The warm vibration of his whisper caressed her cheek and took possession of her senses, her thoughts. She breathed in the tingling starch of his cravat and experienced a moment's dizziness. "Ah, but what fun, eh, Moira?"

She shoved at his shirtfront. "You're insane."

"Oh, go on, admit it. You'd grown weary of the old snake."

She managed to create an inch or two between them, but he stubbornly held on, his arms locked like iron bands around her while his fingertips fondled her back, gingerly exploring the cloth buttons on her gown and eliciting a quivery-cool scattering of goose bumps.

"Aren't you secretly glad I rescued you?" His voice dipped, a warm ocean eddy over rock and sand. He began pressing the buttons up and down her back, playing them like notes on a pianoforte. "Surely you didn't credit his wretched opinions?"

"Stop that."

But he didn't. He only summoned the dimples to distract her. And distract they did with their boyish mischief, their mockery.

Tipping her head back to scowl at him, she discovered something else lurking behind the laughter in his eyes. Something that slipped out at an unguarded moment, not at all lighthearted but—goodness—vulnerable. Downcast. Needful. Her scowl eased as she considered this.

Yes, he very much wished her to concur that perhaps the bishop was wrong, that Graham Foster was not the rogue the family believed him to be. This heretofore unexposed side of him rather touched her heart, albeit she could have boxed his ears for his antics.

She was about to reassure him with some small show of faith that wouldn't also inflate his ego or give him untoward ideas, when footsteps on the drive caught her attention. Stretching to see over his shoulder, she beheld a young dark-haired man who had just descended from a coach parked behind theirs. He carried a leather portfolio in one hand and two or three slender ledgers in the other. A pair of spectacles flashed in the sunlight as he climbed the front steps.

"Isn't that Mr. Pierson?" she asked, pointing. "From Mr. Smythe's office."

Graham turned to follow her line of sight. "I believe it is. Wonder what the devil he's doing here."

"A legal matter, I suppose." Moira shrugged. Pierson didn't notice them, half-hidden as they were behind one of the portico's wide columns. "The bishop is a client of Smythe and Davis just as Papa was. Just as you are."

They heard the front door open and close. Graham said absently, "Mm, suppose you're right. Come. Let's go home."

Home. How easily he spoke the word. How naturally it fell from his lips as he offered his arm to escort her down to the carriage. The house on Brook Street— once her home, now his. But certainly not theirs. Yet he said it with the sort of familiarity he so often bandied about, as though home and family were nothing special, nothing to be cherished or defended or valued above all else in life.

It was this—this lack in him—more than anything the bishop of Trewsbury might have said about Graham Foster that disturbed her most. What did this man, this adventurer, know of home? What did he know of family? Or of the pain in her heart at having lost both?

CHAPTER
10

Moira awoke early the next morning determined to perform a task put off since her
arrival in London.   Going to the clothes-
press in her dressing room, she opened the top drawer
and rummaged through the undergarments she had un-
packed the night before.   There she found the lacquered
wooden box that held paper, ink pot, pen, and sealing wax.

She arranged these items on the bedside table.   Slipping back beneath the bedclothes, she propped the crisp
paper on a closed book and frowned in concentration,
preparing to write a detailed letter to her mother.   Of
course, a great deal of those details would come straight
from her imagination.

*Having a lovely time in London.   Catching up with old
friends.   Attended a brilliant ball last week.   Have positively
been adopted by the Mrs. Augusta Foster and family.*

This last would let her mother know where to direct

her correspondence without raising her concerns for Moira's welfare. After all, Augusta Foster was Everett Foster's second cousin by marriage, or some such relation, and it would not be at all unusual for the woman to take Moira under her wing. Even if, in truth, she hadn't.

She stared down at the blank page while tapping the end of her pen to her lip. She didn't like lying, especially to her mother, but what other choice? Besides, accompanying the missive would be the wages she earned as a maid. She hoped even that small amount might bring cheer to her mother's comfortless cottage, perhaps a small treat or two. Reaching across to the end table, she dabbed the brass nub of her pen into the ink.

Her pillow shifted beneath her, and her effort to catch her balance resulted in a gleaming black splatter across the edge of her pillowcase. Oh, rotten luck, the case happened to be part of the Alençon lace-edged linen set her mother had purchased in Paris several years ago.

Perhaps Mrs. Higgensworth knew a handy recipe for ink stains. In the meantime, the occasion called for a fresh case. After sliding the pillow free, she swung her dressing gown over her nightgown and padded barefoot from her room.

The doorknob of the linen chamber wouldn't budge. Locked? She tried again. How odd. As if there were treasure rather than towels and bedclothes inside. She glanced up and down the empty corridor. As she stood contemplating the puzzle of the locked door, a thunking echoed from the back staircase that led from the attic rooms to the ground floor.

Moira hurried along the carpeted hall, and stepped over a threshold onto the bare floorboards of the service stairwell. A maid descended to the landing, her mouth gaping in a hearty yawn as she reached around to tie the trailing ends of her apron.

"Excuse me," Moira said.

The woman came to a halt, one hand absently tucking a curl into her frilled mobcap. She bobbed a curtsy. "Good morning, ma'am. May I be of service?"

"Yes. Sorry to bother you." Moira stopped, realizing she'd never uttered those words to a servant before. She felt a little silly for it, and noticed the maid eyeing her with a mildly amused expression. Did the girl recognize her as the newest and briefest member of the household staff? "I've just been to the linen chamber to discover the door locked," she explained. "Do you have the key?"

"Why, no, ma'am. Only Miss Foster has the key."

"Oh. It's never been locked before."

"Miss Foster's orders, ma'am." The maid gave an apologetic nod. "As of yesterday. The tea service and silverware cupboards, as well."

"And why in deuced hell would that be?"

Moira spun about to find Graham looming behind her. The sight of him produced prickles of self-consciousness. In the dusk of the service hall, even with the maid present, there seemed something far too intimate about standing before him in her dressing gown and bare feet. Moira felt. . .chilly and exposed and rather regretful she hadn't considered this possibility before leaving her room.

He, on the other hand, looked elegant and entirely at ease in wheat-colored trousers tucked into glossy boots, and a stark white shirt that brought out the lingering traces of Egyptian sunshine on his face and throat. For several foolish moments, she stared, caught like a butterfly in a sunbeam, captured by the beauty, the sheer, simple magnificence of the man in shirtsleeves who filled the doorway and dwarfed his surroundings.

She was so taken by him that she didn't at first notice how intensely he returned her gaze. Then a single dimple winked at her. How did he do that? She blinked and looked away.

Moira Hughes, remember yourself.

"G-good morning, your lordship." The maid dipped an unsteady curtsy and caught the banister for balance. "I don't know why the cupboards have been locked. I-I only know what I've been told, milord."

Graham's gaze lingered on the woman. "Of course. I'll inquire with Mrs. Higgensworth. That will be all."

The young woman made another stiff curtsy in preparation of continuing down the stairs, but Graham stopped her. "What is your name?"

Her face filled with alarm. "A-Anne, milord." Her eyes began to glisten, her chin to tremble. "I'm sorry, milord, I—"

"It's all right, Anne. You aren't in any trouble. You're part of my staff, and I only wished to know your name." He offered a benevolent smile that made Moira-the-former-maid's heart leap with gratitude. "Keep up the good work."

"Yes, milord. Thank you, milord." Anne scurried away, raising a clattering echo down the steps.

"Come with me." Taking Moira's hand, Graham drew her down the hall and around a corner to his sister's room. He rapped his knuckles against the door. "Letty Foster, I wish to speak with you this instant."

A noticeable moment passed before they heard a light scuffle of footsteps inside. The door cracked open little more than an inch. "Yes, Monteith? Why ever are you kicking up such a clamor at this uncivilized hour?"

"Open the door and come out here, Letty." Between gritted teeth he added, "Now."

"Oh. . .all *right*." She stepped into the hall wearing a pretty morning gown of sunny lawn sprinkled with a green leaf pattern. Short puffed sleeves brought grace to her long, lean arms.

Graham glared down at her. "I'm interested in knowing, Letty, why we are suddenly locking doors in this house that have never been locked before."

Letitia sniffed, bit her bottom lip, and looked so nonplussed Moira experienced ripples of embarrassment on her behalf. It was like the other night at supper all over again. Moira tried to catch Graham's gaze and issue an unspoken admonishment to be kind, but he seemed not to notice.

"Well?" The word was a growl. "I'm waiting."

Letitia summoned her courage with an up-tilt of her chin. "It seemed prudent."

"Prudent?" His retort made both Letitia and Moira jump.

"Y-yes. There are *strangers* about." Moira supposed Letitia didn't quite intend to level such an accusing gaze on her. The girl shrugged. "One can't be too careful nowadays."

Graham thrust his face close to his sister's. "Is Mother privy to this? Or did you conceive of it all on your own?"

"Mother knows," she murmured and eased away a step.

"The keys." Graham held out his hand. "All of them."

After the briefest hesitation, Letitia spun about, stalked to her dressing table, and returned holding a ring of keys of various shapes and sizes. A disgruntled sigh escaped her as she dropped them into her brother's hand.

He passed the keys to Moira. "I believe you needed something in the linen room. Feel free to help yourself to anything else you desire, even if it might happen to be a handful of silverware."

His sister flamed scarlet from neck to hairline. Hefting fistfuls of skirt, she whirled to trounce back into her room.

"Stop right there, young miss. You and I are going to talk. Moira, will you please excuse us?"

Despite Letitia's less-than-generous disposition, Moira didn't favor abandoning her to her brother's unpredictable temper. Not with that stormy look on his face and that craggy ridge above his perfectly chiseled nose.

"Graham, please. . .I only wanted a pillowcase."

"And now you shall have it."

"Yes, but—"

Too late. He took possession of his sister's elbow and marched her across the gallery to his suite of rooms. Moira knew what a persuasive bully he could be. Poor Letitia. Moira would say a little prayer for her.

♥ ♥ ♥

"Letty Foster, have you taken leave of your senses?"

"*You* have been keeping your study door locked," she countercharged.

"That was to reserve one room in this house other than my bedchamber as completely mine. Besides, this is *my* house, Letty, not yours. I decide if rooms are to be locked or not."

Despite her brave scowl, Letty's shoulders slumped. "I'm merely looking after your interests."

"My interests?" Graham took a stride toward her, his voice soaring several notches. "After the kind of debts you and Mother ran up in my absence?"

"I should think that would be different. We are your *family*, though you seem hard put to act the concerned brother. Meanwhile you bring complete *strangers* into the house. . ."

"Moira Hughes is hardly a stranger. This was her home before it became ours."

"*Precisely!*" Her finger shot into the air. "All the more reason for caution. How do we know she won't try to reclaim what she's lost?"

"Ah, Letty." Sadness dragged at his anger as he wondered, not for the first time, where his high-spirited, charming little sister had gone. "Letty, Letty. I don't think I've ever been more disappointed in anyone than at this moment. Moira's situation should raise your compassion, not your disdain."

She sniffed. "What about that acquaintance of yours? The one who seems to have nowhere else to go?"

"Shaun? What about him?"

"Exactly who is he?" Her chin poked forward. "Who are his family? You say you met him in Egypt. What do you *really* know about him? Why, he could be a vagabond, a criminal—"

"Now you listen here." He paused for a breath and to calm an urge which would yield regrettable results. "Shaun Paddington is one of the truest souls I've ever had the privilege to call friend, and if you so much as whisper an unkind word about him again, I'll. . .shake you till your teeth rattle."

"Oh! You *wouldn't*."

"Try me." He stepped closer, towering over her. The next thing he knew, tears spouted from her eyes.

A knock sounded at the door, opening an instant later upon their mother's startled face. "What on earth is going on in here? I heard shouting. Heavens, Letitia, are you crying?"

"He threatened me, Mama."

Graham massaged a throbbing temple. "What do you know about locking doors against our guests, Mother?"

Augusta's gaze flicked back and forth between them. "Locking the cupboards is just a precaution, dear. It's certainly no reason to browbeat your sister."

"He said he'd rattle my teeth."

"Oh, my darling girl." Her arms opened, and Letty scurried into them. "Monteith, what were you thinking?"

"I'm wondering the same about the two of you." He pinched the bridge of his nose. He didn't want to be doing this. No, he'd much rather be back in the servants' staircase, admiring how Moira's satin dressing gown hugged her luscious curves.

He sighed. "There are going to be changes around here, and if you both wish to remain in this household, you had better accept those changes as ironclad and nonnegotiable."

The women traded wounded expressions. Augusta

dabbed at Letty's tears with an embroidered handkerchief. "I see life in the desert has made you despotic and insufferable, Monteith."

Yes, and how they must desire his return to Egypt, so they might cheerfully continue bankrupting the estate.

Suddenly feeling the need for an ally, he strode to a table by the window, opened Isis's crate, and scooped her into his palm. Then he went to the door, closed it, and took up position in front of it. "Now, then." He cleared his throat to reclaim his mother's and Letty's attention.

"Good heavens." Augusta's lips turned white. Her finger pointed in Isis's direction. "Letitia, is that the monster you spoke of?"

"Indeed, it *is*, Mama." Letty averted her gaze. "Hideous, isn't it? Monteith claims it's harmless, but *look* at it. Ugh!"

"Monteith, what is the meaning of this?" Augusta's eyes flashed outrage. "Step away from the door and let us pass."

"You may walk around me if you wish, Mother." He smiled. "But Isis and I would much prefer you stay until we've all reached an understanding."

"Beastly thing. And in this instance I don't mean your spider. Come, Letitia, let's be gone." She touched Letty's shoulder, giving her a little push. "You first, dear."

"No, Mama." Letty's upper lip curled as she regarded Isis. "I'm suddenly interested to hear what Monteith has to say."

♥ ♥ ♥

Shaun glanced up and down the gallery. Upon confirming that he was its sole occupant, he pressed his ear to the door of Graham's suite.

He'd heard voices—Graham's, Miss Hughes's, and lovely Letty's—all the way from inside his own room. He hadn't liked the sound of those voices, particularly not Graham's and particularly not the way he addressed his sister. As if Letty Foster were some inconsequential wench to be taken to task.

He didn't hear Miss Hughes now. No, she must have gone back to her room.

Miss Hughes was top-notch in Shaun's estimate. No grudges, no axes to grind, just determined to recover what belonged to her and her mother. And who could blame her? Hunting riches was, after all, what he and Graham did, and they employed far more questionable means than Miss Hughes, no mistake about it. No, he couldn't begrudge Miss Hughes her current goal, even if she did chafe Letty's patience at times.

Though presently absent, Miss Hughes nonetheless fueled the debate taking place on the other side of the door. He held his breath and listened.

"What is she after? The fortune is *yours*, Monteith, and she has no right to *any* of it."

Not entirely fair to Miss Hughes, Shaun reflected, but Letty could hardly be faulted. After all, her own father's fortune had been whittled away by creditors shortly after his death, leaving the family on the brink of beggary until Graham was able to send money home.

"Your responsibility," their mother said after Graham grumbled some reply Shaun couldn't make out, "is to marry and produce heirs, not to support distant relatives who wish to impose upon our generosity."

"Our generosity?" Graham's voice became razor sharp. He then launched into a diatribe on the extent to which *they* had imposed on *his* generosity and how things were going to change.

In Shaun's opinion, his friend was being too hard on the ladies. If only Shaun could think of a graceful way to intervene, to get inside that room. With a look, he would quiet Graham and remind him of a proper gentleman's behavior. After so many years braving the Egyptian deserts and dangers, a man did tend to forget the more genteel side of life.

Without warning the door opened. Shaun pitched forward. Tumbling across the threshold, he sprawled without the slightest scrap of dignity at Graham's feet.

"Blazing hell, Shaun." His friend half-laughed, half-scowled down at him. "What the devil are you doing?"

Shaun negotiated his hands and knees beneath him—oh, the ignominy—and lifted a mortified gaze to his astonished audience. He attempted to grin. "Just came to inquire if anyone else was going down to break-fast."

It was at that moment he noticed Letty's face. The tears; the mottled cheeks; the swollen, reddened nose. Sweet *Amon-Ra*, her vulnerability only made her more beautiful. More haunting. Shaun's chest constricted. Her eyes flickered as she caught him watching her. Tucking her chin, she sniffed and turned away.

Great Seti's tomb. An inferno roared through him. Graham had made Letty cry. The sight of those tears upon that tender face fanned a fury Shaun didn't know existed inside him, a conflagration that virtually propelled him to his feet, curled his fist, established his aim on his best friend's face, and spurred him forward.

♥ ♥ ♥

Graham watched Shaun's fist sail through the air, head-ing squarely for him. The act so thoroughly flummoxed him he didn't think to duck or parry the blow. Shaun Paddington was going to clout him? In the face?

Had the earth stopped spinning, as well?

At the last moment, so close Graham felt the breeze of the swing, Shaun's fist opened. The flat of his palm thwacked the side of Graham's head, narrowly missing his ear. The blow stunned, though more from astonish-ment than from any resulting pain. When it was done, Shaun stood before him wide-eyed and unmoving, as if frozen in disbelief.

"Well," Augusta said on a little puff of breath. "I can't say that wasn't deserved."

Her words seemed to shake Shaun out of his stupor. "Graham, old boy, did I hurt you?"

His hand went to his head. "A little, actually."

"You don't say." Shaun broke into a rueful grin.

Graham darted a glance to Isis, sitting serenely on his sleeve as if the disturbance hadn't occurred. She lifted several legs and set them down gingerly again. He regarded Shaun. "Why the blazing hell did you do it?"

Shaun's amusement faded. "I, ah. . ."

His expression sheepish, his gaze skittered over each of the room's occupants in turn: Graham, Letty, his mother. . .then Letty again. Shaun's attention rested on her for the length of a heartbeat, then another. A sentiment flared in his eyes, fierce, brilliant, but so brief Graham almost might have missed it. Letty surely did, for she stared quizzically back, eyebrows converging and tears suspended, her expression now simply one of expectation as she waited for Shaun to explain.

His shoulders squared, and his chin came up. "What kind of gentleman makes his dear sister cry? Graham Foster, you should be ashamed of yourself."

Should he? Letty had been deserving of a thorough set-down since the day he arrived home, probably long before that. She was a conniver and intolerably spoiled. Even now, Graham knew all her tears amounted to so much folderol. What next? An attack of vapors? Besides, would Shaun be as swift to play the gallant if he knew Letty's complaints were leveled as much on him as on Moira?

But, by God, Shaun wanted Letty. Graham had suspected before but had dismissed the notion as passing fancy. Good old stouthearted Shaun. . .and Letty. Who could have guessed? The notion raised Graham's ire all over again for his friend's sake, and he silently swore Shaun would never learn of Letty's sentiments, leastwise not from him.

"Perhaps you're right," he conceded and tipped the ladies a smooth bow. "Forgive me if I seemed overly harsh. However, you know my mind."

Isis chose that moment to scoot across his shirtfront. His mother gasped and muttered something incoherent. Letty stifled a squeak.

"Miss Foster." Shaun stepped forward, the crook of his arm extended. "May I escort you to breakfast?"

She regarded him down the length of her reddened nose. Graham held his breath.

Don't you dare snub him, Letty Foster, or it will be your last mean-spirited act in this house.

She hesitated with a look of uncertainty. Her gaze traveled over Shaun, rested on his features, and turned thoughtful. Then she gave an infinitesimal shake of her head and swept past him, out the door. With a sigh, their mother followed.

Graham's insides clenched. He wanted to sprint after Letty, shake her, and shout that she'd be damned bloody lucky to have a man as fine as Shaun. But to what purpose? During his absence from England, his sister had grown into the young woman she was. He couldn't dismiss his own culpability here.

Shaun stared into the vacant place where she had been, his brow furrowed, expression wistful, as if he might make her reappear simply by wishing it. Then a corner of his mouth pulled, and he blinked. In that instant Graham witnessed the dismissal of a man's hope. He felt miserable.

Shaun met his gaze and shrugged. "Ah, well, offering seemed the gentlemanly thing to do. Shall we go on down?"

CHAPTER
11

B reakfast proved uneventful, a circumstance Graham credited to the fact that none of his immediate family members made an appearance in the morning room. If Moira's pensive silences and Shaun's frequent sighs lent a certain tension to the meal, he felt grateful to have escaped any further dramatics.

Soon after, he and Moira prepared for their sojourn to Smythe's office, where together they planned to search through Everett Foster's financial records with a quizzing glass if need be. He'd have Moira all to himself during the coach ride first, a notion that spread a grin across his face as he descended the stairs to meet her in the foyer.

He discovered his brother there instead, striding to the front door with the pace of a man in a hurry.

"Where are you off to so early?"

With no acknowledgment, Freddy swung the door wide and stepped out onto the portico. In his free hand, he clutched a valise. Graham hurried to follow. "Wait a moment, Freddy. Where do you think you're going?"

Freddy halted on the top step. "I don't believe it's any of your concern. I'm of age, or nearly. I'll do as I please."

"I asked you a simple question."

"Then here's a simple answer. I've no desire to spend another day under this roof." He started down the steps.

Graham caught up again and checked his brother's descent with a grip on his shoulder. "What suddenly brought this on? I can see you're angry, but I haven't the slightest notion why. Is it because of the other day? Should I have left you unconscious in a puddle of ale at the stinking tavern?"

"I'm not the least bit angry." Freddy avoided Graham's gaze, squinting in the sunlight to the street below. "In fact, thank you for rescuing me."

Sarcasm drenched his words. Despite his assertion to the contrary, Freddy was furious. Roiling. Graham recognized the signs. Labored breathing, white-knuckled hold on the valise handle, rigid tension across his back.

He removed his hand from his brother's shoulder. He had already been struck once today, and Freddy's bearing put him on his guard. "Whatever the problem is," he said, "leaving won't solve it."

Freddy forced a humorless chuckle. "I should think you'd be relieved to see the last flick of my coattails."

Perhaps Freddy was right, he should be. One less problem to contend with, one less self-absorbed family member driving him to distraction. Yet for some bloody reason, relief was the last emotion he felt. On the contrary, the idea of watching his younger brother march away filled him with a palpable sense of panic.

He swallowed, took a deep breath, and tried to be rational. "See here, Freddy, do you really think your present circumstances allow you the means to live independently? In any sort of acceptable style, that is?"

"By 'circumstances,' are you referring to my utter lack of means or that I'm a drunk?"

"Don't make a joke of it. What do you wish me to do? Stay out of your way? I will."

"That's just it, big brother. I don't want you to do a thing." Biting sarcasm contorted each syllable. "Living off the fruits of your inheritance was bloody enjoyable while it lasted. Unfortunately, you're part of the bargain."

Graham stiffened against the sting of Freddy's verbal blow. His brother's expression warned of worse to come. He braced, ready for the full brunt of Freddy's antagonism.

"Has this anything to do with my years in Egypt? My staying away so long? You told me the other day I should have been here."

"Did I?" Freddy tossed his head in a gesture very like one of Letty's. "Drunken ranting, so don't flatter yourself. And don't think I begrudge you your illustrious career. You were meant for that life. You prepared for it so thoroughly at university."

Graham's insides clenched. With narrowed eyes, he seethed, close to forgetting everything he knew of tolerance and self-control. "What are you implying?"

"Implying? No, brother, I'm saying quite plainly I despise you." Freddy tossed an offhand shrug and faced Graham full on. In eyes very like his own, Graham witnessed glittering, naked contempt. "I'm saying your years in Egypt proved you're not only a cheat, but a thief, as well. Whatever trinkets you unearthed were not yours to claim, yet claim them you did."

Freddy leaned close, bringing the reek of brandy to burn Graham's nostrils. "I'm saying, dear brother, that of all the faces inhabiting this incomprehensible world, yours is the one that repels me most."

Graham's skin ran hot and then cold. The words rang in his ears like an echo from some far-off source, not possibly having anything to do with him. Yet the reverberations kept on, running all through him, leaving his nerve endings prickling and numb.

Freddy strolled down the steps before Graham recovered even a fraction of his equilibrium, before his temples ceased throbbing enough to allow his vision to clear.

He briefly considered calling to his brother, but the grim set of those retreating shoulders silenced the urge. Feeling dizzy, mildly sick, he closed his eyes, opening them again at the sound of a footfall on the threshold behind him. Moira stood poised in the doorway. A regretful look on her face revealed that she'd seen and heard all, or at least enough.

"He'll come back," she said quietly. Pity hovered in her lovely dark eyes, and he found it astounding that Moira Hughes—fatherless, homeless, penniless—should feel such an emotion for him, Baron Monteith, desert adventurer and treasure hunter.

Blazing hell.

He shook his head. "I don't think so. He's so angry and. . ." He trailed off, too weary to enumerate.

"I don't mean to make things worse." She descended a step and stopped. "In fact, I hope to make them better."

"Is this a riddle?"

"No. I've made a decision." She flashed a smile. "I'm leaving, too. Moving out."

"The devil you are."

Unfazed, she continued down until she stood beside him. "I heard Letty crying as I passed her door. You oughtn't to make your sister cry, you know."

"Letty was being a spoiled brat this morning. And every other morning, not to mention afternoons and evenings."

"Perhaps, but this time I was the cause. I don't wish to be the source of family strife. Certainly not of tears."

"Believe me, Moira, you are not the source. The discord between us began long before you ever set foot in this house."

"That may be," she said a little absently, as if it were a moot point. "Uncle Benedict has graciously invited me to be his guest. I think it would be best if I accepted."

"No, Moira." He reached out, only just preventing himself from taking possession of her arm. It was obvious from the way she flinched that his curtness startled her all the same. He continued more softly, "Not with him. I'd sooner see you return to that lodging house in Southwark."

She grimaced at the mention of her former abode, and he could have bitten his tongue for being so insensitive. "The bishop of Trewsbury isn't all he seems," he said quickly, "albeit he's got that sympathetic old cleric routine down to perfection. He has a devious streak, and few qualms about employing treacherous means to achieve his ends."

"I will grant perhaps in your case, he made a mistake. . ." She trailed off when he slanted a disapproving eyebrow. "All right, in your case he did make a mistake. People do. But I know the bishop to be a man of principles, and I will not hear him maligned so."

"Moira, Moira." Tsking, he reached for her hand. When she didn't resist, he held it in both of his own, which was better than physically trying to shake sense into that beautiful head of hers. "It's naïve to believe someone deserves your trust simply because he is family."

"I've yet to be proven wrong." Those midnight eyes

glimmered with certainty. Heat tingled between their joined palms, making him want to draw her against him, to feel all of her pressed to his length.

She made him want to believe. Made him want to release the past and bury his senses in the taste and scent of her skin. But experience had taught him a lesson too harsh to forget, even at the behest of the lovely Moira Hughes. As easily as perfect strangers, a family could fail to trust, fail to defend, fail to rally around one of their own.

"Please stay here with us." He stroked the back of her hand, then stopped when he remembered that was just the sort of thing likely to drive her away. "I'll even try to be nicer to Letty if you'll agree to stay."

Her glance flicked to their clasped hands. She skewed her mouth in skepticism. "She is your sister. It shouldn't be a challenge to be nice to her. You really ought to value your family, not set them at a distance."

"What I've learned to value is loyalty, whether blood related or not. In fact, I've often found that lack of blood ties makes for a truer friend, one free of ulterior motives."

"I'm sorry for you." Her fingers tightened a little around his. "There are no greater ties than family. No greater joy. You have a mother, a brother, and a sister. You should stop taking them for granted and appreciate your good fortune."

Her admonishment hurt a little; after all, who had

been taking whom for granted?

"Lucky? Ah, Moira, such easy words for you. You, my dear, are one of the lucky few for whom the word *family* holds only good connotations. I, on the other hand, have learned life's greatest disappointments spring from where one's trust lies deepest. Trust is a devilish thing, Moira, and highly overrated in this world. It's a mistake I won't make again."

"They hurt you very badly." Not a question, but a quiet avowal. "Perhaps you should forgive them and move on." Her tone, however, said *grow up* and move on.

He released her hand. "Again, easy words."

"Well." There was a world of sentiment encompassed in that utterance, and the notion that, just as his family did, she perhaps found him lacking. More than any of his mother's admonishments, Letty's complaints, or Freddy's accusations, that one little *well* made him feel inadequate, ungenerous, a cheater.

Her eyebrows rose in the face of his continued silence. "Shall we go see Mr. Smythe?"

"By all means." He offered the crook of his arm, hoping he'd be spared further judgment for the rest of the day at least. There was only so much a man could tolerate in a single morning.

No, there was more to it, much more. His brother despised him; the same brother who once idolized him. The fact of it produced a knifing pain in his chest. He didn't want to be alone with that pain.

Perhaps Moira felt a certain disappointment in him, but she neither despised nor looked up to him, neither vilified nor glorified him. That made her a rather safe haven at the moment.

♥ ♥ ♥

Graham was uncommonly silent on the carriage ride across town, and Moira found it unnerving, even more so than when he teased her and found spurious reasons for touching her. She'd grown accustomed to that Graham Foster, the cavalier who feigned ignorance of civilized manners; the playful, boyish rogue who nevertheless retreated to his corner whenever she said no and meant it. She'd learned how to handle that Graham Foster.

The stranger with her now occupied the far corner of the coach by choice, a great brooding shadow drawn in upon himself, arms crossed, shoulders bunched, head bent. Oh, he liked to pretend imperviousness to life's trials and to his family's idiosyncrasies, but she knew better.

As he'd already proved in dozens of small ways, he wasn't a bad sort, not the cad she'd envisioned prior to meeting him. He was simply, well, a bit lost, and determined to shield his gentler side behind a devil-may-care indifference.

She saw what his brother's words did to him. But she had also detected in Freddy's abominable behavior a perverse sort of reaching out, a desperate plea for

Graham to intervene. Perhaps this same sort of longing accounted for Letitia's petulance, as well. Despite their adult appearances, the Foster twins were two children in need of a father, or at least a father figure. Something Moira understood, being sadly devoid of a father herself these days.

Oh, but not one of these Fosters understood another. Somewhere along the way, events had torn them asunder from the heart outward, and Moira's own heart ached for them, albeit each of them often made her want to dash her head against the wall.

Perhaps, in return for Graham's helping her with her stepfather's will, she might find some way to reconcile this muddle of a family. Of course, the effort would require her to decline Benedict Ramsey's kindness and remain on Brook Street, where she might daily exert her influence. She wondered. . .could she befriend so quarrelsome a creature as Letitia? Win the regard of the flighty, pretentious Augusta? Gently lead Freddy away from the bottle—if he ever came home, that was. And Graham. . .

How to convince him he not only needed his family, but that it was perfectly all right to need them? She'd have to employ subtle means, and not be nearly as obvious in her prompting as she'd been back at the house.

A secretive smile blossomed as she warmed to the task.

"What's so amusing?"

"Oh, nothing." She assumed an innocent expression.

"I'm merely gladdened by the prospect of discovering something useful at Mr. Smythe's office. Do you suppose he'll have Papa's documents ready for us?"

"He'd better." Graham returned to his huddle.

Oh, yes, the man needed her help. His entire family did. As she fell to planning her strategy, she barely noticed the remainder of their trip until the coach rolled to a stop and the footman opened her door.

They discovered Smythe's front office to be strangely quiet. Not only were there no patrons occupying the waiting area, but Mr. Pierson's desk stood deserted, as well, giving Moira the impression of a guardhouse hastily abandoned in the face of an attack.

"How odd."

Graham led the way to the inner door. It opened upon more silence, so ponderous the hairs on Moira's nape stood on end. "If no one is in, why would the street door be unlocked?"

"Is anyone here?" Graham called. His voice filled the corridor, bouncing back at them from the closed office doors.

Moira instinctively reached for his hand, seeking reassurance in his steady grip. He didn't disappoint. His fingers closed securely around hers, instilling a sense of protection.

"Come." His sultry murmur produced chills, or were the goose bumps running down her arms the result of the eerie stillness?

They stopped outside Mr. Smythe's door. Graham knocked. He turned the knob and pushed the door open.

A gasp broke from Moira's lips at the sight within. The room lay in shambles. Papers littered the floor. Drawers hung open or had been pulled free and dumped upside down. The contents of the desktop—ink, pens, desk pad, a lamp—lay in a scattered pile. A small cabinet had been flung onto its side, its doors gaping, a panel splintered.

"Blazing hell."

"Yes, poor Mr. Smythe. He'll be most dismayed when he discovers he's been burgled."

"That's not what I mean, Moira." He raised his free hand and pointed to the floor just beyond one end of the desk.

At first Moira only made out a dark object poking through a spilled sheaf of papers. It was rounded on one side, flat on the other, not very big, and shined a bit in the light of the window. What could so leach the color from Graham's face and cause his fingers to tighten so insistently around hers as though ready to yank her away at any moment? Anchored by his hold, she pressed forward, peering to make sense of that strange black object.

The instant of recognition propelled her backward into his chest; her heart hammered in her throat while her legs nearly buckled.

The object was a shoe. . .connected to a trouser-covered ankle.

Graham's arms encircled her. She turned, pressing her face into his shirtfront. "Good heavens, is it. . .is it. . .?"

"Stay here." He released her, though he hesitated before leaving her side as if to be certain she could stand on her own. Her ability to do so surprised even her. The room spun at the edges of her vision as she watched him cross to the desk. Broken glass crunched beneath his feet. He placed a bracing hand upon the desk's edge and leaned over low. Then lower. His back to her, he crouched and shoved bits of clutter aside.

"Is it?" she asked in a whisper.

"It is."

She stepped forward. Graham whipped around, holding up both hands. "Don't come any closer, Moira."

"Is—is he alive?"

He stared into her eyes, and shook his head. "I don't think so. He doesn't appear to be breathing."

"Oh, good heavens." Her hand pressed her mouth; she spoke around her shaking fingers. "How dreadful. Oh. . .what about Mr. Davis?"

Whirling, she grasped her skirts and headed across the corridor to the other solicitor's office. Before she reached the threshold, Graham caught her from behind, his arms snaking beneath her arms and taking firm possession of her. "But we need to see if he's all right. . ."

"I'll see. You stay put."

She didn't argue. Trembling, breath lodged in her throat, she watched as Graham pushed the door inward.

It opened upon a scene much like the first. Strewn

papers, ransacked drawers. And a body sprawled across the floor, though thankfully this one stirred in response to Graham's approaching footsteps. By the time he reached Mr. Davis, prone at the foot of the bookshelves, the solicitor let out a weak groan and tried to lift his face from the rug.

"Davis? Can you hear me?" Graham squatted on his haunches and gave the man a cautious nudge. The solicitor's chin dropped back to the floor, but he continued to make noises, albeit incomprehensible ones.

Relief sent Moira to kneel at Graham's side. "He's all right, then."

"We'll know better in a moment, but at least he's alive." He reached an arm around her waist and drew her against his side, closing the gaps between their bodies until she could feel the ripple of muscle along his rib cage, the slight crush of his torso against her breast.

Yet the intimacy of their position aroused nothing of his usual irksome, lustful teasing. Rather than wanting to push him away or chastise him, she felt protected, utterly safe.

Mr. Davis stirred again. Graham called his name. The man's eyes opened. He slowly rolled onto his back and attempted to sit up.

"Don't move." Graham placed a hand on his shoulder. "Not just yet."

"Wh-what happened?"

"We're hoping you might be able to tell us," Graham

said. "Do you remember anything?"

Mr. Davis fingered the side of his head. "Not sure. I was looking for a particular law book, when. . ." Pain etched furrows across his forehead. He lay silent for several moments before reaching out a hand. "Please help me up."

"Certainly, Mr. Davis." Moira helped him to a sitting position and, with Graham at his other side, let him lean his weight on her as he struggled to his feet. He swayed several times as they steered him to an armchair. After settling him in, Moira slipped away down the corridor to the meeting room. Nothing appeared disturbed there, and near the head of the long table, she found the brandy cart intact. She poured a generous glassful.

On the way back, an impulse sent her detouring to Mr. Smythe's doorway. His foot lay as they had left it, a scrap of buffed black leather poking heavenward. How forsaken it looked, how alone. A tearful ache pressed her eyes.

"We're so sorry to have left you there like that, Mr. Smythe," she whispered to the toe of that black shoe. "It won't be much longer, we promise."

"So you were searching for a book when the door opened," Graham was saying as she reentered Mr. Davis's office. "Then what?"

The solicitor waited for Moira to hand him the snifter before answering. A gulp produced a shiver across his shoulders. With a deep breath, he continued,

"I didn't bother turning around to see who it was. I knew only Smythe or young Pierson would be entering unannounced. Although, I do remember wondering why I hadn't heard a knock. Then I felt a blinding shock of pain, and everything went black."

"You've no idea who struck you?" Graham perched on the edge of the desk. "You didn't hear anything that might identify the individual? Heavy or dragging footsteps, for instance?"

Mr. Davis shook his head. "I don't remember anything. What about Smythe? Was he attacked, too?"

Graham exchanged a glance with Moira. "We must send for the authorities," he said quietly. "There'll need to be an inquiry. And Pierson appears to have gone missing."

"You didn't answer my question about my partner." Mr. Davis squinted back and forth between them. "Has something happened to Wallace?"

Graham nodded at the floor. "I'm sorry to have to tell you this, Davis. Wallace Smythe is dead."

♥ ♥ ♥

"Damn it, what could be taking so long?"

Graham paced Smythe's front office until a look from Shaun sent him into the nearest armchair. He plunked down into it and hunched forward. "I want her out of here, Shaun. Dead bodies are nothing new to you and me, but for Moira. . ."

"She'll be fine. She's a strong woman."

Graham pushed out a breath. Moira and Mr. Davis were both still in the inner offices being interviewed by the coroner and a Mr. Miles Parker of the Bow Street Runners. Graham could only imagine the kinds of questions those men were asking. Of course, Moira would cooperate, not to mention put up a brave front worthy of a seasoned soldier. She always did, no matter the effort it cost her. "I should at least be in there with her."

"These inspector chaps always want to question the witnesses individually. They believe it gives them an advantage." Shaun paused, eyebrows knit. "You're convinced the burglar meant to kill Smythe?"

Graham knew by his thoughtful tone that Shaun was working it out, searching for clues in the scant information they had so far.

He nodded, unable to block out the memory of the solicitor's bashed head and misshapen features. "Definitely not the unintentional result of a mere blow to the head. The culprit wanted Davis incapacitated, but I assure you he meant to have Smythe permanently out of the way." He winced as the grisly images flashed in his mind. "What's more, the inspectors have already determined that while Davis's office has been vandalized, nothing is actually missing. Smythe's office, on the other hand, was ransacked with a purpose."

Specifically, Everett Foster's records. Vanished. All of them. And to think it had been Graham's orders that prompted Smythe to compile the documents and have them ready today. In effect, Graham had inadvertently made the thief's job easy.

"But why kill Smythe?" Shaun propped his chin in his hand.

"The answer may be hidden in Everett Foster's financial documents. Today's events have proved his last will and testament involve more far than meets the eye." Pushing out of the chair, he began pacing again. "The big question is, what happened to Pierson and how much does he know? Think you can track him down?"

"That's two questions." Shaun shrugged. "Finding Miss Hughes's lodging house was easy. Locating a man who might be intent on remaining hidden is another matter. I've been away from England a rather long time, old man. Don't have the contacts I once had."

Graham approached Pierson's desk, gazing over the contents of the blotter. He lifted a brass fountain pen from its holder, opened and then closed a leather-bound ledger. "You don't suppose he was taken hostage?"

"To what purpose? If the killer wanted him dead, his body would be lying here now. And Pierson is just a clerk, so he's worth nothing as far as ransom is concerned."

Graham nodded. "See what you can find out. I have a lot more faith in your abilities than in the authorities."

The inner door opened upon Mr. Davis, followed by the coroner. "Mr. Parker is finishing up collecting his evidence," the coroner told them. "And I now have the unhappy task of informing Wallace Smythe's family of his demise. Lord Monteith, Mr. Davis, good day to you both." The man nodded at Shaun, as well, and took his leave.

Trusting Shaun to plan a strategy, Graham went searching the inner offices for Moira. He found her curled in a chair at the meeting-room table, her head cradled on her arms.

He lingered in the doorway, watching as her slender shoulders convulsed. Was she crying? The notion gripped his chest and at the same time sent an uncomfortable sensation crawling through him. He considered retreating to allow her a few more minutes of privacy.

Privacy? Bloody coward, afraid of a woman's tears. Yes, he'd rather face an army of honor-bent Bedouins than deal with a crying woman. A man possessed no defenses against that. Couldn't fight through tears with a sword, pistol, or fist. No, a woman's weeping reduced a man to shuffling, stuttering, spineless futility.

But the utter hopelessness of her posture wouldn't let him walk away, either. He tapped lightly on the open door, not wishing to startle her. At first she made no response. Ignoring the urge to give up, he was about to tap again when she lifted her head a fraction, just enough to view the doorway.

And give him a view of her face.

Without another thought, he went to her, crossed

the room at a quick stride and knelt beside her chair. When his arms went around her, he felt none of her usual resistance, no effort to maintain propriety. The saltiness of tears mingled with her warm, sweet scent. Her breath trembled against his neck, and a need to protect, to fix everything that was wrong in her world, rose like a dervish inside him.

"Moira, forgive me. I should never have brought you here today. And for damned certain I shouldn't have let you look inside that office."

She lifted her face from his collar. "I might have come alone if you hadn't volunteered to accompany me. I don't know what I would have done."

Standing, he hoisted her into his arms, sat in the chair, and tucked her into his lap. For a long time she simply leaned against him. He held on tight, chin nestling in her hair.

His chest ached in response to her grief, but he felt something else, too, a surprising and thoroughly unfamiliar contentment, as if he were precisely where he ought to be. As if his shirtfront had been fashioned for no other purpose than absorbing as many tears as she needed to shed.

"I'm an abominable person," she at last said with a sniffle. She sat up straighter and wiped her palms across her sodden cheeks.

He blinked. "What on earth do you mean? You're the best person I know."

"Mr. Smythe wasn't only our solicitor. He was our friend. And. . .and. . ."

He thought she was going to collapse into sobs again, but she only swallowed and drew a deep, albeit shaky, breath. "I'm selfish and horrible because only some of my tears are for him. The rest are because now I'll never know what Papa intended for Mother and me. Our last hope is gone, probably forever. But how can I cry for my own petty concerns? How dare I, when poor Mr. Smythe lies dead?"

"Ah, Moira. You're not horrible, and neither are your concerns petty. I understand how vital your stepfather's promise is to you, and I assure you, hope is not lost. We're not going to sit back and do nothing."

She was no longer looking at him, didn't even appear to be listening. Tears clung to her eyelashes and cheeks but had stopped flowing. Her brow furrowed as she stared across the room to the open doorway. He experienced a vague twinge of annoyance. Here he was at his most gentlemanly, despite the fact that her warm weight in his lap aroused urges that undoubtedly would have earned him a slap if she knew of them. He had put her needs first, and she'd barely noticed. . .

"I just remembered something. That cabinet in Smythe's office. . ." Sliding off his knees, she jerked her skirts into place and took off at a trot.

Graham followed her back to Smythe's office. The body had been moved, thankfully, to the long table in the filing room. Moira knelt beside the overturned cabinet, running a hand along its splintered edges.

"I noticed this when we first came in. It seemed odd to me, but then we discovered Mr. Smythe, and I forgot all about it. But look here, where it's broken. There are tiny hinges hidden within the molding." Her hand traced the panel's edges. "And a recessed latch."

Gaining her feet, she stooped and set the painted cabinet upright. One of its bowed panels swung back and forth, like a door.

"I never knew about this." She thrust a hand into the concealed compartment and felt all around. "It's empty, but. . ." A startled gaze rose to meet his. "There's an identical cabinet at home in your study. Papa bought them on a trip to France, keeping one and giving this one to Mr. Smythe."

"I never noticed the similarity, but now that you mention it—"

Her features went taut with urgency. "I believe I know where Papa's codicil is hidden."

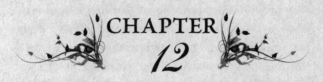

CHAPTER
12

Bonnet bouncing on its strings against her back, Moira ran through the house, sliding to a breathless halt when she reached the study.

There she lingered, unable to step inside, at least not until she'd admonished her heart to cease pattering and she regained a modicum of common sense. The codicil might not be hidden where she believed it to be. Or it might not exist at all outside of her imagination. Papa never did so much as mention the word, although she had been so certain it was what he had meant.

It must exist. It simply *had* to.

With a shaky sigh, she entered the study. On the far wall, beneath the stern glare of the first Baron Monteith captured by bold brushstrokes on canvas, stood the mate to the cabinet in Mr. Smythe's office.

Painted garlands of flowers and leaves festooned a creamy surface, spilling down the sides to gently bowed legs that ended in clusters of carved blossoms. Lovely. Delicate. And today, perhaps, an instrument of fate.

On trembling legs she made her way across the room. Part of her dreaded reaching her destination, fearing the abysmal disappointment she might meet. Then the cabinet was before her. Her hands remained at her sides as the fortitude suddenly drained out of her in a torrent. Her legs gave way. She reached for the wall, teetered a moment, then sagged against the wainscoting until her bottom made contact with the floor.

The door to the study closed softly. She looked up to see Graham approaching, her reticule dangling on its cords from his fist. In her haste she had left it in the coach.

She offered a wan smile. "You look. I can't."

He set her purse on his desk, then bent over her and touched her shoulder, a brief but reassuring brush with the backs of his fingers. Turning to the cabinet, he stood considering it a moment before running his hands along the panels. Moira hugged her knees and shut her eyes.

Through the rushing of blood in her ears came a click, then a squeak as the panel opened. The sound shot through her, striking chords of apprehension, hope, uncertainty. Then. . .nothing. Not a blessed sound.

Still not daring to look, she pressed her palms against her eyes. Was the compartment empty? How would she bear it? How on earth to return home to her mother with empty hands, empty hopes, empty cupboards, and no means of filling them?

"Moira." Her name came as a deep bass note. "Look."

A crinkling of paper forced her eyes open. Graham pulled his hand out of the cabinet, fingers clamped around a tied bundle of papers.

"Please." She paused to swallow and say a quick prayer. "Tell me it isn't a stack of old letters."

He tore at the twine. Her heart slammed her corset stays as he smoothed the pages open. He went still, frowning down at the topmost document before shuffling through the rest. His continued silence raised a mad impatience until she barely kept from grabbing his lapels and shaking him.

"Blazing hell." He slid down the wall to sit beside her. A nervous rustling rippled through the papers. Then he broke into a grin that made his dimples cavernous. "These are ledgers, records of government stocks drawn on the Bank of England."

She regarded him blankly. "Stocks?"

"This is it, Moira." He waved the bundle under her nose. "These are your unentailed funds. Look here." He pointed at a list of figures that meant nothing to her. "See? Most of these stocks were purchased way back in the late 1700s. Do you have any idea what they're worth now?"

She shook her head, the only response she could manage from within the swimming numbness threatening to drown her.

"Are you all right?" He slipped an arm around her shoulders. "Say something. You're frightening me."

"But. . .what about the codicil? Is it there?" Her hands lay limp in her lap. Even now she couldn't summon the strength to reach for the documents that determined her future.

"I don't see it, but frankly you don't need one."

"But without a codicil, these stocks are yours." She slid out of the shelter of his arm, using the chair rail to pull to her feet. Fighting tears, she summoned all her resolve to hold her countenance steady. "I've told you before, I don't seek anyone's charity. I won't take what is rightfully yours."

"Ah, Moira, do you think I'd claim these stocks? Never." He gained his feet and faced her. "They are yours and your mother's, as your stepfather promised. His word is codicil enough for me. This is not charity, but the fulfillment of a dying man's wishes. We need only go down to the bank and authorize the transfer."

A refusal simmered on her tongue. Why shouldn't he claim these stocks as part of his inheritance? Neither the bank nor the law would blink twice. Only her claims dictated he do otherwise, and that made it feel entirely wrong. The thought of accepting charity stung, yet she and her mother needed that money. Badly.

She was about to decline his offer, tell him he was a dear but she simply couldn't accept his generosity, when the enthusiasm in his handsome features sparked an entirely different notion.

"You, Graham Foster, are the greatest liar that ever

walked the face of this earth."

Her words stunned him to wide-eyed, eyebrow-arcing silence. She swallowed the urge to laugh and said, "You are a fraud, my lord Monteith, a charlatan of the most brazen kind. It's been a merry chase, wondering after the true Graham Foster. But you have been found out, my friend." She jabbed a forefinger into his shirt-front. "There is no use denying it any longer."

"Deny what?" His hand closed around hers, holding it against his chest. He looked utterly confused, alarmed. "What have I done now?"

"Nothing. That's just it." Only with the staunchest of efforts did she contain a mouthful of delighted, bubbling laughter. "You pretend to be so cynical, so self-sufficient. Graham Foster doesn't need anyone, especially not his family. You almost had me believing it. And then you go and make such a sweet, generous, completely noble gesture such as handing me these stock accounts. You're no blackguard." Her hand slid out from beneath his and came to rest on his smooth-shaven cheek. "You're a mush."

"A *what*?"

"You heard me."

He shook his head in adamant denial.

She cupped his face a moment longer; he was so beautiful, and never more so than at that moment.

"You're a family man in the truest sense of the word." This time laughter accompanied her words; she simply couldn't help it. Finding the answer to her worries *and* discovering the gentler Graham Foster beneath the arrogant rogue proved more than she could bear. "Why else would you extend such kindness to my mother and me?"

"Yes, but you're not family, Moira." The familiar devilish twinkle returned. He was laughing, too, now. "What are we? Distant stepcousins twice or thrice removed?" He made a feeble show of ticking off the degrees of relation on his fingers. His voice rasped like gravel as he continued, "No, not related in the least. Here, I'll prove it to you."

Before she knew what he was about, his hands closed around her shoulders. He suddenly pulled her to him. A little squeal escaped her, quickly muffled by his lips, absorbed into his mouth. A vague thought flitted through her mind, something about impropriety and the necessity of pushing him away. Oh, but sensation— the strength of his arms, the masculine musk of his skin against her nose—proved stronger, keener, and infinitely more interesting.

And decidedly more frightening and wonderful.

She slid her lips from his to catch her breath, to better anchor her unsteady feet on the floor. "I'd. . .say you. . .proved your point. . .and then some."

"Oh, no, Moira, not yet. Not nearly yet." Tightening his arms about her, he yanked her closer—like a sailor newly in harbor might yank the first doxy to come his way—and Moira let him. Let him and relished it, especially when his mouth again claimed hers. Opened hers. Breathed into hers with an intimacy that thrilled even as it shocked her to her core.

Then, with little hesitation and less apology still, his tongue entered her mouth to sweep her into a whole new realm of sensuality that left her dizzy, burning, throbbing. When his hands smoothed over her bottom, she let it happen and realized, with a jolt, that she trusted him. Trusted the cavalier, cynical, rakish Graham Foster who was not related to her in the least. She harbored no doubt he would lead her safely through this wild adventure.

Safely? Well, no, perhaps not quite.

"Ah, Moira, you're so beautiful." His baritone rumbled deep inside her.

"So are you," she replied, and even his throaty chuckle didn't make her wish she hadn't said it. He *was* beautiful—a golden, desert sun god.

One of his large, ever-so-warm hands wandered over her bodice, exploring her through muslin and linen before slipping into her neckline to fondle bare skin. She ignored the ripping of tiny threads and a lifetime's teachings as he traced a nipple, caught it between two fingers, and brought her to aching desire tinged with a mixture of shame and delight so sweet she felt a tear forming.

All she could do was cling to him, suckling his tongue—dear heavens, was she really?—savoring the rich taste of his mouth and knowing, yes, *knowing* she had suddenly and inexplicably become a wanton and didn't care.

Simply didn't care.

"Moira."

She shivered in his arms.

"Moira." Less gravelly now, but breathless, insistent. "I want you. I could drink you in and consume you whole."

She smiled against his cheek and made a purring sound she had never uttered before. Not in her whole entire life.

He released her bottom and slipped his hand from her bodice with jerky motions that spoke of deep reluctance. He grasped her shoulders again and shook her gently. "I want you, more than you can know. And in another moment, I shall have you, if we don't stop this instant."

Tipping back her head, she opened her eyes. For the first second or two, he was a blur of tawny brown hair and southern sea eyes. Then the handsome features took form. In the taut lines fanning from his eyes and the pull of his mouth, she saw the depth of his self-induced disappointment, his astonishment even, at having put a stop to what they both so obviously wanted.

Their gazes met, and he nodded, stepping back. His hands remained warm and steady on her shoulders, but his look of frustrated yearning persisted. Oh, yes, he'd wanted her, as much as she wanted him. Her eyes brimmed. Alarm sparked in his face, but she smiled through the gathering tears.

"You're a sweet man, Graham Foster. There is

infinite honor in you."

He looked at his feet. "Blazing hell, Moira. You've no idea what's going on behind this oh-so-honorable facade."

"Yes, I do." Her breasts ached with it; her thighs throbbed with lingering need. She blinked away the moisture in her eyes. "Why did you kiss me?"

"You mean besides *always* wanting to kiss you?"

She nodded.

"Because you laughed. Because that was the first time I've ever seen you truly laughing."

"Do you know why I kissed you back?"

"Because I'm sweet?" He cringed as he said it.

"Yes. And because for once, your guard was entirely down."

"You enjoyed that, did you?"

"Immensely."

He peered down into her face. His fingertips traveled up and down her arms, leaving trails of gooseflesh. He pulled her closer, not into an impassioned embrace like before, but a loose-armed hold around her waist. Companionable, affectionate. "Was I right to stop us?"

No. The word sprang into her mind, shocking in its bluntness. In truth, she'd have been content to let their kiss go on and on—although *content* was the wrong word entirely. She would have been thrilled, exhilarated. . .quivery. . .

But whatever had happened between them, whatever temptation inadvertently unleashed, had passed. Already he was reverting to his normal self, the devil-may-care

Graham Foster. Suddenly the reality of why he'd kissed her struck her a dulling blow: she'd been laughing. He'd kissed her for fun. For excitement and adventure. A deflating disappointment-and self-consciousness-swept a hot wave from her neck to her scalp.

"Of course, you were right to stop." She turned away, cleared her throat, and set her bodice to rights. The muslin hadn't ripped after all; he'd merely strained the rows of pin tucks furrowing its front. "No sense losing our heads simply because I laughed and you were sweet."

"Quite so." Stooping, he gathered up the account records that lay fanned across the floor.

Moira drifted to the bookcase, where she hoped, in vain, to avoid his scrutiny. He appeared at her side, his features sober. "In the excitement of discovering these ledgers, we nearly forgot why and how we found them."

"Good heavens, yes." Her head went down, weighted by shame. "Poor Mr. Smythe. How could we be so heartless?"

"I was referring to the burglary." He touched the small of her back briefly before dropping his hand to his side. "This could all be a bizarre coincidence. The thief might have been looking for something that has nothing whatever to do with Everett's will."

She touched the spine of a thin volume: Marlowe's *Doctor Faustus*, one of Everett Foster's favorites. She had flipped through it several days ago while searching in vain for the codicil. She sighed. "My instincts tell me there's a connection."

"I'm afraid I agree. Our first step is to go to the bank, secure your interests, and see if we can find out why Everett hid these accounts."

She turned to him. "Let's go now."

"It's late." His voice gentled as he delivered yet another disappointment, albeit a temporary one. "They'll be closed. We'll go first thing in the morning."

She clenched her fists at the thought of another delay.

♥ ♥ ♥

"What's eating you tonight?" Graham flinched as Shaun's question yanked him from his brooding. They were seated in the drawing room, beside the hearth. Across the room beneath the windows overlooking the terrace, his mother and Letty sat over their sewing. Restless tonight, Moira paced the carpets.

Graham realized he hadn't heard a word Shaun had been saying until his query struck a chord. "What do you think is eating me? There was a *murder* today, you know. Bloody harrowing business."

"Indeed." Shaun flashed him a knowing look. "And ordinarily you'd be trying to solve the case. Out loud."

His friend was right. Smythe's demise wasn't what had him ruminating. His gaze followed Moira as she drifted among the furnishings, running her fingertips over surfaces and leaning to straighten a porcelain figurine here, a bronze clock there.

Was she reliving her experience as a maid? No, more likely she was remembering living in this house, comparing her happy experiences to that of being merely a guest.

The drawing room was long, more a gallery than a room, and keeping her distance proved an easy task as she busily took stock of the knickknacks. Graham leaned, chin in hand, pondering her reasons for positioning the greater share of carpet between them.

He'd overstepped his bounds that afternoon and was deeply ashamed. At least, his conscience suggested he should be. He'd stolen a moment of emotional upheaval—Smythe's death and the discovery of the stock accounts—and pressed his advantage to kiss her. Grope her. And very nearly more than that.

Good God, this lust, for he couldn't in good conscience call it anything more civilized, had been seething since his first sight of her. Now, heaven help him, he couldn't enjoy a single thought without visions of the darkly dazzling Moira Hughes stealing in. Taking over.

She had called him sweet. Honorable. Because he had pulled back from committing an indiscretion of gigantic proportions, but only just.

He groaned into his hand.

"Why don't you simply invite her over to sit with us? Or better yet, go talk to her."

He met Shaun's far-too-penetrating gaze and raised his brows. "Talk to whom?"

"Right." His friend's mouth twisted. Then his gaze wandered to Letty and Augusta. He emitted a thoughtful *humph*.

Letty was hunched over an embroidery frame, jerking her needle in and out in a manner that threatened to shred the fabric. Her brows were tightly knit. She had, these many minutes, been muttering about the tedium of her task. "*Why* must women engage in such *tiresome* occupations anyway? Silly waste of time. Who *cares* if my borders are crooked or these snapdragons are as tragic as real dragons slain by the black knight?"

Her grousing triggered a memory. Letty in a pair of Freddy's trousers, declaring girls' pursuits a sorry waste of time before she had stormed off, revealing the miniature quiver and bow slung across her back.

She had been about eight at the time. On another occasion she had evaded her governess by way of a dumbwaiter. Graham found her an hour later giving three village children rides on her pony. Their laughter had rendered him incapable of reprimanding her, and he had even managed to convince her governess not to report her mutiny to their parents.

Stubborn? Yes, to a fault. But also high-spirited, clever, and generous. Not for the first time, he wondered where on earth that child had gone.

You should have been here. . .

He shoved Freddy's accusation from his mind. Should he be blamed for all the ills of the world? The unfair charges leveled at him at university had forced him to gather the remnants of his dignity and carve out a new life for himself, rather than wallow in what couldn't be helped.

Was it unreasonable to ask his siblings do the same?

But as Letty impatiently tugged her thread, he felt little hope.

With more than mild surprise, then, he watched Moira approach the Foster women and lean over Letty's shoulder. She studied the expanse of silk with a critical eye, then propped her hand on the back of Letty's chair. "You know, if you cross the stitches, they won't pull nearly as much."

Graham braced, anticipating his sister's less-than-amicable response.

"Yes, Letitia." Their mother looked up from her own sewing. "I've been telling you as much."

Letty scowled and continued plying her needle. Graham experienced a moment's exasperation on Moira's behalf; she was only trying to help. But then his sister's brow smoothed. "Why, you're right. It *is* lying smooth."

Moira nodded. "One other thing, if you will. For the centers of the flowers, French knots work to best advantage."

"Really? I'm not sure I know how. . ." Letty pushed the embroidery stand aside and stood. "Show me."

"Certainly." Moira settled into the armchair, repositioned the stand, and angled the frame. "My compliments on your design, by the way. It's lovely. Did you draw it yourself?"

"I did. Drawing isn't nearly as tedious as stitching. It's one of my favorite pastimes. In fact—"

"Now, Letitia," Augusta interrupted, "stitching accomplishes something useful. Drawing does not."

Letty's scowl returned, but only temporarily as Moira prepared to demonstrate.

Moira took the needle between thumb and forefinger and leaned over the frame, elongating the nape of her neck until Graham hungered for the taste of her creamy flesh. "French knots are simple once you know how," she explained. "You go in, then out quite close. . .just here." She gave a gentle pull. "Before passing all the way through, you loop it round, like so."

"That seems easy enough." They traded places, and after accomplishing several knots, Letty paused in mid-stitch. "Thank you."

"You're very welcome."

Augusta's mystified expression mirrored Graham's own astonishment. While Letty's exchange with Moira seemed insignificant enough, it certainly constituted a major foray into the realm of cordiality on Letty's part. And perhaps a minor miracle on Moira's.

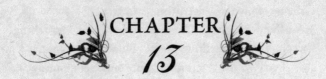

CHAPTER 13

Your affairs seem in good order, my lord. However, these particular accounts have been temporarily closed." The bank clerk, a man with thinning hair and a high forehead, snapped the maroon leather portfolio closed and sniffed.

"There must be some mistake," Graham said from his seat across the desk.

Seated in the chair beside him, Moira made a little noise in her throat and asked, "How *can* they be closed?"

Behind them, the activities of the Bank of England's main office proceeded at a brisk if subdued pace, the quiet footfalls and hushed tones more what he might have expected in a cathedral than in the country's chief financial institution.

"I'm afraid there is no mistake." The clerk sniffed again. "Our instructions were quite clear."

"They are not clear to me, sir. Not in the least."

Moira's impatient comment was snatched up into the vaulted ceiling and dispersed through the room. At the next desk a few feet away, another clerk glanced up, censure evident in the ridge above his nose. Graham angled a challenging eyebrow at him, prompting the man to return his attention to the work in front of him.

"The stocks are being transferred," their clerk continued in his businesslike manner, "to the name of the new stockholder."

"Is that all?" Moira relaxed against the back of her chair and treated Graham to the first truly genuine smile since their indecorous activities of yesterday afternoon. She continued smiling as she turned back to the clerk. "The new stockholder sits before you now."

"I'm afraid not." The balding man folded his hands on the portfolio cover. Despite issuing the contradiction, his expression retained an eagerness to be of service.

Graham cleared his throat. "Am I not Everett Foster's only heir?"

"No, my lord. It would seem there is another claimant." Clipped, professional, like everything else about this clerk: his well-fitted but unremarkable suit of clothes; his carefully trimmed, if sparse, hair; his quick, efficient hands that lay clasped before him when not in use. "We've documentation bequeathing these particular accounts to a second heir."

"There is a codicil." When the clerk nodded, Moira's

grin became triumphant. "We've been searching for it everywhere, and here it's been all along."

"Quite right," the clerk said, then frowned. "However, neither of you are mentioned in it."

"Of course not." She positively beamed while apprehension took root in Graham's gut. "This second heir would be my mother, Estella Foster, the dowager Lady Monteith."

"No, I'm afraid it wouldn't."

Graham had had about enough. "So who, then?"

The clerk gazed at his hands, looking uncomfortable and suddenly not nearly as keen to be of assistance. "I can't say."

"Can't or won't?"

"My lord, I am not permitted. Bank records are kept in strictest confidentiality. You'll understand, of course."

"Can you at least tell us if this heir is a Foster?" Moira's gloved hands fisted on the arms of her chair until the kidskin stood out in shiny relief across her knuckles.

"No, ma'am, not a Foster."

"And not a Hughes, either?"

"No, ma'am." The man's eyes closed briefly beneath raised eyebrows. A show of regret, perhaps; of dismissal, undoubtedly.

With a troubled sigh, Moira started to rise. With a hand on her forearm, Graham conveyed the message that he was not ready to concede defeat.

"Wait one minute." He mustered his most severe scowl and trained it squarely on the clerk seated across the desk. "You are well aware of who I am, and of the extent of my holdings. The barons Monteith have done business with the Bank of England since its inception."

The man's facial muscles twitched; his eyes narrowed fractionally.

"Yes, I believe we understand each other," Graham went on. "But to make matters perfectly clear, I will pull every last farthing out of this bloody establishment this very day unless you give me a name. Just a name, Mr.. . .ah. . ."

The man swallowed. "Bentley."

"A name, Mr. Bentley."

The clerk exhaled. Flipping open the portfolio, he riffled through the documents until he found what he sought.

"Michael Oliphant," he murmured at length.

"I've never heard of him." Moira accompanied the assertion with an indignant toss of her head. "Where does this man live?"

Mr. Bentley looked alarmed. "I couldn't possibly give out that information."

"Come now, Bentley, stop playing games." Graham injected the authoritative air of an aristocrat into his voice. "Where does this Mr. Oliphant reside?"

"You said just a name."

"No good to me unless I know where to find him."

Then, more agreeably, "I promise I'll make it worth your while."

The clerk worried his bottom lip. "I could lose my position. Can you make *that* worth my while?"

Bentley had a point. It would take quite a sum to make up for the loss of his employment. Graham decided on a fresh approach. "The information may be vital to an investigation being conducted by Mr. Miles Parker of the Bow Street Runners. An investigation of a crime that could very well be linked to Everett Foster's estate."

The man's brows converged. "Inheritance fraud?"

"Murder, Mr. Bentley."

The clerk swallowed again. Dipping his quill, he scratched some words across a sheet of paper, folded the page, and held it out.

"Thank you." Graham slipped the notepaper into his coat pocket. "An associate will pay you a discreet visit soon. And now I suppose our business here is concluded."

"Not quite yet." Moira prevented him from standing by gripping his wrist. "Mr. Bentley, can you, or someone else here, at least tell us what manner of man this Mr. Oliphant is, generally speaking, that is?"

"I'm afraid not, Miss Hughes. The transactions were conducted through his solicitor."

The very word sparked a note of alarm. Graham leaned forward. "And who is that?"

The clerk scanned the financial documents and

tapped a page with his forefinger. "The offices of Smythe and Davis."

The name hit Graham like a fist.

"I feel ill." Moira pressed the heel of her hand to her brow.

Graham cupped her elbow, helped her rise, and slipped an arm around her waist. "Steady. We'll get to the bottom of this."

"Oh, dear. Perhaps Miss Hughes would care for some brandy," Mr. Bentley offered, his helpful demeanor once more in place. "There's some in the private office."

"No amount of brandy can cure what ails me, Mr. Bentley." Pivoting out of Graham's embrace, she set off at a crisp march that raised an irreverent echo through the building.

He hurried after her. "Moira, wait. It isn't over. We'll get to the bottom—"

"Don't. And I'm perfectly capable of walking unassisted," she added when he again attempted to hold her about the waist. Her eyes sparked dangerously. "All that money, given to a stranger."

"Not a stranger, apparently. At least not to your stepfather."

Her expression blackened even as her pace quickened. People darted out of her path; a porter hurried to open the street door for her.

"Why?" she demanded to the wind rushing down Threadneedle Street. "Why would Papa do this? He promised me. . ."

"He was ill at the time—"

"He wasn't raving, blast it." A passerby jostled her elbow. Graham steered her toward the waiting carriage. "And all along, Smythe knew. Knew the truth and flat out lied to me. I can't believe it. I simply cannot."

"Perhaps there were debts. Perhaps Everett meant his family wouldn't have to worry because he'd settled those debts with this Mr. Oliphant. He expected you to marry Nigel—"

"Nigel." The carriage door stood open. Graham waited, one hand extended to help her inside. But in the next instant, she whirled and set off down the foot pavement toward the Romanesque structure that housed the Royal Exchange.

"Now where are you going?" He trotted to catch up.

"Nigel. Mr. Smythe." She went still, panting into the gusts racing between the buildings. "Dead. Both of them. The burglary. Now this Mr. Oliphant turns up."

"You suspect a connection between Smythe's and Nigel's deaths and Michael Oliphant?"

Both her features and her voice became deadly calm. "Don't you?"

He gave a reluctant nod, unable to deny her suspicions. There was something more going on here than a misplaced codicil, something elusive and sinister. Perhaps he might have connected the pieces sooner, if not for a stubborn inclination to ignore certain facts.

Nigel. The very name festered on his conscience like an open blister. He'd tried ignoring Nigel's ghost and pretending this one rival for Moira's affections had never existed. But in so doing, had he silenced a vital message from the grave?

He seized her forearms. "How can Nigel have been involved in any of this? His death was an accident."

"Was it?" She shook her head, glaring over his shoulder across the square at the pillared entrance to the Exchange. "Nigel was an expert rider. I'd seen him urge his horse over hedgerows in the driving rain with nary a misstep. He could gallop his mount blindfolded with both hands tied round his back. Tell me. . .how does such a man fall and break his neck on a main thoroughfare in fine weather?"

"Where was he going when it happened?"

"Home. From London. He'd come to secure his interests as the new Baron Monteith."

"Good God." He gave her a shake that imparted merely a fraction of the panic squeezing his chest. Passing pedestrians stared. He forced his voice to calm, his grip to lighten. "Why didn't you tell me this sooner?"

"I would have, but I didn't realize its significance until today." Her face filled with dismay. He felt her trembling beneath his palms, and he instantly regretted his curtness.

"I'm sorry. Come. Let's get you home." Gently he placed a hand at the small of her back and turned her toward the carriage.

"Yes, home. Not Brook Street, but Shelbourne." She climbed into the carriage before he could offer assistance. "I should never have left my mother alone. She could be in danger, as well."

"Let's not jump to conclusions." He summoned what he hoped was a reassuring smile. "However, while I understand why you don't wish to move her again, I insist we do just that. You'll both be safer at Monteith Hall. I shan't take no for an answer." He rapped on the ceiling. The carriage lurched forward.

"What of Michael Oliphant?"

"I'll deal with him the moment I return to London."

She faced him levelly, or as levelly as the swaying carriage allowed. "You'll do no such thing. One and possibly two men may have died because of that man."

"You needn't worry. I'll go straight to Bow Street and enlist the assistance of Miles Parker."

"Let's go see him now. He'll want to know what we've discovered today, especially Smythe's connection to the stock accounts." She leaned back against the squabs, and he resisted the temptation to gather her into his arms, at least in her present mood. "My suspicions concerning Nigel may also be of interest to him."

"We'll make a brief stop, then, to convey our news to Mr. Parker. I suppose he'd best search out Michael Oliphant as soon as possible. Meanwhile, I'm not letting you out of my sight until you're safely installed at

Monteith Hall."

She nodded, but a pensive look clouded her eyes. It was a look he didn't trust, not on the doggedly head-strong Moira Hughes. The sooner he got her away from London, the better.

♥ ♥ ♥

"Moira, darling, you're back."

"I am, Mother. I'm here at last." Hurrying to her mother's chair in the cottage's cramped parlor, Moira sank to her knees in a billow of skirts.

Her heart thudded, both with happiness at the reunion, and with anxiety about how her mother had got on in her absence. And yet, Estella had hardly blinked moments ago when Mrs. Stanhope announced her and Graham's arrival.

"I'm frightfully sorry to have been away so long, Mother. Are you quite well? Did you miss me terribly?"

"Yes to the first, and very much indeed to the second." Estella stroked Moira's cheek. "I told Mrs. Stanhope to hold tea, but now that you're back from your walk, I shall ring for her."

A weight like yesterday's dumplings descended in Moira's stomach. She flicked a glance at Graham and winced at the pity in his eyes.

"I see you've brought Nigel with you." Pleasure filled her mother's voice. "How splendid. It's been a long while since we've visited with Nigel, hasn't it, my dear?"

Laying her cheek in her mother's lap, Moira reached her arms around a waist gone noticeably thinner in her absence. "Mother, this isn't—"

"Lady Monteith." Graham approached the faded petit-point armchair. Bending at the waist, he lifted Estella's hand to his lips. "Ma'am, I am your late husband's relative, Graham Foster. I'm very pleased to make your acquaintance."

"Graham Foster? Not Nigel, then?" Shadows gathered in Estella's dark eyes.

"No, Mother, not Nigel."

"Well, then." She produced a polite smile that trembled slightly at its corners. "Won't you join us for tea, Mr. Foster? You must forgive us, though. We seem to have misplaced our splendid Meissen tea service and must make do with the Minton set I purchased in Staffordshire before my marriage to Lord Monteith. It's quite lovely, mind you, but not nearly as elegant as the other." Her gaze darted about the room. "We seem to have misplaced a great many things lately."

Not misplaced, Moira reflected dismally, but left behind at Monteith Hall. "Mother, would you like to see the Hall again? Return there to live, perhaps?"

"Why, yes, I would, indeed." Her matter-of-fact reply held the question in no higher account than what cake she'd like with her tea. "We should go soon, in fact. Your papa will be waiting for us. He must wonder why we've lingered so long on holiday without him."

Graham's hand closed on Moira's shoulder. She could not help turning toward it and seeking its warmth beneath her chin.

How she'd hoped—prayed—things would be better with her mother by now, that the confusion would have cleared once Mrs. Stanhope had settled her into a routine. On the contrary, Mother seemed worse than ever, her thoughts more mired in the past. Moira wondered if moving back to Monteith Hall would make any difference at all.

The reverberation of the tea cart along the corridor's bare floorboards interrupted her musings. Bare floorboards. Yes, when she last walked the parlor floor, her footsteps had reverberated throughout. Now, however. . .

Gazing downward, she realized her knees were cushioned by a thoroughly unfamiliar throw rug. They certainly hadn't brought this broadloom of green vines on a russet background from Monteith Hall. Another rug lay beneath the front window.

Where on earth had they come from? Or, more to the point, where had the funds to purchase them come from?

"Mother. . ."

Mrs. Stanhope entered the parlor at that moment and positioned the refreshment cart beside her mother's chair. Smiling, the housekeeper whisked a silver cover off a platter. Moira's breath caught at what she saw.

Tea cakes dripping with honey. Clotted cream.

Fruit preserves. Cinnamon biscuits. Good heavens!

A sense of outrage clogged her throat. Such extravagance. Such sinful excess. How was it possible? Even if the funds she had sent had managed to arrive so quickly, the money was simply not enough for luxuries like these.

She pushed slowly to her feet. How *could* Mrs. Stanhope have been so reckless with their meager savings?

"My goodness," that very woman exclaimed as she hurried back into the hall. "I nearly forgot. I've made a lovely bread pudding, as well. I'll be right back with it."

Estella nodded and lifted the teapot. Moira felt as though she staggered at the brink of disaster.

"Excuse me a moment," she murmured and followed Mrs. Stanhope into the kitchen. The sound of the housekeeper's uneven soprano sent her ire soaring with each carefree note.

"Mrs. Stanhope, a word, if you please."

"Of course, Miss Moira." The woman looked up from the worktable, where she was just lifting a linen cloth from an oblong pan. Inside, cubed bread oozed with buttery vanilla sauce dotted with raisins. A warm, sweet aroma set Moira's mouth watering despite her indignation. "I do hope you and the new Lord Monteith brought your appetites."

A deep breath helped contain the urge to bellow. Moira clutched her hands together. "Mrs. Stanhope, what have you done? Sugar, butter, new rugs? What is the meaning of this?"

"I. . .whatever do you mean, Miss Moira?"

Sheer frustration propelled her to the worktable. Gripping the pan, Moira lifted it, then smacked it against the countertop. The bread pudding shimmied within its syrup. Splatters flew.

Mrs. Stanhope flinched. "Why, Miss Moira—"

"Don't *Miss Moira* me. Not after months of meting out every ingredient, of painstakingly rationing our foodstuffs, of barely holding financial disaster at bay..." Her words dissipated on a nauseating wave of fury. Trembling, she clenched her teeth and fisted her hands. "I demand to know where all this abundance comes from."

"But. . ." Mrs. Stanhope eyed her sideways, her wary frown suggesting Moira had quite taken leave of her senses and was liable to exhibit even more deranged behavior at any moment. As well she might. "They were delivered the day before yesterday. Didn't you arrange it, Miss Moira?"

"Delivered?" Several seconds ticked by on the wall clock before she was able to close her mouth, swallow, and form an answer. "I most certainly did not. Who delivered them?"

"Two men in livery came in a coach, which is odd, now that I consider it."

"Livery?" Suspicion hissed through her like a serpent. "What color?"

"Royal blue." Mrs. Stanhope tilted her head. "With

silver trim, I believe." Her eyes went wide. "Why, that's the—"

"The new Monteith livery, yes."

"We left the Hall so soon after the change was made, I'd forgotten." The woman took up the discarded linen cloth and began mopping at the butter sauce dispersed by Moira's tirade. "Are you angry with me, Miss Moira? Should I not have accepted the delivery?"

Angry? Quite right. But not with this trustworthy woman. "Mrs. Stanhope, do forgive me. I don't know what came over me. I'm so sorry. It's just . . .well, never mind. You did exactly right."

The woman beamed, and Moira did an about-face, blazing a path back to the parlor. From the doorway she wagged a beckoning finger at Graham. "Would you mind helping me find something in the coach, please?"

He sat perched on a footstool in front of her mother's chair, his long legs drawn up and his cup and saucer balanced on his knee. Her mother was saying something that had him grinning. At Moira's request, he nodded, set his teacup on the cart, and placed his hand over one of Estella's. "Would you excuse me a moment, ma'am?"

"Yes, but don't be long. Your tea will grow cold, and besides, we have so much to catch up on. Moira, dear, did you know Nigel's been all the way to Egypt? No wonder his presence at Monteith has been woefully scarce these past months."

"Yes, Mother. We'll be back presently." Tugging

Graham by his coat sleeve, she conveyed him out the front door and down the garden path. At the gate, she halted and released him. "All right, you. Come clean. Who stocked the cupboards?"

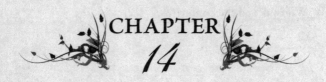

CHAPTER 14

M oira wanted to be furious, but this man made it a devilish difficult task. Especially when the afternoon sunshine gilded the ends of his hair, rekindled the African sun in his skin, brightened his eyes to aquamarine, and—oh, how she hated to admit it—lent him the dashing magnificence of an Egyptian king.

She blinked and banished the pharaoh from her sights, bringing Graham Foster clearly into view. He was trying to smile, yet looked uncharacteristically at a loss as he fidgeted with his cravat.

"There's no need to be angry, Moira."

"Have you not heard a blessed word I've said about accepting charity? When I went to London, it was to secure what I believed to be. . ."

Her voice caught. Blast. What she didn't need now were tears, but there they were, pushing against her eyes and closing her throat until all she could do was hiccup into her hand. She spun away, but Graham caught her shoulders, turned her, and gently drew her to him.

"I was only trying to help."

"Assisting me in my quest is one thing, and for that I'm eternally grateful." A sob rushed out, unstoppable for all she whisked a fist to her mouth in the effort to contain it.

Without a word, he anchored his arms around her and pressed his forehead to hers, waiting patiently to catch whatever utterances made their way past her weeping.

She gathered her breath, stepped backward until his hold loosened, and wiped angrily at her eyes. "Handouts are quite another matter. I will not live my life as anyone's poor, dependent relation. How dare you think so little of me and of my capacity to care for me and mine."

"It was only the other day you called me sweet, Moira." His hands nestled warmly at the curves of her neck. "Have I once more reverted to blackguard?"

"Oh, don't do that. Don't try to be adorable." She shoved his arms away, then regretted it, immediately missing their steadying strength.

"Adorable. Egad." His mouth pulled. "A sweet, adorable blackguard. Please don't tell Shaun. I'd never live it down."

"Oh, you're impossible." She pushed through the gate and strode half the length of the picket fence before halting and doing something she hadn't done in many years. She stomped her foot. "*Why* won't you understand? I'm an able-bodied person. I can obtain some sort of position. A teacher, a governess. I sew tolerably well. I could take work as a seamstress."

"A seamstress?" Quicker than lightning he was beside her, grasping her elbow and turning her to face him again with considerably more insistence than she might have preferred. "And do what, Moira, sit in some garret fifteen hours a day wearing out your fingers and your eyes for a pittance that will keep you merely half-alive? I'd sooner die than allow you to come to that."

"Allow me? Of all the impertinence." Her chin came up. She was about to take him to task when suddenly the admonishments flew from her mind. His expression was fierce, his jaw stony. She realized what he'd said—but had he meant it?

I'd sooner die.

Would he? For her? Her heart swelled at the thought, but. . . Was this simply more of Graham Foster's dramatics? Cavalier sentiments tossed out for effect, for excitement, for sport?

"I will not accept charity," she said. "Not from you. Not from anybody."

"Would you rather your mother go hungry?"

"I—" Her mouth snapped shut. She despised his logic. "You needn't put it that way, as if there were no prospects between the one and the other."

"Damn your pride, Moira Hughes. You're the one

always extolling the virtues of family." He took possession of her face in both hands. He brought his own face
close, until the heat of his breath fell like kisses across her
lips. "You little hypocrite, too stubborn to live by your
own credo. You'd rather starve than accept help, even
from someone for whom that help presents no hardship
whatsoever. Or is it simply me, Moira? You'd rather not
be beholden to *me*?"

Between his palms, she felt her color rise. That had,
indeed, once been the case. She *had* balked at trusting a
man who claimed family meant nothing. Yet, more recently,
she'd glimpsed another side to him, a side that, when
acknowledged aloud, made him cringe and her smile.

Still. . .

"In my place, would you accept handouts? Should I
possess any less integrity for being a woman?"

His hands dropped to his sides. "No." His shoulders bunched; he thrust his hands in his trouser pockets.
"Consider it a loan, then."

"One I might never be able to repay. Especially in
light of what we learned yesterday at the bank."

"You could always don your maid's uniform and work
it off. Of course, it would cost me a fortune in chipped
porcelain. . ." Grinning crookedly at her simmering scowl,
he tipped his head from side to side as if weighing the pros
and cons of the matter. "Then again, watching Letty's
ensuing descent into madness would be priceless."

In spite of everything, laughter came tumbling out.

How could this man so infuriate her and at the same time reduce her to such mirth her belly shook like so much bread pudding?

He threw back his head and joined her in disturbing the quiet and alarming the birds. A rabbit formerly nibbling the crocuses lining the fence darted with undue haste into the trees. New tears trickled from Moira's eyes—and from Graham's, as well—tears that had nothing to do with wills or misfortune or hunger. Tears that had everything to do with generosity, and with the dearness of a man who avowed one thing and did the opposite entirely.

And with the notion of Letty Foster tearing out a golden curl for every chipped piece of china she discovered.

With the backs of his fingers, Graham flicked away tears of merriment. "So you'll accept a loan for your mother's sake?" When she hesitated, he raised an eyebrow. "I swear I do not think you're helpless or lacking in integrity or any other affront to your precious ego. For I fully intend to have every last penny back."

She knew he was lying. But she nodded. "Since you put it so eloquently. . .yes. Thank you. And I *will* repay you."

"Fine."

"Good."

They shook hands to seal the bargain, a single, firm-gripped yank up and then down. He held on longer than necessary and flashed his dimples. Oh, he was always doing that to unnerve her, but this time it produced a notion that zinged her nerves and snatched her breath.

Kiss me.

She wanted him to, and, dear heavens, she thought he might. It wouldn't be all that inappropriate really, in light of their coming to terms as they just had. And it wasn't as if they hadn't done it before. Good gracious, had they ever done it, especially the time in the study. And now, dimples and boyish grin and all, he was being. . .well. . .such a dear.

He gave her hand a little tug. "Come. Your mother is waiting. Let's join her and have our tea. Unless, of course, you'd like to take me to task for something else. Lord knows, my sins are vast and varied."

Oh, impossible man.

♥ ♥ ♥

Home. England.

Those words struck Graham as they never had before as he made his way across the gardens of Monteith Hall and approached the first sweep of the lawn.

The parterres needed weeding; flower beds, replanting. But Monteith achieved an elegance infinitely more genuine by using the best England could offer: a rolling landscape; towering, ancient trees; and a fine morning mist that transformed his surroundings to the muted tones of a watercolor.

Off some thirty feet to his right stood the disordered columns of an orchard left to its own pleasure, gnarled branches tangling in their effort to catch the sun's attention. The sweetness of pears mingling with the tang of apples yet to ripen drifted in wafts and set his mouth watering.

To his left some fifty yards away, a groom led a pair of bays into the nearest paddock, their combined tread thudding a leisurely rhythm on the dusty lane. Through the split-rail fences, he watched the horses entering the paddock, listened with pleasure to their snorts as they strolled, testing the limits of their freedom. Once satisfied no lead rope restrained them, they broke into playful canters.

This was what he'd forgotten. These simple details of home were what he had missed, lacked, so deep at his core he hadn't sensed the emptiness until now.

The realization tightened his throat. Had he truly thought to judge his homeland on faded memories and the dismal influence of London's sooty skies? No wonder he'd been pining to return to Egypt. But *this* was breathtaking. This was home.

And this, he feared, was who he was at heart. Or at least who he might have been if everything he'd believed in as a young man hadn't been yanked out from under him. If only there'd been one person, one soul brave enough to believe in him.

Isis's prodding at his shoulder came as a welcome distraction from the disagreeable turn his thoughts had taken. She'd looked hungry earlier, crouched on her limbs in the doorway of the leafy burrow that occupied a corner of her crate. When he'd reached in to take her out, she'd pounced on his forefinger, but caught his scent before delivering the painful if harmless bite.

He set off now to a row of pine trees bordering the main riding lane. Crouching, he deposited her at the base of a tree where low branches and fallen needles formed a natural lair. Instinctively seeking camouflage, she scooted toward the tree trunk, out of view. Graham retreated a few steps and waited.

If he had once feared losing the spider by releasing her to hunt, he wasted no worries now. He didn't know why she darted back into his palm once she consumed her fill of beetles, ants, or anything else small and crawly; he only knew she did so each time, for all appearances eagerly. Perhaps one day she'd change her mind and seek freedom.

Wait till you're home, girl. You'd be no match for an English winter.

While he waited, he turned to view the gardens and house. He wasn't the only one affected by the beauty of this place, not alone in experiencing the sensation of finally arriving home.

Despite Moira's apprehensions about moving her mother a second time, the joy on Estella Foster's face upon walking through the front door assured them they'd made the right decision. After only one reference to her late husband, Estella had seemed unusually coherent, not to mention cheerful and entirely at ease. She even stopped addressing Graham as Nigel. And following supper, she had been thrilled to discover that the Meissen tea service had not gone missing after all.

Graham had opted to occupy a guest room and allow Lady Monteith to move back into the rooms she had once shared with her husband. The look in Moira's eyes and her whispered thanks had been far more rewarding than fame or glory or gold. Later, as the two women embraced and bid each other good night as if they hadn't a care in the world, he'd experienced a kind of quiet, very private jubilation.

A rustling beneath the pine tree recalled his attention. Isis must have snatched something appetizing. Crouching with hands on knees, he peered beneath the tree.

"I see I'm not the only early riser this morning."

The voice startled him. Apparently, the rustling he'd heard hadn't been Isis appeasing her appetite, but Moira strolling up the riding lane. He got to his feet.

"What were you looking for under there?" she asked, smiling as she came around the row of trees. Against a frock of dusty violet, her dark eyes and sable hair stood out with striking intensity. She wore no bonnet, and her hair hung loose—a rare treat—tumbling down her back and framing cheeks gone ruddy from a brisk morning walk.

Simple and stunning, like the countryside.

Her head tilted, the lovely curve of her chin taking on a mischievous slant. "Cat got your tongue?"

In that instant he knew. Understood. This newfound sense of home encompassed far more than the narrow scope of house and holdings, went leagues beyond misty glens and rolling hills.

Moira. Her smile. Her approval. Her trust. Could he have been capable of appreciating this fine English morning had it not been for her influence?

He doubted it. Very much.

Moira and England. Both brave, honest, and beautiful, and able to face the worst adversity with an upper lip of pure steel. And both somehow intricately wrapped around his heart.

What did that mean for him? For his future? It was a question he couldn't answer, not yet. But at that moment he knew one thing with certainty.

"I'm glad you're here."

Her eyebrows rose. "Are you?"

"Yes. I was looking for you."

"Under a tree?"

"Everywhere."

Her laughter was high and light, like the tumble of water over rocks. Utterly devoid of cares. The sound drew him to her with a single-minded resolve that must have shown on his face, for her eyebrows surged higher and she slung a long stride back, then another.

"Graham?" Her voice rose with uncertainty. With amusement, too. "What are you doing?"

"This." He caught her face in his hands and took

a final step that brought them hip to thigh, breasts to chest. Lips to lips. His mouth smothered hers, feasted. His tongue entered without pausing for permission, without allowing her the chance to demur. Not yet. Not until she knew fully what she'd be turning away.

She tasted of tea with honey and every sweet ideal a man could dream of. Her lips were moist, pliant, and, to his delight, pushed readily against his, seeming as eager for more as he was. Her arms around his neck, her breasts melted into the planes of his chest, and her torso undulated—probably without her knowledge—in a seductive dance that filled the hollow places of his body with the soft, luscious feel of her.

With a hand at the small of her back, he pressed her to him and rocked his hips to match her rhythm. While his arousal nestled in skirts and the suggestion of what lay beneath, his free hand explored, tracing her narrow waist, sweeping the curve of her side, molding the swell of her breast above her corset. His thumb and forefinger closed around a nipple gone taut beneath the fabric. Traced and rubbed the bead it became. A moan rose inside her, passing from her mouth into his. Fire seethed through his brain, in his loins.

How many times had they done this before? Done this and stopped, breathless, burning, fighting what felt, at least to him, inevitable.

"This is no kiss of convenience, Moira." He breathed the words against her mouth. "Nor of merriment or because a bumpy coach tossed us together."

"No. . .no, it is not."

He opened his eyes and pulled slightly back. Her eyes opened, her gaze as brilliant as midnight. He nipped the end of her nose and grinned. "What is going on behind those dazzling eyes of yours?"

"Can't you tell?"

He believed he could. With his arms tight around her, his arousal snug against her, he felt the answer pulsing through him. But he needed to be certain. "I don't like guessing."

"Then let me make it quite plain."

He felt an instant's regret when her arms released him. Then she gripped his shirtsleeves, yanked him to her, and kissed him squarely, a kiss commanded entirely by her. Open mouthed, tongue-touching, saliva-sharing. It drew the last bit of blood from his brain and rushed it like a spring-thawed waterfall to his groin.

The great warrior donned his helmet and leapt to the ready. Here was something completely new, unexpected. He throbbed pure flame while sensation fled his arms and legs and left him tingling. Thrumming. In a state of utter surrender, he let Moira hold him in place while she all but sent him over the brink.

And all he wanted was to do the same for her—and more. Reduce her to writhing pleasure wrought by his hands, his body. . .

She shoved him to arm's length, fingers still bunched

in his sleeves. "Be assured that was *not* for the blazing hell of it."

His reply grated incoherently in his throat. Yet despite having been kissed senseless, he couldn't remain a passive recipient for long. The need to have her rumbled through him. He again took her face in his hands, threading his fingers in her hair as he brought his lips against her ear. "Is your mother awake yet?"

A tremor shook her lower lip. "Not for another hour or so. She's not an early riser."

They stared into each other's eyes, so close he saw the dilation of her pupils against irises nearly as black. He searched for a hint of turmoil, fear. He saw only a raw anticipation that sent his pulse lurching.

Had he truly asked that question, and had Moira quite understood what he meant?

Did *he*? What had begun as little more than an amusing diversion—find the fortune, kiss the woman— had gradually and subtly changed into something of far greater consequence.

Were they truly about to return to the house, race past the servants to one of their bedrooms, and do things that would change the nature of their relationship forever?

Forever. His heart bucked.

She stepped out of his embrace, took his hand, and thus decided the matter. Their fingers laced tightly, irrevocably, as they started toward the house.

They made it as far as the box hedge bordering the lower gardens when Graham brought them to an abrupt halt. "Isis."

With trembling fingers, Moira swept loose hairs from her eyes. Her heart was dancing a country jig, reverberating at every pulse point. She had finally decided what she wanted. What she yearned for. What she could no longer deny. And all he could think of was—

"Your spider? What about her?"

"I left her under a tree."

"Is that what you were looking for?"

"I'd brought her out to hunt. I have to find her before she's lost. She can't survive on her own. Not here." He looked as apologetic as she'd ever seen him. And as ill at ease as she herself now felt. A few self-conscious steps created distance between them. The spell that had propelled them toward the house had broken, and Moira knew there was no recalling the magic. At least not presently.

"Come," she said. "We can't have her falling into misfortune on our account, can we?" They retraced their steps at a run.

Falling to one knee, Graham swept the lower branches aside and let out a whoop of relief. "She's still here."

He came to his feet with Isis perched on his sleeve. He grinned at Moira, and she grinned back, relieved for his sake. But the silence that fell resounded with the acknowledgment of what they had been about to do, spurred by a madness that had taken them both unawares.

Moira sighed her regrets, then wrinkled her nose. "You're really quite enamored of that creature, aren't you?"

He shrugged. "If the truth be told, I believe she's rather enamored of me. She waited here for me, didn't she?" He touched one long, bent, hairy leg. "There, there, my lovely. Safe and sound."

Moira couldn't suppress a shudder. He held Isis closer to her. "I assure you, she's completely harmless."

"She gives me chills."

"She can't help looking ferocious."

"No. . .I suppose not."

"Away from her natural environment in Africa, she's quite helpless. Wouldn't last a single winter here in England."

Her brows converged as she realized what he meant. He and his spider must eventually return to Egypt. Something she'd known all along. Something that suddenly took on new and unwelcome meaning.

She forced her gaze not to dart away from the fat, hairy being on his sleeve. "She's a curious choice of pet."

"You shouldn't judge the old girl solely on her looks." He released a long-suffering sigh. "You might try getting to know her before you discredit her character."

She wasn't sure she liked the sound of that suggestion. "Get to know her how?"

"By holding her. Unless you insist on allowing your fears to rule you."

She huffed and thrust a hand toward him. "Fine. I'll hold her. Just for a moment, mind you."

"There's my brave Moira." As he held out the fearsome beast, her stomach twisted. Despite her best effort to appear brave, her eyes shut tight as a tomb.

"Do you swear she won't bite?"

"Well, no, actually."

Moira's eyes flew open.

CHAPTER 15

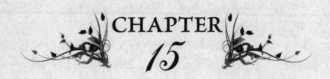

What?" She snatched her hand back and clutched it with the other. Those chills she'd mentioned but a moment ago raised gooseflesh across her back. "How could you?"

Worse still, how dare he have the audacity to laugh? The villain was nearly doubled over. Oh, why *shouldn't* she pick up the nearest stick and dash him about the head?

"Stop laughing." She stamped a foot, an unfortunate habit this man seemed to inspire with increasing frequency. "It isn't funny in the least."

His guffaws mellowed to chuckles. Then he cleared this throat. "Sorry. But the look on your face. . . Never mind." His mouth twisted contritely. "I was joking, Moira. She won't bite, not unless you make a sudden movement that frightens her, or if she's hungry and mistakes your finger for a slug."

She didn't trust herself to reply, not just then.

"I do promise she isn't poisonous." His free hand caught hers before she could whisk it behind her back. "Come, let's sit and I'll show you how to hold her in complete safety."

Gripping her hand tightly enough to prevent it from slipping free, he all but hauled her to a patch of sunlit grass. By the time she sat and settled her skirts around her legs, she had to admit her curiosity had gotten the better of her. Not about how to handle the spider— that she could live entirely without—but how a man who claimed little or no attachment to blood relations could feel such affinity for an alien species.

"Now, then." He held Isis up to the sunlight. Moira shivered when he ran a fingertip over a hairy foreleg. "When you wish to touch her, be very gentle, but don't hesitate or jerk away."

"And if I don't wish to?"

"Now, now. Here, you try."

"J-just her leg?"

"Yes, like so." His fingertip made another gentle swipe back and forth.

"Oh, dear." Extending a finger, she drew a breath and held it. Just as her fingertip almost made contact, Isis skittered a few inches along Graham's sleeve. Moira went rigid.

"It's all right," he whispered.

Her teeth clenched her bottom lip. She reached closer. Short, spiny hairs tickled the pad of her finger.

The leg twitched and rose, pushing lightly back. Moira's breath tumbled out, but she fought the impulse to lurch away and bury her hand in her skirts.

"Not so bad," he prompted, "is she?"

"Hairy. And prickly."

"But kind of nice, wouldn't you say?"

A tiny shrug formed her reply. Her finger traveled slowly back and forth while she marveled as to where her courage came from. Then Isis opened and closed those fearsome pincers at either side of her mouth, or what Moira assumed to be her mouth. She flinched.

"It's all right, she's not going to bite." Graham's free hand settled between her shoulders, warm and steadying. "She moves her pedipalps that way because the hairs there are hollow and they allow her to taste and smell her surroundings. She's merely becoming acquainted with her newest admirer."

"How charming." And yet, the behavior did imply a personality of sorts, making the creature somewhat less of a monster. Moira leaned for a closer look. "Are those her eyes? My word, how many does she have?"

"Eight."

"Goodness. Can she see eight places at once?"

"Of course. The better to keep an eye on you, my dear," he said in a dastardly growl. Moira chuckled—quietly, so as not to disturb Isis. "Would you like to try holding her now?"

"I don't think—"

"Of course, you do. You've come this far. I'll be right beside you." He did better than that, shifting until they sat thigh to thigh. His chest braced her shoulder, and he stretched an arm behind her, cradling her back while bringing the arm that held Isis up beside Moira's.

"Don't." She felt herself shrink into his protective warmth. "That's too close."

"It's all right." His breath grazed her neck, eliciting a shiver. He seemed to misinterpret her reaction as fear, because he said, "If you really don't want to, I'll move her away."

"No. . .wait." With her fingertip she explored the bend in one of Isis's legs. "Maybe just for a moment." But she didn't know if the words came of a sudden desire to hold the spider or to simply keep Graham close.

"Here we go, then." He brought the length of his forearm against hers and held it there. How she wished she had opted for long sleeves rather than the three-quarter ones she wore. Fascination mingled with stomach-sinking dread at the sight of those legs arching and stretching like fingers across a harp. At the first whisper-light tread upon her skin, sweat trickled between her shoulder blades.

"Don't go anywhere," she rasped through a throat gone dry.

Graham placed his arm beneath her own, his fingers wrapping gently round her wrist. "I'm right here."

"Oh, Lord. . .eek. . .it tickles." Panic rose in a

tremulous giggle.

"I know. But it's rather pleasant, isn't it?"

"Look, she stopped. She's staring at me. Whatever could she be thinking?"

"That her hostess is very beautiful, I'd imagine." His words infused her with a heated awareness of his strength, his solid presence lending her the courage to do something she'd never in her wildest dreams do on her own. "She seems pleased to make your acquaintance."

"Likewise, I'm sure." Or was she? As Isis began a slow ascent up her arm, every muscle in Moira's body tensed. The spider's many legs tipped a ticklish path along the sensitive skin of her forearm. Tremors shimmied across Moira's shoulders. At her elbow, Isis paused and explored the edge of her sleeve before continuing up. Alarm tingled through Moira's nerve endings. "She's going too high. Take her off. Take her off now. Please."

Isis was in Graham's palm before Moira drew another breath. Relief flooded her. Feeling as though an enormous weight had been lifted, she drooped back against him as the rigidity flowed from her muscles.

"You did it," he said and kissed her hair. "I'm so proud of you."

She angled her head to gaze up at him. The slant of his jaw revealed an effusive grin. "Joking as usual."

"Not in the least." Transferring Isis to his knee, he stroked his hands up and down Moira's arms as if to warm her. "You did splendidly. I'll have you know other than me, you're the first non-Egyptian ever to hold her. Shaun refuses."

She wrenched away and faced him head-on. "Graham Foster, one of these days the devil is going to roast you on a spit."

His dimples flashed, faded, reappeared in a fruitless display of innocence. "What d'you mean, Moira?"

"'Don't let your fears rule you, Moira,'" she parroted in a deepened voice meant to mimic his. She yanked a handful of foxtail and clover from the ground and tossed it in his face. "I only agreed to hold the dreadful creature because I didn't wish to be considered the only coward in your acquaintance. I wouldn't have touched her had I known *everyone* abhors her."

He combed bits of grass from his hair and brushed it from his shirtfront. "Go on, admit it. Holding Isis was a bit of a thrill, and now that it's over, you're elated you did it."

She pursed her lips. There did exist a tiny morsel of truth to his words, but she didn't have to admit it. He smiled, not the teasing smile of moments ago but one that sped her pulse and sent prickling heat to her cheeks. She couldn't help smiling back.

He cupped her chin. "Brave Moira." His voice dipped, rumbled like an ocean wave approaching the shore. "You amaze me at every turn."

She accepted the praise by simply tucking her chin more firmly into his palm and silently forgiving his prank. He leaned in, at the same time drawing her gently forward until their lips met, without the urgency of their last kisses but softly, like petals opening to the cool touch of rain.

He pressed his forehead to hers. "We were about to make a mistake earlier, weren't we, Moira?"

She understood his meaning. Before he remembered Isis, they'd been rushing back to the house with no illusions between them as to what would happen once they arrived. She should be thankful they'd come to their senses in time. Disappointment welled instead. Her eyes fell closed. His forehead felt smooth and strong and warm against hers. "Yes."

"It wouldn't have felt like a mistake, and afterward I'd have denied the error of it to my dying breath." He broke the contact between them, only to reestablish it with his palm against her cheek. "I swear it, Moira."

"I believe you." Her heart twisted within the depth of that belief. "But it would have been wrong all the same, wouldn't it?"

He nodded, all trace of his dimples fading into sadness. "Wrong to permanently bind ourselves to each other when I must eventually leave England and you must stay. For that is the truth of it. The work Shaun and I do in Egypt is too important to forsake. I have obligations, and I've made promises. Promises I temporarily forgot this morning."

Not for an instant did she fool herself into believing

she could entice him to stay, to give up his adventurer's life in favor of a woman so firmly on the shelf as to have truly earned the title of spinster. Ah, no, a man like Graham Foster thrived on freedom and spontaneity and danger enough to make one's heart pound. He'd languish here, with her.

"I must stay for my mother," she said, and was relieved to feel no regret for this, at least.

Bracing Isis on his thigh with a careful hand, he slipped an arm around Moira's shoulders. The passion that had almost sent them racing to the nearest empty bedchamber had faded, or, more accurately, settled into a calm and comfortable intimacy. Yet the promise of more remained; Moira felt it like a current just beneath the surface, coursing, biding its time, searching for even the tiniest gap in their resolve.

For now she relaxed against him, savoring the luxury of a masculine shoulder and the delicious warmth of the sun on her face. Perhaps lulled to sleep by the streaming sunshine absorbed into Graham's dark trousers, the spider didn't stir.

With a jerk of his chin, he gestured toward the meadows and the more distant hills. "Monteith Hall has made me feel—I don't know—English, I suppose, for the first time since my expulsion from Oxford. This place has made me remember all the good things about being English. For a moment I was tempted. . .truly tempted. But I can't, Moira. I cannot stay."

Plucking at the turf beside her, she let out a breath of frustrated longing. "Is there no one else to dig up Egyptian treasure?"

"Yes. Hundreds of greedy men roam the deserts, raiding the tombs. That's precisely the point. Ever since Napoleon invaded Africa years ago, men have been whittling away at Egypt's treasures."

Her hand went still against the small pile of grass she'd shredded. "I'm not sure I understand what you're saying."

"Have you not seen the exhibit of my finds at the museum?" He chuckled, a sound resonant with irony. "Flashy, isn't it?"

She nodded, baffled.

He stupefied her with a single word. "Worthless."

"How can that be? The artifacts are said to be priceless."

"Rubbish. They're trinkets, nothing more."

Taking this in, she stared off into the distance. Bars of sunlight streamed through lacy clouds and dappled the hillsides. "Trinkets of pure gold and gemstones. And what of the historical worth?"

"Ah." His voice went soft, thoughtful. He wrapped a lock of her hair around his fingers. "Now you've hit upon it. What I've brought back to England are baubles with very little historical or cultural value at all. Think of a pair of your own earbobs, even your most valuable ones. In a thousand years they might be worth something in a sentimental sort of way, could even end up in some historian's private collection. But in comparison with, say, the crown jewels of England, they'll be of no significance whatsoever."

"But. . ." Her mouth worked around gaping incredulity. "What about the jewels you presented at court? The pectoral pendant. . .the lapis scarabs. . .the burial mask. . . And the encrypted tablets."

"All found in the tombs of wealthy merchants and craftsmen. I believe the tablets were an inventory of a family's holdings."

"Graham. . ." His nonchalance sparked a burst of dismay. "You were *knighted* for your discoveries. What if someone should find out?"

"What of it? The knighthood's a moot point now that I've inherited the barony, and they can't strip me of that. I suppose I'd be tossed out of civilized society— again. I'll simply have lived up to my legacy as a cheat and a fraud."

"You are not a cheat or a fraud. At least not the way people think." She brushed the hair from his brow with a familiarity she felt she had every right to claim, for something extraordinary was happening here. She suspected that in the entire world, there were precious few people privileged enough to be granted a glimpse of the real Graham Foster. "What are you doing in Egypt that you don't want your fellow Englishmen knowing about?"

"Fellow Europeans, actually." He continued playing with the ends of her hair while gazing down at the slumbering Isis.   "Ever since Napoleon attempted to occupy Egypt, Europeans have been sifting through the sands under the guise of scientific research, without so much as a by-your-leave to the people whose heritage they're stealing.   And because Egypt is currently ruled by a Turk, the government is doing precious little to stop the pillage.   With the exception of John Wilkinson and very few others, most Egyptologists are a disgrace.   No more than plunderers."

"Where do you fit in?"

"Don't misunderstand."   His voice took on an edge, became almost defensive.   "I went to Egypt with the same delusions of grandeur as everyone else.   Discover the secrets of the pyramids, find riches, and return to England in a blaze of nose-thumbing glory."

"And haven't you?"

He pushed a sardonic chuckle through his teeth. "In a manner of speaking, I suppose."

"What changed?"

"A sheik and his dagger convinced me of the folly of my ways."   A self-conscious smile pulled at his lips. "It was early in my career.   I'd stumbled upon hallowed ground, the site of a shrine the Bedouins had been guarding for centuries.   And like the arrogant, ignorant European I was, I'd have dismantled the place without a second thought.

"Luckily I was caught, and a man named Hakim al Faruq taught me that Egypt's heritage belongs in Egypt, and Egyptologists, for the most part, do not. Shaun and I have been working these past years to help hide anything of true value by erasing all trails leading to it. Ever hear of a boy king called Tutankhamen?"

"No."

"And you won't, not if Shaun and I continue to have our way. He and I have been perpetrating one of the greatest ongoing hoaxes ever pulled off. But make no mistake, Moira. Through my so-called philanthropy, I've profited nicely. So stop looking at me like that and don't call me sweet."

She had, indeed, been about to make that very pronouncement. Dear man, didn't he understand the more cavalier and roguish he tried to appear, the more honorable he became in her eyes? Yet everything he'd just told her convinced her more than ever that he didn't belong here, didn't belong with her. The truth of it squeezed her throat and pricked the backs of her eyes.

She reached for Isis. Awakening before her finger made contact, the spider scurried away over Graham's knee. Then she stopped, turned, and ventured back. Moira opened her palm.

Graham watched her intently. "What on earth? Moira Hughes, you never cease to astonish me."

"Nor you me." She shrugged as she conveyed Isis to her lap. "But I suppose it's all a matter of accepting the truth and trusting it. She's harmless. She can't hurt me."

And neither could Graham Foster remain in her life.

She hadn't realized until now how much she wanted him to stay. All along, without even quite knowing why, she had been searching for signs of honor in this man. Not until this moment had she understood. Honor would be the very thing that drove him away.

And once again, she would be alone. . .

♥ ♥ ♥

Graham stared into snapping flames, pensively sipping brandy. At the card table, Moira and her mother sat with their heads together, quietly conferring.

Earlier, while sorting through some of her stepfather's effects stored in the attic, she had come upon a box of letters, an assortment of correspondence from friends, relations, and business associates. Some predated the man's death by mere days.

Estella had warmed to the prospect of settling down at the leather-topped game table to revisit the travels and daily lives of old acquaintances, but even from across the dimly lit distance, Graham caught the quiver in Moira's fingertips as she unfolded each missive. Occasionally her gaze glittered in his direction, her unspoken question plain: would they discover any clue as to Michael Oliphant's role in her stepfather's life?

He lifted his brandy snifter and sipped. The puzzle of Everett Foster's will no longer concerned Moira and her mother alone, nor was it merely about money. Who was this Michael Oliphant, and what hold had he had on Everett Foster that the latter would neglect to secure the future of his own family? Had Smythe known the answer and paid for it with his life? And what of Nigel Foster's death—accidental or intentional?

Then there was Pierson, Smythe's missing secretary. What part did the bespectacled clerk play in this drama? Had he been involved? Of course, his disappearance alone did not signify guilt. He might have run off out of simple fear. Or perhaps he harbored some personal, completely unrelated reason for avoiding a murder investigation.

To ensure the safety of the women, Graham had earlier met with his steward to establish a more rigorous schedule for the footmen. As of this afternoon, the Hall could no longer be taken unawares from any direction. At every possible approach, there would be a man on guard, night and day. Windows and doors heretofore kept blithely unlatched would be secured, with only the terrace and rear garden doors unlocked during the day. He'd been pleased to discover his gamekeeper and under-butler had served in the infantry during the war. Older men of seeming good sense, they'd been well trained in the use of firearms.

Having set the estate in order, he should have set off for London earlier this evening. Yet he'd put off his departure until the morning despite his certainty that returning to the city was not only the logical course, but the wisest.

Wisest for Moira. And for him. Setting his snifter on the oval table beside him, he gained his feet, beginning a restless circuit of the room.

When he had first arrived back in England, he couldn't wait to return to brilliant desert skies and searing adventures. That notion paled now in comparison to feisty admonishments and cheeky observations conveyed with the thrust of a stubborn chin. He smiled. The way Moira took him to task for the smallest trifles stirred his blood as vigorously as setting foot into the booby-trapped catacombs of a cursed tomb.

More so, if the truth be told. And he could lose himself just as easily and irrevocably in the dark mystery of those midnight eyes.

But he'd made a vow, damn it, even if it was virtually at knifepoint. Hakim al Faruq had presented him with a simple choice: make reparations for yourself and your swinish countrymen's transgressions, or die. Even without the blade drawing a thin trickle of blood beside his Adam's apple, Graham agreed the former choice was the nobler, not to mention the more sensible, of the two.

At the time, his future in England had lain in waste. A lie about which student had copied the other's work, and the cowardice that prevented others from taking sides against a powerful duke's son, had destroyed any prospects Graham had had.

But neither had he envisioned, in those few choked seconds beneath Hakim's dagger, the serenity of evenings spent in the spacious drawing room of a country manor, in the presence of two charming ladies, the elder of whom had captured his heart in the space of an afternoon. Her daughter meanwhile. . .

He retrieved his brandy and welcomed the liquid burn in his mouth. As he drank, he studied Moira's profile, his gaze tracing the curve of her nape as she poured over the contents of a letter. Suddenly her head turned. She caught his eye and gave an infinitesimal shake of the head that summed up tonight's search thus far: nothing.

He strode to a window, not from any interest in the view outside, but because he couldn't risk letting her read his expression. He was glad she'd found nothing. He wanted her out of this. Out of danger. His biggest fear now was she would insist on returning to London with him. He could already hear her arguments: a woman possessed no less integrity, courage, ability, and whatever else, than a man. All well and good in theory, he supposed. But not when people were dying.

He pressed a fist to the windowpane. Blazing hell, every notion about himself, every plan—shot to hell by that woman. He wasn't supposed to care this much. He was a blackguard. A rogue. Not sweet at all, really.

Moira, Moira. She'd sent his world spinning on end that morning, grabbing him, kissing him, and starting him rethinking the only truly admirable commitment he'd ever made in his life.

Not that a woman like Moira wouldn't be worth a

host of broken promises. If only he could be sure he would measure up to the kind of man she deserved. Yes, he'd undergone changes since she had entered his life, but were those changes enough to undo a decade of rash living and a staunch belief in no one but himself?

Enough to settle him into the sort of a family man she so desperately wanted? A man, for instance, like the one she was supposed to have married?

Those notions hounded his dreams later that night, until a tap at his bedroom door startled him from sleep. As he sat up, the door opened, spilling the flickering candlelight across the floor.

"Has there been a disturbance?" he demanded of the faceless figure behind the glare. By the abruptness of the intrusion, he feared one of his footmen had spied something or someone suspicious on the grounds. He reached for his dressing gown at the foot of the bed.

"No. All is quiet." Moira's whisper resonated in the stillness and brought him up short, dressing gown tossed over one shoulder and an arm thrust halfway into a sleeve. "And I've reached a decision I believe you should know about."

She closed the door behind her and set the candle on a cabinet. Golden light gilded her cheekbones, the soft lines of her chin. Deep shadows cloaked her eyes, but he felt the intense heat of their scrutiny.

He knew his mouth had come unhinged, and he didn't doubt he gaped with all the astuteness of a jacko'-lantern. Discarding his robe amongst the rumpled bedclothes, he started toward her, impelled by an almost urgent need to head her off before she advanced any further into the room. . .into the intimacy of the darkness and his arms.

Wrong. For him. For her. Hadn't they decided that only hours ago?

But he was a man. How could he be expected to resist the lure of a beautiful woman whose eyes held all the sultry promise of a moon-drenched tryst?

They came together between the bed and the door, and resolve spiraled away into the softness of flesh beneath a wispy layer of linen, the perfume of her hair, the caress of her cheek against his. His body responded with a shuddering blaze of desire.

"You shouldn't be here," he whispered.

"Will you send me away?"

"No."

"Well, then." She combed her fingers through his hair and pulled his head down for a kiss that scrambled his wits. Together they stumbled toward the bed. It wasn't until the backs of his knees hit the edge that coherent thought emerged from swimming sensation.

"What are we doing?"

"What each of us wishes to do." She took his face between her hands and peered into his eyes, her own dazzling and earnest. "Darling, am I wrong?"

"You're not wrong, and you damned well know it."

His open palms swept her shoulders and traveled down her sides to settle at her waist. "There's no denying what we both want. It is a question of consequences, and of disappointments perhaps neither of us could bear."

She surprised him with an amused look, a breathy laugh. "I thought I was the one clinging to propriety while you tempt and tease and flirt with scandal." Her fingertips stole like Isis across his nape and dipped into the collar of his nightshirt, sending a hot shiver through him. "I do believe we are transforming into each other."

He grasped her arms and shook her, albeit gently. "Think you're clever, don't you? But flirtation is one thing, and yes, I enjoy it. More than that. I relish the game, the challenge. But this is different. This could lead to irrevocable things."

"It needn't." She fondled his chest between the laces of his nightshirt, her fingertips soft and all too tempting against his skin. "I wouldn't try to hold you here."

"You wouldn't have a choice." The words came out more sharply than he intended, resonating with his rising frustration. His growing need to end the discussion and simply be inside her.

Through her sheer night shift, he caught a teasing glimpse of dusky nipples. His resolve to be honorable threatened to shatter. How far did she mean to push him? He'd never wanted any woman as badly as he wanted her, and never had more reasons to stay away. She was no tart, no supposed sultan's daughter sneaking into his camp with a wink and an open palm.

"If I got you with child," he said, "do you think I could leave?"

He winced at the sudden pinch of his chest hairs between slender fingers gone rigid. "If you think I'm here to trap you, Graham Foster, you couldn't be more wrong. As God is my witness. . ."

"Stop." He caught her hands, uncurled the fingers, and brought them to his mouth, kissing each and holding them against his lips. "That wasn't what I meant. Of course, you would never stoop to anything as underhanded as that. But a single rash act can lead to a lifetime of regret."

What was he saying? The woman of his dreams was offering herself with no strings attached, and he chose this moment to become a bloody priest?

Not very gentlemanly of him. He yanked her to him and set his mouth against her neck. Shivering, she emitted a squawk when he drew her flesh between his lips with an enthusiasm certain to bruise.

"You drive me to distraction. Of course, I want you." He sat on the bed and pulled her into his lap. Against the warmth of her thigh, his arousal hardened urgently, painfully. He clamped the insides of his cheeks in an attempt to focus his thoughts. "But, understand. I'm not the man you think I am. I'm certainly not Ni—"

He'd almost said "Nigel," but caught his tongue just in time. Good God, he would have sounded hopelessly pathetic, jealous of a ghost. He wasn't jealous, merely wary of misplaced sentiments.

Her eyebrows angled in conjecture. "You're not what?"

Let it go.

"Something beginning with *N*." Her eyes widened. "Good Lord, you're not Nigel? Is that what you were about to say?"

"Of course not."

"Look at me when you deny it."

Caught, bloody red handed. He might as well speak his mind, then, for good or ill. "Moira, coming home to Monteith Hall has surely reawakened the past for you. You loved Nigel. You were to be married. It's understandable your feelings for him are still very much alive."

Linking her fingers at his nape, she narrowed her lashes and regarded him at arm's length. "You think I've somehow confused the two of you?"

"Not confused, exactly. But I've become so much a part of your life perhaps you may have, well, transferred your feelings for Nigel to me."

"I see." She swept her fingers through his hair, then suddenly clenched them tight, making his scalp shriek in pain. "Liar. This isn't about Nigel in the least, is it?" Without seeming to expect an answer, she used her grasp to turn his head from side to side. "No, indeed, it's not about Nigel."

"That hurts."

"I don't even believe it's about right or wrong," she went on, ignoring his complaint. "Or preserving my honor. This is about your fear of commitment, your inability to trust anyone but your hairy old spider."

"Don't be absurd. *Ouch.*"

"You have pursued me since the Jarvis's masquerade ball, where you lured me under the arbor and licked my wrist, you shameless scoundrel. No, even before that. The day at Smythe's office, you saw how distraught I was, yet you flashed those dimples just to taunt me."

"You're being unfair." He attempted to dislodge her fingers. She only held on tighter, giving a little yank to reclaim his undivided attention. He gave it, at the same time realizing his body's attention hadn't wavered in the least, despite her rather indelicate tactics. Quite the contrary, his genitals pulsed with interest.

"Don't you dare talk about unfair." Her grip, however, eased. Her fingers slid from his hair, only to fist again at the front of his nightshirt. "As I said, you've pursued me from the outset. I practically had to shove you away whenever we went out in your carriage. Yet now that you have me, now that I've come to you, you're terrified. You don't know what to do."

That last part wasn't at all true. He certainly had some quite vivid ideas of what to do with the luscious Moira Hughes across a wide bed in a dark room. But the rest of what she said resonated through him.

He'd never been afraid of any woman in his life.

But Moira wasn't any woman. Moira affected him in all the obvious ways and all the obvious places. But in not so obvious ways and places, as well. After Oxford and his family's betrayal, he believed he had closed the door to his heart and locked it tight. Believed he could get by without binding loyalties. Without love.

Damn the woman's lock-picking abilities.

She yanked his shirt, pulling him close, so close her lips vibrated against his. "Well, my darling? Have you nothing to say? No protest to make? Shall I leave you to your brooding? Or shall I stay and help you face your fears, as you helped me do earlier today?"

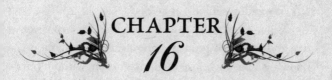

CHAPTER 16

Brave words, Moira. Well done. Now, will he believe them?

Do you?

Yes, partly. She'd certainly spoken from her heart. Mostly. It's what she hadn't said that smacked of dishonesty.

Graham's mention of Nigel had sent a jolt through her, so violent she marveled he hadn't detected it.

Nigel. Dearest Nigel. How few thoughts she'd spared him these past weeks. How fearfully quick she had moved beyond her widowlike grief to. . .to this moment.

And yet, it *was* partly Nigel's death that brought her into Graham's arms now. For years it had been understood that eventually she and Nigel would marry—a comfortable sort of knowledge—and during those years she had felt no pressing need to change the nature of their relationship. Nigel, too, had seemed content to continue as they were, so that even after their engagement became official, they made no dash for the altar. Then Papa died, and, of course, there could be no talk of weddings for a year at least.

What a price she paid for tarrying, for being content and calm and prudent. She lost Nigel without ever knowing what their love might have been, without once awakening the passion that might have grown had they lived as man and wife.

Without having, at the very least, one spectacular memory to cherish the rest of her life.

Or. . .would she have? In truth, had there ever been, between her and Nigel, even a single heart-stopping rush of desire? Had she once experienced that unsettling hodgepodge of perplexity and delight and yearning that so often left her giddy in Graham Foster's presence?

She forced herself now to look into his eyes, unwavering, using all the wiles she possessed to conceal the uncertainty weaving her insides into a hopeless web. She would lose him in the end. That much she knew. But this time she wouldn't be left empty and wondering, or feeling she'd missed a once-in-a-lifetime scrap of happiness.

He'd been watching her, waiting, brooding over his reply, as evidenced by that ridge above his nose. Now his dimples appeared, deepening with the gradual curve of a smile.

"I can think of no headier adventure than facing my fears with you, sweet Moira." He leaned in closer, bringing his masculine scent to swirl around her, envelope her, intoxicate her. His breath was fiery on her neck, his lips a dewy whisper against her skin. "And so the gauntlet is tossed, my dear, and I meet your challenge most willingly."

His hands were already upon her, slipping beneath her shift's hem and lifting, smoothing the fabric upward. Cool air kissed her legs, thighs, hips. Her belly flinched at his light touch. Her breasts ached in anticipation.

A sharp burst of air filled her lungs. His thumbs stroked her nipples, caught her shift against them, and rubbed again, mingling the friction of his hands—so warm—and the cool sensation of linen.

With a gasp she arched her back, offering herself wholly, at the same time reaching for him, wanting to feel him, know him, share this blessedly wicked pleasure. Palm on his chest, she swept the planes of his muscles, the curve of his shoulders. So solidly male. So perfectly beautiful.

Through half-closed eyes he held her gaze, lips parted and tilted in a kind of seductive, triumphant smile. His hands were ever moving, claiming parts of her never touched this way before. She shivered with fearful excitement as his expression darkened, shadowed by mysteries and notions she could only guess at. Only wait for, as a nameless craving billowed inside her.

A craving that threatened to explode when it was no longer just his hands roving her body but his lips, too; when he lifted her arms above her head and slid her shift free. Then his head dipped and he took a nipple into his mouth, releasing a multitude of sensations and creating an urgent need inside her.

His head came up, his lids passion-heavy, but his gaze sharp and clear. "I cannot stay, Moira. Eventually I must leave."

"I know." And in that instant she didn't care. She'd worry about it come morning. Would somehow find the courage to let him go. Tomorrow. Tonight he would be hers. And she his.

One spectacular memory.

She kissed him, openmouthed and with her tongue, to banish any lingering doubts either of them might harbor. His tongue met hers with mutually probing strokes that erased thoughts and worries and all but the feel of him against her body. He made short work of removing his nightshirt, barely releasing her in the process and without breaking their kiss.

Naked. In a naked man's arms. The shock of it thrilled her. She marveled at her courage, her ingenuity, as she discovered him warm in places, cool in others. But, oh, everywhere hard, uncompromising. Reaching down, she dared to touch him, gave a little jolt as his arousal moved against her palm, seeming of its own volition. She curled her fingers around him, filling her hand with velvet flesh that throbbed like a living flame. It frightened her. Fascinated her. Made her breath quiver in her throat.

He had gone quite still, she realized. Eyes shut, head tilted back. Jaw clenched and hands immobile on her breasts as if suspended in pleasure. But then, just like that, he retook control. She found herself tipping onto her side and he with her, until they lay facing each other.

"I learned more in Egypt than how to decipher ancient maps, Moira. More than where and how to find treasure."

"Show me. Teach me what you learned."

His dimples flashed. "My darling, school is in session."

Cupping her shoulder, he turned her onto her stomach. The bed shifted as he sat up. His gaze seared her back, intensified her nakedness. At the first stroke of his fingertips moving the hair from her nape, she shuddered.

"Don't be frightened."

"I'm no such thing." Now who was lying? She was terrified—of the unknown, of how her body would respond, of whether she would lose the control so carefully held in place throughout the past months. Her entire life.

But she was not afraid of him. She knew she'd never come to harm beneath his hands. Only his leaving had the power to wound her. *No.* Such thoughts were not permitted, not tonight.

"Not frightened, eh?" She heard a faint laugh, a husky note that held no mockery but echoed the infinite tenderness of his fingertips, working circles on her neck and shoulders. "You're as rigid as a hewn oak."

Steadily he kneaded the muscles until the tension melted. Until *she* melted. . .

"Mmm. . .feels good."

Another quiet laugh. "It is only the beginning, my

love."

The endearment elicited ripples of pleasure, albeit she knew it was merely that: an endearment. Not a promise. Not a commitment.

His hands worked their way lower, lower still, passing in meticulous, sensual increments down her spine to the small of her back, the slope of her bottom. He pressed deeper, each ministration pushing her breasts and belly and hips into the satin coverlet. Awareness and pleasure spiraled amid the erotic mingling of the cool, slippery texture at her front and the firm, heated caress at her back. A misty sensation like rising steam gathered between her thighs.

"And this. . ." Her words were muted against the bedclothes. She lifted her chin, gathered a breath. "This you learned in Egypt?"

"Ancient wisdom preserved on papyrus scrolls." His fingertips grazed the cleft of her buttocks. Her heart tripped and pounded, then stood still, waiting. He leaned over her, bringing his heat to waft above her, his chest hairs grazing her spine. He traced soft kisses on her neck, leaving trails of hot moisture; he nipped her earlobe, licked her nape. . .

A sigh poured out of her. "Oh, yes, I remember how you like to lick."

"Very true, but do you like it, my Moira?"

She could not but admit she did. Yes, there, at the curve of her shoulder and—ah—there, in the hollow beneath her ear. And—oh, my—when he set his lips there, near the base of her shoulder, why, she'd agree to anything, do anything. . .

Dizzy with leaping, burning desire, she moaned into the mattress. At his hands' coaxing, she widened her legs, reached her arms above her head, and gave herself up to pleasure. To sinful, sacred, soul-baring indulgence. For in those next moments, she did, indeed, bare her innermost wishes and inclinations and needs, without ever uttering a single word.

He simply seemed to know, able to read her body's responses as one might a favorite book, lovingly and ever so thoroughly. Her shoulders, her arms, the backs of her knees. . .her inner thighs. . .the ridges of her spine. . . Even the arches of her feet experienced the rising fever of his touch, his kisses, his breath, his tongue.

"Right to the edge," he whispered. "Let yourself glide right to the edge, and I'll hold you there. I won't let you fall. At least, not yet."

She surrendered to him, lay helpless in his arms as he showed her the brink, each time gently pulling her back an instant before she tumbled.

When she thought she could not bear another moment of it, he lay down beside her and tucked her back to his chest, her bottom to his hips, trapping her legs beneath one of his long, muscular ones.

If she had found the combination of satin coverlet and male hands scintillating, that was nothing compared to this, with his length snug against her back and buttocks and his arousal prodding between her thighs. Arching her in a way that heightened sensation, one hand fondled her breasts, reshaping her nipples into tight little buds. His other hand wandered lower, skimming flesh, combing the fine hairs at the juncture of her legs.

He touched—something. Hidden flesh. Swollen, sensitive, in dire need of. . .being touched exactly as he touched it. A sensation sprang instantly to life, like a flower bursting open. It was a marvel with the power to control all of her—her heart and pulse and breath and mind—as though all of her flowed from that very spot.

"Are you ready now, sweet Moira?"

She didn't know what *ready* meant, but she nodded. He turned her onto her back. Gently he moved over her. In his tensed muscles, his taut features, she glimpsed the measure of his restraint, saw his need very much matched her own, but he had it leashed in tight control.

He pressed kisses to her neck, across her mouth. He dropped lower still, lips playing across her breasts. He used his tongue and sometimes his teeth, nips that wrought cries and whimpers from deep inside.

She experienced a rush of cool air as he disentangled his limbs from hers. She wished to call him back, implore him not to stop. He crawled crablike across the mattress, and she heard the sound of a latch opening. Puzzled, she remembered seeing his overnight bag on the chaise at the foot of the bed. What on earth was he doing?

He returned before she could hazard a guess, bringing his warmth to blot out thought, to press her female places until they begged, ached for all that could be shared between a man and a woman.

One spectacular memory. . .

He peered down at her, his eyes a churning sea clouded by passion and some deeper, raw emotion she'd never seen in him before. "I may despise myself for this. But, darling, I can pleasure you without—"

"No."

"Are you quite certain?"

She nodded and framed his face in her hands. Her lips twitched; she couldn't help grinning. "Unless, of course, you've decided to give in to those fears of yours—"

"Wanton creature." His dimples danced as he reached between their bodies, his hand coming to rest against that simmering place between her legs.

At first he only pressed, and she pressed back, filling his palm, feeling their shared heat pass back and forth between them. With a hypnotic rhythm, he began massaging, manipulating, until moisture sizzled and coherent thought dissolved. Again.

When his hand moved away, she wanted to cry out for its return, but something else took its place, hot and silky soft against her. Something that fit the burning folds of her body in a way nothing else could. He pushed, opening her a fraction at a time, allowing her to stretch, to fit around him, allowing each increment of pain to recede before sliding deeper.

She shut her eyes, afraid that beneath the glimmer of ecstasy he'd detect her pain and stop. He cupped her cheek, insisting she meet his gaze.

"Moira. . ."

She heard the question at the end of her name.

"No words. Only this." She arched, burying him another excruciating, delicious inch, welcoming the pain with the pleasure, glad for it. It was a consuming pain, a deeply erotic pain, intensely arousing and sweetly satisfying. It was a pain that made her. . .

Love him.

The knowledge of it crashed through her as, with a resolute push, he relinquished restraint and filled her. Utterly. Something inside her moved, fractured. With a sweltering whoosh, her virginity bathed her inner thighs.

Graham went still, watching her, waiting. It must have shown on her face when the pain subsided, for he moved again, took up a new rhythm. Slowly, methodically, he swept her up, away from inexperience and discomfort and into a realm where her body knew what to do, how to move, to seek and take and return pleasure.

His strokes intensified, quickened, became furious. She thrust to meet him, welcome him, glory in him until a tempest gathered and raged. The world around her shattered. *She* shattered, as all the breath slid from her lungs on a silent scream.

And then she heard a deep rumbling that built to

a roar, sealing the bargain between them and assuring her that whatever this wondrous thing he had done to her, she had done for him. It made him hers as much as she felt herself his. It took that little burst of love of moments ago and swept it the length and width and breadth of her heart.

♥ ♥ ♥

Rational thought evaporated; control took to its heels. As if from a distance, Graham watched the gentleman he'd meant to be give way to a wild, insatiable buck. He was helpless—*helpless*—to prevent it.

She'd taken possession of him, drew him in, and wrapped him in silken, pulsating tightness. The perfect ecstasy of a perfect fit, rendering him powerless to do anything less than give all, take all, unable to prevent losing himself to sheer physical rapture.

No, not just physical.

Mere moments after collapsing over her, he gathered her in his arms and rolled onto his back. She pillowed her head on his chest, and her hair spilled across his lips, trailed over his shoulder. He would have been happy to spend the rest of the night and all the next day engulfed in her scent, her warmth, her slender arms. For the span of several heartbeats, he knew contentment in a perfect world.

But a single particle of truth nagged.

"Moira?"

"Mmm. . ."

"Darling, why didn't you tell me you'd never before. . .that you were a. . ."

"A virgin, yes. Should that surprise you?"

"I, ah. . ." At his hesitation, she lifted her head to peer at him, brow creased. He hurried to explain. "I'd assumed that perhaps you and, uh, Nigel had. . ."

"Why would you assume that?"

As his tongue stumbled to form an answer that wouldn't offend her unforgivably, she rather surprised him by draping her arms around him and snuggling her cheek against his chest. "Well, Nigel and I didn't."

She didn't elaborate further, and except for a mild twinge of curiosity, he was glad. Bloody glad she had never wandered into Nigel's bedroom in the middle of the night issuing challenges. Yet he also couldn't help enjoying a certain degree of one-upmanship over his cousin, a sentiment all the more petty, he must admit, because Nigel was, after all, dead.

So, what did she feel for him that she hadn't felt for her fiancé? The question startled him, worried him. Made him consider the same question, but turned around. What did he feel for her? Physical elation, completion. Yes, but so much more. More than he'd felt for anyone in years.

Or ever, really.

But hadn't he, just that afternoon, explained the myriad reasons he could not remain in England, why honor dictated he return to Egypt? Hadn't he reiterated those reasons following her knock at his door?

Egypt. He'd learned many things there, some of which he'd shared with Moira this past hour or so. Although if the truth were told, many of those seductive arts had been gleaned from boastful stories exchanged around late-night campfires.

He'd brought something else home from his travels, as well, something he had tossed into his overnight bag weeks ago and nearly forgotten. Tonight he had remembered, and as discreetly as possible had slipped the sheath over his erection before entering Moira's body.

If not for that, his oath to Hakim al Faruq would be rendered null, for he would never consider leaving Moira if there were even the slightest chance of a child. Now he could honor his promise to Faruq. He would be able to leave England with a clear conscience.

Wouldn't he?

Her breathing deepened, and her fingers curled lightly against his chest. He lifted a lock of her hair and brushed it against his lips, eliciting a yearning that bore the sting of a futile wish.

That he'd forgotten or had simply decided not to use that sheath.

"Out of the carriage, Moira."

From across the plush seat, she leaned a little forward to look out at him where he stood in the morning sunshine beside the open coach door. She quirked an eyebrow and harrumphed.

"Out of the carriage, Moira, *please*."

She faced front again and folded her hands on her lap. "I'm returning to London with you."

"Blazing hell you are."

"Don't be silly." She sniffed. "What did you think, that I'd be content to while away my days in the country and live off your largesse, while some stranger named Michael Oliphant made off with my mother's inheritance?"

She narrowed her lashes as she mentioned her faceless adversary, then glanced again at Graham to bestow her disapproval equally upon him. "After last night, doing so would make me a kept woman, which is something I could never abide."

"Oh, Moira, for heaven's sake, I no more wish to make a kept woman of you than I expect you and your mother to live off anyone's charity for the rest of your lives."

He wanted to reach in and haul her out by the scruff of the neck. Instead, he gripped the edge of the open carriage door and counted backward from ten. She continued regarding him with that stubborn, superior, oh-so-Moira Hughes propriety that made him fear, greatly, that in the end he'd lose the argument.

"I thought we agreed Monteith would be the safest

place for you and your mother," he reasoned. "Why else did we come here?"

"I don't know why you came here," she said with a shrug, "but I came to ensure my mother's safety. We've done that and then some. With all the guards you've set on the estate, no one can venture within a half mile of the house without being spotted. But more than that, Mother seems quite clear on where I'm going and why. She understands that I will, indeed, return and that Papa, sadly, will not. I owe that to you."

Her voice had softened, and she offered a fond look that didn't for an instant fool him into believing it was anything other than an attempt to wrap him round her finger.

"Must I tear my hair out, Moira? Dash my head against the wall? Fall to my knees and beg? Is that what you require of me?"

"Don't be dramatic."

"Then don't you be. Stop swashbuckling and stay where you belong. Where I know you'll be safe."

To his surprise she slid closer to the open door, but his sudden optimism that she would, in fact, listen to reason proved hasty. She pried his hand from the door and held it fast.

"Oh, Graham, after last night, do you really wish to put so many miles between us? Can you ride off so easily without me, or did last night mean infinitely less to you than it did to me?" Here her voice trembled and her eyebrows gathered in a display of imminent devastation.

Stubborn, clever woman. As she spoke, her fingertips stroked back and forth across his palm and even slipped beneath his cuff to caress his pulse point. Ah, yes, she'd been an apt pupil, becoming quite adept in the art of subtle and not-so-subtle seduction.

In fact, despite being wise to her ploy, he felt the effects of her little caresses and widened his stance to accommodate the sudden lack of room in his trousers.

"Well, my darling? Can you leave me behind with so little compunction?"

"No," he replied through clenched teeth.

"Splendid, then it's settled. Are we all set to leave, then?" Holding her skirts, she scooted back to the far end of the seat, presumably to allow him room to climb in. She squared her shoulders in preparation of the carriage lurching into motion. "I've already said my farewells to Mother, so if you're ready, let's be off."

"One night and I'm lost," he mumbled under his breath. "Hopelessly and irretrievably lost."

"What was that?"

He scowled. "The footman is securing my overnight bag now." He clambered in and closed the door.

A moment later Estella Foster's face appeared at the open carriage window. She reached an arm inside, extending a letter to Moira. "I very nearly forgot. This is for Benedict Ramsey. When you arrive in London, do deliver it for me as soon as you may. It conveys my congratulations."

Moira leaned around Graham to take the missive

from her mother's outstretched hand. "Congratulations for what?"

"You mean he didn't tell you when you visited with him?"

"Yes, well, my visit with Uncle Benedict was cut suddenly short." She eyed Graham askance.

"Why, dear cousin Benedict is finally to gain a seat in the House of Lords," her mother explained. "He's been hoping for years, but as I'm sure you know, clerical seats are limited, and newly created bishops must wait for, well, for someone to die." She conveyed this information in an undertone, as if it held the taint of scandal. "Benedict has finally gotten his chance."

"So the old cobra's to be a peer," Graham murmured several minutes later as the carriage proceeded through the gates and onto the main road. "Heaven help us all."

Moira shook her head at him. "I understand that he did you a bad turn years ago. But can you not allow that a man can change over time, and perhaps Uncle Benedict may regret the past?"

"Have you forgotten how he spoke of me that day in his house?"

"No. Nor have I forgotten you were eavesdropping outside the window."

As the carriage bumped along the country road, they said little else, the silence taut between them. He slid low on the set, arms crossed, one leg thrown across the other knee. Moira bounced stiffly against the squabs, chin up, bottom lip slightly protruding.

This wasn't right. They should be happy, laughing, holding hands. Last night they'd shared something extraordinary. He'd taken her virginity, a precious and irreplaceable commodity, albeit she had given it willingly. He should be offering something in return, a gift equally valuable, equally earnest. Otherwise he didn't deserve last night, didn't even deserve to be sitting beside her now. Perhaps he should tell her the truth, a truth that had been quietly creeping up on him only to thunder through him last night.

He cleared his throat. "Let's not be angry, Moira."

"I'm not."

Then why the self-righteous furrow above her nose? But he said, "Good, because there's something I wish to tell you. It's about last night."

Before he could say another word, she placed her hand over his where it lay against his thigh. "I know."

He felt a jolt of astonishment. "You do?"

"Of course. I understand you're not a family man. You don't believe in it, and besides, your obligations in Egypt prevent you from forming commitments here. I promised I wouldn't try to trap you into anything you couldn't give, and I've no intention of going back on my word. But that doesn't make what we shared any less special, at least not to me."

"Nor to me." His teeth clamped the inside of his lip. He hadn't been about to say any of those things, yet they were right, each one. He *wasn't* a family man; he *didn't* believe in it. Witness how much damage he'd done his own family through the years. What right had he, then, to even contemplate loving a woman for whom family meant everything?

No right at all. Good God, blurting the truth would only make their inevitable parting that much more difficult; would very likely break her heart. And his.

A good thing she'd headed him off by speaking first. Except. . .

It didn't *feel* like a good thing. He only knew, on an intellectual level, it was.

"That's exactly what I wanted to say," he lied. "Last night was very special to me, too. *You've* become very special to me." He stopped, considering his words. They seemed safe enough. Correct enough. People could be special to one another without having their hearts broken.

He fought past a crippling disappointment and somehow found a grin, the one that displayed his dimples and so often produced that shivery reaction in Moira. "I only hope last night made you happy. That I didn't—"

"You didn't hurt me in the least." She held his gaze and smiled. "Last night was a grand adventure I'll never forget."

Adventure? The irony of the word burned like a brand against his chest. Apparently she couldn't see past the adventurer he was, and didn't see their lovemaking as anything more than a daring exploit.

Her fingers tightened around his hand. "You will

always have a special place in my heart, Graham Foster. But you and I are so very different. You are an explorer, and I am a homebody. You have obligations in distant lands, and I am bound here. You are reckless and daring and bold. I am cautious and practical."

Well, he supposed he deserved to have his own life thrown back at him. "Moira—"

"Oh, but that doesn't mean I don't wish to see this adventure through." She smiled and blinked several times. Good heavens, did he detect the glint of a tear? "I see no reason why we can't enjoy the rest of our time together."

As if to make her meaning clear, she ran her hand along his sleeve, traced his shoulder, and brought it to rest just beneath his necktie. Her fingers inched between the buttons of his shirt.

Everything honorable in him shouted to end it there. If they had no future together, what business had they indulging in present pleasures? He was responsible for this; had flirted, coaxed and teased her into a seduction fueled by a very mutual attraction.

Ah, when she touched him like that. . .sensual and sweet, brazen and innocent. . . His chest flamed beneath her fingertips. He covered her hand, pressed it more firmly against him, and leaned down to kiss her. As their lips joined, he privately admitted his utter inability to end now what must end in time. Acknowledged his weakness where she was concerned. And banished, into the heat of their embrace, all thoughts of the future.

CHAPTER 17

Delightful shivers rippled through Moira as their tongues thrust and parried, as her fingertips forged heated paths inside Graham's shirt.

But a mutinous notion tainted her pleasure. What an accomplished liar she'd become, what a cool manipulator of the truth. Not that she hadn't spoken the truth. They *were* as contrary as two people could be. But that didn't make a blessed difference in how she felt.

She loved him. Loved and adored him. She wanted to stick her head out the window and shout it to the world. Wanted him to make love to her right there in the coach.

Wanted to tell him he must forsake his life's work and his oath to the people of Egypt and stay here with her. But. . .

Would he—could he—ever love her as much as he loved his adventurer's life?

I cannot stay. He'd uttered those words right before he took her, before he had swept her to joyous heights. Heights that had, nonetheless, defined limits. He'd taken precautions. A sheath, he had called it. She had heard of such a thing before. French letters, as they were sometimes called, prevented the spreading of the French Pox. It also prevented children.

Would prevent his child from growing inside her.

Then, no, as fond of her as she believed him to be, he could not possibly feel for her even a fraction of what she felt for him. He spoke of obligation, of honor. Hadn't she, last night, abandoned, or at least set aside, her honor for love of him? Even now she didn't regret it. Would do it again. . .

Graham gently broke their kiss, and she smiled, a gesture formed to fool him into believing she could live with the bargain she had instigated. That she could simply enjoy him for the rest of their time together and not die a little inside at the thought of his leaving.

For now, then, she would sit beside him, laugh, and not flinch each time the carriage conspired to shrink the space between them; grin rather than swat him whenever he schemed to cup her knee, stroke her hand, catch her in a quick embrace.

As his arms tightened around her and drew her to his chest, he needed no excuses for what she readily allowed. Eagerly anticipated. For now, she would be his, and he hers.

She sighed and felt her eyes grow heavy. They'd neither of them slept much last night. With the rocking of the coach, the solid pillow of Graham's chest against her cheek, and his strong arms holding her secure, it was all too easy to drift off, to find haven in a dream.

A noise, a rustling from the floor of the carriage, woke her sometime later. She sat up groggily and pushed a lock of hair from her eyes.

Graham's palm settled against her cheek. "Morning, sleepyhead."

"It certainly can't be morning anymore," she said on a yawn. "How long did I sleep?"

"Who knows? I was enjoying the feel of you in my arms too much to notice the passing time."

His husky tone fanned a little flame to life, one that burned hotter when he added, "Did you know that when you sleep, your breathing deepens until your bosom rises against your bodice in the most delightful way?"

His hands were already there, on her breasts, raising them within the bodice of her carriage dress. He pressed his face to her bosom, kissing, his breath hot through the fabric. Desire coiled. He lifted his head to regard her, beyond doubt witnessing the passion clouding her eyes. His own gleamed beneath lust-weighted lids.

Another rustling reminded her they weren't alone. "We have an audience, or have you forgotten?" She hoisted the crate that held Isis and set it on the seat beside her. Unhinging the top, she reached inside.

A moment later the spider sat nestled in a fold of her skirts. She stroked the arachnid's furry back with her pinky. "Comfy, dear?"

"You two are becoming fast friends." Graham smoothed his hand along Moira's thigh, stopping just short of Isis's broadcloth lair. He wiggled his forefinger back and forth, letting the spider catch his scent while sending a tremor through Moira's leg.

"I have grown rather fond of her," she admitted. "She's not nearly as fearsome as she likes to pretend. The poor dear is simply misunderstood."

Laughter rumbled in his chest. "I know the feeling."

"As do I. After all, you and your family mistook me for a fortune hunter at first."

He angled his face close enough to kiss her, or nearly so. "And you, my dear Miss Hughes, pegged me for a scoundrel."

"Was I wrong, sir?"

"Not in the least." He nudged her chin and made contact with his lips, teaching hers entirely new and exciting ways to open, soften, oh, melt. His hands resumed their thorough and unabashed exploration of breasts straining against their fabric prison.

For that was how clothing had begun to feel. Having experienced the unhindered touch of Graham against her, she found herself yearning for all of him, here, in the inappropriate interior of a moving coach.

Ah, but she, too, stole a privilege. Sliding her fingers

beneath his cravat, she opened his collar, then the topmost buttons of his shirt. His approval vibrated beneath her fingertips. Somehow the buttons on her carriage jacket came undone, and the hooks securing the back of her dress gave way.

Ah, yes, they would enjoy each other. . .for now.

A devilish notion struck her. Last night she'd soared headlong into delirious pleasure at the sensation of Graham's callused hands against her breasts. She wondered. . .despite the hardness of a man's chest, did his nipples respond to the touch as a woman's did? Were his connected by taut cords to places so deep and sensitive the soul shivered with each caress?

To put it to the test, she searched out the spot that proved nearly as velvety as her own. She circled it with her fingertip, then captured the flesh between thumb and forefinger, as he had done to her.

He winced, sucked air, caught her wrist. She knew an instant's mortification. What *had* she been thinking? Then he relaxed. With a grin he released her.

"I'm sorry. I—I didn't mean to hurt you."

"You didn't, you minx. Just surprised the hell out of me." After scooping Isis back into her crate, he slid lower beside her, his expression somewhere between that of a mischievous boy and an insatiable lover. He nuzzled her neck, suckled her earlobe, raising shivers across her nape. "Moira, Moira. Go on, darling, take another liberty. Take several."

She did. And so did he. Hands slid beneath clothing, hers, his. Her skirts inched upward, smoothed by his broad palms along her stockings, then bare thighs. Higher, until the breeze from the windows added its cool kiss to Graham's heated ones. Her own hands traveled wayward paths to forbidden places, wrapping firm, feeling the pulse of his lust hot within her grasp.

Sunlight streamed through the windows while farms and villages rushed by. While Graham's hands worked their magic, a tide swelled and surged inside her, consuming her wholly until there was only rapture and the fracturing of her very self.

His mouth absorbed the soft cries that dissipated into whimpers of depletion and contentment. As awareness returned, she heard a grind in his throat, the rumbling murmur of a lust still gathering, mounting. With a little start, she realized he was still in her grasp, had been all along, her grip opening and closing in counter rhythm to her own rising ecstasy.

She set about pleasing him. His groans and the sway of his body taught her a new cadence, fiercer than she might have dared without his tutelage. His hand burrowed in her hair, holding her fast. With the other he guided her, until suddenly his limbs went rock solid against her, and he thrust forward with a raw, gusting breath.

Long, languid minutes followed. The vibrations of the coach and their shallow breathing filled the silence—a companionable, contented silence. Then they disentangled, sat up, helped each other secure buttons and hooks. Conspiratorial smiles winked in and out of sunlight and passing shadows.

"Just you wait till I have you back in London." He gave her shoulder a little bite. "If you think having Letty and my mother in the house will ensure your safety, you're gravely mistaken."

At the mention of London, a portion of her bliss dissolved. "Will you do something for me when we arrive?"

"Anything, my darling." He traced fluttering kisses down the side of her neck.

She shuddered as pleasure once more shimmied through her. Then, "When we reach London and the coach has been unloaded, will you take me to find Michael Oliphant?"

He stilled for an instant, then spoke into the sensitive underside of her jaw. "I'm going alone. It might be dangerous. I won't have you in harm's way."

"But we've plenty of daylight left." She snuggled her chin in his hair. "What harm can come from standing on someone's doorsill in the light of day? Besides, Michael Oliphant might not be dangerous in the least. Perhaps we've misunderstood the situation, as we once misunderstood each other."

"Do you believe that?"

She released a breath. "No, I'm merely trying to convince you to let me come along. I've a great many questions for this Mr. Oliphant, and I've a right to hear the answers firsthand. Please promise me we'll go together."

"I suppose I can't deny you that much." He pushed up taller, meeting her gaze with as stern a one as she'd ever seen on his handsome features. "If Inspector Parker is available to accompany us, I'll agree to take you along."

She wrapped her arms around him and tried to hide a self-satisfied smile. "Thank you."

♥ ♥ ♥

Fair weather saw them back in London in a matter of hours. As the city's towering walls cast shadows across the coach, a sense of sadness, of having lost something only recently gained, took hold of Moira. Even before she'd quite defined the sensation, she found herself sitting up taller and setting her dress and bonnet to rights.

It was the city itself. The crowds. The dictates of civilization. Here they could not sit with their arms around each other. They could not openly kiss. Could not enjoy each other as they had a mere few miles down the road. What felt familiar and natural in the country would be gasped at here among polite society, and, for Moira at least, respectability would be forever lost.

And so she slid a few inches along the bench seat, reestablishing distance and thus a modicum of propriety between them. Graham seemed to understand. He opened his arms as she eased away, though the instant she finished fussing with her clothing, his hand found hers and clasped it, simply held it for the remainder of the journey.

Mr. Paddington must have spied them coming down Brook Street, for when they arrived in the coach yard, there he stood, a little breathless, waiting for them.

"I know where your brother is," he blurted without prelude or a how-do-you-do. "And it isn't good. In fact, it's damned bloody bad." As he handed Moira down from the carriage, his gaze turned sheepish. "Forgive my language, Miss Hughes."

"Quite all right, Mr. Paddington."

Graham hefted Isis's crate and stepped down to the paving stones. "Where's my prodigal brother got to now?"

"Only found out a short time ago, you understand, or I'd already have gone to collect him. I put out some feelers while you were away and got a reply from an old friend, the Viscount Weston. Seems his mistress's brother knows Freddy and happened upon him last night. They parted ways before night's end, mind you, but—"

"For heaven's sake, Shaun, where is he?"

"In a pub in Wellclose Square. Near the Royalty Theater. Not far from the Tower."

"Stinking drunk, I presume?"

Mr. Paddington shook his head. "Worse. The place

is in a cellar, known for serving tiny glasses of Turkish Raki, which will knock even the most stouthearted bloke flat on his hairy. . ." He pursed his lips. "Sorry, Miss Hughes."

"Yes, quite all right, Mr. Paddington."

"At any rate, the place is infamous for Raki and women of coarse nature and. . .well. . ."

"And what?" Graham and Moira asked together.

"Opium."

Graham lurched forward. "My brother's in an opium den?"

"Is that very bad?" Moira asked, being thoroughly ignorant of the subject. She knew such dens existed, had once overheard Nigel and several of his friends daring each other in whispers to sample the pleasures of just such a place.

Graham cast her a fierce glance. "In Cairo, I watched it destroy far heartier men than my brother."

"Sorry, old man." Mr. Paddington clapped a hand to Graham's shoulder, then jerked away with a little gasp as he finally noticed Isis's crate.

"I've got to get him out of there. Moira, I know I made a promise to you, but—"

"My errand to find Michael Oliphant has suddenly lost much of its urgency," she said. "Go find your brother."

"Thank you." He offered a sad but grateful smile. "I won't be long, and then you and I shall find this

Oliphant fellow."

"I am in no doubt." She pressed her hand to his cheek, wishing she could take all of him into her arms. "Go. And take Letty with you."

"Letty?" He grimaced. "You'd have me take my sister to an opium den? Do you have any idea what those places are like?"

"Of course, I don't, but if it's very dreadful, let her wait in the carriage. Bring an armed footman if you must."

He exchanged a perplexed frown with Mr. Paddington. "Mind telling me why I should bring my sheltered little sister to scrape our debauched brother up off the floor?"

"Because Freddy will know you've both come for him. He'll see that you both care very much what happens to him, and he'll know he's part of a family. I think Freddy needs that more than anything just now, although he may not realize it."

"Ah, Moira." Too quickly to allow Mr. Paddington a chance to demur, Graham passed Isis's crate into his friend's hands.

She couldn't help but notice the sheer horror with which Mr. Paddington greeted his burden, nor the speed with which he transferred the crate to one of the footmen unloading the carriage.

Graham's hands cradled her face, and her surroundings faded into the intensity of his eyes and the slant of a smile bracketed by those fascinating dimples. "You're really quite wonderful, you know." Despite their audience, he brushed a kiss across her lips. "I'll make it up to you, I swear. We'll find Michael Oliphant as soon as I've returned."

"You needn't swear." She tossed a quick glance at Mr. Paddington, another at a passing footman. What must they think? But with the warmth of Graham's lips still moist on hers, she decided she didn't much care. "Just bring your brother home."

Within the hour she saw him off with a protesting Letty, who had had plans to take tea at the home of a friend and simply could not be persuaded to see the sense of trundling halfway across London, as she testily put it, to redeem a brother with little taste for redemption.

"He has a perfectly *good* sense of direction," she reasoned as Graham practically pushed her up the carriage step. "He'll wander home when he's *hungry*."

Moira placed a hand on Graham's shoulder, gone rigid with an obvious surge of temper. "Be patient with them both."

His expression bordered on seething. "Perhaps you'd better come along."

"No." She smoothed the furrows across his brow. "This is your chance to show your family how much you care. Don't squander it."

"Can't bring Shaun, either, then?"

She shook her head. "Only the footman, for protection. Anyone else will seem intrusive."

Grim-faced, he clambered in after Letty.

Once the carriage rolled through the gates, Moira walked to the edge of the garden, where Mr. Paddington stood watching with a skeptical frown.

"Perhaps one of us should have gone with them after all."

"He'll do just fine, Mr. Paddington."

"It's not Graham I'm worried about." His jet brows knotted, a tangle of censure and concern. "Letty Foster has no business being within a mile of a place like that."

"Her brother will take care of her, to be sure. Not to mention that the footman is a rather formidable fellow. Besides, Letty Foster is of tougher mettle than her family gives her credit for."

"By the pharaohs, you're right, Miss Hughes." He raised a fist in the air. "She's got the fiery spirit of Artemis, that one. The Fosters scarcely appreciate her at all."

"Well, then, Mr. Paddington, perhaps you're the man to point out all her finer qualities to them."

What began as a twitch of his bottom lip soon broadened to a grin that declared more than Moira believed she had a right to know. Mr. Paddington's heart was his own business, yet in that instant she glimpsed the whole of it.

But she did hope he wouldn't misconstrue her last comment as mere flattery designed to persuade him to do the favor she was about to ask. She would never stoop so low. Really.

She cleared her throat. "Mr. Paddington, I wonder if you would be so kind as to accompany me on an errand?"

He was still grinning, obviously lost in agreeable thoughts of Letty. "Nothing would give me greater pleasure, Miss Hughes."

That only increased her guilt, for once he learned the nature of this errand, he might very well regret his generosity.

♥ ♥ ♥

"Did you find him inside? Is he inebriated? Oh, is it *quite* a den of iniquity?"

Graham winced at the enthusiasm, and the damned naïveté, of Letty's questions. Her eyes sparking with scandal, her gaze darted beyond his shoulder to continue her first-ever inspection of an establishment of ill repute. Or at least of its facade, for he had ordered her to wait in the coach while he went inside to search for their brother.

But that was about to change.

"I'm afraid you're going to find out for yourself, Letty." He gritted his teeth and signaled to the footman posted at the rear of the coach.

What the devil had possessed him to bring Letty instead of Shaun? Shaun wouldn't have blinked an eye at their task, wouldn't have spoken a word beyond what was necessary to convey Freddy to the coach. They'd have gone in, collected the heap of arms and legs that was his brother, and made their escape wholly without incident. With Letty, however. . .

Even as he bemoaned his rotten judgment, he understood exactly what had gotten him into this predicament. Moira. Ah, Moira, Moira, of the dark, dazzling eyes and the velvet lips that transformed the most preposterous notion into wisdom worthy of the oracle of Amon. With a whisper the woman could undo the most vehement resolution, with a touch crumble the most ironclad oath.

He held out a hand to help Letty down. "I'll need your help coaxing Freddy outside."

He might have spoken Arabic, given her blank stare. Then her brows shot up. "Monteith, I *cannot* walk into a *gentlemen's* club. What would people think?"

"Gentlemen's club? Are you serious? Come along, Letty, we have no choice. Our brother is little more than semiconscious, and what few wits he does possess are only proving a hindrance. He refuses to budge."

More than that. To Graham's chagrin and vexation both, Freddy had spat at him when he suggested they make their exit. Spat! Luckily Freddy's current condition precluded taking aim with any accuracy.

"Besides," Graham added, "I seriously doubt you'll meet anyone you know, and if you do, it's highly unlikely they'll remember."

In truth, he deplored bringing her through that door,

loathed having her see the depths to which her twin had plummeted. He'd seen places like this aplenty in Cairo, and knew what sort of men frequented them. Usually those with little to lose, less still to hope for. They were typically men who'd lost everything from lovers to limbs, whose lives essentially entailed waiting to die.

Why should his brother be among them?

The simple act of descending the steps to the subterranean entrance was like sinking into a netherworld quite distinct from the one they inhabited. At street level the building, its bricks soot-stained but intact, appeared no more menacing than the Royalty Theater a few doors away.

With each downward step, however, the salty breezes from the nearby London Docks waned beneath a cloying perfume that seeped from the door's warped edges, an odor that reached out to claw the senses and drag the unsuspecting visitor into a languid but lethal embrace. As he opened the door, a waft hit them full in their faces. Letty emitted a choking cough. He felt his airways constrict. Even the footman quietly cleared his throat as he followed close behind.

They stepped into a dim interior relieved only by the glow of several stinking tallow candles and a gap in the smoke-browned curtains. Of illicit activities he saw no sign, just that heavy, hypnotic sweetness that permeated every cranny, every breath. The smoking apparatus had apparently been stowed away during daylight hours, not to be unveiled again until nightfall a couple of hours hence.

A single window peeked out onto the foot pavement like a toddler able to glean only knee-high glimpses of the adult world. Beneath it, three men sat at a round café table drinking tiny cups of acrid-smelling coffee. Eyes drooping from sleeplessness slid toward him and Letty with no more than lethargic curiosity, exactly as they'd regarded him the first time he'd entered their lair.

At the time, he had feared having to fight his way in and ransack the place for Freddy. He had even come armed for the likelihood, but a handful of coins had proved effective enough. The obliging proprietors, or patrons, had pointed the way to his brother at the end of a damp, narrow corridor.

He stepped now between the men's inquisitive gazes and Letty as together they proceeded around a scattering of tables littered with ashes and cups of foul-smelling dregs.

Fumbling to open her reticule, Letty pulled out a handkerchief and held it to her nose. From beneath it she whispered, "What on earth is this place?"

He hadn't explained much during the ride except to say the place emulated pastimes popular in other parts of the world. Her imagination had filled in the details, he knew, but even high-strung Letty hadn't imagined this. Not for Freddy.

He cupped a hand to her elbow and guided her toward the deepening gloom of the corridor. The footman followed, a silent but reassuring presence as they skirted a man sprawled facedown on a moth-eaten carpet. Another lay slumped across a bench, a glistening string of drool wending its way down his cheek.

Within her handkerchief, Letty stifled a snort of disgust. Graham slipped his arm across her shoulders. "Let's just get him out of here."

A smoking sconce lit the corridor. They passed several doorways, each draped in fabric that displayed more filth than design. He felt Letty draw closer with each step, heard her breathing become labored, faltering. Once she stumbled to a halt and made a croaking squeak, pointing as some insect disappeared into a crack in the wall.

"Come, he's in here." He lifted a curtain aside and ushered her into a chamber no larger or more appealing than a prison cell. A grating at eye level permitted light enough to reveal a pallet of rugs that filled one entire wall. Lying on his back, an arm thrown across his eyes, their brother uttered a fitful moan.

"Freddy!" Letty swept into the room. Her cry of dismay echoed Graham's own sentiments upon finding Freddy here earlier. The first time he had looked into this chamber, he almost hadn't recognized his brother, had very nearly moved along to continue searching. But a thatch of tawny hair had caught the candlelight from the corridor.

Freddy looked as though he'd been in a fight and dragged senseless through the streets. His trousers were muddied, his coat and waistcoat askew, his shirt stained and torn, and his neck cloth hung limp from an open collar.

Heedless of the packed-dirt floor, Letty gathered her skirts and knelt at her twin's bedside. "Freddy, are you ill?" Her gloved hand nudged his shoulder. "What's wrong with you? Why do you look like that?"

Freddy's arm slid away from his face. He managed a weak smile, quickly eclipsed by a groan that hinted at impending illness. He swallowed audibly, blinked, and turned bleary eyes on Graham. "Wha's he doing here?" The words were slurred but nonetheless barbed. "Thought I sent 'im packing. Make him go 'way, Letty."

"He's rescuing you, you nincompoop. So am I. What *were* you thinking, coming to a wretched place like this?"

"W-wha' were *you* thinking? Shouldn't be here."

"Idiot." Despite her scolding, she pressed a palm to his brow and smoothed damp hairs away. Graham watched, astounded and more than a little touched to witness such tenderness in Letty. Or, at least, in the Letty he'd known since returning home.

"Can you walk, do you think?" she asked her twin in the gentlest of tones.

Freddy shrugged, coughed, moaned again. "Don't know."

"Well, never mind, you can lean on us."

"Wha' if I don't wanna go?" His gaze narrowed on Graham. Despite the haze in his eyes, Freddy's rancor burned clear. He rolled onto his side, his back to the room. "Think I'll just stay here. I like it here."

"Oh, Freddy, *do* shut up. *Look* at this place. The walls are *dripping*, the floor is crawling with the most *revolting* creatures, and, good gracious, the *stench*. *Why* would anyone of sound mind *not* wish to leave?" She sounded more like the familiar Letty then, which oddly brought a smile to both Freddy's and Graham's faces.

Peering over his shoulder, Freddy reached back to grasp her hand. "All right, Letty. To put a stopper in your bellyaching, I'll come 'long like a good boy."

With considerable effort and coordination, they wrestled Freddy from the filthy pallet and onto his feet. He wobbled precariously, supported on either side by Graham and a clearly shaken Letty. The footman moved to lend his assistance, but, remembering Moira's advice, Graham waved him away.

Freddy's head sagged between his shoulders while a chorus of groans slid from his throat, increasing in volume with each step. Graham counted it a small miracle that the contents of his brother's stomach remained where they were.

With little mishap they maneuvered to the main room and headed for the street door, their shuffling feet sending bits of the previous night's debris skittering along the floor. They'd nearly achieved the exit when Freddy's knees buckled. Letty let out an *oomph* as he fell against her side. She lost her grip, and Freddy toppled over backward.

Graham's quick grasp saved Letty from falling, as

well. A nearby table bore the brunt of their brother's weight and tumbled over with him, along with several porcelain cups and a spindle-backed chair. Freddy and the furniture hit the floor with a crash and the screech of shattering china.

Letty stood with a hand pressed to her mouth as she gaped at the wreckage. Graham and the footman scrambled to disengage Freddy from the table's splintered legs, hauling him to his feet and brushing shards of porcelain from the back of his coat. The sour stench of fermented spirits wafted from the fabric.

From behind him, a barrage assaulted Graham's ears, a string of epithets in a language he didn't comprehend. One of the coffee drinkers, heretofore inert and disinterested, now bolted from his chair and bore down on them with a face gone crimson. Once again, Graham foraged into his coat pocket and extracted a palm full of coins whose value he didn't bother verifying before pouring them into the foreigner's hand.

As quickly as Freddy's dragging feet allowed, they made their way outside and into the carriage. Sprawling across the seat, Freddy sneered once at Graham and promptly passed out. Letty climbed in after him and gently lifted his head into her lap. Graham settled into the seat facing them and rapped on the ceiling for the driver to move on.

"What was that awful place?" His sister raised a face sapped of color. "What was Freddy *doing* there?"

"It's an opium den, Letty." Graham pinched the bridge of his nose, weary unto exhaustion.

"Opium? Isn't that what laudanum's made of?"

He gave a nod.

"So it's like medicine, then?"

God. Why had he brought her? Why the devil had Moira suggested it? He should have known better, should have realized what seeing such a place would do to Letty's naïve assumptions about the world.

"Such a den is where men go to escape," he explained in a voice gone flat. "Where they go to forget who they are when drink alone is no longer equal to the task."

Absorbing this information in silence, she stared down at her twin's prone form. Her fingertip traced his chin, identical to her own. "I'd no idea. I knew he was drinking, but all men his age do that, don't they? I never thought—"

"You're not to blame, Letty." *No.* He tipped his head back against the seat. *I am.*

Yes, he was to blame for leaving, for not staying and contesting the charges against him at university, for not returning when their father died, for. . . Christ, the list went on. A dull pain knifed his chest as he regarded his brother's gray features, then Letty's pinched ones.

In that instant he realized exactly where his mischievous but engaging little sister had gone. Nowhere. She was simply hiding, keeping safe. The affectations, the attitudes, the ridiculous ringlets were all merely part of the shield Letty had erected around herself when

Father died and left them nearly penniless. He could only imagine a young girl's horror to see both her family and her future—her very security—dissipate like sand sculptures on the tide.

"Is it very deadly? The opium, I mean." Her forehead puckered. Her eyes pleaded for reassurance.

Graham hesitated before replying. It could be damned deadly, depending on how much and how often a man imbibed. Not information he planned on sharing with her. He was determined not to see her hurt again; was resolved to be patient and heedful and everything an elder brother should be.

With a colossal effort he summoned a benign smile. "He'll be just fine as long as we keep him away from that place and others like it. But he's not of a mind to heed me, Letty. Will he listen to you, do you think?"

Her chin pressed forward, suddenly bearing little resemblance to the slack curve of her twin's relaxed jaw. Her voice, when it came, held none of the childish complaint or girlish simper that had become so familiar of late, but bore a decidedly adult and, God help him, eerily Moira-like conviction. "I'll *make* him listen. I'll box his ears if I have to, but he'll listen."

And Graham knew Moira had been right about bringing Letty.

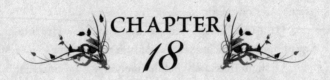

CHAPTER
18

W e're looking for Mr. Oliphant. Is he. . .is
he in?"

Moira's heart tapped an anxious rhythm
as she waited for the woman in the doorway to reply. Perhaps now she would have her answers, finally understand
why her stepfather had bequeathed a small fortune to a
virtual stranger.

Mr. Paddington stood on the step directly below her,
so close at her back she could hear his breathing, made all
the heavier by his disapproval. He'd vehemently protested
coming here, particularly when they hadn't been able to
locate Miles Parker at the Bow Street Office. When she had
insisted on continuing with or without Mr. Paddington's
assistance, he had relented, however reluctantly.

Using the directions she and Graham had acquired
from Mr. Bentley at the Bank of England, they had proceeded south on Bow Street to the Strand. Passing palatial

homes along the way, her ire had steadily risen with imagined notions of Michael Oliphant's home, which in her mind had burgeoned to a lavish town house purchased with the funds from her stepfather's estate.

After circling St. Clement's Church and turning onto Essex Court in the heart of Butcher's Row, however, her half-mumbled indignation had lodged in her throat. Now, standing on this crumbling stoop from where she could see, beyond the woman's shoulder, walls blackened with mold and the vapors of second-rate coal, Moira saw no sign of the opulence she had been so ready to resent.

The woman leaned against the peeling doorjamb and boosted the baby in her arms higher on her hip. His pink little fist bunched the fabric of her bodice, thin and faded from countless washings.

"He ain't in."

Moira's stomach dropped several notches. The baby, a few months old, made *blubbery-blub* sounds through his lips. Despite her disappointment, she smiled at him and was rewarded with a dribbly grin. Reaching out, she smoothed her fingers through his feathery blond wisps. The child snatched her forefinger and gripped it tight.

"Perhaps you'd be good enough to tell me when you expect Mr. Oliphant," she said to the mother, a young woman close in age to her but as different in circumstance as could be. Then again, perhaps not so different, for Moira's boardinghouse in Southwark had certainly boasted no greater distinction than this centuries-old tenement.

The woman shook her head, a nervous, twitchy motion that sent strands of lank brown hair drifting in her face. "I ain't seen him in weeks."

"Does he not live here? Oh, but. . ." She stopped just short of revealing how Mr. Bentley had broken bank rules by divulging Michael Oliphant's direction.

Flashing a dimpled grin that reminded her oddly of Graham, the baby chose that moment to attempt to insert her forefinger into his mouth.

His mother's lips formed a thin line in a face that should have been pretty, fine-boned and elfin as it was. Years of harsh living, too few comforts, and far too many worries had robbed those features of youth and allure. "Wot did ye say yer name was?"

"Hughes. Moira Hughes." She allowed her finger to reach the baby's lips before pulling it back and wiggling it against his nose. Delighted laughs filled the doorway while Moira's spirits plummeted. "Would Mr. Oliphant happen to be your husband?"

"Brother. But like I said, I ain't seen him in a good while. Comes and he goes. Wot d'ye want him for?"

"It's a business matter. Concerning a mutual acquaintance."

"'E owe ye money?"

Indeed. But Moira waved the notion away. "Nothing like that. Does he live nearby? Perhaps you might direct us, Mrs. ah. . ."

"It's Miss. Miss Oliphant. My brother's a drifter.

Don't know where 'e might be stayin' just now."

"Oh. . .I see." She reclaimed her hand from the baby's grasp. "Would you know if your brother was acquainted with the late Baron Monteith, also called Everett Foster?"

The woman shifted the baby to the other hip and blew strands of hair from her cheek. "Never heard of 'im, ma'am."

"No, of course not." Disappointment sapped Moira's strength; her shoulders sagged beneath the burden of another dead end. "Thank you for your time."

Miss Oliphant began backing away, closing the door. Moira wanted to stick out her foot to prevent the door from shutting in her face, but there was nothing else to say or to ask. Nothing to do but return home empty-handed.

The baby smiled then and held up his hand, opening and closing tiny fingers in an approximation of a farewell wave. Something in his sweet, cheerful countenance called directly to Moira's heart.

"Wait." An impulse sent her digging through her reticule. Whatever money Michael Oliphant had gleaned from her stepfather, his sister and her child seemed none the richer for it. She pulled out several shillings and poured them into the woman's hand. "For your little boy."

Miss Oliphant closed her fist around the coins. She held Moira in her gaze for a long moment while her wary expression turned pensive, almost sad, or so Moira thought. "Sorry I can't be more 'elp, ma'am." She shut the door.

Moira regarded the door with a maddening sense of failure. She wanted to beat her fists against its rotting boards, break it down, and barge inside, demanding answers. She wanted to dash her head against it, sink to the stoop, and cry.

She pivoted, seeking the street but marching instead smack into Shaun Paddington. The impact sent the breath rushing from both their lungs. Recovering first, Mr. Paddington steadied her with a hand at her elbow, then released her and stepped promptly out of her way.

"Oh, Mr. Paddington, what am I to do now?"

"Don't you worry your lovely head, Miss Hughes. We'll find him." He matched her stride on the cracked foot pavement.

A boy, his lean form swallowed by a ragged shirt several sizes too big, scuttled from an alley between the houses. He stopped a few feet away, holding a begrimed wooden box in the crook of his elbow. "A ha'penny to shine yer shoes, sir."

"No, thank you, lad, haven't the time." Without breaking their stride, Shaun tossed the child a coin. They'd gone only a few paces more when a girl wearing little more than a soiled shift came trotting across the street.

"A flower for the lovely miss?"

Moira regarded the dirt-streaked face and matted hair, the handful of wilting carnations. She raised her reticule.

Shaun pushed the purse back to her side, flipped a second coin to the girl, and hurried Moira across the street. "They'll be on us like locusts if we don't leave now, Miss Hughes. Never should have brought you here." He opened the door to their hired hackney. "Don't want to imagine what Graham will say when he finds out."

"I'm not in the least bit afraid of Graham Foster, I assure you, Mr. Paddington."

"Yes, but you're not the one he'll take to task, are you?"

"Don't worry, I'm sure he'll be busy enough with his own concerns. And we met with no danger here, merely disappointment."

Merely. The word echoed through her mind like a child's singsong mockery.

She was settling her skirts around her when an emphatic hissing caught her attention. Gazing out the open coach window to her left, she scanned the building front until she spied a stout figure beckoning from an open doorway. Weathered skin, a sharp nose, and a tuft of grizzled hair gave few hints as to the gender, but layers of colorful shawls pronounced the individual a woman. A leathery hand gestured from within the shapeless garments.

"Whatever can she want?" Moira asked Mr. Paddington, who had just slid in on her right and shut the coach door.

"A handout, to be sure. Never mind, Miss Hughes. It'll be dark soon. Let's be gone from here."

"Psst. You there."

"I believe she wishes to have a word with us." Moira considered the swaddled figure and decided the elderly

Lisa Manuel

woman could pose no danger, especially with Mr. Paddington along She opened the door and hopped down to the street.

"Now, Miss Hughes, please get back in the coach. I say, Miss Hughes. . . Ah, hell."

Like a faithful hound, Mr. Paddington slid out after her, shadowing her as she approached the old woman's doorstep.

"Do you wish to speak with us?"

A rheumy gaze darted right and left before settling on Moira. "I saw you talkin' with Susan Oliphant. Lookin' for her brother, are you?"

"Indeed, we are. Would you happen to know where he is?"

To Moira's complete shock, the old woman flung her head aside and spat over the stair rail. "He ain't been around, and good riddance. I mean to warn you, ma'am. He's a mean little blighter for all he puts on gentleman airs when he wants to." She made a strange gesture in front of her, like a hex to ward off evil. "A fine young lady like yourself don't want no business with the likes o' Piers Oliphant."

"Piers Oliphant? No, no, you're quite mistaken." She experienced a rush of relief that they had not, in fact, been discussing the same person. "My business is with Mr. *Michael* Oliphant. Do you know him?"

A frown deepened the already considerable creases in the woman's brow. "No, I ain't never 'eard of a Michael Oliphant. Could be there's another brother, I s'ppose,

296

but I ain't never seen him round 'ere." A crooked finger pointed in Moira's face. "You'll stay clear of that Piers, though, if you know what's good for you."

"Yes, I'll be sure and do that. Good day and thank you." Disheartened yet again, Moira backed away toward the street, only to tread on poor Mr. Paddington's toes. Well, he needn't hover quite so close, need he?

"Crazy old coot," he murmured, gripping the hand strap as their coach swerved west onto the Strand. "Reminds me of our gamekeeper's wife when I was a lad. Always going about the estate hiding the heads of dead chickens in the oddest places. Claimed it warded off all manner of calamity. Scared the other servants silly, till Father demanded she stop or pack her bags."

She only half-listened to his reminiscence, her mind far more occupied with deciding how next to proceed. Return to Mr. Bentley at the bank? He'd already risked his employment by helping her once. Begin another search through the house, in hopes of finding. . .what?

Or finally admit defeat and return home to her mother. Such a bleak prospect, such grim finality. . .

"Gamekeeper," she exclaimed, her mind seizing upon that single word from Mr. Paddington's boyhood memory. "Good gracious, why didn't I think of it sooner?"

He eyed her in sidelong puzzlement. "Do you hunt, Miss Hughes?"

"What?" She shook away her preoccupation. "No, Mr. Paddington, I do not hunt. But tell me, who in every household knows precisely the affairs of each of its members? Who keeps abreast of every new development, every crisis, each and every well-guarded secret?"

His brows gathered. "Never was much good at riddles, Miss Hughes."

"The servants, Mr. Paddington, the servants."

He mouthed a silent *ah* but didn't appear any more enlightened. She slapped her palms against the seat in a burst of impatience. "Is there no way to coax our driver to enliven the pace?"

"Right you are, Miss Hughes." In this, Mr. Paddington showed no hesitation in the least. Putting his face to the window, he stuck two fingers in his mouth and emitted a sharp whistle. "Driver, there's an extra quid for you if you get us to Brook Street within the half hour."

As if eager to match the leap in Moira's pulse, the horses broke into a trot.

"You went *where*?"

Though it was Moira's matter-of-fact announcement that prompted Graham's interrogation, his exasperation centered directly on Shaun. "What were you *thinking*? You *don't* take a woman like *Moira* to a neighborhood like *that*, especially when there's already been at least *one* murder committed in all of this *mess*."

And *why* was he sounding remarkably like Letty, aping her habit of emphasizing every other word?

He stepped back, perched at the edge of his desk, shut his eyes, and brought his temper under control with a deep breath. Between his exploits with Freddy this afternoon and now this. . .

He opened his eyes to find Moira standing within the vee of his splayed knees. Her arms went around his neck, her sweet touch imparting the contrition reflected in her eyes. Her muslin-clad breasts brushed his shirtfront, sending his anger for a headlong tumble into desire.

Little conniver, trying to win his sympathies, and doing a splendid job of it, too.

"You mustn't blame Mr. Paddington," she said. "The fault lay entirely with me."

"I don't for one minute doubt that. However. . ."

She stopped his words with a kiss that brought her length snugly against him. As lust leapt to a roaring flame, he heard Shaun clearing his throat and shuffling his feet.

No, he supposed he oughtn't to blame his friend for Moira's dangerous foray, for he knew as well as anyone the extent of the woman's persuasiveness.

He savored the taste of her lips another moment before raising his mouth from hers. "All right, my dear, we'll deal with your headstrong inclinations later."

She smiled sheepishly at him, then turned serious. "How is your brother?"

Changing the subject—a good strategy. But the

warmth of her hands closing around his own spoke of her genuine concern for Freddy. "Sleeping safe and sound in his bed."

"And Letty?"

"A bit shaken, but keeping guard at his bedside." He gave in to the temptation to lower his forehead to hers, losing himself for a few precious seconds in the feel and scent of her. "I have to thank you. Turns out you were right about bringing Letty. She surprised me today, appealing to Freddy as part-sister and part-regiment commander. He'd never have come along had it been me alone." He shook his head. "He despises me."

"Don't be silly." She nudged his chin. "Your brother doesn't despise you. If he did, he wouldn't go to such lengths to attract your notice."

He met her gaze. "Is that what he's doing?"

Her sigh pronounced him hopeless. She suddenly tugged his hand, leading him past a rather relieved-looking Shaun and into the corridor. Before they'd progressed many paces, however, she stopped and called over her shoulder, "Mr. Paddington, why don't you see if Miss Foster needs anything." Then she began hollering Mrs. Higgensworth's name.

They discovered the housekeeper at the rear of the house, in the ladies' parlor. On bent knees, the woman was carefully sweeping a bristle brush back and forth across an armchair's gold moiré cushion.

"When I discover which servant spilled water on

this costly fabric," she griped under her breath, "there's going to be a very loud, very uproarious to-do."

"Ah, Mrs. Higgensworth?" Moira hovered on the threshold, her momentum abruptly stalled.

"Yes, dear, what can I do for you?"

"The spilled water. . .er. . .that would be me."

The housekeeper sat back on her heels. "I suppose I might have guessed. Well, never mind. If the stain won't come out, I'll set another pillow over it."

"Yes, but do leave it for now, please. There's something I wish to ask you. But not here. Is anyone in the morning room at present?"

"Quiet as a tomb. I'll have tea sent up directly."

At the morning-room table, Graham's curiosity spiked as he watched Moira sip tea and nibble her watercress sandwich. He kept his questions to himself, however, fairly certain her sudden interest in speaking with the housekeeper bore some connection with her illicit ride to the Strand.

"Mrs. Higgensworth, you've been here for many years, haven't you?"

"Indeed, Miss Moira. I came when your stepfather first became Baron Monteith. I was a parlor maid then."

"So you must be fairly familiar with Papa's acquaintances."

"With those acquaintances who have visited the house." The woman stirred her tea absently.

"Can you tell me, did you ever hear of a Mr. Michael Oliphant?"

The spoon clattered, sending dollops of tea across the linen tablecloth. "Who?"

Moira regarded the stains, then exchanged a glance with Graham. "You heard me, Mrs. Higgensworth. And I daresay you've heard the name Michael Oliphant before." Her gaze, sharp and glittering, rose to meet the other woman's. "Please, you must tell me all you know of this man."

"Oh, now, Miss Moira, why would you want to go poking into matters that don't concern you?"

The apprehension in the woman's voice raised the hairs on Graham's neck and made him wish he'd been the one conducting this inquiry, without Moira present.

Moira leaned over the table. "Doesn't concern me? Mrs. Higgensworth, I'll have you know this Mr. Oliphant has made off with a portion of my stepfather's estate. A portion that by rights and all that is decent should belong to my mother."

Dismay spread across the wide, kindly face. "Your mother's a goodly soul and as generous a mistress as a body could hope for." Her voice fell to a whisper. "She didn't deserve it, Miss Moira, and neither did you."

"Deserve what? Did my stepfather fall into debt?"

The housekeeper angled a despondent look at Graham, obviously wishing herself elsewhere. He wished it, too, dreaded the unknown thing about to be said, but realized it was too late to stop this particular boat from sinking. He nodded gently. "You needn't fear the consequences, Mrs.

Higgensworth. Just tell us what you know."

She sighed. "A debt of sorts, yes. Of the moral kind. It's a tale I swore I'd never speak aloud, especially not to you, Miss Moira. My sweet lamb."

At the endearment, Moira reached across the table to clasp the woman's hand. "Have no fear of speaking the truth," Moira assured her. "The truth can't possibly hurt me more than all these secrets have."

The housekeeper denied this with a tearful shake of her head. She frowned down at the slender hand covering her own plump one.

"I did meet a soul by the name of Michael Oliphant last winter. It was as cold and black a night as can be imagined, and I'd only just crawled beneath the bedclothes when a pounding shook my bedroom door. It was your stepfather, Lord Monteith. Without a word of explanation, he bade me don my heaviest dress and cloak and follow him out to the carriage house.

"We left Mayfair and traveled to a neighborhood the likes of which make hearty men tremble in their boots. I don't know where we were. It was so dark and I was shivering so badly I couldn't retrace our route for all the gold in America."

"That's all right," Moira said, and Graham doubted anyone but he could have detected the impatience in her voice. "What did you find when you arrived?"

With shaky hands Mrs. Higgensworth lifted her tea and took a sip. "You're quite sure you wish to know, Miss

Moira?"

A breath slid from her throat, her frustration evident.

"So be it, then. What I found in that squalid dwelling was a woman laboring to bring forth a child." Her gaze bore into Moira's. "I had been brought to attend the birthing. Michael Oliphant entered the world that night."

"My goodness! Could that be the baby boy I met today? Then I must be seeking whomever his mother named him after. She called herself *Miss* Oliphant, so the child is obviously not named for his father. One of his uncles, perhaps? But I don't understand why you and Papa were—"

"No, Miss Moira, there is no uncle by that name. It wasn't the mother who named the babe. His father named him. His father bestowed his own middle name on the child."

That last statement, drawn out in a plunging whisper, hung between them all like the echoing beats of a drum. Graham didn't know what they meant. He only knew they sapped the color from Moira's cheeks and left her shaking.

"Dear God." She lurched to her feet, sending her chair crashing behind her.

"Moira, what is it?" He gained his feet in an instant.

"It can't be." Backing away from the table, she stumbled against her chair's upturned legs.

He darted to her side, reaching to steady her. Her wrist trembled in his hand. "What can't be? Mrs.

Higgensworth, what does this mean?"

"I swore I'd never tell." The woman's gaze brimmed with remorse. "I wish I'd kept my oath."

"Tell what?" He caught Moira's shoulders. Horror slowly spread across her features, engulfing them. "Moira, what don't I understand?"

Eyes gone bleak and misty met his. Helpless, he watched the dazzling spark he adored extinguish like last night's embers. Though she peered into his face, her gaze traveled through him, to some unspeakable sorrow beyond.

"He gave the boy his middle name. Just as he left him an inheritance to see him through life." Her voice was flat, devoid of all expression save resignation. "Why shouldn't he have done so? The boy's father, you see, was Everett Michael Foster."

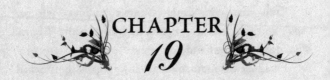

CHAPTER 19

"Moira, please open the door."

Please go away. She turned her face into her pillow. She had tried rising this morning, intent on going down to breakfast and greeting the others with a brave face. She had even managed to change into a morning frock, braid her hair, and pin it into a fair imitation of a respectable chignon. But then her fortitude had deserted her in one great wave of despondency. She had drawn the curtains closed and crawled back in between the bedclothes.

At Graham's entreaty now, she said nothing, hoping he would believe her asleep. Or perhaps simply give up as he'd done last night after knocking at her door for some minutes and begging an entry she had found no stamina to grant.

He tapped again. "I thought you might be hungry. I've brought up a tray."

She didn't want anything. Not food, not company,

not solace. She certainly didn't want any of his teasing affection, his playful lovemaking, no, nor those enchanting dimples that tricked the unsuspecting woman into forgetting everything she knew to be true and right.

Then again, what had she ever known? About anything? All her assertions about family bonds and loyalty amounted to. . .what? Nothing. Nothing laced with bitterness. And she wished to be left alone to savor the taste of it.

Everett Foster had been her father nearly all her life. She had loved him. Trusted him. Believed him the finest and truest of men. Her mother had believed so, too. Never in their wildest imaginings could they have predicted his betrayal nor his leaving them virtually penniless.

Yet the birth of his illegitimate son had accomplished exactly that.

What a perfect deceit Everett had wrought on the naïve females in his life, a duplicity all the more ghastly for the love he had taken from them, valued so little, and squandered.

Gone. Not just the money but everything—*everything!*-she had ever believed in. Staked her life upon.

"Moira?"

Why wouldn't he go away?

And yet. . .the thought of Graham hovering outside her door holding a tray of food somehow penetrated the anger and self-pity and roused her conscience. She rose up on an elbow.

"Thank you," she called out. "It was sweet of you,

but I'm not hungry."

There, perhaps now he'd stop haranguing her. She dragged the lace-edged bed linen higher over her shoulders.

"But you can't have eaten since our tea with Mrs. Higgensworth yesterday, and I know you consumed but little then."

Flinging the bedclothes aside, she sat up to better project her voice to the other side of the door. "That is precisely when I lost my appetite."

And the joy of every memory she'd ever held dear.

"We all missed you at supper last night. Me most of all," he added, his murmur barely audible through the bulky paneling.

She heard a thump and could only imagine he'd dropped his forehead to the door, his face bowed over the unwanted breakfast tray in his hands. Her conscience raked like the claws of a stretching cat, emerging whether the creature willed or no.

"Letty's been asking after you."

Oh, all *right*. She went to the door and flung it wide—and barely managed to catch the tray as he stumbled forward. She thrust the burden onto a nearby bureau and attempted to step around him. He moved too quickly for her. He caught her hand, drew her against his chest, and fastened his arms around her.

"Don't." She shut her eyes to his handsome face, those dimples that danced, not with humor now, but bewilderment.

Still, they had their effect on her, rousing sensations and images that made her want to slink back beneath the bedclothes. Graham licking her wrist, jostling against her in the coach, tugging her through Benedict Ramsey's drawing-room window. Always, always he'd flashed those teasing grins, those devastating dimples that made her melt. Until at last at Monteith Hall. . .good heavens . . .where she had. . .they had. . .

Oh, they should *not* have.

Groaning, she stopped struggling in Graham's hold and shut her eyes. How could she have forgotten, even temporarily, the very thing he had made so obvious from the beginning? Courting her was a game to him, an adventure, like hunting treasure. It wasn't his fault; it was simply his nature.

But not *her* nature, at least never before. She'd been raised on certain principles, taught to observe the strictest propriety. Guided by example in the proper behavior between men and women. Her mother. . .her stepfather . . .oh, yes, hadn't their lessons been exemplary?

Feeling ill, she slid her hands between them, palms flat to Graham's chest. "Please release me."

He hesitated an instant, his arms tightening with a possessiveness that threatened her resolve. Then his arms fell away. "Why have you been avoiding me?"

"I'm not." No, not avoiding *him*. Avoiding her own disastrous impulses. He was rash, reckless. He brought out the same in her.

No, more than that. He occupied her heart so entirely her joints ached from the restraint of not wrapping herself tightly around him even now.

Only what she had learned yesterday prevented it. Only the replacement of a lifetime's belief system with the hard, ugly truth held her in place. There were *reasons* people tended not to marry for love—logical, sensible reasons. Because if someone who seemed as steady and sure as Everett Foster could do what he did. . .

"Please excuse me. I wish to visit with your sister. You said she asked for me."

He reached behind him and swung the door closed. "You'll visit with me first."

An unsettling sensation fluttered in her stomach. She stared past his shoulder to the sealed door, afraid of what might come out of her mouth if she risked speaking. Afraid, too, of the silence sizzling between them as he stared down at her.

"I understand you're upset," he said at length. "But it's no reason to shut me out."

"The door was unlocked."

A dimple flashed, then disappeared as he worked his jaw. "I don't believe in barging in uninvited."

Yes, as she had done at Monteith Hall, sneaking to his room and challenging him, throwing herself at him.

She groaned again.

He had been honest, had told her quite plainly he couldn't stay. Wouldn't stay. He hadn't lied as many men would have done, professing eternal love and making promises he had no intention of keeping.

The shame of her behavior roared through her, making her dizzy. Those things they did. . .things he had learned in Egypt. From how many Egyptian women? How many Egyptian by-blows awaited the return of their English father? Or had he remembered to use a sheath then, too?

Hand pressed to her forehead, she turned her face away. He caught her chin on the ends of his fingers, sending a mutinous tendril of heat coiling through her.

"I've no wish to upset you further," he said. "But Shaun and I both agree the facts concerning your step-father's codicil don't add up. Not by a long shot."

"You told Mr. Paddington about. . ." She yanked her chin away. Anger and disgrace rose like bile to burn her throat. On shaky legs she groped her way to the chaise beneath the window. "How could you?"

He followed and crouched at her feet. "If anyone can help unravel this mystery, it's Shaun. And I trust him completely."

"What mystery? All is revealed. And now it's time I went home." Home, where she would be safe from the temptation of him. She covered her face with her hands, speaking into her palms. "I'm going as soon as I decide what to tell my mother."

"Don't be in such a hurry." He cupped her knee, the warm weight of his palm eliciting a shiver. Perhaps misinterpreting her tremor as a sign of distress, he anchored his other hand at her hip and held her firm. That only made the gathering ache sharper.

"There's more to the story than we've learned thus far," he said as if unaware of the turmoil he created inside her as his fingers splayed over her hip, stroked her knee. "Otherwise, why all the secrecy? Why was Smythe murdered, the office robbed? Where is Pierson, his clerk? And why did Susan Oliphant lie about knowing your stepfather?"

She focused on his words and tried to ignore the yawning desire begging to be filled. "Isn't it obvious? My stepfather must have sworn her to secrecy. He didn't want my mother learning of his betrayal. As for Mr. Smythe and the robbery, a dreadful coincidence."

"No, Moira. That's one too many coincidences for my palette. Are you forgetting Nigel? You yourself questioned how an expert rider was thrown from his horse in fine weather."

Why was he tormenting her with particulars that no longer mattered? Why were his fingertips kneading her flesh with such rhythmic tenderness? She brushed a lock of hair from her damp forehead. "So what do you suggest?"

"I think we should pay Miss Oliphant another visit. Confront her with our questions."

"No." She pushed his hands away and leapt to her feet, but he just as quickly pushed to his, blocking escape.

"Why shouldn't we?"

"Because the inheritance belongs to her son. If you

wish to help, go back to the bank and insist the transfer of those stock accounts be concluded immediately. I shudder to think of Michael or any child living in the kind of squalor I saw yesterday."

"What about you and your mother?"

"My stepfather dishonored us in the most unforgivable way, and yes, I'm confused and so angry I could smash something. But I will not take it out on the child. It's over." Her hand shot out in a gesture of finality that sent him flinching out of the way.

"The arrangements my stepfather spoke of before he died were for his family—his *other* family. He wished to secure the well-being of his son, his only natural child." Her voice broke somewhere between those last two words, ripped wide open upon a gush of emotion she could not contain.

She shoved at the arms he attempted to put around her. He encircled her nonetheless, encompassing her struggling limbs with his strength, holding her when she would have run from the room. "I must go. You can't keep me against my will."

His hold gentled, but his arms remained around her. "Am I?"

She might have pushed free if she tried. But it was more than simply his arms holding her. It was his very essence—that high-seas, open-air, fresh vitality that permeated her senses and stole her breath. Her heart stumbled in its beat and she clung, fistfuls of linen shirt caught tight between her fingers, her face pressed to the strong column of his neck.

"Moira." He buried a hand in her hair, tilted her face to his. Her gaze lighted on features gone taut with some powerful emotion akin to fury, intense and fearsome. . .but beautiful and irresistible, too. "Don't push me away. You need me now. You know you do."

She did. God help her, she did. That was the worst of it. Needing him not just now, but for an always she couldn't have.

Despite her shattered, unworkable heart, her body didn't seem to care about the future or what would never be. Inescapable need compelled her onto her toes and sent her mouth seeking his.

His lips both hard and warm, breathed life in and out of her, and tumbled her thoughts until there seemed nothing beyond the flame of their kiss. Her fingers tangled in his hair as she groped for more, as her feet suddenly left the floor and the world tipped precariously.

Together they fell onto the chaise. She lay beneath him. Her mind flooded with images from that night at Monteith, but she no longer wished to shove those memories away. No, she would savor them, indulge them, give them life. Desire ruled her, set her breasts aflame, and pooled hotly between her thighs.

When his hand slid along her leg in search of her hems, she helped him yank skirts and petticoats aside, helped him fumble with his buttons. Within her straddled thighs, she guided him, using her hands and little cries muffled against his lips to assure him of what she wished. She felt him against her, smooth, burning, prodding for entry.

Then suddenly, horribly, he went still.

She opened her eyes to find him staring down at her, his gaze fierce, wild, barely that of a civilized gentleman. "We shouldn't be doing this." His voice was raw, strangled.

"*Why* shouldn't we?" She tried to pull him down, recapture his lips. He wouldn't budge despite her repeated tugs. The desire rippling through her turned painful, became a sharp-edged vortex of disappointment. "Whom are we hurting? What laws are we breaking that haven't been broken millions of times already?"

"Not this time, Moira. Not like this." He rolled off her, secured his trousers, and sat up. Extending a hand, he helped her upright, then compounded her confusion by smoothing her skirts over her legs as if she were some wanton piece of baggage. "It isn't right."

The irony of his comment sent a chuckle to her lips. "Was it any more right at Monteith? What difference—"

Realization silenced her and brought her to her feet. One thing had been different at Monteith Hall. The sheath. He didn't have one now. They would have risked making a child.

"I see." Her voice fell flat and cold in the quiet room. "I wouldn't wish you to compromise your scruples, Lord Monteith. If you'll excuse me."

Yes, she wished to leave before he saw the pain etched on her face, before—heaven forbid—tears should begin to fall. It shouldn't hurt so much, his pulling back and being sensible, reducing their lovemaking to such rational terms. If she became with child, he would be trapped. He would lose the life he loved so much.

No, it shouldn't hurt. He had been honest from the start. Dear God, but it did. It galled her, too, even if she couldn't explain exactly why. Escape beckoned at her closed door, but he grasped her arm before she took many steps.

He spun her around to face him. "Why are you angry? I stopped us for your sake, not my own."

"My sake?" She treated him to as cool a glare as she could produce. "It's your future at stake, isn't it? You who must single-handedly save a civilization's history. Far be it for the likes of me to stand in the way of that."

"What are you going on about?" His hands closed around her shoulders. "I stopped us because it didn't seem right, not with you so upset, so devastated by what we learned yesterday."

"What we learned. Ah, you mean that even the best of men betray their families. That none can ever be fully trusted."

He replied with the knotting of a facial muscle, the beading of his jaw. His hands fell to his sides, leaving her shoulders feeling exposed and chilled. "You can trust in this, Moira. I intend taking care of you. And your mother. Neither of you need ever worry."

"As my stepfather took care of us?" A laugh escaped her, harsh, acerbic, beyond her control to prevent.

He pulled back if she'd slapped him. "I am not your stepfather."

With that he stepped around her. A lick of remorse sent her reaching out, fingertips grazing his shoulder.

"Forgive me. I didn't mean that."

He faced her again, and they simply stood there saying nothing, each harboring emotions they could not or would not share. They seemed to have reached some barren place where neither understood the other, where they all but spoke different languages. Part of her knew he'd been right for stopping their lovemaking. Part of her hated him for it. Her heart threatened to choke her.

Clutching her skirts, she swept past him and hurried from the room.

Graham stood in Moira's room for several minutes trying to collect his composure, attempting to still the tremors running hot and cold through the length of his body.

Good God. By all that was holy, he'd wanted her. Wanted her so acutely, even now, the rage of his need threatened to send him after her, refute his damned principles, and take her wherever he found her.

When exactly had he grown this burdensome thing, this conscience, and what sort of devil was it to drive him to insult a woman by *not* making love to her when she all but begged for it?

Had he been wrong? She'd certainly made him feel wrong. A true cad. But the act would have seemed too much like. . .sex. Like groping, lustful sex devoid of the tenderness that should accompany lovemaking. He hadn't been altogether certain they'd done the right thing at Monteith Hall, but it had *felt* right. Had felt like heaven.

This had felt entirely wrong.

He wondered who was at fault. Him? Everett Foster? Certainly not Moira. Her world had fallen apart. Her faith in people had been thoroughly dashed, cruelly, leaving little in its place but hurt and confusion. Ironically, he knew exactly how she felt. Understood firsthand how that sort of disillusionment made a person's heart twist and bleed and finally shrivel, impervious and numb to future hurts.

Ah, but not completely numb, at least not to Moira. She'd taught him something these past weeks. Despite the disappointments and betrayals of his past, he could, indeed, still feel. Still hope.

Still. . .God help him. . .love.

But he hadn't been able to say it. Hadn't been able to convince himself it *should* have been said.

Her pronouncement the other day at Monteith echoed through his brain. *You and I are so very different. . . You are reckless and daring and bold. . . I am cautious and practical. . .*

Why fight the truth? Why pretend he was more than he was? Whom would it benefit? Moira? He shook his head as he traversed the corridor to his bedroom suite. She deserved a better sort of man. Not a reckless, cynical blackguard.

Alone in his room with the door closed, he poured a brandy. Then another. It didn't help, didn't dull the sense of failure that hounded his every thought. He finally set the snifter down and strode from the room.

His feet took him to Freddy's suite. Freddy, another of his failures. Baxter had assured him earlier the worst of Freddy's illness had passed, and he'd slept through the night. Graham would just poke his head in the door, to make sure.

He never expected to find the room occupied by both Moira and Letty, seated side by side in armchairs next to the bed. Less expected was the sight of their clasped hands bridging the small gap between them. Their backs were to him.

"Mama doesn't know," Letty was whispering. "The truth would make her distraught, so I told her only that Freddy felt under the weather. She sat with him before supper last night, while he was awake. Somehow he pasted on a brave face and attributed his ailment to corrupt oysters."

"I shan't breathe a word to the contrary," Moira promised.

"She wasn't at home when we brought him in. Good thing, too, for he became ill shortly after." A shudder traveled her shoulders. "Violently ill."

"Perhaps that was best, to purge his body of the poisons."

Letty nodded. "Poor Freddy. I didn't realize how unhappy he's been."

Graham winced at the simple comment, knowing his absence from England was at least partly to blame.

"We all have our trials." Moira tightened her hold on Letty's hand.

"Yes, but I should have sensed that he needed help. I am his twin. That makes me closer to Freddy than anyone. But I've been selfish, too immersed in my own affairs."

"Perhaps you haven't been happy, either, dearest. It's difficult to watch over others when our own needs go untended."

"Perhaps." Letty paused, regarding their brother. "But if I don't look after him, who will? I am the elder twin, after all."

The assertion stabbed at Graham's conscience. Ah, Letty, berating herself for what should have been his task. His responsibility.

His privilege.

"The years since Papa died have not been easy for us," his sister added.

God, no, especially when their elder brother had abandoned them, as well. All those years he had considered himself the injured party. Even upon returning

home a few weeks ago, he had griped about his self-in-
dulgent brother, spoiled sister, and spendthrift mother.
His hand closed around the door frame; he wanted to rip
it from the wall.

"Oh, but who am I to complain," Letty went on,
"when you've only just lost your father?"

He saw Moira's shoulders go rigid. "Stepfather."

"Yes. How cruel to have lost two fathers."

Cruel, indeed, yet Letty had formed the observation
without drama, without the histrionics Graham had come
to expect from her. It had taken a near-disaster to reach
her, but the true Letty, the better Letty, had been roused
from her slumber. Her courage made him proud.

And rather ashamed for lingering in the hall, eavesdropping while assuming he wasn't needed or wanted
inside. The same useless convictions had sent him from
England and his duties all those years ago.

As he stepped into the room, their heads turned,
noses nearly brushing as each peered over her shoulder.
A hesitant nod of acknowledgment from Moira and a
quizzical twitch of Letty's brow exhausted the entirety of
their interest in him and they turned back to Freddy.

Unwanted, unneeded. The sentiments breathed a
cool whisper in his ear. He ignored it, or rather, resolved
to endure it. "Can I do anything for you ladies? Do you
need anything?"

Before they could answer, Shaun entered the room.
"Graham. Miles Parker is here. He's waiting in the

drawing room."

"Parker? Now?" He let out a breath. "Tell him I'll be there presently."

"He wants all three of us. You, me, and Miss Hughes."

"Please inform Mr. Parker that I'm currently occupied," Moira said without turning.

"I'm sure Mr. Parker wouldn't have come all this way if it weren't important."

A tiny shrug acknowledged Graham's observation while seeming hardly to agree with it.

Letty settled the matter. "Go ahead, Miss Hughes. Perhaps I'll stretch out on the settee for a nap."

"If you're quite sure. . ."

Letty nodded. "We'll be fine, Freddy and I."

Moira rose from her chair, then hesitated. "Miss Foster, we are cousins or nearly so. May we not be Moira and Letitia to one another?"

"No," Letty said rather severely. Her brows gathered while her lips pursed in her most petulant pout. Then a softer, wholly different expression spread across her countenance, bringing, if not beauty in the classical sense, an engaging charm to her angular features. "We may be Moira and *Letty*. So long as Mama isn't within hearing. She cringes at my pet name."

"Letty it is." Moira kissed her cheek. "I'll look in on you later."

Parker awaited them in a corner of the drawing room, ensconced comfortably in a wing chair and nursing a brandy. Graham poured three more and handed one each to Moira and Shaun.

"I do hope you haven't inconvenienced yourself on my account," Moira said to the inspector. She settled beside Shaun on the settee, the significance of which was not lost on Graham. He remained standing, leaning against the mantel. "The matter I came to your office to speak with you about yesterday afternoon," she continued briskly, "has been settled quite to my satisfaction."

Parker eyed her curiously. "I'm here to talk about Wallace Smythe's murder."

This announcement met with a collective silence. The inspector cleared his throat. "We've all wondered what happened to Mr. Smythe's clerk, Pierson. I've found a witness who saw a man exit Smythe's offices by the alley door the day of the incident.

"A street sweeper described a man of middling stature, youngish, perhaps twenty-five give or take, with close-cropped brown hair. The individual was dressed, so this street sweeper reports, in the usual plain dark suit typical of office clerks. The street sweeper also happened to notice a flash of sunlight on what might have been a pair of spectacles in the man's hand. I've never met this Pierson fellow. Does the description fit?"

"Certainly sounds like the man I remember." Graham set his brandy on the mantel. "Was he alone?"

"According to the witness, yes. Here's a clue that may clinch it." Parker dug into his coat pocket, extracting a pair of silver-rimmed spectacles. "Upon inspecting the alleyway, I discovered these at the bottom of a trash bin. Did Oliver Pierson wear such an item?"

"Indeed, he did, Mr. Parker." Moira craned forward, studying the eyeglasses in the inspector's hand.

"Oliver Pierson. . ." Beside her, Shaun rubbed a hand absently across his chin. His eyes narrowed.

"Rather curious, isn't it. . .a man tossing his spectacles away, hiding them, actually, beneath a mound of trash. Unless. . ." Parker sipped his brandy, less, Graham thought, out of a desire to moisten his mouth than to prolong and thus heighten the effect of his next comment. "Unless he never needed them in the first place."

Graham's pulse quickened as he caught Parker's meaning. "You mean they might have been part of a disguise?"

"Precisely. Consider this. What reason would Pierson have to disappear, unless he's guilty of the crime? But why would a humble clerk murder his employer? Secure positions are not easy to come by, even in a city of this size."

"Perhaps Mr. Smythe sacked him," Moira suggested, but Graham doubted a mere disgruntled employee would resort to murder.

"Oliver Pierson," Shaun mumbled again. "Pierson. . ."

Graham cast him an annoyed glance, then ignored him. "If the clerk was not really a clerk," he ventured, voicing his thoughts as they formed, "but someone with ulterior motives, murder might be the only way to protect his interests. Especially if his identity or purposes were detected."

Parker nodded, turning the spectacles over and back. "Yet I keep running smack into a dead end. What could Oliver Pierson's ulterior motives have been?"

"Where the devil have I heard that name before?" Shaun scratched his head, sipped his brandy, stared into the air.

Parker regarded Shaun, and frowned. "Have any of you ever encountered Pierson anywhere other than Smythe's offices? Think. Anywhere at all. Even a bakery, a street corner."

Graham had a niggling sense. . .

"Why, at the bishop's house." Moira thrust a forefinger in the air and for the first time met Graham's gaze. "Remember? When we were. . ." She trailed off, color suffusing her cheeks. Yes, he remembered pressing her hand to his heart, abducting her out the bishop's window and plying her with teasing caresses.

Ah, Moira, let me tease again, and you can scold me all you wish. Just don't be bitter and cynical. Don't become like me.

"Who's the bishop?"

He swallowed a sip of brandy. "Benedict Ramsey, bishop of Trewsbury. He's also a cousin of the Fosters."

"One of Papa's closest friends, actually," Moira added in a voice tinged with sadness.

"And you saw Pierson at this man's home?"

"He arrived just as we were leaving," Graham said.

"But Miss Hughes says the bishop is also a client of Smythe and Davis, so Pierson's appearance there was nothing unusual."

"I shall pay the bishop a visit." Parker swirled his brandy around in its snifter. "It wouldn't hurt to ask him a few questions."

"Pierson. Oliver." Shaun cocked his head.

"What are you going on about?" Graham snapped, becoming more than a little irked by his friend's pointless mutterings.

Moira's spine went rigid against the settee. "Mr. Paddington, what did you just say?"

Her inquiry sounded nothing like Graham's, not impatient and testy, but taut with urgency. She deposited her little-touched brandy on the sofa table and shocked them all by taking Shaun's face between her hands. "Say it again, Mr. Paddington."

"Pier. . .son. Piers. . ."

"Good heavens, you're right. It's got to be."

"Got to be what?" Graham and Parker said as one.

"Oliver Pierson. Piers Oliphant." She glared—black eyes snapping—into Shaun's astonished face, then up at Graham and over to the inspector. "Mr. Parker, I believe your dead end just burst wide open."

CHAPTER 20

Leaning forward from her reclining position against the foot of Freddy Foster's four-poster, Moira plucked another slice of spicy mince pie from the tray in front of her and met Letty's pointed glance with one of defiance.

"I know this is my third piece, but can you blame me?"

"Not a bit." Freddy held out his teacup. "More sugar, please, Letty."

His sister's disapproval turned on him. "You mustn't overdo. We don't need it all coming back up on us. *Again.*"

"Oh, do stop bullying. I'm much better now. Besides. . ." He waved the cup beneath her nose. "It's only tea and sugar. You're here to ensure I slip in neither whiskey nor laudanum."

"As if I could stop you if you didn't wish to *be* stopped."

Still scowling, she lifted the sugar bowl from the

nightstand and spooned a heaping mound into his cup. Then she tucked her skirts around her crossed legs and said to Moira, "We both know that consuming every confection in the house *won't* hasten Monteith's return."

They were waiting for Graham and Mr. Paddington to return from another trip to Susan Oliphant's flat. Upon deducing that Oliver Pierson and Piers Oliphant were, indeed, the same man, Moira thought it prudent, if unpleasant, to explain to Mr. Parker the man's connection to her stepfather. Upon hearing the tale, the inspector had leapt to his feet, declaring the importance of bringing Miss Oliphant and her child into custody, partly for their safety, partly because the woman might, after all, be involved in the crimes.

At the mention of Graham now, Moira lowered her face and indulged in an extra-large bite of pie. She didn't know if she wished to see him or not. No, that wasn't true. She did wish to be with him—truly with him as a woman should be with the man she loved. Ah, but therein she had broken the rules. A grand adventure, a challenging conquest. One spectacular memory to last a lifetime.

But love? Not for Graham Foster. He had made it abundantly clear that permanence had no place in his life.

What business, then, did she have playing love games with a man who would never be hers? She had grown so accustomed to having him at her side, to their easy familiarity and, oh, yes, the desire, those great leaping flames that licked up at the slightest provocation, at the mere sound of his name. Even now, knowing all she knew about him, and about men in general, she longed to be with him, and missed him so much she ached.

She glanced up to see Letty eyeing her with a speculative expression. She changed the subject. "I do wish I hadn't agreed to remain behind. It's an insult to have been left at home." She swallowed another mouthful of sticky mince. "The matter concerns my late stepfather, my late fiancé, and my late solicitor." Her brows shot up. "Good heavens, I hadn't thought of it in exactly those terms before." Her hand snaked toward the cake tray, only to receive a gentle swat from Letty's fingertips.

"Becoming as big as a house won't help. Besides, Monteith was right. It would have been too dangerous. That *beastly* man, Oliver Pierson or Piers Oliphant, may have killed poor Mr. Smythe. What if he should decide to come after you?"

Freddy drained his second cup of tea. "Why would he come after Moira?"

"Because, jingle brains, she's searching for the very same inheritance these dreadful Oliphants are determined to hide. Perhaps they fear she'll make a claim, since the child is, sadly, illegitimate." Her eyes went wide. "That sets Monteith at risk, as well. He *is* the rightful heir."

"I'm sure our brother is quite safe, Letty," Freddy said gently. "After all, he's with the inspector and his rather resourceful friend."

"Mr. Paddington. . .yes, I suppose you're right. . ."

"He's forever making eyes at you, you know." Freddy grinned.

"Who?"

"Shaun Paddington, goose, that's who."

"He is not." She picked an almond from her anise biscuit and flung it at him.

"Is, too. . ." He caught the offending morsel in his palm and popped it into his mouth.

"I believe Freddy is right, Letty," Moira concurred with a smile. "Mr. Paddington appears to have taken a fancy to you, and you must decide if you wish to encourage him or not."

Letty's bottom lip crept between her teeth. She tilted her head and considered. "Are you certain?"

Moira nodded.

Freddy gave a self-satisfied harrumph. "Told you so."

Letty flicked another almond at him.

Watching the Foster twins revert to their childish antics, Moira questioned, however briefly, the wisdom of confiding in her stepcousins. Of course, the alternative would have been a lonely, maddening wait by a window, chewing a hole through her lip while imagining all manner of violent encounters between Graham, his companions, and Piers Oliphant.

At any rate, Letty and Freddy were Fosters. The matter concerned them nearly as much as it did her. And it hadn't hurt to occupy their thoughts with something other than Freddy's recent disgrace. Awakening an hour earlier in a reassuringly lucid state of mind, he had promptly announced the return of his appetite, thus instigating a foray down to the kitchen.

She must admit lounging on Freddy's bed and indulging in pilfered delicacies had been fun. She felt. . .oh, part of a family again; part of the easy, unthinking acceptance among those who simply belonged together for good or ill.

Liar. She had confided for none of those reasons. They were merely a happy by-product of her having done so. No, her motives had much more to do with the simple—no, desperate—need to turn her thoughts to matters other than Graham.

He arrived home within the hour. Minutes after she heard the rumble of carriage wheels, he appeared on Freddy's threshold to regard them all with eyes smudged with fatigue, and something more. Disheartenment. Regret. She had heard it in his reluctant footsteps dragging along the corridor, and saw it now in his veiled expression.

She suppressed a shiver of yearning as his dimples made a halfhearted attempt to dance. "What a cozy scene."

She looked away, unable to endure the emotion burning in his eyes, or the yearning pulsing inside her. She contemplated the design of the coverlet. "Is Susan Oliphant in custody?"

When he didn't respond, she stole another glimpse at him. He sidled a look at his brother, another at his sister.

Freddy shrugged, but Letty met his gaze unblinking.

"We know all about it, Monteith. Moira's told us everything."

He looked back at her for confirmation.

"I saw no reason not to tell them," she said. "They are Fosters, after all."

He released a breath and nodded. Pushing away from the door frame, he approached them with head bent, broad shoulders bunched. "We discovered no sign of Pierson or any trace of Piers Oliphant. And nothing at all to link the one identity to the other. It gets worse."

Dragging a chair closer to the bed, he settled into it with a sigh that traveled under Moira's skin and left her nerve endings tingling. "Parker's superiors down on Bow Street refuse to invest the manpower to pursue Oliphant unless someone can reasonably prove he's also Pierson."

"But that makes no *sense*." Letty swung her legs over the bed to face him. "Moira's *presented* the proof. Everett Foster's will. *That* is what connects Oliphant to Mr. Smythe, and thus to Pierson."

"True enough, Letty, but the inspectors feel the codicil hardly gives Oliphant a motive for murder." Graham ran a hand over features gone pale with fatigue, drawn with frustration. "Since the funds are not entailed to the Monteith estate, there is no question that the inheritance legally belongs to Piers Oliphant's nephew. As Michael's closest male relative, Oliphant is the trustee, which gives him a good deal of power over the funds. So while Pierson may have had some purpose in disposing of Smythe, Piers Oliphant seems to have had none at all."

"Piers, Pierson. . ." Letty gave a snort. "It makes one's head positively *spin*."

"Yes." Graham's expression was grim. "And once again Inspector Parker is up against a wall."

"But he must have questioned Susan Oliphant," Moira said. "Could she provide no clue at all? Didn't anyone think to ask why she continues living in that squalid flat when those stock accounts could provide a decent home? Even if the accounts are still on hold, she could easily obtain credit."

He leaned forward, elbows on his knees, clasped hands resting on the mattress. He drew closer to her, so close she might have tousled his sun-tipped hair, stroked his shoulder, caressed his cheek. She gripped her hands together.

"I'm afraid it is to remain a mystery for now," he said. "No one was able to ask Susan Oliphant anything. She and the baby have vanished, and none of the neighbors will admit to having seen them leave."

♥ ♥ ♥

The trip to Susan Oliphant's flat had left London's lingering odors of soot and grime on Shaun's clothing. He returned to his room, intending to change as quickly as possible. He had stripped off his coat and waistcoat and even his shoes when a thought—no, a revelation—struck him a blow that sent him racing across the upper gallery in shirtsleeves and stocking feet.

He slid to an abrupt halt in the doorway of Freddy's room just as Miss Hughes said, "I fear for the child. Susan Oliphant's disappearance can only mean she is an accomplice in her brother's crimes."

He paused to catch his breath and straighten his shirt before calmly entering the room.

"Ah, Shaun, we could use another viewpoint." Graham gestured to an empty chair. "Join us. You all right? Looking a bit flushed, old man, not to mention a little unkempt." Without waiting for an answer, he returned his attention to Miss Hughes. "Susan Oliphant may not be guilty. Or perhaps no more than an unwilling accessory. I'm beginning to suspect some legality is preventing Oliphant from controlling the funds, and he's attempting to cover it up."

Miss Hughes regarded him a moment in silence, then shook her head. "If only they had left some clue to the direction they took."

"They may have left no clues," Shaun put in before Graham could comment, "but that doesn't prevent us from making an educated guess."

"Whatever do you mean, Mr. Paddington?" Miss Hughes asked.

"Just this." His gaze encompassed the little group: Miss Hughes waiting expectantly, Graham half-dubiously,

Freddy Foster with mild curiosity, and Miss Letty Foster—lovely Letty—with a regrettable pout of impatience.

He sighed. "There are only so many roads out of London. A man traveling with a woman and child would certainly use one of the coaching routes, wouldn't he? Any other would slow a fugitive to a dangerously sluggish pace."

Miss Hughes held up her hands. "But once beyond the city, there's no telling which way they might head."

"No? They'll want a town with a bank, won't they?" Shaun grinned. "In order to draw funds from the inheritance the moment they become available, or perhaps arrange a series of transfers to some final destination."

"Good grief, Shaun, you're a genius." Graham flashed his first genuine smile in hours.

"That does narrow the field," Freddy agreed.

And Miss Foster. . .Letty? Shaun's pulse thudded as he waited for. . .yes, for *that*. The little ridge of perplexity above her nose disappeared and then reemerged as something altogether different.

Interest? Regard? Or—dare he think it—admiration?

"They want a means of disappearing, too," he pressed on, emboldened now. "Once the inheritance is at their disposal, why shouldn't they leave the country? They'd be much harder to trace on the Continent. My guess is they're headed for a port."

Graham's eyes narrowed. "They might have boarded

ship right here on the Thames."

"That was my first guess, but it takes time to reach the mouth of the Thames, and a ship can be boarded and searched anywhere along the way. I think they'll likely take an overland route to a port city."

"A first-rate deduction, Mr. Paddington." One of Miss Foster's golden eyebrows arced. "But there are numerous ports along the coast, with numerous destinations."

"True enough, Miss Foster. But remember, they must wait for their funds before they travel. They'll want a busy city where they'll blend in. They'll also want a swift journey once they embark. I would rule out Portsmouth and all ports west of Dover due to the more lengthy distance across the channel. Dover itself is a possibility, although perhaps too obvious a one. They'll know we'll send men looking for them in Calais. That leads me to suspect they might try a more easterly port, perhaps Margate or Southend-on-Sea. From either of those, they might disappear into the Netherlands."

"How very astute of you, Mr. Paddington." The corners of Miss Foster's delicate mouth curved into a smile that added several beats to the rhythm of his pulse.

"Another matter occurred to me, as well," he said, speaking now as if Letty Foster were the only person in the room. "Mr. Parker aside, the Bow Street inspectors are leery of our suspicions concerning Oliver Pierson and Piers Oliphant."

"Morons," the lady declared with a disdainful sniff.

"Indeed, Miss Foster, and I thought. . .if we only had a picture of Pierson to show Susan Oliphant's neighbors, we might very well achieve a positive identification and sway the officers to our cause." He paused, swallowed, and prepared to be as forward as he dared. "Do you not draw, Miss Foster?"

"Why, yes, I do, Mr. Paddington, and I believe I understand what you are suggesting. I am acquainted with the man in question." Her gaze darted to her brother. "I met him before you came home, Monteith, when Mr. Smythe opened the house for us." She turned back to Shaun, face positively radiant with eagerness. "Perhaps you'll be so good as to help jog my memory, Mr. Paddington, to ensure I get it right."

Ah, darling Let, anything. Anything at all. Aloud he said, "I would be honored to be of service, Miss Foster."

Reaching beside her to the nightstand, she lifted a platter whose hideous brown contents, as glistening and lumpy as flies trapped in molasses, quivered from the movement. "Would you care for some mince pie, Mr. Paddington?"

He schooled the distaste from his features. "Indeed, I would, Miss Foster."

♥ ♥ ♥

The house was hushed, vacuous. As Graham passed Moira's door, no light beckoned from beneath. He was tempted to try the knob. Was she awake? Still angry with him? He wished to explain again—better this time—why he'd brought things to a halt earlier that night.

Wanted to take her in his arms and assure her it hadn't been for lack of desire.

Or would he only compound the damage? It seemed they couldn't be alone without losing their heads.

Then again, was that really such a terrible thing? The notion raised a bit of a grin. He'd deal with Moira in the morning, when they were both fully awake. Thoughts of her constantly filled his mind, true, but it was concern for someone else that presently kept him from his bed.

He continued across the gallery and turned into the east wing. At Freddy's threshold, he stopped and pressed his ear to the door. Not a sound issued from within. Setting his candle on the hall table, he carefully turned the knob and stepped into the nearly pitch-dark bedroom.

He preferred the shadows. Freddy slumbered with nary a sound, his outlines a too-slender shape beneath the bedclothes. He'd lost weight, even in the few weeks Graham had been home.

If only he had been alert to the signs sooner, the warnings that contradicted the notion of Freddy over-indulging in similar fashion to the other young bucks of his set. No, Freddy's excesses were of a far more sinister nature. He was wasting away inside and out, and until today all anyone had thought to do was disapprove.

The chair Graham had dragged to the bedside earlier

was still there, as though awaiting his return. Sitting, he leaned over the bed, hesitated, and lowered a hand to his brother's brow as Letty had done countless times the night before.

No fever, nothing to indicate permanent damage. Freddy stirred, and a soft groan whispered through his lips. Graham moved his hand away, then set it lightly on Freddy's shoulder.

He had been almost ten when the twins were born. From the very first, they'd been angelic conspirators, devilish schemers. Despite, or perhaps because he was nearly a decade older, they'd toddled and then clambered after him, racing to keep up with their big brother.

The big brother Freddy these days looked upon with loathing.

He was glad Freddy was sleeping. He had something to say, but he doubted his ability to say it to a countenance that judged and found him so entirely wanting.

"They were right about me, Freddy," he whispered. "The university, Benedict Ramsey, our parents, everyone. I cheated, just as they all said I did. Except that it didn't involve another student or any pointless examination. It was you. You and Letty. I've cheated you both for years, and I realize saying I'm sorry won't begin to make amends. You have every right in the world to despise me. It's perfectly all right that you do. Only don't. . ."

He swallowed against a burning sensation and waited for his throat to reopen. "Don't despise yourself,

Freddy. Give me all of your contempt. I deserve it. You don't. Neither does Letty. You have to understand. You determine your future, and whether or not you'll ever know any measure of happiness. You and no one else. Don't waste your life, Freddy. Don't be miserable because your buffoon of a brother didn't realize the worth of what he had."

He sat back. There, it was said and done, while Freddy snoozed peacefully on. Better that way. At least Freddy couldn't turn away. At least he hadn't spat.

Graham stood up but lingered at the bedside. He hadn't quite said all. There was one thing more, the most important of all, perhaps. Of course, it was the hardest to say and probably the very thing Freddy would least wish to hear. He decided it was better left until his brother was wide awake.

What, after all, did he have to lose?

Graham rose to the first gray glimmers of dawn, well before anyone else, or so he thought. He was surprised a short time later to find Moira already in the morning room, standing at the sideboard and spearing a slice of fried ham with a fork. She flinched when he bid her good morning. He took in her pleated skirt with its matching jacket. A bonnet lay on the table beside her coffee cup.

"You're up early," she said in a decidedly accusing

tone. A guilty light flared in her eyes.

"So are you."

She gave a little shrug and returned her attention to the platters on the buffet.

"Where are you off to?" he asked.

Her next selections of toast and preserves resulted in spilled crumbs, a clattering spoon. "Who says I'm going anywhere?"

"Your carriage dress. Rather jittery this morning, aren't you?" He took her plate from her hands and carried it to the table. "Can't have you ruining another morning-room rug, now can we?"

Her eyebrows twitched to a frown. "You shouldn't sneak about, startling people."

She tried to slip past him to the table, but with a quick side step he blocked her path. "You haven't told me where you're going."

"I have some errands to do."

"Where?" A step brought him closer to her.

"Here and there." She backed away. "You needn't be concerned."

"Needn't I?" He prowled closer still and grasped her shoulders, halting any further retreat on her part. "I am head of the Foster family, and you are still a member of it, last I checked. I'd like to know ahead of time where you're going and with whom. For your own protection."

Her lips parted and plumped on an indignant huff, one he felt sorely tempted to swallow with a kiss. "And if you don't happen to approve?"

"Then you don't go."

Her frown became a genuine scowl. "Am I a prisoner?"

"Do you wish to be?" He met her scowl with a wide grin and pulled her to his chest. He couldn't help it, neither the smile nor the need to feel her against him. Right or wrong, good or ill, he could no more resist her than an explorer could resist the lure of uncharted territory. She stirred his blood like a bracing desert wind, tinged with mystery and the promise of adventure.

He held her past the moment of resistance, when the rigidity left her and the gaps between their bodies closed. Her scowl dissolved. He stole the opportunity and nipped her lips, and felt well-rewarded when she nibbled back.

Her arms slid around his neck. "Yes, in answer to your question, blast you, in a way I wish I were. Then I wouldn't have to make decisions I loathe. Not have to think so bloody much about. . ." Her sigh warmed the skin of his neck. Her fingers tangled in the hair at the back of his head, pulling none too gently. "*Why* do we keep doing this? It's as if we *are* prisoners. Ones who hold the key to their shared cell but refuse to unlock the door and escape."

Her gaze met his with a flare of conflicting emotions. Naked longing checked with fear, a desire to trust tainted by uncertainty.

Damn Everett Foster for that.

But no, it wasn't all Everett's fault. Graham wanted to soothe her fears and doubts the way he now soothed her brow with a caress and a kiss. "Damned if I know how to let you go, Moira, or how to set my feet in motion even if the cell door stood wide open."

"And yet you will," she murmured, sending a dart of truth shooting through him.

A maid carrying a fresh pot of coffee entered through the swinging service door. His arms opened, and Moira stepped out of them, shuffling to put a respectable distance between them.

She fussed with her hair, brushed at her bodice. "Yes, Mr. Paddington's suggestion was brilliant," she said loudly, as if hoping to fool the maid into believing they'd merely been having a conversation. "Letty has composed two sketches of Piers Oliphant, one with spectacles and one without. Both are uncanny likenesses."

"Good work." He watched the maid bustle at the sideboard before retreating through the swinging door. Then he said, "And yet my original question goes unanswered. Where do you intend going today?"

Moira stood beside her chair. "Oh, all right. While you and Mr. Paddington meet with Inspector Parker again, I'm going back to Essex Court to show the sketches to the Oliphants' neighbors. There was one old woman in particular—"

A single stride brought him to her. He gripped her hands. "You most certainly will not."

"You're hurting me."

His fingers relaxed, but he did not release her. "Forget it, Moira. You're not going."

"Don't be ridiculous. The Oliphants are gone, and it's broad daylight." Managing to slip her hands free, she sat down and picked up her fork.

He stood gritting his teeth and glaring down at her. Then he slid into a seat opposite and fixed her with a level gaze. "The safety of that neighborhood aside, all the evidence points to Piers Oliphant having killed Smythe. We have no idea where he is at present or where he might turn up next. And to tell you the truth, Moira, it's becoming damned burdensome to have people engaging in self-destructive behavior on my account."

She looked up from her breakfast, mouth going still around a bite of ham. "What is that supposed to mean?"

He raked a hand through his hair and thought briefly of Freddy, somewhat better now but still ravaged by the wounds that had driven him to opium. "It means I'm sorry about what your stepfather did. I know he hurt you very much. What I don't understand is why it all seems to be my fault."

Her eyes went wide. "I never implied any such thing."

"Yes, you did. With each cool word, each chilly glance, you seem to be visiting your stepfather's sins upon me. I've thought about it a lot these two days." He stopped just short of admitting he'd lain awake nearly two entire nights. "Because Everett betrayed your trust, you feel you can no longer trust me. As if you're certain I'll hurt you as he did."

"Is that what you think?" Her lashes fell. She wrapped her hands so tightly around her coffee cup he feared for its safety. "It's true that of all men on this earth, my stepfather seemed least likely to ever betray those who loved him. And yet he did." Her gaze rose, shimmering darkly.

"And if *he* could, then surely a swaggerer like me will?"

"That isn't it at all." She pressed her fingertips to her eyes. "I simply think we should stop doing the kinds of things we were just doing."

"Caring about each other and showing it?"

"We've strayed far beyond that, and you know it."

"At your prompting." When her mouth fell open, he held up a hand. "I only meant you seemed happy enough in my arms until you learned of Everett's broken promises."

"Yes, well, you have made me no promises and thus there are none to break." She sat back, her spine stiff against the chair's spindles. "You are sworn to return to Egypt. That is your commitment. Your future."

"What if it wasn't?" he murmured before stopping to consider the ramifications. The very notion set his blood racing, his thoughts reeling. This was something he hadn't dared consider before, a notion he had refused to entertain, and yet. . .hadn't every moment in Moira's arms led him to this very suggestion?

"Then you would be disavowing your oath to that

sheik, wouldn't you?" Her chin squared in challenge. "Breaking a solemn promise."

"So I'm damned if I do and damned if I don't."

"This is pointless." With a flick she deposited her napkin on the table and set her bonnet on her head. Scuffing back her chair, she came to her feet.

"Moira, wait." He caught up with her in the doorway and seized her hand. "Why am I guilty before I've committed any crime? I am not your stepfather. How can I make you believe you're safe with me?"

"You could be Ni—" Her mouth snapped closed.

"Be what? Whom? Nigel? I could be Nigel? Blazing hell. Was he such a paragon you'd never suspect in him what you're so ready to condemn in me?"

"You still don't understand." She snatched her hand free and gripped it with the other. "Nigel would have stayed. He'd have been content and not pined for more. Excitement to him meant racing his horse across the dales in the morning and reading a rousing good book in the evening. He was. . .like me."

"Ah, Moira, I'm beginning to believe you and I are more alike than not." He reached for her, but she pulled away.

Her ebony eyes glistened, but in their midnight depths defiance glinted, too. "Life's greatest disappointments spring from where one's trust lies deepest. Your words. But you didn't have it quite right. The greatest disappointments spring from where one's *love* lies deepest. And I'm sorry, but I simply don't dare risk loving you."

CHAPTER
21

M oira strode through the house, away from
Graham and out the front door. She didn't
think he would follow, didn't want him to.
Her flight came of a need to expend energy on something
other than regret. Regrets were such a useless waste of time.

Outside on the foot pavement, she stopped to catch
her breath, gain her bearings. Where should she go? A
stubborn voice suggested Essex Court.

Graham would be angry. And he'd be justified, for
she couldn't refute his arguments against her going. Putting herself at risk would only hamper the investigation.

She lingered at the bottom of the steps like a lost,
loitering figure, when the sound of her name sent her pulse
for a leap and transformed her next breath to a gasp.

One quivering with relief.

That instant compelled her to admit, silently, that
yes, she *had* wanted him to follow, wanted it with the en-

tirety of her being. Irrationally, ill-advisedly, her world had come to revolve around this man, and she could not envision what it would be like when he left.

Her thoughts churned as he descended the steps to stand beside her, so close he had to tuck his chin to look down at her. His scent, fresh and vibrant and uniquely his, surrounded her and traveled through her, making her crave his arms and ache for the feel of him against her. She concentrated on breathing, on not allowing even a hint of her longing to reach her features.

"I was wrong," he said, "entirely wrong. All those things I said about family and loyalty and disappointments. All of it was rubbish. Good grief, I was wallowing in self-pity, babbling nonsense. You shouldn't have listened. I didn't think you had. Throw it all back in my face if you must, but don't believe it, not a single blessed word of it, Moira."

Ah, when he stood so close and looked like that. . .his eyes sea-bright with remorse, his tanned face aglow with self-blame. . .how easy then to shove her qualms aside and simply believe, as he so obviously wished her to, that they wanted the same things in life. That they could make each other happy in the years ahead.

She placed a hand on his cheek, smooth from his morning shave. "I'm so sorry. I was mean to you inside, and it was wrong of me. I—"

"Don't." When she might have taken her hand away, he pressed his palm over it as if to savor the contact, never let it end. "Don't apologize. Don't be sorry. I'm not."

She understood what he meant. Even now she would not undo their time at Monteith Hall. Could not, for all it would have made the days ahead easier. Fool that she was, she'd rather have that one memory to cherish, even with all the anguish that went with it, than trade it for the luxury of walking away from him with a light heart.

"You spoke of love before you ran off," he said.

Yes, in a moment of wretched madness, she'd said too much. She reclaimed her hand now lest the feel of him beneath her palm compel her to reveal more secrets, convince her to ignore too many truths. She stepped back.

"What I meant was that if we continued what we began at Monteith Hall, I might run the risk of falling in love with you. It is a risk I will not take."

His nostrils flared; his blue eyes frosted. "I see."

That was all. No protestations, no arguments assuring her of his love. Only a despondent look that mirrored the heaviness of her own heart. The truth was, they cared for each other, a great deal. Of that she had no doubt. She simply didn't believe those feelings could weather a lifetime.

She raised her skirts, preparing to retreat back up the steps into the house.

"Lord Monteith!"

They both started at the sound of the hail. Gazing to the street, they watched as Miles Parker stepped down from a hackney.

"I've news," he told them without pausing to exchange pleasantries. "The Oliphants may have been found."

Moira couldn't prevent the cry that burst from her lips.

"It's not the best of developments, I'm afraid." The inspector hesitated and made an unnecessary adjustment to his cravat. "Not what we hoped for."

"Don't keep us in suspense, Mr. Parker." Moira swept closer to him. "Where are the Oliphants?"

The man hesitated, clearly uncomfortable. "My lord, may we discuss this inside? I think you both should sit down."

"Of course. This way." Graham ushered them into the house and to the nearest room off the main hall. In the dining room, he bade them be seated near the head of the long table. "Now then, Parker, explain what's happened."

Mr. Parker gave a brisk nod. "I received a report early this morning that a family fitting the Oliphants' description may have boarded a coach at the White Chapel yard. A porter there remembered them because the man paid the driver extra to start out an hour early, before daybreak."

"Were your men able to catch up with them?" Moira's hopes raced along with her heartbeat.

"In a manner of speaking, yes. But we're not entirely certain it's them." Mr. Parker inclined his head. "That's why I'm here. I'd hoped the two of you might come along to identify the pair."

Graham was shaking his head no. "Not Miss Hughes. It's too dangerous."

"Oh, but Graham—"

The inspector held up a hand. "If these are the Oliphants, I can assure you they pose no threat. You see, there was an accident. The coach slid off the road and rolled down a ravine. There were. . ." He swallowed. "No survivors."

Don't let it be them; oh, please, don't let it be.

The words rang through Moira's mind as Mr. Parker led the way into the barn turned makeshift morgue. She could barely draw breath while images at the corners of her eyes faded into a blur. It was like walking into a nightmare, knowing that what lay within the wooden structure had nothing whatsoever to do with farming or coaxing anything to life, but quite the opposite.

The surrounding fields stood unnaturally quiet despite the bevy of onlookers, neighboring families who'd come to assist or simply view the carnage. They stood scattered about the barnyard in small clutches, whispering among themselves. Others had gathered on the porch of the nearby stone-and-timber farmhouse, their straw hats and gingham bonnets pulled low over bleak, bewildered faces. Their murmurs ceased as Moira,

Graham, and Mr. Parker cut a somber path through their midst.

When the inspector opened the barn door, Moira was bombarded with the arid scents of hay and feed. Something else, bitter and metallic, assaulted her nose and mouth until she nearly gagged. Inside, the thatched roof emitted occasional shafts of sunlight to spear the dusty shadows. She spied sacks here, bales of hay there, farming implements in yet another corner. She understood that this was not an animal barn, but a warehouse for the harvested yield, nearly empty now in early summer.

But no, not empty. Several tarps lay stretched across the packed-dirt floor, and on them were five heaps that looked like piled clothing left to molder in the damp. A part of her that simply refused to acknowledge such horror felt indignation that the laundress should have been so negligent.

"Ye be the inspector from London, then?"

She jumped at the gruff voice behind her. Turning, she beheld a sinewy man with thin, grizzled hair and a leathery complexion. With one weather-browned hand he held out a lantern to them. "Ye'll be needin' this."

"Yes, thank you." Mr. Parker took the lantern. "Which ones are they?"

"The couple what had the babe?" In answer to his own question, the farmer crossed the floor, skirting one particularly large mound, a figure so broad of shoulder as to form a triangle with his upper body. The driver, undoubtedly.

"How do you know which of these. . .these people had the baby?" Moira asked.

"Besides the lady and gent, there were only two elderly men and the driver, ma'am," the farmer replied. "None else what could have had a babe in their keeping."

She nodded, angling her gaze away from the bodies. Beside her, Graham clasped her hand. He hadn't once left her side since Mr. Parker's disclosure in London. "Can you do this?" he whispered.

She wasn't at all certain she could. She squinted into the shadows. "I don't see the little one. Do you?"

He shook his head. "Perhaps they laid him in the house."

Poor little Michael, her mysterious adversary for so long. Until she'd learned who he was, she had thought of him only as the person who had cheated her and her mother out of a secure future. Oh, but he wasn't that at all. He was only a child, completely innocent of the sins of his elders. No matter who had committed the crime, Michael didn't deserve to suffer. Didn't deserve to be one of these desolate heaps.

"Lord Monteith, Miss Hughes. . ." Crouching beside the third figure from the door, Mr. Parker beckoned. "Is this the man you knew as Oliver Pierson?"

Still claiming firm possession of her hand, Graham murmured, "Can you?" The severity of his expression promised a swift departure at the slightest shake of her head.

"I'll be all right." Yet her hand convulsed, clutching

his tighter. Together they moved to the body.

It wasn't as bad as she'd thought. . .and yet it was more horrible than she had imagined. The scarcity of blood on the charcoal suit coat and white shirtfront surprised her and brought a perverse moment of comfort. She certainly didn't wish a violent death on anyone, no matter his crimes.

But then Mr. Parker laid his hands on either side of a head angled in a most abnormal direction, as if, while peering over a shoulder, it had become wrenched in place. As the inspector rotated the face upward, the stiffened neck gave an awkward lurch as if wholly unconnected to the rest of the body but for a layer of flesh.

"That's him. That's Pierson." The assertion came from Graham, for all Moira could do was stare at the lifeless face and use the entirety of her will to prevent her stomach from heaving.

"And the woman?" Mr. Parker released Pierson's head, letting it flop back sideways. He shifted to the next body. "Miss Hughes, is this Susan Oliphant?"

She shut her eyes, sidestepped, opened them, and beheld a death far less quick and tidy than Pierson's. There was blood, gobs of it, clotted across the torso, stuck in the folds of the dress, webbing the fingers, and sealing the gray lips.

She clenched her teeth and swallowed against nausea and pity and yes, even sorrow, for the woman she'd met only a day ago. A young woman who had a baby, a future, and now—neither.

"Yes. That's Susan Oliphant." The words tangled in a throat gone dry. She turned away. "Where is the child?"

"Up at the house," the farmer replied. "Th' wife's got him."

"May we see him?"

Graham swung an arm around her. He said nothing, just held her, his arm a steel girder supporting her as a wrenching burst of grief sapped the strength from her legs.

"I expect he's sleeping, ma'am," she heard the farmer say, "but you can look in on him."

Her head jerked up from Graham's shoulder. "Sleeping? He's alive?"

"Aye. Found him near the top of the ravine, half-hidden by the weeds. Must have been thrown clear of the carriage when it first rolled."

She gave a cry, a short burst of laughter, then pressed a hand to her mouth lest the spectators outside believe she found something amusing in a barn filled with death. "Why, this is wonderful," she whispered between her fingers. "Graham, let's go get him. Inspector, may we take Michael back to London with us?"

Mr. Parker nodded. "It's either you or the foundling hospital, I expect."

She turned to Graham. "Do you have any objections?"

"He's welcome in my home. We are kin, he and I. Second cousins twice removed and then some, but still kin. But are you quite sure, Moira? Sure you can bear to look upon the cause of so much unhappiness in your life?"

"He's not the cause at all, but one more victim. I could never blame an innocent child for my woes."

"No, of course, you wouldn't." The backs of his fingers grazed her cheek. "Brave Moira. Let's go collect him."

They were nearly at the barn doors when he stopped, gazing down at Piers Oliphant's body.

"What is it?"

He didn't answer but sank to one knee and leaned over the body. "I remember something. I wonder. . ."

Reaching, he astounded Moira by not only touching the lifeless figure, but slipping his fingers inside Oliphant's shirt collar. With thumb and forefinger he yanked a gold chain from around the man's neck. The lantern's coppery glow danced across a medallion's gold surface.

"More than likely stolen," she surmised, wondering why Graham studied the piece so intently. What could it matter now? She wanted only to hurry to the house and secure the well-being of the child who had the other day claimed her forefinger with such enthusiasm.

His eyes narrowed and thoughtful, Graham pushed to his feet. "Moira, you go get little Michael. I need to speak with the inspector."

"I'll take you up to the house, ma'am." The farmer held the barn door open for her. Moira followed him, her steps quickening as the crowd outside once more grew silent.

♥ ♥ ♥

As the carriage rumbled west toward London, Graham thought about the first time he'd laid eyes on Moira in Smythe's office. He had found her stunning, a dazzling beauty. That Moira, he realized, had been but a shadow of the woman before him now—Moira with a baby in her arms. She was positively radiant, glowing, transformed by an instantaneous love given wholly without conditions, reservations, or regrets.

To their infinite relief, the child had suffered minimal injuries. A slightly raised bump on the forehead, a scrape across the knee. Nothing else of note. Almost as if he had slid out of the rolling coach into some waiting angel's arms.

He appeared now to be sleeping, his pink cheek a tender bulge on Moira's shoulder, his fingers tangled in a web of ebony hair he'd worked loose from beneath her bonnet. The serenity on Moira's face, leaning ever so gently atop the child's downy head, made Graham believe wholeheartedly that Michael had found a second angel this day.

Alone on the opposite seat, he couldn't help feeling the odd man out, an observer but not quite a participant in their intimate crush.

Could he change that? It would take more than words to convince her he'd changed these past weeks; more than promises, which could be, after all, so easily broken. Inside his coat pocket his fingers tightened around a single hope. Mr. Parker had stayed behind at the farmhouse to await the arrival of the other victims' families. Graham would meet him later at the Bow Street office to discuss a new development.

He stole another glance at Moira to discover her watching him.

She cleared her throat. "I've decided. . .that is, I'd like your permission to take Michael home to Monteith Hall."

"You don't need my permission. Monteith is your home, too." Good God, they suddenly sounded like polite acquaintances, not at all like two people who'd shared adventures, dangers, and intimacy of the closest kind. He wanted to move beside her, ached to encircle both her and Michael in his arms. He released a breath. "What will you tell your mother?"

"I haven't quite decided yet." Her mouth plumped to a rueful half smile. "Not the truth. At least not all of it."

"I'm sure you'll think of something. But as far as Monteith is concerned, you may bring there whomever you wish, whenever you wish."

"Actually, I thought I might also suggest your brother and sister accompany us. I think it would do them both worlds of good to be away from London for a time."

"I've no doubt you're right. But tell me, am I welcome, as well?"

Her gaze strayed to the open window. "Monteith is yours."

He regarded her another moment before taking her cue and feigning fascination in the greenery streaming by outside. *Have it your way, my dear. Protect yourself if you must, but someday soon you might see there is nothing to protect yourself from.*

When they reached Brook Street, a waiting footman admitted them into the cool but welcome shadows of the front hall. The house lay quiet, but not for long.

"Great good heavens, what *have* we here?" Letty leaned precariously over the upper gallery rail, craning her neck. Then she started down the steps. "Why, I suppose that must be. . ."

"It is." Moira's upturned face beamed above the baby's golden head. "This is Michael."

"Oh, he's *lovely*." Letty quickened her descent.

"But in need of changing, I'm afraid. Perhaps Mrs. Higgensworth might be imposed upon to provide us some cotton fabric." Moira pulled a face. "After having him in my lap for more than an hour, I fear I'm in need of a fresh frock, as well."

Her pronouncement stopped Letty's descent several steps shy of the landing. "Oh. *Ick.*"

"One of the hazards of young children." Moira chuckled, a light, airy sound that touched a cord inside Graham. He resisted the urge to gather her in his arms as she added, "Nothing a good soak in the laundry tub won't set to rights."

Letty touched a finger to the baby's dimpled wrist as

if he were made of fine porcelain. The child contemplated her in return, blue eyes wide and staring, one hand fisted securely around the collar of Moira's carriage jacket.

"So you found them," Letty said, a note of awe in her voice. "Was there a *frightful* row? Did the Oliphants resist? Were *pistols* drawn?"

"What have you been reading lately, little sister?" Graham shucked one of her curls. "American cowboy novels?"

A huff formed her answer.

Leaving the ladies to tend the baby, he retired to his suite to change his clothes, eager to rid himself of the stench of barn and blood and tragedy. Piers Oliphant, perhaps, had met his just end. He wondered about the sister. Had she followed her brother willingly? Been aware of his crimes? Living as she had been off Butcher's Row on the Strand, had she even understood the extent of the inheritance that should have seen her settled in far more hospitable surroundings?

So far he had learned from Mrs. Higgensworth that Susan Oliphant never worked here in Everett Foster's London home. Moira confirmed the woman had never been employed at Monteith Hall, either. So if she had not been one of Everett's maids, how had a liaison between a nobleman and a poor commoner begun?

These were questions that, with a little luck and prodding, he intended to answer before the passing of many more days.

Leaving his bedroom in a fresh suit of clothes, he was confronted by the sound of voices surging from the drawing room in a manner most peculiar to this house. The sheer volume took him aback, then raised his concern. Had something happened, some emergency? Was little Michael all right?

Then, heading in that direction, he understood. These were not the sounds of a crisis, but the sort of din created by people talking over one another, offering unasked-for observations, forgetting to be polite.

This, he realized, was the clamor of *family*.

He discovered them all—his mother, brother, and sister, Moira, Shaun, and baby Michael—gathered in the drawing room. Despite the room's ample seating, the adults sat, sprawled, or lay propped on elbows on the floor between the furnishings. Looking remarkably contented among so many strangers, Michael stood teetering against the sofa table, banging the flat of his hand on its painted surface before stretching the other in pursuit of a brass candlestick.

Freddy snatched the sought-after item with barely a second to spare and deposited it onto an end table behind him. "You'll knock someone out with that. Me, more than likely."

Seeing his treasure whisked out of reach, Michael skewed up his features in preparation of howling, an eventuality forestalled by Letty thrusting a small, clothbound book into his hands. "Just don't eat it," she advised.

"Come here, little one." Their mother eased the boy into her lap. He went willingly, apparently far too interested in flipping the pages of his book to spare a thought for where he sat or who held him.

"I do hope he doesn't tear the pages." Thus far Moira had been quieter than the rest. Watching the baby intently, she seemed thoughtful, preoccupied.

"Never mind." Augusta ran her fingers through Michael's blond wisps. "We've books aplenty in this house. Don't we, little one? Don't we, don't we, yes, we do. . ."

Bouncing the baby in her lap, Augusta made a cadence of *yes, we do, oh, yes, we do. . .*

It sent Graham's memories tumbling back some nineteen years, to a time before things had gone so damnably wrong, when the twins were adorable imps and Augusta Foster a happy young mother whose greatest quandary lay in her newborns having pet names that rhymed in the most undignified manner.

"Such a sorrowful shame about your friends, Moira," she said now. "Too young to be so tragically cut down, and leaving this darling boy orphaned."

Graham had wondered what to tell his mother about Michael, but it seemed Moira had already taken care of the explanations.

"My heart positively breaks for them." Augusta dabbed at a tear, real or imagined, and happened to glance up. "Monteith, why ever are you hovering in the doorway? Do come in and help entertain our guest."

Shaun twisted round to regard him. "A capital little fellow, this one."

Graham strolled to the outskirts of the group but remained standing. Somehow, coming closer simply didn't make him part of the group, not in the essential way he would have liked. But there existed an issue between him and every person present—Freddy, Letty, his mother, and now Moira, too. Even Shaun had taken a swing at him just the other day. Only Michael seemed to bear no grudge. The boy raised his pink little face and made saliva bubbles at him.

Using the sofa table for leverage, the baby pulled out of Augusta's lap and toddled to where Freddy lay stretched across the carpet, propped on his elbows. Michael released the table and collapsed across Freddy's shoulders with a gleeful yelp.

"*Ooof.* I suppose you want a ride, then. Is that it?" Freddy peered over his shoulder at the boy draped across his back. Michael let out a happy squeal.

That incited cheers from the others and cries of *giddyap, Freddy.* As Letty grasped Michael's tiny hands to stand him upright, Graham stole the opportunity to note the changes in his brother: the restored color in his face, the easy laughter, the fresh shave. He wore a crisp suit of clothes, albeit he'd shed his coat and his waistcoat lay unbuttoned. Far from the derelict state in which they'd found him two days ago, Freddy now seemed very much a gentleman in a fit state of health.

But however much Graham might wish it, he doubted Freddy's troubles were over.

Rising up on hands and knees, Freddy caught Graham staring. The comical grin faded beneath gathered brows and eyes narrowed in speculation. Graham's neck prickled. Was Freddy remembering their one-sided conversation last night? Would his brother toss his furtive apologies back in his face? Declare his regrets too little, too late? At Freddy's age, that's what he would have done. What he *had* done, when he abandoned England for Africa.

Freddy's gaze angled away. "Hop on, Michael, my boy, and away we'll gallop."

"Don't be ridiculous," Letty scolded. "He'll topple off."

"So hold him."

"Oh, but he might need changing. Mama, you check."

Augusta reached over and gave the baby's bottom a pat. "Dry as an autumn leaf, dear."

"Come along, then." Freddy bounced on his palms as though bucking. "The pony can't wait around all day."

Letty lifted the child and set him on her twin's back, and Freddy proceeded to approximate a pace as close to a gallop as hands, bent knees, and Letty's encroaching skirts would allow. Laughter came first in bubbles and then shrieks as Michael warmed to his ride.

When Letty's feet nearly tangled with Freddy's legs, Shaun jumped up to relieve her of her duties. Augusta and Moira, meanwhile, shouted cautions concerning tables, lamps, and a prized Sevres vase.

After some minutes, a panting Freddy stopped and reared, allowing Shaun to swing the child from his back and nestle him in Moira's skirts. With a groan Freddy reassumed his human posture and made his way to Graham's side. Too quietly for the others to hear above the baby's gurgling and their own cooing, he said, "Thanks for getting me out of that place. And for not raising a fuss."

Graham's astonishment was coupled with an indescribable surge of relief. Gratitude. Optimism. All of those and more. He held his brother in his gaze. "You're welcome."

"Been a bit of an ass lately."

"I know. I'm sorry."

Freddy's lip curled. "No, I meant me."

"Oh. Yes, well, me, too, I suppose."

Freddy responded with a slight shrug and a wisp of a grin before swinging into a nearby chair. That was all, but Graham counted it a huge stride forward.

With the abruptness of a lamp sputtering for want of fuel, Michael began yawning and pushing away the neck cloth Shaun had twisted and tied to resemble a dove. Augusta declared it nap time, scooped the boy up, and bustled off with Letty to prepare a place for him to sleep. Moira rose to follow, but lingered, and approached Graham.

He knew an instant's elation that she would seek him out.

"Do you see a resemblance at all?" she murmured.

Elation dimmed to disappointment. He set it aside. A quirk in her brow suggested her thoughts were troubling ones, deeply so. "To Everett, you mean?"

She nodded. "I keep looking for it. In the hair color, eye color, the shape of the chin, the ears. . ." Here she smiled faintly, then just as quickly sobered. "I simply find none."

"It's difficult to say. I didn't know Everett well."

"He was dark-haired with hazel eyes. And his ears. . .they were rather large, and one stuck out more than the other." She sighed, shaking her head at her own observations. "Perhaps the resemblance is there in those sweet little features, and I simply refuse to see it."

"Or the boy takes after his mother's side."

"He looks nothing like his uncle, thank goodness."

Before Graham could affirm the sentiment, she excused herself and left the room.

He turned to Shaun, reclining now on a settee. "How did Letty do on the sketch of Piers?"

"First rate. Quite a talent, that sister of yours."

"Do you think if the two of you put your heads together, you might also make a sketch of Susan Oliphant?"

Shaun considered. "I don't believe your sister ever met the woman, but perhaps if I described her in detail, we might produce a tolerable likeness. Perhaps Miss Hughes can help."

"Why do you need a picture of Susan Oliphant?"

Freddy pushed to his feet and began buttoning his waistcoat. "She can neither tell us anything new, nor come to any more mischief."

"True. But I want to know where this woman came from and how the devil she entered Everett Foster's life. I've a growing hunch about her, and I need to find some answers."

"Care to enlighten us?"

"No, Shaun, not yet. See what you and Letty can accomplish. In the meantime, I'm going to pay a visit to Mr. Stuart Davis, of Smythe and Davis, Legal Consultants."

He started across the room, but movement at the corner of his vision brought him to an uncertain halt. Freddy had ambled to the brandy cart. He stood before it, his gaze pinned on a crystal decanter. As Graham watched, hoping for any outcome but the one he dreaded, Freddy's hand curled around the cut-glass stopper. His palm cupped it a long moment. The stopper clinked as it slid free. Graham held his breath.

Don't, Freddy.

A quick glance confirmed that Shaun was watching, too. Graham snatched at the first idea that entered his mind. "Freddy, want to come along?"

Stopper in hand, his brother slowly turned. "Trying to keep me out of my cups?"

"I thought you might wish to get out of the house."

His thin lie raised a chuckle. "You know you can't

keep an eye on me all the time."

"I don't intend to."

Freddy squinted down at the stopper, running his thumb over its facets. "Can't make any promises."

"No one's asking for any."

His brother nodded and slipped the stopper back into the decanter's neck. "At least I won't likely puke in the carriage again."

CHAPTER
22

Graham was minding his distance. Respecting her wishes. Keeping his hands to himself.

Moira should have been grateful. Relieved.

So why, then, did she feel this oppressive disappointment? This illogical resentment. Not to mention the desire to demand how his acceptance of her newly established boundaries could be so swift and so complete. Were his feelings for her as fragile as all that? Or was she the fragile one, demanding distance while in her heart of hearts she wanted—yearned for—just the opposite.

But, no. Her yearnings only led her into trouble, made her believe in things that weren't true. Made her forget who and what she was. Moira Hughes, daughter of the Reverend John Hughes, who died many years ago. Yes, John Hughes, a man she never truly knew nor had any memory of, had been her father. Not Everett Foster, a man she had loved so much.

So very much. And who had betrayed her so utterly. The notion awakened demons, ones that chanted the word *fool*, that. . .

Stop. Breathe. Do *not* cry.

There.

She smoothed her skirts, tidied her hair, and lifted Michael from the blanket she'd spread out on the floor for him to play on. His cradle occupied a corner of her bedroom, and the trunk beside it held baby clothes retrieved from many years' storage in the attic.

Together they set out for the morning room, Michael happily humming and blowing through his lips while Moira's thoughts scurried against her will to Graham.

It was a fortunate development, really; he'd suddenly found much to occupy his time. This morning he had again included his brother in his mysterious errands, a fact from which she derived considerable satisfaction. She had, after all, set out to mend the rifts in this tattered family.

Still. . .

She'd like to know what he was up to. Mr. Paddington had no inkling, surely, or she and Letty would have coaxed the information out of him last night while piecing together another sketch, this time of Susan Oliphant. Even Letty's most coquettish inquiries had failed to draw particulars from Mr. Paddington, leading Moira to conclude his ignorance was sincere.

"I do wish the men would get over their need to be so hush-hush about everything," she said to Letty as she placed Michael in the younger woman's lap. She poured a cup of coffee and took a seat beside them at the breakfast table.

"If you're so eager to know what they're doing, why don't you simply *ask*?" Leaning back in her chair, Letty stood Michael on her thighs and shook her curls at him.

The child responded with a delighted squeal. He snatched one golden brown corkscrew and tugged.

"Ouch!" Letty's head snapped forward. "Oh, *do* let go! No, *don't* yank. Moira, *help!*"

Suppressing a chuckle, Moira set down her coffee cup. "There, there, Michael, you're hurting poor Auntie Letitia."

Using nonsense words to distract him, she gently unclenched his tiny yet determined fingers one by one, a task that proved more difficult than she had imagined. Letty groaned while angling her head to relieve the pressure of the child's grasp.

"If you don't want him tugging your hair, dear, you should wear it up as I have today. I learned my lesson on the carriage ride home yesterday." Ignoring Letty's pout, Moira bit her lip to hide a grin. "Oh, and your earbobs. He's sure to find them as tempting as your curls. There now, you're free as a bird."

"Here, you take him while I finish my breakfast." Letty lifted the boy into Moira's arms. "He's a positive *danger* to civilized society. Besides, I believe he needs changing."

"He seems dry to me."

"I believe I detected a whiff of. . .the *other*." Letty wrinkled her nose.

Moira sniffed at the air. "Oh, I believe you're right. Come along, then, little one." She paused in the doorway. "Do you want to come? To learn how, I mean."

"Whatever for?"

"Someday you'll have children of your own. What do you intend to do then?"

"Why, instruct their nurse to do it, of *course*."

Graham arrived home to find Moira below stairs in the scullery. She had Michael lying on a linen towel on the work counter beside the washbasin, and was just then securing a fresh changing cloth around him. She sat the baby up and slipped a gown over his head.

"Letty told me I'd find you here," he said, leaning in the archway and enjoying the sight of Moira fussing over the boy, smoothing the gown's embroidered front and straightening the gathered sleeves. Michael, meanwhile, found entertainment in trying to snatch the silver bracelet dangling from her wrist.

"You're back sooner than expected." She lifted Michael from the counter and settled him on her hip.

Graham merely nodded, disinclined to reveal the reason why and hoping she wouldn't press for an explanation. To change the subject, he said, "Teaching

Michael to wash pots and pans?"

She acknowledged the jest with a small shrug. "The scullery is the easiest and quickest place to change and bathe him. I don't like asking the servants to haul bathwater upstairs each time."

"I daresay you remember all too well what it was like hauling heavy burdens up and down those stairs."

A blush rose at this reference to her masquerade as a servant. He strode closer, boots loud on the wide board flooring. Michael babbled in greeting, thrusting a little hand toward him. Graham offered a forefinger, experiencing a tug in his chest when fingers nearly as delicate as Isis's legs closed around his.

"Your mother said both you and Freddy wore this gown," Moira said. She used her free hand to gather up the linen towel and crumple it into a ball. With a faint smile she regarded Graham from head to toe. "Difficult to imagine."

"Difficult to imagine me this small or compliant enough to endure such ridiculous frills?"

"Both."

He grinned. Some impulse prompted him to reach for Michael. Perhaps it was the effect the child had on Moira, the way she glowed from the inside out whenever she held him. Would he experience the same transformation?

Or would Michael squall and twist and push away? One never knew with babies. But as Moira held him out,

Michael leaned forward and went willingly, one might even say happily, into Graham's arms. He even slid an arm around Graham's neck.

Such a slender arm, so slight and helpless. Indeed, it didn't spread a glow through him at all. It frightened him, made him feel huge and oafish and dangerously powerful in comparison.

What a perplexing challenge it presented, holding a baby securely but gently enough not to hurt him. And yet women—Moira, certainly—accomplished the feat with no apparent effort.

With a few awkward shifts, he managed to tuck Michael snugly against him. The lad made gurgling noises and fisted his free hand in Graham's neck cloth. His air passages constricted.

"He's certainly a playful fellow," he rasped, trying in vain to coax Michael's hand away from his cravat.

"Yes. I find myself wondering why he doesn't cry." She combed her fingers through wisps of wheat blond hair. "Doesn't he miss his mother? Shouldn't he raise a fuss to be surrounded by so many strangers?"

"Perhaps he's too young to understand the difference." Michael finally released his grip, and Graham filled his lungs.

"Or perhaps he doesn't miss his home because it hadn't been a happy one. I laid awake last night for the longest time while fretting over the trials of his short life."

You might have awakened me, Moira. I'd have sat up worrying with you, if you had let me.

"He seems much thinner than a baby should be," she went on, oblivious to his broodings. "And that awful flat they lived in. Oh, Graham, the walls were nearly black with soot and damp. I hope it hasn't affected his health."

She leaned in closer to press a kiss to Michael's forehead, and Graham found himself immersed in her warm, sensual scent. It triggered a maelstrom of sensations merely days old, yet powerful enough to fill him with a painful yearning to kiss her, to gather her to his chest along with Michael and create. . .blazing hell. . .a family. A wholly new one where none had existed before.

But she wouldn't have him. Wouldn't take the risk.

For now.

Carefully he hugged Michael closer and forced his voice past a wretched constriction that had nothing to do with his neck cloth. "It was a happy day for this child when you entered his life."

That radiant light flared again in her eyes before her gaze dipped. "He looks tired. Time for his nap."

She took the baby from his arms and started past, leaving a cold and hollow sensation where the child had been. But that empty chill helped clear his mind and restore his focus. He had business to tend to, business that involved Moira.

He trailed her across the scullery and through the kitchen. "While he's sleeping, we have an errand."

She turned, looking startled and not a little puzzled.

"Mr. Parker requested we meet him at his office this

afternoon. I suppose he has a few more questions for us before wrapping up the case." With raised eyebrows he affected innocence and hoped she'd forgive this small white lie. They *would* be meeting Parker, just not on Bow Street or for the reason he told her.

"I fear there will be no 'wrapping up' of this case." She gave a sad shake of her head. They started up the stairs, the rhythm of their steps echoed by an enthusiastic *bah, mah, gah, mah!* from Michael. Moira bounced him in her arms and sighed. "We'll never know the truth, not with Piers Oliphant and his sister gone."

Of its own volition, and whether she wished it or no, Graham's arm snaked round her waist. "You mustn't give up hope. Who can say what might turn up?"

CHAPTER
23

T he bishop is not receiving at present."

"Then please inform him that we'll call again at a more convenient time." But when Moira turned to descend the steps and return to the coach, Graham simultaneously caught her hand and shoved a foot in the threshold, preventing the bishop's footman from shutting the door.

"Tell him it's urgent."

"Graham, *please*. Uncle Benedict isn't expecting us. It's rude to keep insisting." Moira tried to tug him away.

His features stony, he showed no signs of yielding.

"He cannot be disturbed, sir." The footman maintained an outward show of patience, much more than Moira presently felt.

"Tell him it's a life-and-death matter."

"Graham, you know perfectly well—"

"Just tell him that." He pulled to his full and quite

considerable height, towering over the footman's shorter, slighter frame.

"What in the world are you doing?" she hissed after the servant reluctantly ushered them into the sparsely and uncomfortably furnished waiting room off the foyer. "Have you the faintest notion how ill-mannered you're being?"

"Your mother asked you to deliver her letter, didn't she? And I know you've been carrying it around in your purse since we left Monteith. I glimpsed it in there just this morning."

"Graham Foster, I don't for one moment believe this has anything whatsoever to do with Mother's letter. We're supposed to be meeting Miles Parker on Bow Street. Why are we here? I want the truth. And don't you dare flash those dimples at me."

"You like my dimples, don't you, Moira? I never did particularly, until I noticed that little shivery thing you do whenever you see them."

"Oh, of all the. . ." Her heels raised a loud clacking on the marble floor as she retreated across the room, which suddenly felt much too small for the two of them. She turned and faced him, wishing she could put more space between them, yet realizing the futility of doing so. No distance could diminish the vigor that sped her pulse, the passion that left her aching and weak-kneed. The quivery sensation he'd spoken of hid behind a decidedly forced show of bravado. "What are you up to?"

"Moira, Moira." He tilted his head and regarded her through half-closed lids, a leisurely perusal that left her senses tingling. "I must entreat your patience for the next, oh. . ." He consulted his pocket watch. "Thirty-odd minutes."

His mood had changed considerably since leaving home. He'd been so sweet and clumsy with Michael, hardly the brash cavalier she'd come to know. But that devil-may-care arrogance had since resurfaced, and it set her on her guard. "And what in return for my thirty minutes? Sarcasm? Evasiveness?"

"Dimples?" She glared at him, and his expression sobered. "Moira, trust me. I promise this will all—"

"The bishop will see you now," the footman announced from the doorway.

Graham flashed a triumphant grin and yes, his deeply entrenched dimples, before following the servant into the hall. At the foot of the stairs, however, he balked.

The servant cast a curious glance over his shoulder. "His lordship is upstairs in his study, sir."

"We'd prefer to meet with him in his drawing room."

"I'm afraid I don't understand, sir."

"Now what on earth are you doing?" In her astonishment she didn't even bother whispering.

"In the drawing room," Graham repeated, and strode across the hall. "Explain to the bishop that the sooner he meets with us in his drawing room, the sooner we shall leave him to his private pursuits."

With a scowl of utter bafflement, the footman climbed the stairs. Her own features taut with a similar emotion, Moira hurried to follow Graham and tell him precisely what she thought of his behavior.

"You are impossible, incorrigible, intractable—"

"Yes, Moira, it's what you love about me."

Oh, he made her so angry she couldn't help stomping her foot. "Why must you always tease when you know—"

"You haven't the faintest inkling what I know." His smile vanished, and he came at her in a rush of motion, a sudden squall blown by a dangerous wind. Even as she backed away, he reached her, gripped her shoulders, and gave a little shake.

"You've convinced yourself of what must be true. I am a blackguard, cannot be trusted, will hurt you if given the chance." Though quiet, the words were raw, dagger-sharp. "But see here, my darling, dazzling Moira. Even when you were willing to give up, I pressed on. I'm still fighting for you. Whether you wish it or not."

She was trembling in his grip and fighting the sting of tears whose source she didn't fully comprehend. Outrage? Fear? Of what? The storm in his features. . .or losing him?

The faltering approach of footsteps broke them apart, sent her scurrying to the window to dab at her eyes.

"Why, Moira, my dear, Barryman should have told

me immediately that it was you calling. I'd never have kept you waiting so long had I known."

As she turned to face Uncle Benedict, Graham stepped between them. "No, I imagine I'm the reason you weren't receiving. Our reunion is long overdue, my lord. It's a pleasure to see you again."

"Indeed." Uncle Benedict fingered his cravat, tied loosely around the slack skin of his neck.

An awkward silence fell as the two men regarded each other. Moira opened her reticule and found her mother's letter. "This is for you, Uncle Benedict. From Mother."

"A letter from Estella? How delightful." His pudgy hand gripped the missive. "Nearly as delightful as a visit from Estella herself." He slipped a finger beneath the seal and fished a pair of spectacles from his waistcoat pocket. "A note of congratulations. Isn't she thoughtful?"

"I'd like to add my congratulations, as well." The lightheartedness had returned to Graham's voice, underscored with a razor's edge. Moira tensed, wondering what he was about. "It will be a pleasure working with you in the House of Lords."

"Then you've claimed the Monteith seat?" The bishop's gaze darted to Moira, then slid back to Graham.

"I intend to shortly."

Her breath caught. Did claiming his seat mean he planned to remain in England and shoulder the responsibilities of his rank? Did he suddenly believe in duty and commitment and the principles of authority? Perhaps, but then many an English lord staked his claim only to spend the next many years abroad.

"Since we will be working toward the same ends from now on, my lord," Graham continued, "I thought it time to let bygones be bygones. If you're amenable, that is."

Moira felt a burst of hope. Dared she believe in the sincerity of his overture? Was that why they'd come?

For a long moment the bishop stared as if confronted by a spectacle beyond his comprehension. Then a tentative smile etched deep folds around his eyes and mouth. "Why don't we all sit down and be comfortable. I shall ring for refreshments."

"Splendid idea." Graham winked at Moira as he strode past, heading for a settee near an open window.

She chose an armchair opposite, where she might keep an eye on him, not that it would do her a smidgen of good. She'd held no sway over his erratic conduct thus far, and saw little chance of achieving any now.

After ringing for tea, Uncle Benedict waddled across the room, making his way to the chair beside Moira's on the other side of a small oval table.

"My lord, I've brought you something to commemorate your considerable achievements." Though affable, Graham's tone held a baiting quality that set Moira's nape prickling. She sat rigid in her chair and waited.

"A gift?" The elderly man clapped his hands softly.

"Good heavens, lad, you needn't have."

"Ah, but I did." He reached into his coat pocket.

Moira gasped. In his palm lay the pendant he'd taken from around Piers Oliphant's neck. In the sunlit drawing room, the embossed image of a coiling snake flashed liquid fire.

Beside her came a wheezing breath. Uncle Benedict's face drained of color as he gaped at the ornament.

"I apologize," Graham said mildly. "What I should have said is that I wish to *return* a gift to you. For I've given it once before, haven't I?"

"I. . .I have no idea what you're talking about." The bishop's hands convulsed around the chair's armrests.

"No, I don't suppose you realized it was from me the first time. It came signed by the English consulate in Egypt, thanking you for your contribution to the King George Museum of Art and Antiquities in Cairo." Graham swung the pendant by its chain and gave a laugh. "I must say, Shaun did a first-rate job on the signature and seal."

"Uncle Benedict, is this true?" Moira swallowed against a sensation akin to hands gripping her throat. "Does the piece belong to you?"

"Shaun will certainly attest to my having sent it," Graham answered for him.

"Now that you mention it, I vaguely remember receiving such a gift." The elderly man shifted his weight in his chair. "Years ago. I barely recall the circumstances.

Such an outlandish trinket. I put it away and never gave it another thought."

"But you do recall your donation to the museum?" Graham spoke with deceptive calm, as though trading pleasant reminiscences with an infirm but esteemed acquaintance. "Ironic, isn't it, both of us supporting the same institution after you very nearly destroyed my future in the field of antiquities. But who knew the events at Oxford would lead me to acclaim and fortune? The way things have turned out, I'm more than willing to forgive you for the past."

"*You* forgive *me*?" The bishop's face darkened to a worrisome scarlet. "Of all the gall."

Moira had no wish to become entangled in the old feud, but she nonetheless burned to understand a very immediate puzzle. "Uncle Benedict, how on earth did Piers Oliphant come to possess that pendant?"

"I couldn't say. I'm acquainted with no such man."

"Oh, but you are, Uncle." Understanding his mistake, she reached to press a reassuring hand over his. "He worked for Mr. Smythe under an assumed name. Oliver Pierson."

"Ah, yes, Pierson. The clerk." His hands relaxed on the chair's arms. "That explains it, doesn't it? The man had access to my home on more than one occasion. He obviously came upon the pendant and stole it."

"Are you always in the habit of leaving your jewelry lying about the public rooms of the house?" Graham made an exaggerated show of glancing at nearby tabletops. "I don't see any now, although for a man bent on thievery, that gilded snuffbox would serve nicely."

"I haven't an inkling where or how he found it."

"No? I certainly understand his reasons for wanting this pendant. Melted down, the gold would bring him more than he'd earn in months. But then why was he wearing it? Why hadn't he sold it?" Graham shook his head, smiling faintly. "My guess is, he didn't steal it at all. He had no reason to steal it because you gave it to him."

"For what possible reason?" The bishop's words were measured, quietly challenging.

"To seal a bargain, perhaps?" Graham rose from the settee and drifted to the open window.

Moira suddenly felt like a spectator at an exceedingly tense tennis match and uncertain whom she wished to prevail. The bishop had been an uncle to her nearly all her life. But Graham. . . Despite his abominable behavior, she hoped—believed in her bones—his reasons for doing this were admirable ones. Surely his intentions were worthy, even if his judgment showed a want of prudence.

"I've had business dealings with Smythe and Davis for a good twenty years," Uncle Benedict asserted, "but I've never spoken more than a dozen words to their clerk."

Graham turned from his perusal of the gardens. "What can you tell us about his sister, Susan Oliphant?"

"I've never met any such woman."

Moira winced at the abruptness of the reply.

"Really?" Graham smoothed his fingers along a billowing edge of curtain. "I'm told she worked here."

Moira lurched forward in her chair. "Susan Oliphant worked here? How long have you known this? Why didn't you tell me?" Her gaze darted to Uncle Benedict. "If Susan worked here, then surely you must have known her brother's identity."

Her uncle held out his hands. "How would I know the name of every maid who ever worked here? Perhaps my steward can help you. He does the hiring. But what difference does any of this make?"

"It makes a bloody great deal of difference." Graham sauntered to the back of the settee and leaned his hands on its mahogany frame. "I keep asking myself why a man would commit murder over an inheritance rightfully belonging to his nephew. It doesn't follow. But if the inheritance were wrongfully bestowed upon the nephew. . ." He raised a hand, forefinger aimed at Uncle Benedict. "There's the motive. Inheritance fraud might certainly drive a man to kill, especially if his nasty secret was in danger of being discovered."

"Surely you're not suggesting Uncle Benedict had anything to do with—"

"I'll explain everything, Moira, if you think you can bear one more disappointment in your life."

His words chilled her; she made no reply.

He held her gaze steadily, relentlessly. "Once I realized what questions to ask, and where to ask them, the facts began falling into place." He offered a grim smile, one that barely raised his dimples. "Shaun gave me some advice he learned from you. Question the servants." The smile vanished and he shot pure, naked contempt at the bishop. "Aren't you wondering why the maid hasn't come yet with the refreshments?"

With an agitated twitch, Uncle Benedict twisted around to view the drawing room's vacant entrance.

"Miss Briggs no longer works for you. She and I both knew you'd dismiss her if she told the truth, so I saw no choice but to offer her employment in my home." He again regarded Moira, his disdain melting to concern and regret. "I learned from Miss Briggs that Susan worked here as a maid for more than a year. Piers served as Benedict's secretary during that time, until his sister very suddenly left. Then Piers moved on as well, though he didn't go far, as we know."

"A brother and sister worked in my home for a short time." Defiance shaped the bishop's otherwise indistinct chin. "What of it?"

"Stuart Davis, of Smythe and Davis, Legal Consultants, told me yesterday that he hired Oliver Pierson on your recommendation. Moreover, he can conceive of no reason why Pierson might have visited your home last week. He maintains there were no documents that needed signing or delivering."

"I sent for Pierson. I needed to convey a legal matter to Smythe. But then he died."

"Yes. Conveniently."

"Are you insinuating that I conspired to have him killed?" He turned wide-eyed indignation on Moira. "You know the kind of life I've led. Surely you can't believe these accusations."

Did she? She had known the bishop most of her life. He'd been her stepfather's closest friend. She had never, ever found reason to distrust him. And yet. . .

The silence stretched as her focus settled on Graham and saw him—truly saw him—for the first time that day, without her own disappointments or sheer exasperation coloring her perceptions.

His earlier activities, whatever they were, had left him looking disheveled and wind-tossed, his gold-tipped hair tousled and his clothing rumpled. How beautiful he was, how spontaneous and dashing and cavalier. How easily she could imagine him riding the deck of a ship at full sail, slicing over brisk ocean waves. That was his life and where he belonged, heading for exotic, sun-drenched locales she would never see, and from which he might never return.

"Please don't continue with this," she said, the words raw and stinging. She spoke without looking at Graham, afraid to. Afraid to acknowledge that he was everything she could love in a man, and everything she was afraid of loving. She clung to the meager world she had known before he entered it. "Uncle Benedict is a man of God and a peer. Your accusations make no sense."

"There is sense, Moira, I promise. Miss Briggs provided me with the final detail that brought order to chaos. It concerns an incident that occurred last summer, when your stepfather spent a night here as the bishop's guest."

Benedict emitted a snort. "Am I to be branded for my hospitality?"

"Let me finish. According to Miss Briggs, Everett passed out at the table, and it took two footmen to convey him to a guest room. Moira, was your stepfather in the habit of overindulging?"

"No. Not once have I ever seen him inebriated."

"I thought not. Yet that night he became so deep in his cups he lost consciousness. And shortly after, Susan Oliphant left her position here, very much with child."

"Everett didn't know what he was doing that night." Defensiveness lent a tremor to Uncle Benedict's voice. "Forgive me for saying it, Moira, but he obviously took Miss Oliphant into his bed."

"While he was so deep in his cups, he landed face first in his supper plate?" Graham tsked. "It would have been rather difficult to perform, if you'll forgive me for being blunt. And let us consider the dates of these occurrences."

He came around the settee and paced the carpet as he ticked off the facts on his fingers, reminding Moira of Inspector Parker's brisk manner. "Miss Briggs told me the night in question occurred in early summer. She remembers clearly because Everett had a weakness for gooseberry pie, and she'd been able to find fresh gooseberries at market that day for the first time that season. As you know, the first crop isn't available until June. Now, according to Mrs. Higgensworth, Michael was born in January." He came to a halt. "That makes seven months. Doesn't add up, does it?"

Benedict shrugged. "Many a child comes early."

"True." Graham nodded. "But few of them survive. And though rather thin, this child doesn't appear particularly small for his age. In fact, he's all but walking even now."

"Then you mean Michael isn't. . ." Heart lashing beneath her breast, Moira pushed to her feet.

"Indeed not, Moira. It's highly unlikely that Michael is Everett's son. And extremely likely he's *this* man's son. I'd stake my life on it." Upper lip curling, Graham aimed a finger at the bishop. "Somehow the old cobra orchestrated a scenario that convinced your stepfather Michael was his. What did you do, old man, slip Susan into Everett's bed while he slumbered unaware, then have her tell him some wide-eyed lie in the morning?"

Feeling light-headed, sickened, she clamped a shaking hand to her mouth. Graham was at her side in an instant with an arm about her waist to support her. "I'm sorry, darling. I know this hurts, but I thought the truth would sting less than the falsehood."

She forced her gaze to the bishop's face. "Is it true?"

"He's grasping at straws in order to impress you, my dear." The man's hands opened like a suppliant's. "Why would I do any such thing?"

"There's your answer, right there." Graham gestured to her mother's letter, bearing mute witness on the tabletop where Benedict had placed it. "Your seat in Parliament. You didn't dare risk a scandal."

"Ridiculous."

The protest, tendered a beat too late to resonate with truth, only fueled the anger fomenting inside Moira. Yet in the next instant, she realized it wasn't anything the bishop said or did, or even the newly revealed facts that made her certain of his guilt. Rather, it was the intensity in Graham's face, the grim earnestness, the utter lack of dimples. Only a burning truth could rob a cavalier so thoroughly of his arrogance.

Though an erratic panting threatened consciousness, she somehow gathered breath enough to speak. "Uncle Benedict, you'd never have been considered for the House of Lords had it become known you'd sired an illegitimate child on one of your own servants." Certainty propelled her toward him with the desire to strike, though she held her hands stiffly in the folds of her skirts. "You'd likely have lost your bishopric if Papa hadn't provided an easy escape."

"I've endured enough of this nonsense." The bishop heaved his bulk forward in preparation of gaining his feet. "I want you both to leave this instant."

"Not just yet." Graham dipped a hand carefully into his coat pocket—the opposite one from which he'd taken the pendant. Then he placed the same hand on Benedict's chest. "Don't move. Not so much as a muscle. If you do, she'll likely dart straight for your neck and sink her fangs into you."

"What the devil are you going on about?"

Both Moira and the bishop followed Graham's line of sight straight to where Isis sat twitching her pedipalps on the man's bulging waistcoat.

Benedict's arm jerked upward, but Graham caught his wrist before he could swat the spider away.

"Don't. A sudden movement may prompt her to leap. She'd very well land on your face or neck, and the bite would be instantaneous. Even for a man of your size, the poison would spread within minutes."

"By God, get her off me." Beneath the bristly line of his eyebrows, the bishop's eyes nearly crossed as he gawked at his chest. "She. . .she isn't truly poisonous. . .is she?"

"Yes, quite."

"Moira?" He sought her confirmation without moving, without so much as drawing a breath.

"I'm afraid she's very deadly, Uncle Benedict. I don't dare go near her."

The trembling man's gaze darted back to Graham. "Why didn't she bite you?"

"She knows my scent, knows I'm the hand that feeds her. Tell us the truth, and I'll remove her."

Benedict leaned as far back as the chair allowed, glazed eyes widening in horror as Isis ventured several steps across his stomach. A single word fled his lips. "Laudanum."

"You drugged Everett?"

The man nodded almost imperceptibly. Isis went still as if fascinated to hear the tale. "Laced his wine. Susan was several weeks along. Her brother found out and tried blackmailing me, but I'm not a wealthy man. This house and everything in it belongs to the bishopric. Oliphant threatened to destroy my career, everything I've worked for—"

"What a familiar story." Grasping Moira's hand, Graham calmly led her to the settee where they settled side by side as if awaiting tea and cake. He smiled at the bishop. "Do go on."

"I conceived a plan that would satisfy Oliphant and keep him quiet. Then—" The rest dissolved into a wheeze as Isis tapped his watch fob, each step as dainty as a ballerina's.

"And then months later," Moira finished, the words raising a bitter taste, "Papa accepted an illegitimate son born two months early."

At a half nod from the bishop, Graham pushed away from the settee and lowered his wrist to Isis. She readily clambered up. Benedict's relief rasped through lips gone pale, the upper one awash with perspiration.

Graham held Isis out to Moira. Without a moment's

hesitation, she took the spider in her cupped hands and transferred it carefully to her skirts. The bishop's reaction came in a grunt of indignation.

She shook her head at him in disgust. "Did you never once consider how your deceit would affect my mother and me? And poor Papa. He must have been devastated, believing he'd used that woman in a drunken stupor."

"At first he was. He dreaded your mother finding out." The man Moira knew as Uncle Benedict regarded her with the indifference of a stranger. "But the boy delighted him. He believed he'd fathered a son, his own natural child. He did love you, Moira, but you were another man's daughter. Not at all the same thing."

"No? Michael is yours. Your own flesh and blood, you cobra. And do you give a tinker's damn what happens to him?" Graham lurched toward Uncle Benedict, stopping short a pace away. "If you weren't a fat old man, I'd call you out."

"Graham." When he turned, Moira caught his gaze and held it. "Don't. He isn't worth your ire. He's pitiable."

Perversely, the old cleric smiled. "Pitiable? Why? Should either of you decide to gossip, no one will believe you. It will be the word of a respected bishop against that of a scoundrel who was expelled from university and fled the country in disgrace. People will term it a pathetic attempt at revenge and discount it."

"And what of my word?" Moira scooped Isis into

her palm and held her higher for the bishop's benefit.

He blanched but remained undeterred. "You? You're merely the poor young chit who threw herself at the scoundrel's head."

The assertion sent a flood of heat to her face but no words of denial to her lips.

"Not everyone will discount Lord Monteith's story."

She jumped at the sound of the male voice, neither Graham's nor Benedict's, but nonetheless familiar. Twisting around, she saw a black shoe and gray trouser leg appear through the open window, followed by the stooping figure of Miles Parker of Bow Street.

Once inside, he straightened his coat and tugged his lapels aright. "I'm fairly certain I won't be accused of harboring a motive for discrediting you, my lord."

Benedict's smug expression had turned to outrage. "Who the devil are you?"

"Uncle Benedict, this is Inspector Parker of the Bow Street Runners." Despite her calm reply, Moira felt utterly taken aback by Mr. Parker's sudden materialization. Ah, but not Graham, whose satisfied grin revealed the success of a well-laid plot.

"Forgive me for eavesdropping at your window," Mr. Parker said in his most polite tone, "but I've heard enough here today to warrant a formal inquiry into the matter."

"What matter?" The bishop took no pains to conceal his disdain. "I did nothing but convince a foolish man he fathered a child. I made Everett *happy*. And I certainly never forced him to leave the child a farthing."

"Perhaps not," Moira countered, "but I'll wager you were quick with the suggestion."

"And let's not forget the bishop's part in having Oliphant installed in Smythe's office," Graham interjected. "A convenient method of looking after both their interests."

"I never asked the man to commit murder." Benedict leaned heavily on the arms of his chair and heaved to his feet. "You can hardly blame me for his indiscretion."

"Then you're admitting your connection to Oliphant."

"I am admitting nothing."

Mr. Parker offered Moira a nod of greeting, then started to say something more when his eyes widened to saucers.

"It's all right, Mr. Parker, Isis is quite harmless," Moira assured him, and enjoyed the sight of Benedict's scowl.

Looking dubious, the inspector returned his attention to the bishop. "I have a theory about Wallace Smythe, my lord. I believe he knew of the fraud perpetrated on the late Lord Monteith and was willing to help you cover. Until, that is, Miss Hughes showed up with her quest for the truth. Perhaps his conscience began to nudge. Or perhaps he feared being implicated if the truth got out. Either way, Oliphant needed to silence him, or he'd lose access to the money wrongfully left to his nephew."

"What about Nigel?" Moira asked softly, her fingertip stroking the hairs on Isis's back.

"What *about* Nigel?" the bishop parroted with no small amount of sarcasm.

"It's my guess," Graham said, not to Moira or Benedict but to Mr. Parker, "that if we show my sister's sketches of Oliphant around the vicinity of Nigel Foster's death, someone might remember seeing him there."

"Poor Nigel." Moira sighed. "He must have discovered something suspicious when he came to London to secure his rights as Baron Monteith. Perhaps he began asking questions and. . ." The notion pricked her eyes until they throbbed. She buried her face in her hands. "Oh, Nigel."

"You'll never prove anything. Not even that Michael isn't Everett's son."

The bishop's assertion forced Moira's head up and dried the tears that had begun to brim. Her intended retort died unspoken, however, when Graham knelt in front of her and took her hand.

"Are you all right?" When she nodded, he regarded the bishop over his shoulder. "You may be correct. We might never prove a thing but, ah, the scandal. Your career shall likely never recover."

Benedict treated him to a sneer. "So after all these years, you finally have your revenge."

Graham gave a laugh. "Believe it or not, you old cobra, this has nothing whatsoever to do with revenge.

Nothing to do with you at all really. After today you'll no longer even exist for me." He turned back to Moira. His dimples flashed, and his smile conveyed a tenderness that stole her breath. "Everything I've done has been for one person only."

He brought her hand to his lips, holding it there a long moment. "All I've wanted was to convince you that Everett didn't betray you. The codicil was merely his way of meeting a responsibility he'd accepted. His actions were those of an honorable man, Moira, for at the time he believed your future, and your mother's, secure with Nigel."

He eased closer, blocking out the bishop, Mr. Parker, the room, everything but his bright ocean eyes and gold-tipped hair and reckless, devil-may-care spirit that had swept her off her feet from her very first glimpse of him. "Moira, darling, not all men stray. Not all disappoint."

Those last words shot forth in a whisper, fierce and adamant. Sincere. Her heart splintered—painfully—with the memory of each unfair charge she'd leveled upon him these past days, whether spoken aloud or merely thought.

"I'm sorry. So sorry. . ." The apology lodged in a blistering throat. She turned away, but he caught her chin and turned it gently to him.

"There are some men, an incredibly lucky few, who do realize the value of what they have. Or even. . .of what they don't have."

She leaned more fully into the warmth of his hand. "What a blazing coward I've been. . ."

"We're all cowards when it comes to our hearts. Me most of all." His thumb brushed across her sodden cheek. "I know I couched my feelings in jests and foolishness. I've said one thing when I've meant another. I was afraid, afraid to trust. To love. But you've made it impossible for me to go on pretending. Because of you I've faced my demons. And my angels. You're *my* angel, Moira. You're my. . .oh, hang it, please stop crying and tell me if I'm saying anything at all right here."

His words only made her cry harder. His arms went around her, hands smoothing through her hair, pulling her bonnet off and making shambles of her tidy coif. She burrowed her face in his collar and held on; she realized she had *been* holding on since first accepting his help in finding the codicil. Deeply she inhaled the essence of male strength and knew herself for the pretentious, prideful fool she was.

She had wanted to be self-sufficient, had insisted upon her independence, and yet. . .this self-described blackguard who shunned the notion of family had been her rock, her haven, the very framework holding her together through everything.

Had she ever truly believed she might willingly see him off to Egypt, that his honor was too important to be sacrificed for the sake of her heart? When she had rejected him, thinking to protect the very same wretched organ, hadn't she secretly prayed he'd do exactly as he had done—pursue her, fight for her, defy her every spoken wish?

And throughout all of it, there had been but a single honest moment: the one that sent her to his bedroom that night at Monteith Hall.

"You're much too quiet."

She lifted her face, her cheek grazing the reassuringly rough stubble of his.

"I do hope you're not thinking things over, Moira." He smiled and dabbed at her tears with his fingertips. "It won't likely turn out in my favor."

A laugh escaped her, albeit a despondent one. Their future still held what it had held all along. *Don't leave.* She wanted to shout it, wanted to insist at the top of her lungs that he let honor and obligation be damned. But hadn't she done enough damage thus far with words?

If her one sincere act had been a physical rendering, then. . .

Framing his face in her hands, she leaned and pressed her lips to his in a kiss that held back nothing, not the love bursting from her heart, or the passion and lust she felt for him, or the burning length of her tongue.

His approval rumbled through her, beginning at her lips and settling with a thunderous resonance in her soul.

From somewhere beyond the rapture of their joined mouths, a cough reminded her they were by no means alone. Graham pulled back, grinning, not looking embarrassed in the least. And though her hand whisked instinctively to her lips to wipe away the telltale moisture, she realized, much to her shock, she wasn't embarrassed, either. Mr. Parker might think what he would. And the bishop. . .well. . .bother the bishop.

"Shall we go home?" Graham held out his hand.

"I'm ready," she said and slipped her hand into his.

"Parker," he said as they stood, "we'll leave the remainder of the investigation to you and your associates."

"If you ever seek employment, my lord, rest assured we've a place for you down on Bow Street."

"I'll bear it in mind." At the open window Graham paused, one foot balanced on the ankle-high sill. "Benedict, I thought you might be wondering why I sent you the cobra pendant."

The question raised only a halfhearted shrug.

"It's cursed," Graham told him with a smile. "Not that I believed in curses, mind you, but I enjoyed the irony of bestowing such a token on the man who'd nearly destroyed my career and my life. Seeing how things have turned out for both you and Oliphant, I believe I'll revise my belief system to allow for the occasional hex." His gaze caressed Moira's face. "And for that matter, the occasional enchantment."

Hand in hand, they stepped through the window. Despite everything he'd said, Moira wondered. . .had their kiss conjured enchantment enough to change the future. . .to make him stay?

CHAPTER 24

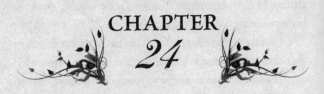

He held her in his arms on the ride home, thankful she let him and relieved with each revolution of the coach's wheels that she didn't pull away with one of her stoic, quelling looks. She tried to speak once, but he pressed a finger to her lips, only to reiterate his demand for silence with a kiss. He was afraid to do more, afraid to shatter this delicate peace between them.

All he wanted was to reach home and discover what she had meant by that mouth-numbing kiss in the bishop's drawing room. Good God, what else *could* it mean? But no, he wouldn't assume, wouldn't build up an illusion only to have it dashed. He had reached a decision. He only hoped Moira would agree.

They entered the house through the garden terrace. All lay still in the Gold Saloon and the ladies' parlor. Not a sound issued from the morning room. But if he had entertained notions of finding some quiet corner in which to be alone with Moira, he found himself sadly mistaken. As they reached the main portion of the ground floor, an explosion of voices bounded down the corridor at them.

Trading startled looks with Moira, he sprinted toward the dining room. Just before he reached it, Freddy stumbled out through the archway, head bowed and nose cradled between his hands. Blood trickled through his fingers.

"You harridan!" he shouted. Unaware of his audience, Freddy came to a wobbling halt at the foot of the stairs and groaned. "I think you bloody broke it."

"What's going on here?" Graham demanded at the same moment Moira cried, "Is Michael all right?"

"I'll give you *broken*, Frederick Foster." Her fist raised, curls bouncing, Letty stormed out of the dining room after him. Nose still in hand, Freddy scooted onto the steps and crouched, cowering behind the banister.

"Hit me again and I'll have you arrested, I will."

Letty spotted Graham and swung about as if to strike him, too. "He's been *drinking* again, Monteith. The little *sneak*."

"I have not. You knocked the glass from my hand before I had the chance." Freddy peered out at Graham from between the carved newels. "And then she hit me."

"Oh, you make me so *angry*!" Letty waved her fist in the air.

Graham grabbed her wrist. "That's not the way to prevent him from drinking, Letty."

"Then why don't we simply drive him back to that *horrid* place, if he's so determined to *destroy* himself."

"Will you please hush?" Freddy darted a look up the stairs. "Mother will hear you."

"Perhaps it's time she found out what a *miserable* little coward her son is."

Despite Letty's sharp words, Graham heard the quiver in her voice, saw the tears gathering in her eyes. He pulled her into his arms. "That's enough now, Letty. It's all right. You stopped him this time. Perhaps next time he'll stop himself."

"Oh, Graham, did I *actually* break his nose?"

Despite the drama, the hysterics, and the salty tears ruining his coat, a warm sensation filled his chest. Letty had finally called him Graham again. He patted her hair. "Don't you worry, we Fosters are more resilient than that."

"No. . .no, it *is* broken." Freddy glared from over his fingertips. "I'm sure of it."

"Let's have a look." Moira knelt below him on the bottom step. "Take your hands away."

"It hurts."

"Yes, I know it hurts, dear." She pried Freddy's hands free with the gentle determination Graham had discovered to be uniquely Moira's. She secured them in one hand—well, Freddy let her, really—while pulling a handkerchief from her reticule with the other. She dabbed carefully at the wounded appendage. As blood seeped through the ivory cotton, she examined her patient. "Let's see, now. . .it looks fairly straight. Hmm. Did you always have that bump?"

Freddy's eyes ballooned. "What bump?"

"Only joking." She grinned. "That perfect Foster nose has prevailed."

"Thank *goodness*." Letty poked her face out from Graham's collar. She heaved a breath of relief, the sound drowned out by a sudden squalling from upstairs.

"That's Michael." Moira pushed to her feet.

"Don't go." Graham moved to her side and barred her way with an outstretched arm. "Letty, would you please tend to him?"

Moira looked puzzled. Letty positively balked. "After such a long nap, he's sure to be *sopping* and goodness knows what else."

"I'll just get him, then." Moira stepped around Freddy and started up. Determined not to let her slip away, Graham took the stairs two at a time until he caught up to her.

"We need to talk."

"Yes, I know, but—"

"I'll get the baby." Using the banister for leverage, Freddy hauled himself to his feet, his free hand pressing Moira's handkerchief to his nose. "You two lovebirds can have your little talk."

Graham didn't know whether to thank his brother or swipe the back of his insolent head. The next thing he knew, though, Letty was pounding up the stairs in pursuit of her twin.

"You will *not* tend to that child, Frederick Foster. Not in your condition."

"I told you I hadn't so much as a sip. . ."

Graham held Moira's hand to his chest and released a sigh. "Pure bedlam, this family. I wouldn't blame you if you demanded an immediate return to Monteith Hall."

Her fingers spread over his shirtfront, her palm pressing warmly against him and filling him with a hope so sharp it knifed his insides.

"When I do go," she said, "I'm taking them all with me, if they'll come. But I won't leave until you do." She stepped closer, infinitely close, until her dazzling dark eyes filled his world. "I'll stay till then."

"And what if I don't leave?" There, he'd said it. Damn his pride, he'd finally said it. The effort left his lungs aching, his heart knocking.

She took an interminable time in answering, leaving him dangling between fates like a felon on the gibbet. Finally, she said very quietly, "That is a question I cannot answer for you. I will not."

No, she was right. He was still hedging, still playing it safe. Ah, the past wounds had left deep scars, sure enough. But just as sure, those wounds would scar his future if he didn't find his courage. The whole of it, and right now.

He sucked a draft of air into his lungs and plunged.

"I'm staying in England, Moira. I'm not returning to Egypt."

He hadn't counted on his announcement raising such a frown, but then one never knew with Moira. "What about your oath? What about that man who threatened to kill you if you didn't help him hide Egypt's treasures?"

Blazing hell, was she going to toss all that honor and obligation nonsense in his face again? So be it. He smoothed his hand through the ebony tresses he'd brought to ruin earlier.

"Hakim al Faruq will have to understand that I have responsibilities here that preclude my oath to him. My family needs me. I abandoned them once. I won't do it again." A little ridge formed above her nose. Her hand started to come away from his chest, but he held it firm. "I'm right to stay, aren't I?"

Before she could answer, Shaun's voice called from the landing above. "Did I just hear you correctly? You're not going back to Egypt?"

"That's right, my friend."

Shaun descended the stairs slowly. "But Hakim. . ."

"Will have to travel all the way to England if he still wishes to slit my throat." He grinned when Moira flinched. "Don't worry, darling, the man's terrified of water."

Shaun stopped on the step above. "Won't be the same there without you."

"Then don't return."

Shaun shrugged. "Might as well. Not much for me here in England, really."

"Then there's something you can do for me." Graham reached into his coat pocket, waiting until he felt Isis scramble into his hand. "Will you take her back for me? I'm afraid she won't last the winter here."

His friend cringed. "Ask me anything. Anything but that."

"But she'll most likely die here. You don't want that on your conscience, do you?"

"Don't I?" His features contorted. His gaze darted from Isis to Graham to Moira and back to Isis, a perusal concluded with a murmured curse. "God will get you for this, Foster. You secure that crate good and tight."

"Will do."

"What should I tell Hakim?"

"Tell him. . ." Graham met Moira's expectant gaze and nearly drowned in an upsurge of emotion. "Tell him I stayed for a woman. He'll understand."

Shaun nodded and started back up the stairs.

"Don't stay away too long, Mr. Paddington," Moira called to him. "There's more here for you than you guess. I shall miss you dreadfully. But I'm not the only one. Do come back. Come back for Letty."

The tips of his ears flaming, Shaun stared down at her a long moment before continuing up the stairs.

"And what of me?" Graham asked when they were alone. He glanced down at Isis, now climbing from his cuff to his shoulder. "Does someone care for me more than I dare hope? And does that person understand even a fraction of how much I love her?"

"Do you, indeed?" she replied brusquely, with a note of indifference that sent his confidence tumbling. "A moment ago you told me you were staying for your family. Now you claim you're staying for me. Which is it, Mr. Foster? Which of us finally tamed the blackguard?"

"Now see here, you little tease." He sank to the steps and drew her down beside him. Their shoulders and thighs pressed, their faces so close the warmth of her cheek imbued his. "It's both. I'm staying for you *and* my family, but we both know deuced well, you alone tamed me. Tamed and inflamed me."

He brought his mouth against the corner of hers. "Moira, Moira, whose name forms a kiss on my lips each time I say it. What do you say? Will you have me? Or must I abduct you and force you to marry me?"

"Always the cavalier." She leaned a little away, angling disapproval from the slant of her brow. But laughter danced in her eyes and along the curve of her lips. "No one has tamed you in the least. And no one ever will."

"Yes, well, if you'll remember, my stubborn darling, this cavalier has made love to you, and at your own prompting, I might add. I will not be responsible for any more illegitimate Fosters running about."

She looked thoroughly perplexed. "What about the sheath?"

"That? Not completely reliable. Far from it, in fact. Honestly, I wouldn't be at all surprised if there was already another little Foster on the way."

Scandal sparked in her eyes. He closed his hand around hers where it lay against her thigh. Isis chose that moment to scoot down to his wrist and leap onto Moira's arm. "Look, even Isis believes we belong together. If you continue to resist, I'm afraid I shall be forced to use my dimples to persuade you."

"Hmph."

"You like your blackguards with dimples, don't you, Moira?"

"I've never heard such nonsense."

"And let's not forget my perfect Foster nose."

"Take it out of the air this instant."

"Yes, Moira."

"And kiss me, you adorable blackguard."

"With pleasure, my darling, dazzling Moira."

For more information

about other great titles from

Medallion Press, visit

www.medallionpress.com